LONGBOURN
to LONDON

Linda Beutler

Meryton Press

Oysterville, WA

Also by Linda Beutler

࿇

THE RED CHRYSANTHEMUM
2013 Silver Medal, Independent Publishers Awards

LONGBOURN TO LONDON

ISBN: 978-1-936009-36-7

Cover design by Zorylee Diaz-Lupitou
Layout by Ellen Pickels

Introduction

Longbourn to London was my first attempt at writing Jane Austen fan fiction (JAFF). If you read this perfected version carefully, you will recognize the exact moment Lizzy asks Darcy a question I would love to ask Jane Austen —should I ever have the chance—and thus was born *The Red Chrysanthemum* (Meryton Press, 2013). At the moment both stories were finished, I realized the second story might be more publishable than the first, so it was the one sent to Meryton Press, and thus was my debut.

Wise people that they are, the folks at Meryton Press suggested I join the Meryton Literary Society, and post anything I had lying around at A Happy Assembly, a forum for JAFF writers and readers. Imagine my surprise to find a whole world of people like me! Until that point, I had been reading printed novels, and I was unaware of this vibrant online universe with hundreds of new stories by great authors, many as yet unpublished. I began posting *Longbourn to London* there, after determining that it was sufficiently unique to be worthy of such an astute audience.

Why did I think *Longbourn to London* was "sufficiently unique"? After reading even more JAFF, I became aware that there are "what-ifs" in abundance—the *variations,* if you will—taken from the *Pride and Prejudice* original plot. There are ample sequels, too, which take Lizzy and Darcy all over the world, set them many trials, and usually require some sort of physical mayhem be visited upon one or the other of them, if not both. But when I was first thinking of even attempting to summon hubris enough to put pen to paper, I wanted to do something few others had tried.

With that motivation in mind, I turned to Jane Austen's masterpiece, looking for gaps. There are some; the biggest and most often commented upon is the dearth of detail about Lizzy and Darcy's official engagement. We know only that Mrs. Phillips made a vulgar pest of herself, letters to family were written, Caroline Bingley strove mightily to stay in everyone's good graces, and Lizzy required Darcy to provide a thorough reckoning of how he came to love her. Jane gave us no first kiss, no flights of hysteria by Mrs. Bennet as she planned a double wedding, no pre-wedding night jitters for Jane, and none of Lizzy's undoubtedly active curiosity about what would befall her as the wife of Fitzwilliam Darcy.

Since there would be no harrowing Hunsford, no catfight with Lady Catherine, and no wickedness from Wickham, it seemed at first that nothing would happen. But thanks to the beautiful screenplay by Andrew Davies for the 1995 BBC adaptation, and the portrayals of Lizzy and Darcy by Jennifer Ehle and Colin Firth, my couple had faces and voices, expressions and mannerisms, making it only necessary for me to provide their thoughts. Somehow, a rudimentary plot laid itself before me.

Then a bigger picture developed as I wrote. In this story, both Lizzy and Darcy are quite stunned by their individual felicity being wholly based on making the other happy. Darcy has some rudimentary idealized notion of this, but the reality of Elizabeth Bennet has him overawed. For Lizzy, the astounding thing is Darcy's playfulness. That he is amused by her from the very beginning is a given, but in canon Lizzy thinks he needs to learn to be teased. I believe the contrary is true. Darcy has watched her affectionate teasing of those she loves, and he longs to be teased by her; it is a sign of her fondness and acceptance. And he has the temerity to tease *her*! From the beginning of *Pride and Prejudice*, although we don't know it fully until the end, he is a more accurate observer of her than she of him.

This story does dwell on the development of their physical relationship: how they approach the wedding night and all it symbolizes for their future. Darcy's willingness to calm her worries with wry asides and silly observations is a revelation to Lizzy. She expects "marital relations" to be weighty and serious encounters. He clearly wants something much different and altogether more to her liking: he wants them to be equals in the marriage bed as well as in their day-to-day life as master and mistress of Pemberley.

—*Linda Beutler, June 2014*

Acknowledgments

It has been my great privilege to work again with editor Gail Warner, and I hope she will always be so willing to go to bat for my stories, without hesitating to turn said bat on me when necessary. She is simply the best and makes me better. I thank everyone at Meryton Press for their support, efficiency, and unfailing *joie de vive*.

And I thank my best friend, Jacqueline Martin Mitzel, who has spent more happy-hours listening to my daft ponderings than anyone should ever be subjected to.

That the unvarnished version of *Longbourn to London* was embraced by the sometimes difficult-to-please audience at A Happy Assembly was so heartening that I started frequenting the chat room. It is populated by a worldwide array of JAFF writers and readers who encouraged me to publish my first story second. It is to them, the Chat-Chits and our one Chat-Chap, that I dedicate this improved version of *Longbourn to London*. It is an honor to know you, write for you, meet you, and share your lives.

Prologue

"Love me!...Why?"
William Shakespeare, *Much Ado about Nothing*

It may be generally assumed, with few examples to the contrary, that a betrothed maiden faces the coming of her wedding night with some sense of disquiet, if not a complete and thoroughgoing fear. Even young ladies of some wit and good sense may become rather addled at the notion of engaging in the ultimate intimate act with a relative stranger of the opposite sex, no matter how beloved—an act with which they have little, if any, prior knowledge, and completely alien to all previous experience. It is an act able to reveal much about a gentleman's character, which might otherwise remain unknown.

In the case of Miss Elizabeth Bennet, and even more so for her elder sister, Miss Jane Bennet, the details of their wedding plans did little to distract from the event that would follow much later that same day. The sisters, dear confidantes from infancy, were to be married in a double ceremony to men who were the best of friends. These men were completely unlike in temperament and physical attributes, although both were tall.

Jane Bennet, fair and blue-eyed, perpetually sweet-natured and believing the best in everyone, was to marry Charles Bingley, a neighbour recently arrived with the lease of an estate, Netherfield Park, which shared a corner boundary with Longbourn, the smaller Bennet estate. Jane and Bingley met at an assembly in the nearby market town of Meryton. It was to themselves and most observers love at first sight, or nearly so. For this well-matched couple, the road to betrothal was not as swiftly travelled as their feelings would have led one to expect, but they had been engaged a fortnight when this story begins.

For Elizabeth Bennet and Fitzwilliam Darcy, who first set eyes on each other at the same assembly, the path to betrothal was a good deal more fraught. A heedless remark made by a petulant Darcy, and unluckily overheard by the acute Elizabeth—known within her family circle to have hearing like a fox—led to a subsequent misreading of his character. Over time, Darcy's caustic remark bred contempt. But as has been known to happen, it is not so very difficult for passionate hate to develop, in the right circumstances, into a deep and ardent love. So it was with Elizabeth's fond regard for Darcy.

Darcy fought his attraction to Elizabeth from their first meeting, although she fascinated him with her luscious dark hair, ready smile, intelligence, and lively manners. She did not fear him or defer to him. Whenever provided the opportunity, she laughed at him. On their third meeting, she refused to dance with him. Generally, she disagreed with any point he made in conversation, if only for the excuse to argue. Elizabeth did not examine the cause of this provocation and, had she done so, would have been most dissatisfied to discover a spark of attraction to his handsome features and elegant physique. Nor would she have understood it.

For both, the dark warm eyes of the other were arresting. In Darcy's case, by the time he acknowledged, towards the end of a party at Lucas Lodge, an appreciation for Elizabeth's fine eyes, his heart was quite beyond redemption.

A first proposal from Darcy to Elizabeth the previous April was nothing short of a catastrophe. It had not occurred to the conceited and arrogant Darcy that Elizabeth might view him with disdain. Darcy was vain of his position and worth, and expected the gently bred, though poorly connected, Elizabeth to appreciate the condescension exhibited by allowing his passionate regard for her to overcome his scruples.

She did not.

Her refusal was particularly illuminating in its minute delineation of his character flaws. He departed in anger, of course, but was also alarmed at the resonance of truth in her description, and it was this shock that lead Darcy to appreciate Elizabeth all the more. He came to own the veracity of her assessment and sought redemption even without hope of ever seeing her again.

When Darcy and Elizabeth did later meet, quite by chance, he was a changed man. She was a changed woman, too, thanks to a letter he had written defending his actions—if not his character—in matters about which he felt Elizabeth had misjudged him for want of true information. The letter tacitly invited Elizabeth to question her perceptions. As she believed her first impressions of people to be rarely incomplete and never wrong, it was an exercise she had not previously undertaken.

That Elizabeth and Darcy accepted love and abandoned hate brings us to the tale of their six-week engagement and the earliest days of their honeymoon, which to some may appear uneventful. These weeks were, in fact, full of countless small adjustments to their understanding of each other, as well as the deepening of regard necessary to convince a maiden that living with a gentleman might have more advantages than one initially assumed. The time also served to further convince a man who has lived in the world —and one who admittedly needed little further encouragement for his passion —that an unconventionally educated country miss with good principles and ready humour would make a worthy partner in *every* particular.

As we begin, Darcy and Elizabeth had been engaged less than a week, and the larger world was only just realising that a handsome man of great consequence—one of the most coveted bachelors of his day—was marrying for the love of a young lady with teasing charm and a pleasingly healthy figure. Their immediate families—his, small with just a younger sister, and hers, large and mainly female—had given their blessings, extended families and friends had been written to, and the neighbourhood of Meryton was awakening to the approach of an event of great significance: the double wedding ceremony of the two eldest Bennet sisters.

In the first days, Darcy and Elizabeth attempted to explain to each other the various turns of their minds as they grew towards a mutual regard, but many more particulars of growing affection awaited revelation. In private moments, the previously guarded Darcy offered love to Elizabeth with every breath; now that she had accepted him, he need not hold back. Elizabeth's expressive eyes looked upon him with thrilling admiration, although her words were often as impertinent as ever. Darcy was not surprised.

Chapter 1
The First Kiss (or Two)

"I wish my horse had the speed of your tongue."
William Shakespeare, *Much Ado about Nothing*

Fitzwilliam Darcy, as he had anticipated, was able to intercept Elizabeth Bennet's early morning walk as he rode on horseback. It was the fifth day of their engagement. He knew she was fond of walking the countryside from the earliest days of their acquaintance, and, in April, his estimation of her had increased as he encountered her morning rambles through Rosings Park. It was outside his country home, Pemberley, on the west sloping lawn, that their paths miraculously crossed in July. His second proposal, the one she *had* accepted, happened along a lane less than a mile from her home. At just this moment, they were mere steps from that sacred spot.

The fact that Elizabeth had rarely bid him more than a nod as she passed him at Rosings Park, and said little when he tried to engage her in conversation, should have been an indication—and would have been to a less proud man—that his attentions were not welcome. The man he was then could not apprehend that *any* woman he deigned to notice would not regard him positively, let alone might despise him. Reflecting, as he often did, upon the errant proposal—when all his words were ill chosen and the entire effort ill starred—he now saw it had the added disadvantage of being delivered in a sitting room rather than in the open air.

How much had changed! Now when Elizabeth saw him on the paths, she ran to reach him, her cheeks flushed and her eyes brightened. Such welcoming delighted him and left no doubt of her affection. If she had not already removed her gloves, she did so when they met. They walked holding hands, or with her hand clasped to his elbow as he stroked it fondly. If he traced circles on her palm, she would watch with rapt attention. He was keenly aware that the sensations he was producing caused her pulse to race.

If their conversation turned lively and amusing, as was often the case, Elizabeth would embrace his arm, sometimes quite fervently, and her bosom would brush against him. She was unaware of it, and he found this inflaming and a happy portent of a demonstrative nature—something he intended to test further on this day by attempting a first kiss.

Just the day before, as Jane Bennet was in the Netherfield front hall awaiting the carriage after touring the house and taking tea with Miss Caroline Bingley, Charles's mordant younger sister, Darcy spied Jane and Bingley in a secret embrace and kiss. If Miss Bennet, sedate and serene Jane, could be moved to respond to Bingley's attentions, how would his more energetic Elizabeth respond? Although Darcy would not advocate for the anticipation of their wedding vows—his sense of honour and concern for her comfort would not condone it—he did mean, in as subtle yet thorough a manner as possible, to indicate he would welcome her responses to his ardour. He had no desire for a wife to "just lie there."

Darcy was appalled at the men of his club who spoke meanly of their wives. These were men who had not married for love and did not appear to want it to develop. Their wives were merely receptacles for their seed to produce heirs. These men went to the added expense of keeping mistresses if their bent ran to fornication. Darcy felt sorry for them and sorrier still for their wives. It seemed a ridiculous business to marry a woman one did not care for and then to bear the added cost—often considerable—of maintaining another woman whose honour would no longer be respected and often could not be trusted. Darcy dreamt of Elizabeth behaving as a mistress while actually his wife; in fact, he dreamt of it more and more often. It was his belief that such a felicitous circumstance was not only possible but also entirely likely. Her every look and gesture assured him that, with his loving and patient guidance, his private wishes would become hers, too.

Does she know Jane and Bingley have progressed to kissing? How deep is their sisterly confidence? Thus were Darcy's thoughts employed as Elizabeth repeated the list of invitations starting to arrive at Longbourn as a result of the announcement of their betrothal.

After a few moments, Darcy realised Elizabeth had grown silent and he had not heard a word she said.

"How will you bear it, sir, the scrutiny of Meryton society from now until the wedding?"

Darcy shook his head to clear it. "I am sorry, Elizabeth. I have not been attending you." He stopped and turned to her.

She released his arm. Her eyes flickered to his and then away. "I pray, sir, will you tell me what you *were* attending? You seemed miles away."

He remained silent until her eyes drew back to his. "No, Elizabeth, I am not miles away. I am here."

He saw her eyes widen but not from fear. He understood her quizzical response well enough. With a crook'd finger he raised her chin, thankful the brim of her bonnet was shallow. *In the days to come, I shall remove our hats when we kiss.* Her lips looked moist, and Darcy felt his mouth go dry, but he drew closer. She closed her eyes, her thick lashes brushing her cheeks. His lips met hers squarely, his mouth closed at first, and then his lips parted. He longed to taste her but stopped himself. He pressed harder instead. Her lips separated. She pressed his, too, following his lead. After a gentle moment, Darcy started to pull back, but Elizabeth's lips pursued him, unwilling to break the connection. His hand under her chin slipped to the corner of her jaw then held the back of her neck, his fingers entwining in escaped tendrils on her nape. He tilted her head without making a conscious decision as his tongue lightly touched the delicate mid-point of her upper lip and withdrew. Her lips parted further as she drew in a gasping breath, and to his pleased surprise, her tongue touched his lip. Darcy exhaled and pulled away.

Elizabeth's eyes were full of dancing light. She blushed and murmured, "I hope that pleased you, Mr. Darcy."

He kissed her rosy cheek. "You seem to have a natural gift, assuming it *was* your first kiss."

"Yes, sir, it was!" she protested as her blush deepened. "Mr. Darcy, are *you* teasing *me?*"

"I am." He kissed her nose. "Was it everything a maiden might wish it to be?"

"Certainly the company was as I have hoped—as to the rest, modesty forbids I reply."

"Surely you know *I* do not forbid it, and other than your dear self, who is there to hear?"

She had not withdrawn or stepped away from his touch and his hand still caressed her neck. "If you were to absolutely insist, I would not resist you in any way should you attempt such a liberty again."

He smiled slightly and leaned his forehead against hers. "Elizabeth."

"Fitzwilliam." She said his given name for the first time.

"Dearest Elizabeth."

"Dearest Fitzwilliam."

He pursued his fondest impulse, and enjoyed her lips again. They were already parted, ready to respond to any new stimulation. He found himself sucking her plump lower lip into his mouth, tasting it fully. Elizabeth gasped faintly but he persisted.

Elizabeth had been aware of his reluctance to kiss her these last five days despite several opportunities. She felt light with relief that he was finally kissing her, and she savoured the moment. *Oh goodness! Was anything ever more heavenly?* Her breathing grew rapid, and she dared to lean towards him as his thumbs stroked her earlobes. She was lost in appreciation of the strong sensations previously unknown to her when suddenly her awareness was drawn to how easily she might be seduced by her feelings. Slowly she began to back away, and Darcy gently released her lip.

Their eyes opened and they smiled.

"I am in some danger from you, Fitzwilliam Darcy," Elizabeth said, her eyes laughing.

"Surely not, Miss Bennet, surely not. I would not have you fear for your virtue."

Instantly serious, she whispered, "I do not fear for my virtue, Fitzwilliam. I trust you with that. The danger is to my soul." She caught his sleeves, resting her cheek on his lapel, and felt him draw in a deep breath.

"Your virtue, your love, and even your soul, I hope, will all be safe with me. Now that you have consented to be my wife, it is my duty to protect you, and all that is yours. Your soul is your own, Elizabeth, but I shall guard it."

She smiled against his coat. *Now that he has let down his guard, he says the most astonishing things. How am I to remember them all?*

Darcy put his hands around her back and held her. Elizabeth turned her head and looked at his hat, wishing she knew what was allowed. She longed to run her hands through his hair. As she pondered what latitude she might have, the corner of her lower lip was caught by her upper teeth.

This habitual pose of her lips when she was concentrating or trying not to smile had long been a pressing source of temptation to Darcy. He surrendered to the desire that beset him from nearly their first meeting and placed his lips on hers, teasing her lower lip free with his tongue, then their mouths met properly for further exploration.

"Oh!" Elizabeth seemed disappointed when he released her.

Darcy gazed into her dark eyes and smiled, indicating he read her response to this escalation of their intimacy quite clearly. He knew very well that he had left her wanting more. He was profoundly happy with his restraint and her responses. She would follow where he would lead. All had gone extremely well.

Elizabeth took his hand, and they started to walk. "I must admit, Fitzwilliam, I had begun to wonder why you had not sought my favours before now."

"You must acknowledge that, given past responses to requests for your affection, I would wait until I could be more certain of your...agreement."

"Oh, dear. Did my ill-mannered behaviour at Hunsford make you timid?"

"Shall I tell you what resolved me to act today?" His tone was decidedly conspiratorial.

"Please do!" She sounded intrigued as she embraced his arm.

"I should not tell you this, but I spied your sister and Bingley in a rather ardent embrace yesterday while she was waiting to depart after taking tea with Miss Bingley."

"You are *certain* it was *my* sister?" She laughed. "Bingley has the advantage of us, I suppose. They have been engaged at least ten days longer than we."

"If we apply ourselves, Elizabeth, do you think we can catch them?" Darcy was joyful and in a mood to tease.

"Would that please you, sir?"

"Indeed, and I hope it would please *you*, madam. Let me compliment you again upon your early efforts."

"You will find I respond uncommonly well to praise."

"Is that so?" He looked upon her as they strolled with their hands swinging between them. He was a man quite delighted with what he saw. She seemed in easy spirits. He looked ahead and felt his heart expanding. He grinned.

I, of all men, am making Elizabeth Bennet happy. Will wonders never cease?

"Look at you, so pleased with yourself. You look like the cat that stole the cream." She scolded him but could not suppress a melodious chuckle.

"Yes, it is true. I am pleased with myself because I have pleased you. That is something few men can say. 'I have pleased Miss Elizabeth Bennet.' Who else can say that with any truth? No one but me, I hope."

"Yes, yes. This once I shall allow you to be full of yourself. I am too happy for censure."

They continued to stroll in companionable silence. Finally, Elizabeth began to speak of her original topic. "Invitations are arriving for us, Mr. —ah!—Fitzwilliam. One is quite remarkable."

"How so?"

"Mrs. Long is determined, given my love of the outdoors, to hold a garden party in our honour on Sunday week. In November! It seems quite daft and very sweet, but she certainly tempts fate."

"Indeed she does. I remember last autumn, before the ball at Netherfield, there were many days of rain one after another. Perhaps a week of it?"

"I remember! The Hertfordshire autumn rains are due at any time, but she is requesting muslin gowns and frock coats. We shall all freeze, but I think we should accept the invitation. It will be diverting in any case."

They laughed and Darcy recalled the muslin dress she wore when he came upon her unexpectedly at Pemberley in July. As Elizabeth was walking with her aunt by the trout stream and into the sun, the shape of her legs could be seen through her summer gown. The remembrance held a smile on his lips. Elizabeth was speaking of other social engagements to come, and again Darcy's thoughts tended towards activities they would not do in company.

His mind wandered through the Pemberley woods to places he knew she would like. He wondered whether she would be willing to join with him in the open air. *There are a million places.* He imagined riding to remote vistas with a bottle of May wine and a blanket in his saddlebag.

"Do you ride, Elizabeth?" He blurted his question, quite interrupting her.

She stopped and looked at him quizzically. "This is a new tendency, Mr. Darcy, not to attend me when I speak. Do not think I have failed to notice. It is not an altogether pleasing habit to form, I must say. Your mind does wander."

"Yes, but you were with me where I wandered."

"Oh? And where were we?" Her eyes sparkled, her expression impertinent.

"We were riding through the Pemberley woods to the distant places that cannot be reached on foot." He imagined her hair wild and loose, a riding habit pulled to her thighs as she lay upon a blanket with a decidedly come-hither look in her eyes.

"Ah, and that begged the question... I see. Well, sir, I have only ridden our Nellie. She will not gallop nor even cantor. Now you will think me unaccomplished."

"Nonsense. It is merely one additional activity with which I shall have the pleasure of acquainting you. I believe you will look quite smart in a dark blue riding habit, or perhaps dark green?"

"Additional activity? In addition to what other activity?"

Darcy was stunned, and his face coloured vividly from his cravat to the brim of his hat. He looked down, mortified by what he had implied. But what would she infer? *Any other woman would have been distracted by the offer of new clothes, but not my Elizabeth, oh, no... How carefully must I mind what I say for the next few weeks? Oh, damn.*

Elizabeth watched his blush. He could not meet her eyes at first, but then he looked at her with a longing to be forgiven for some unknown infraction. She cocked her head to meet his gaze. *What activity can he mean? He is a map of embarrassment. What...? Ooh!* Elizabeth started to blush. *Oh! He is referring to acquainting me with marital relations, I think. What else could possibly cause him to blush? He implies it is an activity he knows but which I do not. On a horse? No, surely not. Someplace where we can only go by horse to engage in such an activity?* Elizabeth regarded him with confusion. She gave her head a little shake to no avail. Her thoughts would not proceed in any logical manner.

Darcy heaved a great sigh. "Elizabeth, you must accept my apologies. I have discomfited us both. Please let us confine our thoughts to simply this: you have not had much occasion to ride, and I enjoy it. I would share something with you that gives me joy. I shall find a good horse for you at Pemberley next spring—an animal you can trust—and I shall teach you to ride... that is, if you are willing."

"Yes... yes, certainly, sir. I have no objection to improving my skill with horses." She turned her head away and smiled, saying, "Indeed, I look forward to instruction from you in many things."

Darcy looked in the opposite direction, his blush remaining. He took her hand and they turned towards Longbourn, his horse following them peaceably if ironically.

Chapter 2
Unsolicited Advice

*"Marry, sir, they have committed false report; moreover, they
have spoken untruths; secondarily, they are slanders; sixth
and lastly, they have belied a lady; thirdly, they have verified
unjust things; and, to conclude, they are lying knaves.*
William Shakespeare, *Much Ado about Nothing*

Darcy did not kiss her again on that occasion, but he thought Elizabeth's welcome more than usually friendly—and was relieved to receive it—when he arrived at Longbourn for a scheduled visit later that afternoon.

Jane and Mrs. Bennet were in Meryton helping Catherine Bennet, called Kitty within the family circle, select fabric for a new gown. Because Elizabeth and Jane were standing up together, they were each *ipso facto* the bridesmaid for the other, and what with Kitty's favourite sister, Mrs. Lydia Wickham, married while away from the family, Kitty was feeling the opportunity to be a charming and important bridesmaid slipping away. Jane and Elizabeth suggested a new gown to raise her spirits, and Mrs. Bennet was happy to help any of her daughters acquire new clothes.

Mr. Bennet emerged from his library when Darcy arrived. The need to chaperon his Lizzy was an unaccustomed impulse, and he fidgeted with a newspaper in his drawing room chair while Elizabeth acquainted Darcy with the volume of invitations she had received.

"I have divided them into stacks, the first being those we need not accept."

"Is there such a thing?" Mr. Bennet asked over a lowered corner of his paper. "I had thought a lady must accept all invitations."

"Indeed, sir!" Darcy smiled a little. "I am more interested in that pile than any other. I should make a study of how to extend an invitation into society in such a way as to have it not accepted, and then I shall give lessons to all of these others."

Mr. Bennet smiled and nodded. "Very wise, Mr. Darcy."

Elizabeth extended them an arch look. "Are you quite finished, the two of you?"

Darcy said, "Proceed, Miss Elizabeth," at the same time Mr. Bennet said, "Proceed, Lizzy."

She sighed.

"Here is a pile of events I may attend without you." She patted a short stack of cards.

"Why without me? Who would not want me to grace their society?" Darcy feigned affront.

"Well, there are people of my acquaintance who do *not* know you, and there are those who *do*, and that pretty much covers the whole of it."

Mr. Bennet laughed from behind his paper.

"Mr. Bennet, I would not have you encourage your daughter's impertinence. She torments me constantly already. I cannot think why I proposed to her."

Darcy was looking into Elizabeth's eyes as he said the last sentence. He winked at her, and she smiled at him with unspoken praise. She liked that he was playing to her father.

Mr. Bennet peeked over the paper and caught the exchange. "Perhaps, sir, men of your station require practice in the exercise, and you did not think of actually being accepted by a woman of such discernment as my Lizzy."

Mr. Bennet did not understand why they both burst into laughter. It took Elizabeth and Darcy several moments to regain their composure.

Elizabeth finally calmed enough to address a third pile of invitations. "In this pile are the invitations extended to us both. These, I think, we ought to accept. I would like to discuss them."

The presence of Mr. Bennet allowed for candour, but his wry comments about their neighbours were also a distraction. Within moments, Elizabeth perceived she would not get far in the pursuit of dissecting social engagements. She also perceived that Darcy would follow her lead amongst Meryton society, trusting her to help him avoid the silliest and most ignorant; those who would too profoundly try his forbearance had already been trying hers for a good many years. Elizabeth relented, allowing her father and her betrothed to make sport with her plans.

That evening, Darcy and Bingley took a family dinner at Longbourn, into which much planning had gone to give the meal an unstudied air. Mr. Bennet had begun to join the two couples as they awaited the men's horses or carriage under the modest Longbourn portico, and Darcy was vexed when no further opportunity to kiss Elizabeth would be immediately forthcoming. As Jane and Elizabeth took their father's proffered arms to return indoors, they noted a certain amused smugness in his expression that neither daughter quite liked.

THE NEXT AFTERNOON BROUGHT A party at the Phillips's apartment in Meryton. Mrs. Phillips was Mrs. Bennet's elder sister and not a pleasant woman. She shared her sister's fits of nerves, and her lack of education amounted to a carefully cultivated ignorance of world events or anything that might be called science. Add to this her prurient interest in marital relations, a will to be scandalised, and a tendency to strong drink, and one can easily comprehend Elizabeth's inclination to become curt and quiet in her company.

A number of local ladies had been invited to drink tea, and once everyone was assembled, the two eldest Bennets were alarmed to see they were the only unmarried ladies in attendance. They sat together on a small sofa surrounded by a phalanx of old family neighbours and acquaintances, all with one subject in mind.

"You must never let your husband kiss your person anywhere but upon your mouth and cheeks, girls," Mrs. Long advised. "I speak of the cheeks on your face, of course!" The ladies tittered like a demented Greek chorus.

Jane closed her eyes and inhaled. Elizabeth opened her mouth to ask a question, became confused, and bit her tongue. Jane clutched her sister's hand and shook her head subtly, imploring Elizabeth to remain silent.

Mrs. Phillips continued the dispensing of advice. "And never, ever, under any circumstance, should you *ever* let them know you find any night time occurrence pleasurable. If you do, they will be at you constantly with the excuse that *you* wish it. They will find any opportunity to...impose themselves. I do feel especially sorry for you, Lizzy, as I think Mr. Bingley can be managed, but how *you* are to control a man who looks at you as Mr. Darcy does, well, I am sure I do not know. Perhaps you may establish a sitting room for yourself where your privacy must be maintained, as Charlotte Collins has done. But I despair for you, Lizzy. You will have your hands full to overflowing, I should think." At this last remark, the married ladies giggled raucously.

"Oh yes!" cried Mrs. Goulding. "Just look at his hands and feet."

"His hands and feet?" Elizabeth asked and immediately wished she had not. Jane squeezed her hand in mortified disapprobation.

"Big hands, big feet, big cock!" crowed Aunt Phillips.

The shrill laughter grew louder. Even Mrs. Bennet was laughing at her daughters' embarrassment.

By the end of two hours, Jane and Elizabeth were irretrievably out of temper. When the Bennet carriage arrived, they would not ride in it and instead chose to walk home to avoid further commentary from their mother. After marching along in silence half the distance to Longbourn, Jane began to express some gentler explanation of the proceedings. "Did you notice our aunt dribbling something from a flask into her tea? I cannot imagine she would have spoken as she did if she were entirely sober."

"That is *some* excuse for our aunt, though a poor one, but what of the others? What of our mother! How can I face any of them knowing they think so ill of Mr. Darcy?" Elizabeth's pace quickened. "There is nothing you can say, Jane—nothing—to explain such a display of vulgarity."

"I must tell you, Lizzy, it was their...*glee* that was most inexplicable. I cannot account for it. They knew we were made uncomfortable. Yet the more they saw our embarrassment, the more they hectored."

"It was as if by design, Jane."

"Oh, no, Lizzy, I cannot think so."

Elizabeth pulled off her right glove, displaying her hand covered with the imprints of Jane's fingernails. "Think well of them if you wish, but I *know* what you felt through the whole of it."

THE BENNET FAMILY DINED AT Netherfield that night. Again, there was no convenient occasion for either couple to be alone for more than a moment. But Elizabeth was not formed for ill-humour, and being with Darcy produced an easing of her temper.

Early the next morning, Elizabeth hoped to take a walk, but was, with

Jane, purloined by their mother, who had awakened in an excitable state. Mrs. Bennet was in the mood for list making, noting every nuance of the coming nuptials with which her daughters must, at that very instant, familiarise themselves.

Since Darcy and Bingley had invited a few local young men to Netherfield that evening to learn billiards, Elizabeth and Jane attended an impromptu soiree at Lucas Lodge. Before the card tables were brought, the two eldest Bennets found themselves in another group of married women where they were again subjected to the improper ravings of their aunt, abetted by wine punch taken to excess. The more she drank, the more lurid grew her tales, until even Mrs. Bennet blushed and herded her daughters to the card tables.

Elizabeth and Jane were so shocked and distracted that they made poor partners. At home in their bedroom, they said only what was necessary as they prepared for bed, and although each knew the other was awake for quite some little time after blowing out their candles, neither spoke.

Chapter 3
Elizabeth's Dream

"What, with my tongue in your tail?
Nay, come again Good Kate; I am a gentleman."
William Shakespeare, *The Taming of the Shrew*

L izzy was lying on a large bed in a dark room. Off to her side was the dull glow of a waning fire, and from above her head, perhaps from a tall bedside table, came the light of one flickering candle. She realised she was naked, or nearly so. A swath of soft, silky fabric covered one shoulder and draped across her chest, flowing onto the bed. Was it a dressing gown?

Her pulse began to race. Her head and shoulders were propped on pillows, and she could look down at the rest of her body. There was her belly and the dark patch of hair that hid, or in this case seemed to draw attention to, the secret place, which Mama had always insisted must be cleaned but in no other way touched. Except that now her legs were spread and bent up at the knees, and someone was touching her there. A man was there! Between her legs!

Lizzy inhaled sharply. The feelings coming from her forbidden flesh were thrilling, and some sort of tension was building. She realised with a shock that she was moist. How mortifying... Had she wet herself? Was it her time; was she bleeding? She could see no evidence on her thighs, and she tentatively put her hand down to where she ought not, encountering... the hair on a man's head! Her hand acted without her direction. Rather than pull away as she wanted, her arm would not obey, and her fingers, now both hands, stroked and caressed the masculine dark hair.

Inside Lizzy's mind, words were flying about in fractured thoughts... I must *stop this—it is improper. I must stop him...stop myself... How could he behave so? I should not allow this... Oh!*

She watched with a strange, detached awe as the man's head moved between her legs, and her mound of short dark hair seemed to writhe with expanding desire. What is he doing to me? She was becoming wetter, and she could not stop her fingers from encouraging what was happening by running through the man's hair.

How could this be? Is he? Oh good god... He is kissing me there... The realisation of what was taking place coincided with the sensation of such a release of pressure that she moaned and raised her hips up to meet the mouth she could not see. Then the face rose from between her blushing thighs. It was a dear familiar face, darkened by a gaze of such wanton, unrepentant lust as she had never before seen. Mr. Darcy!

"*What do you think, Elizabeth? Should I continue?*"

BEFORE SHE KNEW SHE WAS awake, Elizabeth was standing beside her bed, staring down at it. She was panting, flushed and light-headed. Her heat was followed by a cold tremor; she realised she was indeed wet between her legs, her nightgown damp. Her flesh and bones still perceived the waves of passion induced by the dream, now draining away. *So, I really felt it...* This was unlike any nightmare she ever had as a child. She experienced no true fear within the dream, yet she was horrified at herself upon awakening.

Moonlight filtered into the chilly room. Elizabeth grabbed her dressing gown and went to the washstand where a basin of fresh water awaited her morning ablutions. With a tentative gesture, she pulled up her nightgown and ran her hand quickly in and out of the union between her legs. She sniffed at it. It was not blood or urine; it smelled salty, musky. She washed her hands, confounded. After she dried them, she continued to stand by the basin for several minutes, her mind numbly searching...*for what? What could provoke such a dream? I must be more nervous about marrying than I knew... I have heard nothing these last few days but licentious tales from all my female relations... Every married woman we know has forced their advice upon us.*

Of course... Relieved a little by this explanation for the unseemly and vivid nature of her dream, Elizabeth went back to her bed, but she could not make herself lie down. She had lost, for the present moment, all trust in sleep. She sat upon a window seat, searching the eastern horizon for any sign of daybreak. At last, she determined a course of action. She comprehended that her anxiety, as was usually the case, came from a lack of knowledge.

Neither she nor Jane had any regard for the sagacity of their mother's advice regarding conjugal relations, and they felt she had purposefully misled them in some particulars. Jane was reluctant to address the topic with Elizabeth under the best of circumstances, but if Elizabeth started the conversation, Jane would contribute her opinions when pressed.

Their Aunt Phillips, if in her cups, would continue to offer unsolicited advice and tales of intimate behaviour meant to scandalise and embarrass them. Indeed, she had started doing so years before when learning from Mrs. Bennet that Elizabeth had begun receiving her "monthly visits" at age thirteen. Elizabeth and Jane avoided such situations whenever they could manage, but now that both were engaged, Aunt Phillips only grew worse. The Lucases' soiree had been unusually fraught.

During the brief visit the Wickhams paid at Longbourn immediately after their wedding, Lydia sought to thrill, but in fact, appalled all her sisters with tales from her marriage bed. The fact that she had been bedded by her husband for nearly a month before the ceremony—a shameless Lydia revealed that relations had begun even *before* her elopement—seemed to concern her not one jot. Lydia's principal target was Elizabeth, to inspire her sister's envy since Lydia believed herself to have scored a great triumph by securing a man first regarded favourably by an elder sister, and by marrying before any of her siblings. While Elizabeth was of no mind to pay heed to Lydia's ranting, she perceived that at least some of what Lydia said had frightened and confused Jane

After becoming thoroughly chilled sitting at the window, and finding no solace in the view of the frozen night landscape, Elizabeth remembered the two disturbing books she had once found hidden in her father's desk. Although the Bennet daughters were welcome to use their father's library, only Elizabeth, and Jane to a lesser extent, did so. Once Mary's prim tastes settled on reading topics to improve her morals, she found few books in her father's collection rewarding. Kitty and Lydia took no pleasure in reading except for fashion magazines and gossip in the London papers. The latter rarely held their attention as they knew few people in town, though over the winter they noted several mentions of Fitzwilliam Darcy, which they trumpeted to the family.

All the girls, however, were admonished never to disturb the sanctity of their father's desk. Mr. Bennet could have locked it but would not be bothered. He feared he would misplace the key, and he had no reason to believe any child of his would disobey him. Only Elizabeth, the most curious female in the house—and, most likely, in all of Hertfordshire—breached it at age fourteen.

She found little of interest except for the drawer containing two books of illustrations. One appeared to be of Oriental, or perhaps Indian, origin with captions and text of an unknown language. In fact, on her first perusal of the book, she thought the words were illumination-like decorations used to frame the images, later realising the squiggles and dots of repeated shapes must be words. The pictures were quite disturbing, and at the time, she deemed it for the best that she could understand none of it.

The other book was in French, and she determined from what little of the language she understood that the drawings were meant to be amusing. She delved into her French studies with rather more enthusiasm than previously shown. Once she mastered a better knowledge, she crept into the book once more, and found the cartoons not particularly diverting, even perhaps as unsettling as the more exotic publication. She never sought the books again—until now.

The house was still, and as Elizabeth passed the hall clock, she could just make out it was three-thirty. It would be an hour before the earliest servants stirred. She avoided the squeakiest steps as she descended and entered her father's library. The books were still in their drawer. She sat cross-legged on the floor in a pool of moonlight with the tomes in her lap. Gathering her courage, she opened the first, the one in French. Pictured were cavorting couples—sometimes trios!—in various states of undress, just as she remembered. The women had ridiculously large bosoms and the men were outrageously endowed, except in one or two drawings where men with small reproductive parts were derided by other fellows and ladies. There were representations of men and women with their mouths all over any and all parts of the opposite sex. The captions indicated the characters found all of these variations immensely pleasurable. *Oh, dear . . .* Elizabeth shivered.

She was just putting the French book aside when she detected a swirl in the air. She startled but suppressed any sound. Looking up, she saw Jane joining her on the floor.

"What are you doing, Lizzy?" she asked, settling herself next to her sister so their knees touched.

Elizabeth whispered, "How did you know where I was?"

"You awoke with such a start, you roused me. I thought you had a nightmare. When you were in the window seat, I nearly dozed off but then you left, and I thought you might have come down for a little brandy to help you sleep. You did not return, and here you are..." Jane looked at her sister questioningly.

Elizabeth decided not to confide the particulars of her dream. "Jane, have you ever ventured into Father's desk?"

"No."

"I thought not. There are two books here of an intimate nature. I discovered them some years ago and understood very little, but they seemed to cover rather thoroughly the topic of conjugal relations." She assumed Jane was blushing in the dark. "I am decided to try to learn as much as I can about what is to befall us on the wedding night. I am not of a docile nature, as you well know. I cannot face something so momentous in a state of complete ignorance."

Without a second of hesitancy, Jane held out a hand.

"How is your French?" Elizabeth asked in a whisper, handing her the book she had just closed.

"Passable," hissed Jane, flapping the cover open.

Elizabeth opened the book of Oriental drawings and both sisters sat in silent absorption for many minutes.

"Lizzy," Jane whispered. "What is a frisson?"

Elizabeth looked at her sister and gave her head a little shake. "I do not recall ever knowing the word. Here..." She hopped up to retrieve the French-English dictionary from its shelf. She found the English translation and held it to the moonlight. "It says, 'a brief moment of emotional excitement often experienced as a shudder or shiver; as used by the French, an intensely pleasurable physical response generated in either sex by physical stimulation of one's self or by another.' Oh dear..."

"These are just silly." Jane quietly closed the French drawings.

"Yes," mused Elizabeth, returning to the Oriental book. "I thought so, too."

Jane leaned against Elizabeth's shoulder to look at the other book. After sharing a page or two, Jane shook her head to banish the images she was seeing and turned away. "Learn what you can, Lizzy, if you must, but I cannot bear it." She started to rise.

"Fitzwilliam and Charles are Englishmen, Jane, and gentlemen. Surely, they are not such savages. I have not the least hope these drawings are helpful. I can only say they are... unsettling. Perhaps what is shown here is possible, but I cannot think any of it at all likely."

"Come, Lizzy. Let us go back to bed." Jane noticed her sister still held the dictionary. "Put that away." Elizabeth shrugged but complied.

Upon gaining their bedroom, the sisters sat on Jane's bed holding hands. Thus, they met the rising sun, having not uttered a word since returning upstairs. Sleep at the present time was not their friend.

Eventually, Elizabeth rose to dress. There was every chance Darcy would look for her on her accustomed morning walk. *How shall I face him?*

"Will you meet Mr. Darcy?" Jane ventured.

"Yes, I expect so," Elizabeth replied, realising Jane would have spied their morning meetings when they stole away by the eastern paths. "If only he had been with me last evening or if Charles had been there for you. I do not know to what further depths our Aunt Phillips and Mrs. Long can sink. What terrible things they expect of Mr. Darcy on my behalf."

"You must not let yourself believe them. But you are very brave to face him this morning. I do not know how I shall face Charles."

"Yes, I am brave, Jane. I have to be. Just look at the man I am marrying! I am convinced I am the only one in the world who ever stands up to him. It is why he loves me. And you will face Charles later today, quietly as usual and blushing in a most becoming manner, which he will observe without assuming anything at all amiss because you always *do* blush."

Elizabeth shrugged on a spencer, took up her gloves, and was gone. Jane sat at the window seat and saw her sister emerge from the servants' door, putting on a bonnet as Darcy appeared next to the far shrubbery. Usually, Elizabeth ran to him and took his hands without gloves, but now she approached him almost timidly. Jane feared for her.

Elizabeth greeted Darcy but did not reach for his hands. He held out an arm for her, and as if moving through cold molasses, Elizabeth tucked her gloved hand into his elbow, maintaining only the most tenuous connection. They moved slowly out of sight. Jane sighed for her sister and turned away to dress.

Chapter 4
An Awkward Awakening

"Thou and I are too wise to woo peaceably."
William Shakespeare, *Much Ado about Nothing*

D arcy awoke even earlier than usual. His man, Murray, was not yet about with his coffee, so Darcy drank a glass of water and dressed for walking. Usually, at least for the last few days since the announcement of their engagement, Darcy would meet Elizabeth somewhere on the paths between Longbourn, Meryton, and Netherfield, but this day he walked all the way to the furthest reach of the Netherfield estate where it touched the Longbourn property without encountering her. He made so bold as to leave the public lane and enter the Bennet garden. He saw the kitchen door open and immediately drew back until Elizabeth stepped outside.

She looked at him from across the lawn and walked rather than ran to him, producing no beaming smile and wearing gloves. He did not venture to meet her—some intuition kept him close to cover. *Has our routine been discovered? Does she know someone is watching?* When she reached him, she met his eyes, and he could see, even in the pale light, she was awash with blushes.

"Elizabeth?"

"Good morning, Fitzwilliam." She was still saying his Christian name as if trying it on for size. Other than the persistent blush, her face revealed nothing.

"Will you walk with me?" He held out his arm and was relieved when she took it. They started, not at their usual near-gallop, but instead with slow measured steps.

"Elizabeth? Are you not well?" he asked as soon as they reached the cover of trees along the cart path.

"I must confess, sir, I spent the night very ill."

"You did not sleep." It was a statement, for he could see her eyes were dull and the increasing dawn revealed circles under them.

"Hardly, sir, and when I did sleep, I got no rest from it." She shivered.

"You had a nightmare?" He halted their progress and looked at her. She would not meet his eyes and blushed anew. "You may tell me about it, you know. Surely when we are married, we may console each other's nightmares, though I cannot imagine having one with you in my arms."

Elizabeth took a sudden inhale of breath, let go of his arm, and turned away.

"Elizabeth, please."

"It is nothing; it is just silliness . . . " She turned back to him, but she was looking down.

He waited. She silently reached for his elbow, and they continued their walk.

Elizabeth considered how she should proceed, for clearly Darcy had enough knowledge of her to know she was in a tumult over more than just a little lost sleep. Since the announcement of their engagement, his observation of her in public society was even more acute and was remarked upon by others. In mixed society, friends and neighbours said he looked at her with a most charming affection, and was in every way improved. But in the confines of female conversation, the old married hens warned her that he appeared to be a very passionate man with designs to be "at her all of the time" once their vows were said. "At her," like in her dream? She shivered again, wondering whether it was a frisson—*no, what I feel is not pleasurable. I am most decidedly uncomfortable.* She shook her head to vanquish the vision of his leering smile from between her legs.

Before long, they came to a wayside where a generous soul had cleverly carved a fallen oak into a bench. "Elizabeth, you should rest." They sat.

"You are unwell. You have been doing too much, and we have been too much in company. I shall return you to Longbourn." Darcy started to rise and take her arm to assist her.

"No, Fitzwilliam, no." She remained firmly seated. "I know I am slow at confiding what disquiets me, but I do intend to do so."

He sat again. "It is unlike you to be at such a loss for words."

"The topic is one having a vocabulary with which I am utterly unfamiliar. You may laugh at me, and I daresay in a year or even a few months, I will laugh at myself, but at this moment, I can only rely upon your forbearance."

"You are one of the most thoroughly educated women I know, Elizabeth. I find it hard to imagine a topic to puzzle you."

She was bemused, and smiled briefly before catching the corner of her lower lip under her upper teeth, silent and considering. Finally, she looked at him and gave a determined nod. "It seems *all* the married women of Jane's and my acquaintance are bidding us consider, to the exclusion of everything else, a subject of which she and I have no practical knowledge. Do you take my meaning?"

She looked most earnestly into his eyes, and he returned her gaze quizzically at first. Then she saw his eyes narrow and his face become rigid. Darcy angry was indeed a fearsome thing, as Bingley had warned her once in jest, but she now knew him well enough to know she was not the source of his pronounced disapproval.

Darcy stood abruptly and began pacing before her. *Damn them all! The old tabbies have been at her.* "God's blood, Elizabeth!" he cursed in a low tense voice. "Jane, too?" Elizabeth nodded. "How I wish I had thought to spare you this." *All my work of gaining her confidence, ruined. Now she will expect herself to be like every other meek wife...*

"But how could you? You cannot be always with me. And you do not know what ladies can be."

Oh yes, I do! He tossed his head back, losing his hat. "Ladies! Ha! Ladies you call them. I could easily, aye and joyfully, wring the neck of every one of them."

This conjured a mental picture for Elizabeth that she found deeply gratifying, and she smiled. Then she started giggling, and finally she laughed at the image of Fitzwilliam Darcy, in evening clothes for some reason, throttling her Aunt Phillips. *Oh, yes, a scenario devoutly to be wished.* Her eyes were dancing with merriment, and she shared *this* vision with him when he turned to look at her as if she had lost what little was left of her wits.

"I am heartily glad to see you smile, but I assure you, I am serious. Who has been telling you these strange tales?"

"Honestly, Fitzwilliam, every one of the married ladies I know has importuned me in some way. Jane was at Netherfield yesterday, so goodness only knows what she has been privy to that I have not."

"Surely Louisa would not speak so in front of both her sister *and* Jane?"

"Fitzwilliam, think on it. Does Caroline not appear to know more than she ought? I think so, and I lay it at Louisa's door. Then there is Charlotte Collins, from whom I had a letter yesterday, stating she and my cousin will be here in a few days to stay with the Lucases until our wedding. You may well imagine my trepidation about *her* advice."

"God in heaven," Darcy swore again, shaking his head.

"Last night, Jane and I conferred, and as you know us well, you may imagine we have decided on differing strategies to see us through until the wedding."

"Dare I ask?"

"Jane's strategy is to try to avoid the old hens, not read any letters we might receive from Lydia"—here Darcy interrupted with a louder, meatier oath—"and in general, she means to attempt, through her natural serenity and trust in Charles, to meet her wedding day with some measure of equanimity."

"Sadly, this is entirely too passive a plan for my Elizabeth." Darcy smiled and sat down again. "I both love and fear that you are so inquisitive."

"Yes, sir, you may depend upon it. I am bent on such research as I can manage and yet maintain my—our—dignity." She nodded her head, determined.

"Elizabeth, I truly do shudder to think..." He took her hand, removed its glove, and held it in his. "I pray you, dearest Elizabeth, do not pursue this. It is for you and me to find our way. That is what is proper."

"If I am to judge from what I have already heard, I comprehend this is not an unimportant part of married life. I have received so much conflicting information that I am not able to ignore it. Like you, I find it unpleasant to be made sport of when I am at such a disadvantage. And I am not without resources." She lifted her chin.

Darcy was filled with foreboding. "You are not?"

"I plan to write to my Aunt Gardiner. She has a happy marriage and shall not seek to jest at my expense. What she is unwilling to commit to writing, I shall ask her to say to me in private conference when she and my uncle arrive in a week."

Darcy sighed in relief. Mrs. Gardiner was indeed the most sensible woman he knew in Elizabeth's family—or in his own, for that matter. Perhaps not too much harm could come of this.

"And then there are Papa's books."

"What?" Darcy was incredulous. "Your father keeps..." He nearly sputtered "erotica," but stopped himself. "Your father keeps such books in his library?"

"Yes, there are two books secreted in his desk where we daughters are forbidden."

"For all the good forbidding has done..."

"Oh, I found them years ago."

He saw she was ineffectively attempting nonchalance and nodded for her to proceed.

"And have not looked at them since. But after last night, the evening party at Lucas Lodge—it was uncommonly arduous and provoked a most disquieting dream."

Aha! She has admitted it!

Elizabeth paused and drew in a deep breath. "When I awoke in the night, I sought the books. Jane followed me. It is *my* intention to make a study of them, but she will not."

"Dear God, Elizabeth, is there anything I can say to dissuade you?"

"I imagine not."

"What can you tell me about the books?"

She offered with a shrug, "One is French and quite silly, but there may be some facts buried within the cartoons. The other is more foreign. The language is nothing I have the means to translate, but it has many drawings."

Darcy was blushing. *This gets worse and worse; nothing good can come of it.* "If you will not obey your father and leave them alone, is there anything I can say, *anything*, to halt your research?"

Her chin lifted further, defiant. She blurted, "Am I correct that you are not a virgin, Mr. Darcy?"

There it was, the question he dreaded most. And worse, he was Mr. Darcy again. She was asking him the most intimate question he could imagine as if it were an accusation.

The silence was heavy between them, and Elizabeth could barely breathe. She had inferred from overheard snippets of conversations with his cousin Colonel Fitzwilliam and with Bingley—many things were said in a billiard room that a woman with keen hearing might find useful—that Darcy experienced some adventures of a carnal nature during his grand tour of the continent after his university years. She prayed he would not lie.

"I shall answer your question, but first I must say this. Our experiences, relative to each other, ought not to be a source of competition. It would be an unpropitious foundation for a marriage."

"I agree, sir. It is knowledge I seek, not experience. Do you only want me to know that which *you* want me to know?"

"Elizabeth, this is no time for stubbornness. Honestly, yes, I only want you to know what *I* want you to know, and yes, I am not a virgin." His voice was tight.

Her emotions exploded into motion and she stood. "Sir, I think we should walk." And she rapidly took off down the path away from Longbourn, nearly running.

Darcy easily caught up to her, his hat in his hands, and continued by her side. After some time, she finally stopped. They had made an arc around the perimeter of Netherfield, and they were on the far side of the estate. The sky darkened.

"How the weather has caught my mood!" Now a little calmer, she tried to make light of her feelings. To cool herself, she took off the one glove she still wore, realising how ludicrous she must have appeared, marching along wearing only one glove. She hoped Darcy still possessed its mate.

"Elizabeth, what do you want to know?"

She looked down. "Am I likely, sir, to ever meet a woman with whom you have...?"

He raised her chin to look in her eyes. "No. Not unless you plan to frequent a certain exclusive brothel in the south of France and two in Vienna." He spoke gently but with thinly veiled mirth.

France, oh dear. Elizabeth recalled one or two images from her father's French book that depicted the actions in her dream. She lowered her gaze but soldiered onward. "You have never had a mistress here? You never supported an actress in London?"

"What on earth?"

"Newspapers."

"Newspapers lie, Elizabeth, but I shall not. Other than at the age of one and twenty, in Cannes and Vienna, I have never been with a woman for sport, or for love."

"And you are now nine and twenty?"

"Yes."

"So you have not... there has been no one..."

"For eight very long years." He looked away, smirking.

"Well!" She tossed her head. "I do not call that so very much *experience.*" She embroidered the word by elongating it.

The conversation reminded him of a circumstance he had met with recently regarding a beautiful, unbroken filly. All that could be done was to let her run until she tired and became docile. His first instinct was to defend his youthful exploits until he remembered he was not jousting with a friend but, in fact, was wading through the mire of a damned tricky negotiation with his future wife. He drew himself up to his full height. "I believe you will find me knowledgeable enough in five weeks' time, and that is all I shall say."

"Sir... Fitzwilliam..." she looked up at him with more trust and open affection than she had shown all morning. "I rather hoped *you* might also be a source of information."

"Under different circumstances, with clearer heads, I may be prevailed upon to elaborate what I hope from you and what you may hope from me, but we are too overwrought now."

"Oh. We are?"

"Yes. But I do have one question for *you*. Will you not tell me something of what you dreamt?"

She met his supplication with an implacable gaze.

"I assure you, Madam, my imagination will run quite wild, and we do not want that, do we?" He tried to sound jovial but realised it was merely his own prurient interest he sought to assuage rather than offering her any solace.

"Elizabeth," he whispered.

At first, Elizabeth did not at all like the tone of his voice, but when he whispered at her ear beseechingly, her eyes widened, and for the third time ever, a single strong shiver shuddered through her with a verbalised inward gasp. "I cannot." She shook her head, raising and lowering her forearms ineffectually.

She could see the beginnings of alarm in his piercing eyes.

"Please. Give me this much... You were with a man—passionately with a man?"

He was too vulnerable, and while she found she could not speak, she also could not break his gaze or risk hurting him. She nodded.

"It was I?"

She nodded again, and finally murmured, "Dearest Mr. Darcy. Of course it was you."

Darcy closed his eyes and released a long-held breath. "That is all then . . . Nothing else matters."

"I am pleased to know so little will give you comfort." She managed a weak smile.

"Perhaps comfort is not precisely the word you want." He smiled enough to deepen his dimples. Without her leave, he embraced her, and started laughing as the brim of her bonnet bumped against his chin and fell off. He caught it as it tumbled down her back, and she put her hands on his arms. They both laughed with relief.

"How long has it been raining?" Darcy asked. He released her and replaced her bonnet, scattering raindrops.

"It cannot have been for too long. I am not very wet."

They joined hands and, still laughing, ran for the shelter of the manor.

CAROLINE BINGLEY WAS NOT A woman given to gazing at views from windows, for she was in no way a romantic, but in Netherfield's small breakfast parlour, the atmosphere darkened so precipitously that she stood up from her food and looked outside. At the far end of the broad lawn, where the stone path passed through boundary shrubs, a movement of colour drew her attention. It was the rust bonnet and spencer of Miss Eliza Bennet, standing in serious conversation with Darcy. The rising wind was whipping her skirts against their legs but neither seemed to notice.

"Louisa," she whispered, "attend this."

Her sister joined her, and together they watched the couple. "I believe our Mr. Darcy and his Miss Eliza are having a disagreement," snickered Louisa.

It looked as if Darcy and Elizabeth were executing a symmetrical formal dance: Darcy stepped to Elizabeth and spoke. She looked away. He stepped away and Elizabeth pursued, he looked away. Back and forth they went until, suddenly, they were smiling, he embraced her, and the couple turned and ran hand-in-hand for the house.

"I swear, Louisa, between the two of them, they have not the sense God gave a goose," Caroline snorted, and turned back to the table.

"Such a country saying, Caroline," her sister tut-tutted.

"Who has no sense?" asked their brother, who entered the room rubbing his chilled hands. He made for the coffee urn, followed by Louisa's husband, Marcus Hurst. The men had left the house early, though not so early as Darcy, hoping to provide some pheasant for dinner. The sudden cold rain chased them back, guns unfired.

"Mr. Darcy and Miss Eliza, Charles. Unless Louisa and I are much mistaken, they have just had a spat and reconciled, and will be bursting upon us any minute." Caroline turned from the window. "Heaven spare me from nursing another sodden Bennet sister." Bingley glared at her. She did not notice.

WHEN DARCY AND ELIZABETH REACHED the overhang of the house outside the kitchen entrance, he caught her in another embrace. They were both laughing and panting for breath. Darcy removed Elizabeth's bonnet and shook it with his hand behind her back, whilst keeping her within the circle of his arms.

"I shall call for Bingley's coach and send you home."

Elizabeth returned his smile, staying close. Then she stopped smiling but continued looking into his eyes. He saw her lips part and met them with his. It was, he thought, for a third or fourth kiss, quite satisfyingly executed. Their lips were soft together until he pulled away.

She was flushed from running, which he found enchanting. "I love you, you know. You will not forget between now and when Bingley and I arrive for tea?"

"No, Fitzwilliam, I shall not forget, nor have I forgotten for a single moment since"—she hesitated—"Hunsford."

Darcy smiled and opened the door into the kitchen, producing a great to-do amongst the servants as they scattered, bowed, curtsied, assisted with the removal of outer garments, and generally made way for the hurried progress of the couple from above-stairs.

Darcy and Elizabeth did indeed burst into the breakfast room and fell upon the coffee urn as if it dispensed manna from heaven. "Bingley, I found this bedraggled creature in a hedgerow and have ordered your carriage to take it home."

Caroline could not resist being snide. "Mr. Darcy, are you quite certain she will not take ill? In my experience, Bennet women become chilled with uncommon ease."

"Caroline!" Bingley was as vexed as Elizabeth had ever seen him. "You malign both Miss Elizabeth and my bride. I must insist you stop."

Caroline's observations were ignored by Darcy and Elizabeth. As Elizabeth warmed her hands on her cup, she thought to ask, "Mr. Darcy, have you a glove of mine in your coat pocket?"

"Of course, let us fetch it." They exited the room with as much commotion as they had entered it. In the entrance hall, Darcy called up the stairs, "Murray?"

After a moment, his man appeared. "Mr. Darcy, sir? Do you require a lady's glove?" He held Elizabeth's twisted glove for them to see.

"Ah!" Darcy bounded up the stairs. "You found it. Good man." He was back at Elizabeth's side in no time. "Shall we re-join the others?"

Elizabeth shook her head. "Make my apologies to the Bingleys. I am too tired to spar with Caroline. I shall await the carriage here, and thank you for arranging it."

"I shall wait with you." Darcy took the hand not holding coffee. "Once Bingley and I arrive at Longbourn, I do not imagine we shall be alone again for the rest of the day."

"Look at it rain." Elizabeth tipped her head towards the windows next to the front doors. "There will be no more walking today."

She seemed distant again. "Elizabeth." Holding her gaze, Darcy kissed the back of her hand, then turned it over and kissed the palm. She caught the corner of her lower lip with her teeth. He stepped to her, lowering his lips as she released hers. Again Darcy was the one to end their kiss, but he rested his forehead on hers, whispering, "Promise me you will try to nap until we arrive?"

"Yes, I shall. It seems, sir, whether awake or asleep, I deny you nothing." Her voice trembled

Darcy became dizzy at this confession. The carriage rolled by the windows. Elizabeth placed her coffee cup on the hall table, put on her bonnet, and picked up her gloves. The sky had opened, and Darcy moved with her to the door, now held open by a footman. The rain was nearly deafening.

"Were you afraid?" he murmured.

She met his eyes with a troubled brow. "No, I was not—not until I awoke and could judge what was being done…what was happening.

"Stay here. Stay dry." She turned and darted for the carriage, where the footman handed her in, and she found a maid waiting to ride with her.

Darcy stared after her, too stupefied to move.

As the carriage bore her away, she reflected, *I do want to tell him about the dream. Someday…someday when I know a great deal more than I do now…*

Chapter 5
Some Letters

"Neighbours, you are tedious."
William Shakespeare, *Much Ado about Nothing*

What just happened? Darcy slowly shook his head as he watched the Bingley coach leave with Elizabeth aboard. He thought about her parting words and her remembering that he loved her since hearing his proposal at Hunsford. *Those few months from Hunsford to Pemberley—did she start to love me, even then?* Nothing less than half a bottle of fine port, added to an extended period of quiet and solitude, would allow him to sort the meaning of everything Elizabeth said.

But there was to be no such opportunity in the immediate future. An urgent note must be written to Elizabeth's father, and there was an equally urgent need to confer with Bingley in private. Darcy was about to stick his head into the breakfast room when he heard raised voices, and he paused at the partly opened door.

"I say, Caroline"—Hurst was speaking—"that is a damned fool notion, and based on what? You are blind! He is head over heels in love, and it is not the sort of trifling affection that burns itself out. He has been in love with her since last autumn. Are you *all* blind? You think he will tire of her? You are mad!"

"Mr. Hurst, such language!" fretted his wife.

"It is true," Bingley chimed in. "Think, Caroline! You are not in love with Darcy. You have shown him no true affection. He simply has connections and consequence you wish to assume. You think of nothing but position and wealth. You would make him miserable. He wants a partner, not an ornament, and certainly not a harridan. You would have the Pemberley servants fleeing, Darcy House in an uproar, and I do not know what-all."

"It is astonishing. I have no encouragement from my family!" Caroline spat, and flung open the breakfast room door to find Darcy glaring at her. In spite of her rouged cheeks, she turned white and frozen.

Darcy cleared his throat. "Excuse me. This is clearly a family dispute, and I have no wish to intrude. Bingley, would you have time for me in, say, half an hour, in your study? I would be greatly obliged."

Bingley was agitated and florid. "Of course, Darcy. I think we are finished here. Would you like to confer now?"

"No, Bingley, I thank you. I have a letter to write, which you may wish to sign with me. I shall prepare it and meet you." Darcy withdrew, bowing to the Bingleys and Hursts. He heard Caroline gulp.

"Oh, Darcy," she started, as usual assuming an intimacy to which she was not entitled, "I am so sorry, of course. Let me apologise for my family."

"Miss Bingley." Darcy met her fawning gaze with narrowed eyes and a fixed jaw. "You need rather apologise to me for yourself alone, and you have needed to do so since insulting Miss Bennet and Miss Elizabeth this morning. I have never believed you to speak for your family."

He turned and walked to the Netherfield library where he knew there was an escritoire more private than the one in the drawing room. Sitting, he stared at the blank paper, sighed disgustedly at having to write, and then did so.

15 October 1812
Netherfield Park

Dear sir,

It has come to the attention of Mr. Bingley and me that your two eldest daughters have discovered books of a most disturbing nature in your library desk. Miss Elizabeth admits knowing of their existence for some years, but quite recently, the two ladies have begun consulting these same, thinking the books may aid them in preparation for married life. Although we understand Miss Bennet has stated to her sister that she will not continue to make a study of them, Miss Elizabeth will make no such promise. Please be aware that Miss Elizabeth told me of these circumstances in confidence. Miss Bennet is not aware that Mr. Bingley or I know she has consulted the books.

We beseech you, sir, to remove these books from the desk where they currently reside and take them from Longbourn or secrete them where they cannot possibly be found.

It is to be feared these books have already unsettled the delicate sensibilities of your daughters, but at least we may prevent any further harm.

Your daughters have endured a veritable assault on their peace of mind by local married women revealing, or so they think, the mysteries of conjugal relations, and although perhaps in some cases well intentioned, this advice was not well received. Please ask Mrs. Bennet to desist on this topic, and help Mr. Bingley and me to ensure that Miss Bennet and Miss Elizabeth are in company with Mrs. Phillips as little as possible.

Any assistance you are able to render will be greatly appreciated.

Gratefully,
F. Darcy
C. Bingley

"GREAT GOD, DARCY!" CRIED BINGLEY after reading the letter in his study and signing it while Darcy paced. Darcy poured them generous portions of brandy, and they sat together in front of the fire.

"Too early?" he asked as he handed a tumbler to Bingley.

Bingley shook his head. "Not on an occasion such as this. Did Miss Elizabeth give you any description of what they saw?"

"She is such an innocent, Bingley!" Darcy ruefully shook his head. "She mentioned only one book was French, and she described the drawings as cartoons. The other is in a language foreign to her—Sanskrit, I would wager —with drawings much more explicit, intended to instruct rather than amuse."

"Oh, God..." Bingley sat forward, his head in his hands. "My poor Jane..." He was too overwrought to drink.

"We should have foreseen this and brought our families to London to avoid the local tabbies. *They* have done more damage than anything read in the library at Longbourn."

"Certainly you know the same thing could happen in town." Bingley sighed.

"Yes, of course, but their circle would be much smaller, and there would be the Gardiners, who are, by far, the most sensible people in Jane and

Elizabeth's family. I shall be glad when they arrive." Darcy turned his attention from what-ifs to the matter at hand. "I shall not put a return address on this, nor seal it with my signet. Other than Elizabeth, no one there has seen my writing. Do you have anyone unknown by the Bennet household who could deliver it directly to Mr. Bennet? I do not think I exaggerate when I say Elizabeth would kill me if she knew of this letter. If she does try to find those books again and they are missing, let her think what she may, but at present, she must not know our actions."

Bingley considered. "I shall ask my man, Mansfield, to take it. I do not believe he has any association with Longbourn."

Darcy sealed the letter with the tip of a knife in the wax and Bingley left the room to seek his valet.

MRS. BENNET WAS WAVING A fretful hanky at Elizabeth from under the Longbourn portico as she was handed down from the Bingley carriage. "Oh, Lizzy, how you do vex me! You have scared us to death! It would be just *like* you to take cold and *die* before securing the most eligible bachelor in the whole of England!"

Elizabeth lifted her chin and brushed past her mother, out of the rain. "Mama, I thought you were of the opinion that people do not die of 'trifling little colds.'"

"Whenever did I say such a thing? What nonsense. You do try my nerves. You must take care of yourself. So... you have come home in the Bingley carriage?"

"Yes, Mama, I was near Netherfield when the rain started. I am hardly wet at all."

"You must have a hot bath and some warm broth, and I shall write to Netherfield and tell Mr. Darcy not to come today."

"We need not trouble the servants on my account. I have a letter to write. Then I shall rest until the gentlemen arrive. Where is Jane?"

"She had a headache after breakfast and is in her room. Pray, write your letter in the small sitting room so you do not disturb her."

"I must change out of my boots, Mama. I shall not bother Jane."

Elizabeth dashed up the stairs before her mother could argue further. Jane was reading in a window seat, much as Elizabeth left her, except now she was dressed. "Lizzy! I was watching for you! You are not drenched?"

Jane stood; Elizabeth clasped her in a tenacious embrace and, without warning, burst into uncharacteristic tears. "Jane, oh Jane!" They rocked where they stood.

"Lizzy!"

When Elizabeth could speak, she led Jane to the closest bed, and they sat. "Oh, Jane... why do I do this to myself? Fitzwilliam is so kind. He is all that is gentle and patient. It is not right of me to get so anxious and mulish. What could I say? I was not sensible at all. I insisted he reveal secrets about himself. I should not have asked. He is a marvel indeed if his affection survives this."

Jane began removing her sister's short boots. "In him, I think you have found the deep love you have always sought. We both were uncommonly foolish last night. We must not let the married ladies disturb us."

There was a tap at the door. "Yes?" responded Jane.

A maid stuck her head in the door. "Mrs. Hill wants to know if anything is needed."

"Thank you, Annie," said Elizabeth. "Is there any juice?"

"There is fresh cider, Miss."

"Please bring us some?"

"Yes, Miss." Annie bounced a curtsy and closed the door.

"Lizzy, have you given up your quest for knowledge?" Jane asked. "I have reflected on it, and I feel you should."

"I intend to write our Aunt Gardiner. Fitzwilliam agrees she is calm and sensible. She and Uncle may know his heart better than any of my relations, even you. After meeting him at Pemberley, they exchanged visits and formed a happy acquaintance, especially after Lydia's... business." That the Gardiners formed a warm attachment to Darcy was widely known throughout the family. "Does that seem imprudent?"

"I hope it will soothe your mind, Lizzy."

Elizabeth found a pair of slippers and padded to her desk. She was just drawing parchment from a drawer when there was a tap at the door, which Jane answered. Annie entered with a tray holding two glasses of cider.

"Thank you, Annie," said Elizabeth without looking up.

As Annie placed the cider on a side table, a knock at the front door was heard echoing up the stairs. Jane crept to the landing, looked down, and was filled with wonder to see Bingley's valet—who had been introduced to her during a tour of Netherfield—enter the front hall. He spoke in a low tone to Mrs. Hill, and he was admitted to their father's library. Thinking the circumstance odd and not wanting to excite Elizabeth's curiosity, she decided to say nothing of it.

⊙⊙

15 October 1812
Longbourn, Hertfordshire

Dear Aunt,

It is with a troubled mind that I write you. Since the announcement of our engagements, Jane and I have been so inundated with unsolicited advice on what we are to expect of conjugal relations that we are driven quite frantic. Although you will be here in a week's time, I long to have some words of reason and sense from my dear aunt, the one woman in my family who knows my future husband and his heart better than anyone currently around me.

There is so much I do not know and little means to learn of it. Mama is useless and seems somehow less than truthful, and the very approach of my Aunt Phillips now fills me with dread, even though both Jane and I want to believe her tales are ridiculous.

Do please respond soon, and if what you need to say ought not be put to paper, merely promise you are willing to confer with me privately as soon as may be upon your arrival. Jane reports I am foolish, and I expect, as usual, she is right. Things I have no knowledge of make me apprehensive. If I have no need to worry, I shall trust your word.

Your loving niece,
E. Bennet

Elizabeth handed the letter to Jane. She read it, and sighing, said nothing. Elizabeth went downstairs to seek Mrs. Hill and have the letter posted immediately.

"A strange gentleman is with your father," Mrs. Hill whispered, eyeing the closed library door.

Just then, the door opened and Elizabeth scampered up the stairs, turning at the landing to see the stranger's back as he exited.

"Papa has had a visitor," Elizabeth reported to Jane.

"Has he?" Jane tried to sound disinterested and did not look up from her book.

Elizabeth drank her cider, kicked off her slippers, and lay down upon her bed. She fell into a fitful slumber lasting over an hour.

MR. BENNET READ THE LETTER from his two future sons-in-law with mounting alarm. He sat before Bingley's valet in as profound a state of mortification as he had ever endured. Was he always to be found in some state of parental defect by Darcy? The valet awaited a verbal response as the Netherfield gentlemen had bid him. Mr. Bennet cleared his throat.

"Please tell your master and Mr. Darcy that I shall undertake everything they have asked me to do. Tell them further, I am abjectly sorry they have found the need to write me thus. And thank you."

Mansfield bowed and left the room. Mr. Bennet heard him quit the house and sat in stunned silence. *Once again, I have revealed myself to be the most lazy and dilatory of fathers ever to exist.* The idea that he, through negligence, had perhaps reduced his Lizzy's standing with the man she appeared to love so ardently overwhelmed him with remorse. That his earlier unconcern had cost Lydia her reputation meant little to him now, as Lydia had made her own bed, and others had expended a great deal more effort and expense than he had to set the family reputation upright. This present matter, however, was much more private, much less likely to be broadcast, and yet carried just as much potential to do lasting damage to his two favourite daughters.

Mr. Bennet drew open a desk drawer and looked at the offending books. Until this letter from the men of Netherfield, he had forgotten their existence. The two volumes were gifts from Sir William Lucas for services rendered nearly ten years ago. Because Mr. Bennet was known to be developing a library and enjoyed art, and Sir William, who could not imagine wasting time or money on any book not amusing or arousing, decided these volumes constituted a gift of "art." Thomas Bennet slung them into the drawer upon receipt, and three weeks later wrote a note of thanks. Then he thought of them no more.

Now the two volumes were leering at him, and even though they might have some useful monetary value, Mr. Bennet tossed them into the fireplace and watched them suspiciously for the hour it took them to burn. He drew a sheet of stationary from his top desk drawer and wrote:

15 October 1812
Longbourn

My dear Gentlemen,

With the most profound mortification, I find myself yet again revealed to be the poorest quality of father. I feel keenly that the gravity of the current situation requires more, much more, than the verbal response you requested, which I trust I made to your satisfaction. Please be now advised that the two offending and offensive volumes have been burnt to the last cinder and have been replaced by a volume outlining proper deportment for young ladies upon their debut in society, dated 1795, and a fashion magazine of Kitty's that found its way into this library. As to the conduct of Mrs. Bennet and her sister, I shall endeavour to remedy all I am able, by interview and instruction in the first case, and by avoidance in the second.

As the proud father of two of the least silly girls in England, please understand I know them well enough to admit that the curious and inquisitive nature of my second eldest has been known to embroil my eldest in matters about which she would, if left to herself, not take an improper interest. However, given this specific instance, I hope you will further understand that there is no proper way for a father to address such matters directly. In any other case, I would interview Elizabeth to clarify and settle any confusion.

However, I shall send word to Mrs. Gardiner, who is prodigiously sensible and has taken particular interest in my eldest daughters, having a high regard for each of them. She arrives here in a week's time, and I am certain she will know exactly what to say.

In the meantime, please, I beseech you, do not think ill of my two eldest daughters. You are fine men. You honour me by selecting my Lizzy and my Jane to be your wives, and it would break this old man's heart to know my actions, or lack thereof, have cost them the love of either of you. It has been my fondest wish for both of them to spend their lives with partners whom they could love and respect. If I have cost them this, I do not know how I shall bear it.

Most sincerely yours,
T. Bennet

Mr. Bennet called for the footman to deliver the letter to Netherfield immediately. He wanted the gentlemen to receive it before their arrival to spend the afternoon and evening with the family.

AS DARCY AND BINGLEY AWAITED the return of Mansfield, Darcy decided sending an express to Mrs. Gardiner would not come amiss. Bingley left him alone in the library to compose the following:

15 October 1812
Netherfield Park, Hertfordshire

My dear madam,

This express is sent to alert you of a letter perhaps already on its way to you from your niece Miss Elizabeth Bennet. Although I do not, of course, have any direct knowledge of its wording, Miss Elizabeth has made me aware of the general topic, and I believe some history of her motivation in writing it will help form your response.

Please understand, I write this with my longstanding deep affection and regard for your niece, of which I suspect you are already quite well aware, and my profound regard for you and your husband foremost in my mind. Miss Elizabeth has two aunts and I have two aunts, and between the two of us, you are the only relation to whom we can turn for sage advice and sensible direction. And thus I write.

Since the announcement of our engagement, Miss Elizabeth and Miss Bennet have been assaulted—no, I do not think it too strong a word—with bad or worse advice about what they may expect of marital relations. The alarming nature of the various reports and predictions they have received has disquieted your nieces, and you, better than I, may imagine with some accuracy what is being said.

Both are experiencing affected sleep, and Miss Elizabeth only this morning alluded to a disturbing dream about me which has temporarily—I hope —adversely interrupted her usual happy manners. You know her, as I do, to have an inquisitive nature, and she will insist on research, as she calls it, stating it is what she does not know that frightens her. She has accused me of wanting her to know only that which I want her to know—her words—and she is perfectly correct. I make no apology.

She and I have agreed that she should write you as the likeliest source of comfort and truth. It disturbs me more than I can say to think she might approach our wedding night with fear and distrust. I would never consider doing anything to scare her, hurt her, or cause her ever to think I would put my own selfish desires before her continued happiness.

You may safely assume I am embarrassed to write of such things. Anything you can say to calm her will calm me, too. I am certain she will wish to have an interview with you when you arrive at Longbourn, and I hope you will grant her this request.

You have my blessing for whatever you choose to say, as I feel certain you will be our ally in this.

Gratefully,
F. Darcy

Chapter 6
The Taming of the Flibbertigibbet

"'I can see he's not in your good books,' said the messenger.
'No, and if he were, I would burn my library.'"
William Shakespeare, *Much Ado about Nothing*

Thomas Bennet opened the door to his library and called for his wife. After waiting a few moments, he called for Mrs. Hill, who came to him immediately.

"Mr. Bennet, sir?"

"Ah, Hill. Where is Mrs. Bennet?"

"In her sitting room above stairs, taking some tea and making lists of things, sir."

"So she should have heard me when I called just now?"

"I should think so, sir. I heard you from the kitchen."

"Has she been taken deaf, do you think?"

Mrs. Hill smirked and shook her head. "Would you like me to fetch her, sir?"

"No, Hill. It is time the insubordination in this house was dealt with as it should have been long ago." Mr. Bennet took the stairs as briskly as Mrs. Hill had ever seen him, and he entered the open door of his wife's sitting room.

"Mrs. Bennet! Did you not hear my call?"

She looked up with surprise. Her husband usually sent a servant for her, or forgot what he wanted if she ignored him. It was much more exhilarating to make lists of wedding details than to attend to whatever petty issues Mr. Bennet might raise.

50

"Mr. Bennet! Is there some emergency? Are Mr. Darcy or Mr. Bingley ill?" This was her chief concern as the wedding neared, that an errant infectious disease might carry off either groom.

Mr. Bennet closed the door to his wife's sitting room, and took a seat facing her. "Mrs. Bennet, let me first say that, when your husband calls you, he expects a response. I do not think, after nearly twenty-five years of marriage, that expecting courtesy is too much to ask. Do I make myself clear?"

"Oh, Mr. Bennet, if you have come in here to argue with me, I pray you leave at once."

"I am here, Mrs. Bennet, because you would not come to me, and we have a matter of immense and immediate importance, which we must discuss."

Grumbling under her breath, Mrs. Bennet made a great show of setting aside her lap desk and turning her attention to her husband.

"It has come to my attention, madam, that you have been relating stories of married life to Lizzy and Jane, which our daughters find most unsettling, and these, by extension, reflect upon me in a poor light."

"Nonsense. Of what can you be speaking?"

"How do you know it is nonsense if you claim not to know the topic? Oh, never mind... My point is, Mrs. Bennet, you have told the girls disturbing stories about marital relations and what they may expect, and it has frightened them. I want you to correct what you have said and cease discussing the topic with them if you cannot or will not be truthful."

"And may I ask how you came by this knowledge? A father should not know of this. My daughters would *never* discuss such a thing with their father. It is a mother's place to prepare daughters for what may happen in the marriage bed."

"Both of our daughters have complained to their intended spouses." Mr. Bennet was not above stretching the truth to carry his point. "They have been vague as to details, but so completely forthright about their attendant fears as to make what was told to them completely apparent."

"Mr. Bennet! I shall not be criticised on this subject. The girls have no idea what to expect on their wedding night, and I believe it prudent that they be made to expect the worst. I consider their behaviour to their intendeds to be highly improper, implying *any* of what should be talked of *only* amongst women, and I shall scold them, sir. Make no mistake."

"Fanny, you will do no such thing."

Voices were raised. From their bedroom, Elizabeth and Jane could hear the tone but not the content. They looked at each other with open astonishment.

"Mr. Bennet, on this point I shall stand my ground. It is a mother's duty to protect daughters from false hopes of the marriage bed."

"Have you no consideration for their future husbands, and therefore madam, no respect for what they may infer *our* relationship has been? Have I been a brute to you? Have I *ever* made unacceptable demands upon your person? If you speak of horrors you yourself have not experienced, the girls will infer you *have* experienced them, and at my hands!"

"Mr. Bennet, that is ridiculous! The girls do not think of you and me in such a way."

"No indeed, I believe they did not until you felt you needed to see that they enter the married state expecting the worst, as you say."

"And so they should!"

"Mrs. Bennet! You will speak of this subject to Lizzy and Jane no more, except to say you have no reason to believe either Mr. Darcy or Mr. Bingley are brutish, unkind, or perverted in any way. They are gentlemen and will be kind at the very least. You do no one any good service by painting all men with the same brush. You *will* stop this."

"No, sir, I certainly shall not. This is not your concern, Mr. Bennet—not your concern at all!"

"Fanny, I shall lock you in this room until the wedding if you leave me no other choice. No details, no lace, no shopping, no hectoring Miss Bingley and Mrs. Hurst—none of it."

"Oh, Mr. Bennet! You cannot mean it!"

"Do not try my patience further, madam. You will apologise to Lizzy and Jane and amend the untruths you have foisted upon them, or I shall have you kept separate from them until they are wed. I have never been unkind to you in our marriage bed, and I shall not have you implying to anyone that I have. You have no idea the harm you have done, and I shall see it does not continue. The choice is yours, Mrs. Bennet." He stood and began pacing in what little space was available in front of his wife.

"This is most improper, Mr. Bennet—most indelicate. Fathers of daughters must not concern themselves with such things. This was Lizzy, was it not? She's gone telling tales, has she? Only Lizzy would ever think to seek counsel in such a shameful way."

"Lizzy and Jane should not approach their wedding in a spirit of fear and misapprehension; you and your gossiping sister have overstepped yourselves. You give Lizzy and Jane the advice better used on Lydia, who is now married to one of the vilest seducers we are ever likely to meet, no thanks to ourselves..."

"Oh, Mr. Bennet! Lower your voice..."

"No, Fanny. I shall not be moved. You have a decision to make. Remain in your room until the wedding, or amend your advice to Lizzy and Jane. And no more social engagements with Mrs. Phillips. She is no longer fit for civil society—drunk or sober!"

Husband and wife stared at each other with fury. For several long moments, neither of them moved nor blinked. It was finally the weaker-natured Mrs. Bennet who relented. "I am appalled, sir, that you would interfere with a mother's care of her daughters in this manner, but since you are determined upon it, I shall speak to the girls and amend what I have said. And you must allow that, although I can certainly cease inviting my own sister to meals and gatherings here, I cannot control what others may do and who may wish to invite her in our larger society."

"Thank you, Mrs. Bennet. I wish to be informed of all invitations coming to this house between now and the wedding. Lizzy and Jane will not be accepting invitations to small parties where their aunt is in attendance. In large parties, I am confident they can and will avoid her themselves, and will have Mr. Bingley and Mr. Darcy to defend them.

"That is all for now, Mrs. Bennet." He dismissed her, even though he was in her room. Mr. Bennet paused, bowed briefly, turned and slammed her door behind him. The start of a new tirade, delivered in soliloquy, was heard over his shoulder.

"Well I never..." Mrs. Bennet began, ranting to no one. She rose from her favourite rocking chair and sat at her desk. She was angry over the scene just endured and blamed Elizabeth. The only thing to be done was to—as far as propriety would allow—disavow herself of her second eldest daughter and her wedding plans, even if she was marrying a man with ten thousand a year. She would write to her brother's wife, who seemed to understand Elizabeth as she herself could not, and beg assistance. Mrs. Bennet did not like writing letters other than extending social invitations and responding to them, but in this case she wrote with alacrity. As silly and blathering as Mrs. Bennet was in her manner of speech, in her habits of writing, she tended to be concise even when prevaricating.

15 October 1812
Longbourn, Hertfordshire

Dear Sister,

The plans for Lizzy and Jane's wedding are quite over-taking me, and I find I must write to request a favour, which, if each daughter were having a separate ceremony, I would not need to ask. May I prevail upon you to assist with Lizzy's wardrobe for the event? Mr. Bennet has set a budget of £75 for the trousseau. While I wish it were much more, I trust you to help Lizzy with her decisions as she may not understand what she needs or purchase enough. Perhaps you may find fabric for her gown in town, such as may be used by the local dressmakers, and when you arrive later in the week, other items may be ordered.

It is inconvenient for me to be shopping for both Lizzy and Jane at the same time. I cannot keep all of the details separated properly. Please say you will consent to providing such assistance, and think of it as practice for when your own dear Alyse and Sophie plan their nuptials.

Fondly and gratefully,
F. Bennet

Simultaneously, in the Longbourn library, the following letter was being composed.

15 October 1812
Longbourn, Hertfordshire

Dear Sister,

I shall safely wager you will find, in the next hours and days, your correspondence inundated with missives from Hertfordshire. Indeed, His Majesty's Postal Service may have need of a new man just to handle the Gardiner volume. Yet, I find I must now add to the man's burden.

You will certainly be receiving a letter from Lizzy, and likely one from

Mr. Darcy if I have become any judge of the man's character. They write about a situation arising in part from the officious and ill-natured attentions of my wife and her sister, though I would not doubt every married woman of Lizzy and Jane's acquaintance had a hand in causing the chaos and misapprehension now lodged in their minds.

You may now well imagine where my thoughts tend. Lizzy and Jane have both, usually together, received the foulest warnings and slanders of what to expect of married life. They have spoken, or at least Lizzy has, to their betrotheds of the resultant fears that have developed, and as you may well apprehend, both men have expressed their alarm to me.

I have proved no help in the matter, as it must be further confessed that two books on the subject, which I had quite forgotten I owned—past tense as they are now both ashes—have been consulted by the girls under cloak of night.

I have prevailed upon Mrs. Bennet to retract what she has said of the matter, and at the behest of Mr. Darcy and Mr. Bingley, we at Longbourn will endeavour to separate Lizzy and Jane from their Aunt Phillips when necessary, and to avoid her society between now and the wedding.

Now you see what pandemonium awaits you and Edward upon your arrival. You and I have ever been Lizzy's allies against the silliest elements of the Bennet household, and it will be, more than ever, thus from now until the wedding day. I am certain her mother will blame her for the current situation, when in truth, if Mrs. Bennet at least—there is no accounting for her sister—had been truthful and sensible with the girls about their expectations of living with a gentleman, this entire debacle could have been greatly diminished, if not avoided entirely.

This letter comes to you as something of a warning. I know Lizzy will apply to you for the comfort and honesty she will find in short supply from her mother. The men who love her best, and Jane and her Bingley, too, look to you for help and guidance.

Gratefully,
T. Bennet

Mr. Bennet carefully folded and sealed the letter, and stepped to the hall to call for Mrs. Hill. As it happened, she was bustling past him to answer the front door. The two gentlemen from Netherfield had arrived. Mrs. Hill took the letter and noted the address with wonder.

Mr. Bennet slipped into the drawing room to receive the betrotheds of his two eldest daughters, but they only had time to nod to each other in complete understanding before Mrs. Bennet entered, her haughty countenance looking as if her behaviour had never been censured in the whole of her life. Her actions were, however, somewhat changed for the better, and she showed an unusual deference for her husband that grew more pronounced once her two eldest daughters entered the room. This was much remarked upon by the gentlemen after their departure later that evening, and also by Jane and Elizabeth. Even Mr. Bennet told his wife he was proud of her before lodging himself in his own bedchamber for the night.

Chapter 7
Aunt Gardiner Saves the Day

"Pause awhile, And let my counsel sway you."
William Shakespeare, *Much Ado about Nothing*

Mrs. Madeleine Gardiner was surprised to receive an express from Mr. Darcy. It arrived while the children were enjoying an outing in the park with their nursemaid; therefore, she had the opportunity to address its contents immediately. The topic—Elizabeth's newly awakened curiosity about the particulars of marital relations—was disturbing to be sure, but Mrs. Gardiner also regarded Darcy's unrest with amusement. *Men!* Darcy's letter did not require a response, so she sat in wait for Elizabeth's, and pondered whether to share this unlooked-for development with her husband.

When Elizabeth's letter appeared a day later, accompanied by letters from both her parents, Mrs. Gardiner was alarmed until all the missives had been read, then she found herself highly diverted indeed. Before responding to any, she gathered them all and proceeded to her husband's study.

"What in the world is happening in Hertfordshire, my dear?" Mr. Gardiner asked with a laugh after reading them.

His wife smiled. "I wanted you to be apprised of the circumstances surrounding our arrival on Saturday. Who knows what questions may be directed at *you*, by the gentlemen."

"At me! Oh no, the men do not need help. I think *you* are the designated font of marital wisdom. If you can keep me out of it, I should be quite grateful."

"You seem to have the reputation of keeping a sensible wife happy. You will just have to put up with it."

"How little they know!" Mr. Gardiner was laughing as his wife deposited herself in his lap.

He patted his wife's newly noticeable belly. They were content with the symmetry of their family—two girls followed by two boys—and had not looked for further blessings. After four conceptions and four unremarkable deliveries, Mrs. Gardiner thought she knew the counting of her months forward and backward; her tendency to fertility was greater midway between one course and the next. However, love *had* been in the air—and between the sheets—during their short stay at Lambton, and Mrs. Gardiner had simply lost track of time. To have been travelling so amiably out of their normal routine, and to have met the infamous Mr. Darcy and found him to be a charming and obliging man who appeared to be in love with their favourite niece, had been...exhilarating.

"Any quickening yet, Maddy?"

"Not yet, but it is just about time. I still think it would be a lark to name this child Lambton..."

"Not Pemberley?"

"I fear that would embarrass our soon-to-be nephew too greatly. Lambton would be bad enough!" They laughed.

"Well, I am just sorry you must travel during this time. I know you will be more easy in a rollicking carriage after another few weeks."

"Yes, even though we are to spend Christmas at Pemberley—my, how well that sounds—and the journey is much farther, I look forward to it a great deal more than the few hours it will take to get to Longbourn. And now to act the part of mother-of-the-bride to poor Lizzy! The letter from Fanny concerns me greatly."

"Then you had better answer it now. And Lizzy's too. Feel free to send your responses by express, my dearest, I think the situation warrants it. I know my sister's nerves."

Mrs. Gardiner grew contemplative. "Edward...do you suppose we might not be aware of showing such marked partiality for certain of our children as Thomas and Fanny do? I cannot think it right, and would be offended to find I was behaving in such a manner."

"I pray neither of us do, my dear. But I know to whom to apply for an answer. Our children love their cousin Jane. She would tell us, should we ask, whether any of them have remarked on any consistent preference shown by ourselves. As you say, we may be unaware."

Mrs. Gardiner nodded. "If the topic arises during our visit, I shall ask Jane. I would be mortified to know I was behaving like Fanny."

"I know you would. Now off with you; you have letters to write, and I must finish reading this contract from our shipping company before asking your opinion of it."

Mr. Gardiner helped Mrs. Gardiner to her feet, and she kissed his balding forehead before withdrawing to her escritoire in the drawing room, where she produced the following two letters.

17 November 1812
Gracechurch Street, London

My Dear Sister,

Please rest assured I am prepared to take on whatever tasks you may wish to assign me to prepare Elizabeth for her wedding. How well I can imagine the confusion a double wedding might bring about. I recently saw some lovely fabric, and with your permission and subsequent approval, I plan to purchase a length of it and present it to Lizzy as a gift. If you do not like it, she may use it for something other than her wedding ensemble, but I believe you will approve. It is a sheer type of mesh of a unique colour called candlelight. The edge of the fabric has a wide band of embroidered leaf outlines in various shades of green, and I think this would do very well as a petticoat border under a solid-colour gown, or as the outer layer of a multiple-layered skirt. I shall secure it tomorrow morning, and you may judge for yourself when I arrive. If I can purchase enough, it would also be suitable as veiling. It put me in mind of Lizzy the moment I saw it.

This is a joyful time coming upon us, and your brother and I are looking forward to seeing Jane and Lizzy happily settled. We believe you will discover Mr. Darcy improves greatly upon further acquaintance. You may find this hard to believe, but we are convinced his affection for Lizzy is quite as long-standing as is Mr. Bingley's for Jane. I shall speak more of this when we are together.

Fondly,
M. Gardiner

And to her niece, she wrote:

My Dearest Niece,

Of course, dear Lizzy, you find me more than willing to meet in private when your uncle and I arrive at Longbourn. We may certainly include Jane, if you wish it and she chooses. I own I am surprised by the topic of our discourse, but rest assured, I act as your advocate in all things with all of your family and acquaintance. I suspect you are not the first young woman to be sent into turmoil by rumours and unfounded tales of married life. While I do not wish to discuss any particulars herein, let me say that I am quite certain, knowing Mr. Darcy as I do, that you have nothing whatsoever to fear. My observation of him, and conversation with him, leads me to believe he adores you in just the way I would wish your future husband to, and I have no doubt that, on the occasion, his thoughts will only be for your pleasure and happiness.

But let me repeat, it is for your peace of mind that I am concerned, and I shall speak to you for your benefit alone, and not at the behest and prompting of Mr. Darcy. He will not know of the material points of our conversation unless you tell him. I am your instrument in this; make no mistake.

Your loving aunt,
M. Gardiner

The express was on its way to Hertfordshire by ten the following morning after Mr. Gardiner had reviewed, at his wife's request, what she had written. "You always strike just the right tone, my dear." Mr. Gardiner beamed at her over his desk.

THE PACKET OF LETTERS ARRIVED at Longbourn before four o'clock, and Elizabeth had just returned from a vigorous walk. The lanes were quite muddy from the previous stormy night, and she was changing her clothes when Mrs. Hill tapped at her bedroom door.

"An express from your aunt in London, Miss."

"An express? Thank you, Hill."

"There is one for Mrs. Bennet, too, Miss, but I brought yours first rather than wait for my mistress to return." Mrs. Hill gave Elizabeth a knowing look.

Elizabeth nodded. "Ah, I see. I am indebted to you, Hill, indeed."

She and the housekeeper exchanged wry smiles, and not for the first time.

Hill withdrew, and Elizabeth was able to read her letter in peace and quiet, as all the men had gone shooting, and her mother and Jane had not yet returned from Meryton. She wondered when she would suffer the affliction of shopping for wedding clothes with her mother.

Presently, Jane and Mrs. Bennet returned and rushed upstairs to begin their preparations for dining at Netherfield. When Jane entered the bedroom, Elizabeth was just putting on her evening slippers. "Jane, an express arrived from our aunt. You may read it."

Jane took it from Elizabeth and began reading. At the mention of Mr. Darcy, she put the letter down, unfinished, and blushed. "There, Lizzy. She hopes to put your mind at rest. At least you may be calmer now just knowing she will hear you."

Mrs. Hill's appearance at their door prevented Elizabeth's response. "Miss Elizabeth, your mother would speak to you. I gave her the express from your aunt when she came in," she said with a sly smile.

Jane gave her sister a quizzical look, and as Elizabeth left the room, she whispered, "Mama does not know of my letter."

"Ah, Lizzy," Mrs. Bennet began pleasantly when Elizabeth entered her mother's dressing room. The interruption did not hinder the maid's preparation of Mrs. Bennet for the evening. "I have just had a letter from Mrs. Gardiner. It seems, my dear, that I am over-taxing myself trying to prepare two daughters for the same wedding. Your aunt has kindly consented to assist me with your arrangements. She says she will bring some fabric from London she thinks you might like, and the two of you can take it to Miss Cassandra's in Meryton and see what you can make of it. Here, dear." She handed Elizabeth the letter.

Elizabeth felt more and more relieved as she read the description of the fabric that would arrive with her aunt, whose taste more suited her own than her mother's ever could. Elizabeth detected the slight by her mother, and although it was painful, her main sensation was one of liberation. The idea of shopping for her wedding ensemble and trousseau had instantly become much more palatable.

"How kind she is to me, Mama. Thank you for letting me read the letter. I am full of curiosity now for her arrival." *In every possible way.*

"Yes, dear," her mother said absently as her hair was being dressed. "I thought you would not mind if she helped you. Are you wearing *that* this evening?" Mrs. Bennet eyed her daughter's choice of gown dubiously. "I am sure Mr. Darcy has seen that gown too many times to count. What about your ball gown, dear?"

"I have heard Mr. Darcy remark in jest of Miss Bingley's tendency to wear ball gowns for regular evening dress. He thinks her pretentious. I would not have him think so of me. And I only have so many gowns, Mama."

Mrs. Bennet huffed. "Soon you will have enough to fill all of the closets in this house put together."

"I doubt quite as many as that, Mama."

"Lizzy! You must learn to live up to your new station. Mrs. Elizabeth Darcy..." Mrs. Bennet finally smiled upon her second eldest daughter. "How well it sounds. I knew you could not be so clever for nothing." Mrs. Bennet began humming to herself, and Elizabeth sensed she had pleased her mother by agreeing so easily to the arrangements for obtaining her wedding clothes, however undeserving she might be of becoming Mrs. Elizabeth Darcy.

When the Bennet carriage arrived at Netherfield that evening, Mr. Darcy was awaiting it. With a great show of magnanimity, Mr. Bennet stepped aside so Darcy could hand Elizabeth down from the carriage and walk her into the house. They had seen each other only in company during the three days since Elizabeth's revelations and the letters sent to Mrs. Gardiner. Elizabeth found she had to force herself to be easy with him in public. Not usually missish, she nevertheless had surrendered to her trepidation and changed the timing of her walks to start at midday, and she followed paths known only to the local populace. She had seen Darcy riding the day before—perhaps looking for her?—but she did not draw his attention. Now, having received her aunt's missive, she began to feel her confidence returning.

Once they were a safe distance from her family, Elizabeth whispered, "I have had a letter from my aunt, Mr. Darcy. She says she will gladly meet, and that she has the deepest regard for you and high expectations of your behaviour." She sent him an impertinent sidelong glance, "So you have deceived *her*, at least..."

Darcy chuckled, pleased to have a few private words with her, and that she was teasing. "No, I do not suppose I have. Your Aunt Gardiner strikes me as a woman few can hoodwink." Darcy held out his arm, and Elizabeth tucked her hand in his elbow.

"Jane and I had an odd conversation with my mother yesterday afternoon before dinner."

Darcy composed a tart comment but thought better of speaking it, asking instead, "Did you? And the topic?"

"The day I told you of my dream, Mama and Papa had a fearful row. Jane and I could not hear all of it, but the subject was what Jane and I have been told to expect of..." She paused and sighed. "...Of our wedding nights. Papa demanded she recant most of what she told us, else he would lock her in her bedroom until after the wedding! It seems she wished to prepare us for the worst. I am wondering how my father learnt of the nature of Mama's advice to us, or perhaps he merely surmised?" Another sidelong glance was delivered.

They had entered Netherfield's front hall, and servants advanced to take the Bennets' outerwear. Elizabeth held back so her pelisse and bonnet would be taken last, and Darcy stayed behind with her. He was embarrassed to reveal his communication with Elizabeth's father, but he would hide nothing from her as now several days had passed from that strange and sensational morning.

"It must be admitted, Elizabeth—I shall confess—Bingley and I were alarmed to learn of your ordeal at the hands of the local married ladies. We wrote to your father, asking him to do what he could to spare you too much time with your Aunt Phillips. And your mother."

Elizabeth had taken his arm again and now they were nearly to the drawing room doors. She stopped their progress and looked at him with a knowing smile and a slight shake of her head. "I thought as much. I own I do not know whether to be grateful to you for the results or very cross for the interference. Mama is treating Papa with unprecedented deference, but she is annoyed with me although she tries to hide it. She blames me for expressing my concerns."

"I hardly know how to respond, Elizabeth! I would not have you in your mother's bad books."

"It is hardly an unusual occurrence, sir." She chuckled.

"Before we enter the drawing room, Elizabeth, there is something else you should know."

"Indeed?"

"On the same morning of which we are speaking, the Bingleys also had a family set-to. I only heard part of it. Hurst and Bingley attempted to give Caroline some correction in her behaviour towards myself and to you. So far, I see no change, or if anything, she is worse, and I want you to be on your guard. Netherfield has taken on a surprisingly uneasy atmosphere unless Jane is visiting. She always lightens the mood."

"*That* is what Bingley and I have been trying to persuade you: Jane is uniformly angelic! You should have wooed her when you had the chance, and you would have had a much more amiable wife than you deserve or are likely to get."

Darcy chuckled. "I am getting exactly the wife I want and deserve. Of *that* I remain firmly convinced." They smiled openly into each other's eyes for the first time in days. Both breathed a sigh of relief.

When Darcy and Elizabeth entered the drawing room, Caroline swept to Darcy's other side and offered to bring him some refreshment in an unnecessarily obsequious manner while ignoring Elizabeth. Darcy gave a curt bow and a brusque, "No, thank you, Miss Bingley," before turning his back and seating Elizabeth upon the only settee in the room where there was space for her, which was next to Hurst. That gentleman made his allegiance clear by springing up in a rapid manner rarely seen and insisting Darcy take his place.

"I shall have the singular opportunity, Darcy, of taking the chair nearest my wife." With a bow, Hurst strove to make amends for his sister-in-law's rudeness. "May I bring you something to drink, Miss Eliza?"

"You are very kind, sir; yes, I would take some wine punch if that is what I see in the bowl." Elizabeth turned her eyes to Darcy with a little surprise.

His response was a raised eyebrow. "You see how matters lie?" he whispered.

She nodded in reply then looked up to Hurst with thanks as he returned.

"Miss Eliza," Louisa Hurst called as her husband settled himself with a generous goblet of wine in the chair next to hers. "Have you begun the selection of your wedding clothes?"

Elizabeth leaned forward to answer and did not notice, as Darcy did, the glaring look sent Louisa by Caroline. "Indeed, we have just had word from my aunt in London, who is bringing a fabric she has admired and thinks would suit me. She arrives the day after tomorrow. My Aunt Gardiner knows my taste well, and I am most pleased to have her exert herself on my behalf."

Caroline moved in hopes of catching her sister's eye to pull a face of scorn, but Louisa would not look in her direction. She asked instead, "This is the aunt we had the pleasure of meeting at Pemberley?"

"Yes, the same." Elizabeth nodded. She was wary, but to all appearances, Louisa was distancing herself from the unbridled disdain that marked her sister's discourse.

"She seems to be a lady of fashion. Her travelling pelisse was beautifully tailored. I am sure you could not be in better hands." Louisa seemed sincere.

Elizabeth decided to try her further. "Yes, she has a modiste on Bond Street to whom she has extended her custom for many years: a Miss Camille. Have you heard of her?"

Louisa could not hide her surprise. The Gardiners must have a vast deal of wealth for Miss Camille to condescend to create gowns for the wife of a tradesman. Elizabeth chose not to reveal that her uncle's company had made a fine carriage for Miss Camille's use as she made calls for in-home fittings to London's best addresses, and that a bargain by way of barter had been struck to keep Mrs. Gardiner in the latest fashions. *Let them assume what they like*, Elizabeth thought, and wondered whether, in her own way, she was not displaying a certain smugness she would have discouraged in her betrothed.

Louisa's eyes flickered to those of her sister, who appeared thoroughly astonished and then looked away.

Dinner was announced. Darcy was further vexed when, after extending his right arm to Elizabeth, Caroline Bingley took his left, steering them both to where she wanted Elizabeth to sit, between Mr. Bennet and Mr. Hurst.

Again Louisa intervened. "Pray, excuse me, dear sister, but I thought I had informed you of my seating plan. Mr. Darcy, you are on Miss Bennet's right, and Miss Eliza, you are to his right."

Caroline blushed angrily. "How silly of me, Louisa. My apologies. I had thought you would sit as hostess tonight, rather than I."

"Yes, dear," Louisa responded, "and you will sit on my right, since we have too many ladies."

Caroline was quietly livid; *she* was the extra lady!

WHEN THE GARDINER CARRIAGE ROLLED into the Longbourn paddock, Elizabeth was annoyed with herself for being nervous. She was filled with a strange fluttering and prayed this was not some early evidence that she might become more like her mother with age. She knew there would be no time for a lengthy conversation anytime that day, and took several deep breaths to calm herself enough to join her sisters in greeting their London relations. Nevertheless, Elizabeth could not resist inundating her aunt and uncle with embraces delivered with excessive velocity and vehemence, for such was her relief at their arrival.

After dinner, which included Mr. Darcy at the Gardiners' particular request, the ladies examined the fabric brought for Elizabeth's wedding ensemble, and even Mrs. Bennet seemed to approve. It was her intention to decorate Jane following the newest fashion of dressing brides in white, and Mrs. Bennet was heaping onto Jane's gown as many ruffles and laces as her daughter's statuesque figure could carry. To a disinterested observer, the effect would be not unlike an all-white Maypole. The fabric offered for Elizabeth, candlelight in colour with a naturalistic leaf embroidery, suited her second daughter admirably without any danger of diminishing Jane.

When the men entered, they were laughing. Mr. Bennet revealed that Mr. Gardiner had been regaling them with a fishing story from Pemberley, which ended with Mr. Hurst and Mr. Bingley completely soaked in pursuit of a trout little bigger than a minnow. The story was retold for the benefit of the ladies, but was not quite so amusing with the absence of Mr. Hurst's colourful oaths.

There was no time or opening for Darcy to speak to Elizabeth about her abandonment of their morning walks. That she was reluctant to be alone with him was obvious, and although he had not thought of anything suitably clever or persuasive enough to encourage her to take up the habit again, he did mean to try. She did not sit near him, though she smiled when meeting his eyes and gave every appearance of friendliness. But Darcy knew perfectly well he was not as trusted as he had once been.

The couple avoided Mrs. Bennet's whist table, but Elizabeth was drawn into a conversation about Kitty's new gown, which had not yet arrived, and it seemed she had assigned herself the duty of describing it in agonising detail to her aunt. She was actually quite amusing on the topic as she teased Kitty, but Darcy was not inclined to do anything except observe her with the fixed gaze that had so marked his first evenings in Elizabeth's society a year ago. She glanced at him often, smiled, nodded, and attempted to include him, but he was having none of it.

After an hour of hearing nearly nothing from Darcy, Mrs. Gardiner turned and caught his eye. She glanced at Elizabeth and back at him, raising her eyebrows in acknowledgement of her niece's behaviour. She gave a little nod, and for the first time that evening, Darcy returned a restrained half smile. He was evidently pleased that the Gardiners had arrived.

At the end of the evening, Mr. Bennet accompanied Elizabeth to see Darcy away in his carriage, and Mrs. Gardiner, to whom the notion of imparting a married woman's wisdom-of-the-ages to her niece had seemed something of a lark, began to take her responsibility more seriously. *Mr. Darcy was not happy, and Lizzy is losing the confidence he appreciates. This will not do.*

THE NEXT MORNING, MRS. GARDINER was surprised to see Elizabeth join the family for breakfast. It was just starting to rain; however, the sunrise had been bright, and an early riser like Elizabeth could certainly have enjoyed an hour of exercise.

"Lizzy! No walk this morning?" Mrs. Gardiner was accustomed to the rhythm of Longbourn with Elizabeth always the first to rise but the last to break her fast, bursting into the dining room with flushed cheeks and a handful of flowers or some other treasure found in the hedgerows, souvenirs from her rambles.

"I have been taking my walks at midday." Elizabeth looked out the dining room windows. "Now the rain has come, it seems I have done myself out of the activity that has become so necessary. Perhaps I can convince Jane to practice dancing if Mary will play."

"Jane and I must get to Meryton for a fitting the very instant this rain stops," her mother informed her. Mrs. Bennet was unwilling to risk her eldest daughter to wet weather, unlike the year before. "I shall not have you set her all aglow before we must be at Miss Cassandra's, Lizzy. I shall not have Jane perspire on her bridal gown. Let Kitty dance with you."

So this is how it is, Mrs. Gardiner observed. *Fanny gives Lizzy no quarter. Why did I think the security of seeing two daughters very well married would change her?* "Lizzy, if it is no inconvenience to your mother, perhaps we can converse privately in the small sitting room. I have some suggestions for your gown and trousseau, and *nightgowns*... and so forth."

Elizabeth's eyes widened; she nodded and looked down at her plate, which she had scarcely touched. Mrs. Gardiner noticed Elizabeth had not taken her usual hearty helpings, and was chasing a morsel of ham around her plate without seeming to want to catch it. Mrs. Gardiner reflected upon the previous evening and recalled it had been much the same at dinner, even with Mr. Darcy by her side. Elizabeth was too discomfited to eat.

"Oh, yes, Lizzy! You and your aunt must make lists first; it so aids the shopping. You will be much less likely to forget anything. No one needs the back sitting room now, Sister." Mrs. Bennet was delighted to have Elizabeth out from underfoot and in someone else's charge. "Take as long as you like. Once you have organised yourselves, you can begin placing your orders tomorrow."

"Thank you, Sister, you are most obliging," Mrs. Gardiner replied, perceiving the motives of her sister-in-law. "Whenever you have finished eating, Lizzy, we can take our tea in there."

Once settled across from each other in two armchairs behind a closed door, Mrs. Gardiner had the chance to examine Elizabeth particularly. It was extraordinary to see her vivacious niece sitting still, staring at the folded hands in her lap. Elizabeth looked tense and tired. Mrs. Gardiner was sincerely cross when she said, "Elizabeth Bennet, I am astonished to see you behaving like a lamb being led to slaughter."

Elizabeth met her aunt's eyes with alarm.

"You, of all people, should know to think sensibly and consider the source of all you have heard. To put it bluntly, your Aunt Phillips is the town sot, and your mother wishes to make marital relations sound horrific so neither you nor Jane will anticipate your vows. I prefer to believe you and Jane will be *most* pleasantly surprised when the time comes, especially you, Lizzy."

Elizabeth gaped at her aunt, her mouth opening like a beached perch.

"Close your mouth, dear. You will catch flies. Now honestly, Lizzy, what are you afraid of? That the man you adore will not treat you with consideration and affection? To have earned the love of a man of Darcy's intelligence and nobility, to say nothing of his obvious *physical* superiority to any other man *I* have ever seen, well, it should make you proud of yourself, not fill you with trepidation. He is ready to dote on you if you will get out of your own way and let him!"

"He *is* gorgeous, is he not?" Elizabeth whispered. "I have never told him so, but now we are betrothed, and he looks at me the way he does, Aunt, it is all I can do not to *throw* myself at him. I am much more fearful of myself than of him." She looked into her aunt's kindly eyes, and continued. "The dreams I am having! I am certain they are provoked by what I have been told will happen, but I am appalled to not be more...ashamed by what I have envisioned. I judge myself a thorough wanton when I awaken. Yet, what I dream seems so real and *so* overwhelming. I have dreamt that he—"

Mrs. Gardiner put her hand up. "Stop right there, Elizabeth. I have no wish to know your dreams. Do not disparage them, to be sure, but only share them with Mr. Darcy. Do not encourage other women to envy you."

Elizabeth looked confused. "Envy me?"

Mrs. Gardiner started to chuckle at herself. "I may seem like an old married woman to *you*, my dear, but I am not *dead*. I am only a year older than your betrothed, you know."

Elizabeth considered the implications of her aunt's remarks. "Oh. I was rather hoping you would tell me whether I am normal or I am...fallen."

Mrs. Gardener started laughing. She shook her head, trying very hard to stop. "Oh, Lizzy. I am sorry...to be laughing. I have never known you so grave and serious." Mrs. Gardiner removed a handkerchief from her pocket and dried the mirthful tears at the corners of her eyes. Elizabeth was not amused and looked it. "It is just, oh, you remind me so much of me! I have no intention of telling you tales of your uncle and myself, so do not ask, but I *do* see so much of myself in you. Such innocence and such desire!"

"Is *that* what I feel?"

"Yes, and it is healthy. It is what you *should* feel. Once you are married, as *soon* as you are married, you may act upon the desires you feel now."

"What if Mr. Darcy thinks me too forward? I do not fear him, truly, but I do dread his disapprobation. What if he thinks me indecent?"

"Oh, I highly doubt he will think *that*, my love. More likely he will be flattered, perhaps dumbfounded, but I promise you, he will be thoroughly pleased if you are bold."

"What if he thinks me unchaste?"

"I suspect there will be ample evidence to the contrary."

"Will it hurt so much as that? I have been hoping what I have been led to expect is a complete exaggeration."

"It is impossible to say if, or how much, the first time will hurt. Each of us is different, and so is every man, I am told. You may bleed a bit, but you are used to that. It will be not as much as what happens every month. And after the first experience or two, any discomfort will cease and you will find it all very pleasant."

"Pleasant? Not arduous?"

"Pleasant. Not arduous."

"What if he wants to undress me?"

"Let him."

"And to *see* me...undressed. Naked." Elizabeth reddened.

"Let him."

"What if he wants to sleep in the same bed?"

"Let him."

"What about if he wants to...during the day, instead of at night?"

Mrs. Gardiner waved an impatient hand. "I doubt *instead* is the word you want, more like in addition to, but let him!"

Elizabeth remembered the disquieting conversation she and Darcy had after he kissed her the first time, and he blurted he wanted to teach her to ride horseback. "Aunt, I think, if I inferred correctly, and the way he blushed, I am sure I did, that Mr. Darcy might want to...to have relations with me...*outside*. In the woods or...somewhere."

"You will have a large estate, Lizzy, and if you feel the place he chooses is sufficiently private, by all means, *let him*!"

Chapter 8
Walking to Oakham Mount

"Sit by my side, and let the world slip: we shall ne'er be younger."
William Shakespeare, *The Taming of the Shrew*

Elizabeth left Longbourn seized by energy, determined to walk to Oakham Mount with or without Fitzwilliam Darcy. It was two full days after conferring with Aunt Gardiner—full in every sense—and there had since been no opportunity to have the private, lengthy conversation with Darcy that Elizabeth had settled upon as the next necessary step of their relationship.

The day after the important conference saw the arrival of Georgiana Darcy and Colonel Fitzwilliam at Netherfield, and Darcy had spent the day with them. Elizabeth and Jane had been invited thither to dinner, with an evening musical interlude featuring Georgiana on the harp and pianoforte, and Bingley's sisters singing and playing duets. Those assembled politely requested a performance by Elizabeth, but she had demurred, which Darcy did not like but understood. The performance was a gift to the betrothed couples and Elizabeth felt it rude to display herself. She was grateful her sister Mary was not in attendance, for *she* would have had no such scruple.

Elizabeth had also spent the two days shopping for wedding clothes with her aunt after receiving very particular—if not particularly helpful—instructions from Mrs. Bennet. Those went largely ignored. Aunt Gardiner had her own ideas about what would suit the occasion for Elizabeth and later to please Mr. Darcy.

Just the evening before Elizabeth's expedition to Oakham Mount, the

Bennets hosted Darcy, Georgiana, and Colonel Fitzwilliam to a family dinner as the Bingleys were engaged elsewhere. It was the first opportunity for Georgiana to meet the younger Bennet sisters, and her shyness prevailed. Elizabeth had prepared her sisters and mother for this likelihood, and even the often oblivious Kitty was slightly subdued. Mrs. Bennet showed Georgiana every civility without her usual heavy-handedness, for which Elizabeth was grateful.

Kitty was privately disappointed that the colonel did not wear his regimentals, and thus was less inclined to put herself in his way. Elizabeth observed that the colonel paid Jane rather too much attention but felt reasonably certain no one else noticed as he was known for his pleasant manners in company. Elizabeth was seated between her father and Darcy; the men chatted like old friends, each having learnt the style of comment likely to raise a smile from the other. Their sources of amusement were discovered to be more alike than not, and they included Elizabeth in their sport whenever they could.

After dinner, Mary played for Georgiana followed by the reverse. Mary's appreciation of the abilities of Miss Darcy was slow in developing, but Mary did, by the end of Georgiana's third piece, begin to understand humility.

During the playing, Darcy leaned to Elizabeth's ear and whispered that his cousin had brought him a most pleasing letter of congratulations from Darcy's aunt and uncle, the Earl and Countess of Matlock. They were in such despair of their nephew ever marrying that they cared nothing for his intended's wealth, connections, looks, or education; the list of attributes they did *not* care about went on at some length. The earl and his wife were concerned only that she still be of childbearing years and healthy. Colonel Fitzwilliam had assured them that Miss Elizabeth Bennet was merely one and twenty and of uncommonly robust health; therefore, that branch of the family was most favourably disposed towards her. Elizabeth was highly diverted. *Clearly, Lady Catherine's sway within the family is not nearly so wide and commanding as the lady thinks. Her practical sphere of influence seems entirely limited to the parsonage at Hunsford and her poor daughter!*

WHEN DARCY DID NOT APPEAR for her early walk, Elizabeth returned home out of spirits and convinced Jane to send an immediate note to Bingley, ostensibly about the coming evening's entertainment at Netherfield. Jane just *happened* to mention that Elizabeth was planning to visit Oakham Mount on foot and she would set out after the Bennet family's breakfast.

As often happened when excessive tension was bound within her, Elizabeth began to trot and eventually to run up and down the rolling lanes until the paths became too narrow and uneven, beginning the steady rise to the mount. She had slowed to a brisk walk when she heard the cantor of a horse approaching and turned to look behind her. She could not help smiling when she saw it was, at last, Darcy.

"You have been running, Miss Bennet." Darcy slid from his horse and took her ungloved hand, kissing it. He found her skin delightfully warm. "I own, I have been watching you."

"Please do not reveal it to anyone, Mr. Darcy, as it leads to a scolding at home. Mama thinks a lady running is quite deplorable, unless, of course, one wants to run after officers. *That* is the sort of running of which she heartily approves."

He did not let go of her hand and joined in her laughter. "It pleases me that you run for exercise and not for any *other* reason."

"You may suppose my motive for running is as you say, sir, but I have always thought I run because I have energy that cannot be expended in any more productive way, which may be seen as a fault. The activity does seem to dispel my ill humours. Now I may continue my walk in a more contemplative and circumspect manner."

"I am pleased that we begin to have these little secrets between us. I like knowing things, which—although I find them charming—you would not wish me to share with the world." Darcy's dimples punctuated his approbation.

She blushed a little, and her voice dropped to a whisper. "Will you join me as I walk, Fitzwilliam?" She knew she should wait for him to ask whether *he* could join *her,* but Elizabeth felt such ceremony unnecessary. It seemed one propriety had already been breached and possibly more.

Darcy held the reins of his horse in one hand and offered his other arm. Elizabeth tucked her bare hand into the bend of his elbow. They walked along quietly. After several minutes, Elizabeth found herself again becoming perturbed. *Why does he not speak? Has he no questions for me? I certainly have a few for him! Where is his native curiosity? Or does he already know what was said?* Just as Elizabeth thought she might have to increase the speed of their climb to oust her uneasiness, Darcy began to speak.

"Elizabeth, are you aware that Mr. Gardiner has made your aunt acquainted with every particular of his business?"

"No!" She was confounded at the direction of their conversation. "I suppose I have never thought of it. The news does not surprise me; he seems to have every confidence in her. Her powers of organization are the stuff of legend within the family."

"It has been a great education for me to become well-acquainted with your aunt and uncle. They are fine people, and they have an unexampled marriage. We would do well to emulate them."

"I am inclined to agree. The Gardiners have provided proper guidance to Jane and me where my own parents are found wanting. It is a pity the expansion of their family has prevented my younger sisters from knowing them better. But tell me, Fitzwilliam, where do these reflections tend?"

"The Gardiners have inspired my desire to teach you the workings of Pemberley estate management if you are willing to study it. I am eight years your senior, Elizabeth, and it would be a comfort to know, should anything happen to me, that you could pass the knowledge onto our children, to continue Pemberley and make improvements." He stopped to assess the effect of his words in her luminous eyes.

Elizabeth looked up at him slightly breathless. "You do me a very great honour, Fitzwilliam, very great indeed. I would be most pleased to learn about the estate. That you would allow me to help you, to support you, in so material a way is highly gratifying. I assumed I would run the house —but in truth Mrs. Reynolds does it all—and plan neighbourhood entertainments. I do love to garden, and I am very good help in a stillroom. There will be tenant visits, I expect, and tending new mothers and the ill, which will naturally fall to me now rather than Georgiana. But to learn about the planting of crops and the husbandry of sheep, and, I suppose, investments? This degree of trust, I had not envisioned. Thank you, Fitzwilliam, for your faith."

Darcy lowered his head towards her face as she stood on her toes to meet him with parted lips. They closed their eyes as their mouths met. Darcy barely touched her with his tongue, but he felt her respond by briefly leaning her body against his. They separated, each mirroring the other's satisfied half smile. Darcy dropped the lead of his horse and removed his gloves. His hand joined hers, fingers entwining as they walked more casually.

"I want you to be my partner in all things, Elizabeth."

"So I have been given to understand." She avoided his eyes and felt her colour rising, her aunt's words still foremost in her mind. *A willing and responsive partner,' Aunt Gardiner said. 'Do not just let him do things to you, respond!'*

Elizabeth's bonnet blocked her view of Darcy's countenance. He stopped again so she had to look up to see him gazing tenderly at her. In a gentle voice, he asked, "What does your understanding encompass, dearest Elizabeth?"

"You wish me to be happy with you...or rather, perhaps it is that you wish to make me happy? You wish to be the means of my happiness?" He nodded, encouraging her as she refined the accuracy of her phrasing. "Your parents were uncommonly devoted to each other, you have said, as are my aunt and uncle. These marriages are characterised by mutual respect and good humour and...a passionate regard, which you also wish to find in married life. With me." She shook her head in astonishment. "With *me...*"

"Yes, Elizabeth, you and I together. Your aunt told me about your explorations of Derbyshire prior to visiting Pemberley, how fearlessly you scrambled over the tors, scaring her to death! She said you admitted feeling you could spend the rest of your life there.

"So why was I searching in the *ton* for a woman who did not exist in that sphere? I know you bear society and unknown company with infinitely more grace than I, but if I understand your true nature, you are most yourself outside in the open air as we are now. How I would have loved to see you climbing the Peaks."

"I did not recognise it at the time, but perhaps those two days in Derbyshire —before we met at Pemberley—were a preparation after a fashion. The very country you live in was preparing me for you." She looked seriously into his face, hoping he understood the depth of her feelings.

"Elizabeth!" Her words thrilled him. She was in his arms without either of them realising he had embraced her. "Elizabeth..." he whispered.

"Please, let me finish my thought." She chuckled, bending away to watch his face without leaving his grasp. "The country around Pemberley has a handsomeness not wholly tamed, and you are of that place. When I saw Pemberley so civilised and well situated, elegant within the wilderness with no useless finery, it was as if I was seeing *you*. I have already spoken of all the kind words Mrs. Reynolds said of you. When I saw your portrait with its observant smile, I only then remembered it had been sometimes fixed upon me, and I fell deeply in love. Now I see how every circumstance of those days led to truly seeing you.

"Had we not met, I would have spent that night, and surely many after it, completely bereft and heart-broken. I would have realised I had been loved and was in love myself, at last, all to no avail. But I had no time to dwell upon what might have been because I went outside and there you were. Embarrassed confusion snuck into my heart before abject despair could. But when I learned of Lydia's actions, I *did* despair. I believed you would think ill of me and the association of my family with *him*."

"I chose love, Elizabeth."

She met his gaze to reveal tears at the corners of her eyes. She was filled with pride on his behalf, just as she had been when she first learned he had secretly helped her family solve the tumult caused by Lydia.

"Elizabeth," Darcy spoke in a low voice, "you will think me a rake, but may I remove your bonnet and kiss your hair?"

She smiled. "Yours are not the eyes of a rake, sir."

He inhaled the scent of her and kissed the top of her head where the hair parted in curls framing her face.

Elizabeth continued, "You have always looked at me with love though I was too stubborn or distressed to recognise it. When I told Lydia's news in Lambton, you stood at the door looking at me for a long moment before you left. I assumed you were congratulating yourself on a narrow escape from all things Bennet. But it was, in truth, not such a look. You were trying to give me strength. I was too abashed to understand, too broken by events."

"Let us not speak of that." Darcy nodded his forehead against hers, a gesture in which he found great comfort.

"With your forbearance, Fitzwilliam, I do have a question about that day I have never asked."

Darcy felt they had discussed every particular of the interview a dozen times. "I cannot imagine what I have not said about finding you in such a dreadful state and learning its cause."

"But I have never asked why you came to be paying me a visit. You did not arrive with the intention of comforting me—you arrived with some intention of your own. And it was...?"

Darcy stepped back and smiled. "Ah! You are quite correct. You have never asked, and I never thought to say." Elizabeth returned his smile. "My intention... We had seen each other the day before, when you and your aunt called. You were so kind to Georgiana, protecting her, and I knew, whatever your feelings about me might be, that my letter had some softening effect. You joined me in keeping Georgiana safe from the thoughtless insults of Caroline Bingley.

"That evening, Georgiana played for us, and I mused all the while about Hunsford and all you had said of me. I hoped, in the brief time we had thus far spent at Pemberley, that you had seen my improvement in civility, but I had done nothing to relieve Bingley's suffering.

"He made it clear he *was* still suffering. His only topic of conversation was the miracle of you being in the neighbourhood—a miracle I was not insensible to—and how he longed to hear you speak of his Meryton friends, but I was not deceived. There was only one person of whom he wanted to speak, and it pained me to realise he felt that he must speak privately with you to mention Jane. He feared I would evidence some displeasure if he let slip her name in my hearing.

"To begin his relief, I determined to see you before you arrived for dinner to let you know I was certain Bingley's affections had not waned, and to measure whether you would trust me enough to reveal Jane's feelings. I planned to ask you to enter into a conspiracy with me, its purpose to reunite Bingley and Jane.

"But to be honest, I simply could not wait to see you again. Had I found you reading happier letters from home, and had you shown any amount of approval of my visit and its purpose, I cannot account for myself. I might have asked for a walk, or I might have asked you to begin a correspondence with Georgiana so I could maintain some rudimentary connection to you, or...I might have renewed my addresses. I might have asked your uncle for leave to court you."

Elizabeth's smile broadened as his answer lengthened. "If, as you say, Jane's letters had only carried trivial news from home, I expect I would have entered into any conspiracy you cared to suggest. And if you *had* renewed your addresses, I would not have refused you. No, Fitzwilliam, I could not have refused you *again*. I was in love by then, though I had not yet time to frame it as a complete thought."

She took her bonnet from his hand, hooking it over the pommel of the saddle. As she took Darcy's arms and wove them behind her, she whispered, "I am still in love with you. It is my vow to you: I shall remain so."

Darcy finished the embrace she had initiated, pulling her to him with their arms folded together behind her back. He kissed her with more intensity than he previously allowed himself. Her mouth responded hungrily; her lips parted willingly and welcomed his tongue. She turned her head allowing him to taste her more deeply, and she brought a hand up to the back of his collar, pressing him to maintain contact. *She does not fear an ardent kiss, at least.* Darcy was intoxicated. He continued until the pressure of her hand eased and released him as she gasped for breath.

"Oh! I am not yet as proficient as I would wish to be, Fitzwilliam. I am grateful for the opportunity to practice." She spoke in a low breathy voice he found utterly beguiling.

"We both want practice, dearest Elizabeth." Darcy brushed his lips against hers again, briefly. "The breathing is the trick." *Oh, I am too enthralled. I am aroused. I must pull back.* He stepped slightly away. Their eyes met, each reading the other's depth of desire. *She does not understand her power over me.*

"Fitzwilliam, may we speak, just for a moment, about your expectations of me?" Her voice was firm, though she coloured slightly and cast her eyes down.

"I thought we were."

"Yes, we were speaking of my duties as mistress of Pemberley. Perhaps I should not be so self-assured, but I am confident of my success in that regard. You will be patient, and I shall be eager. No, I refer now to my duties as a wife. As *your* wife..."

There was an awkward pause. Elizabeth jumped in, unable to bear it. "We need not, of course. You deem it unseemly. I understand."

"No, in the present case, I think you do *not* understand. To speak plainly, to talk of you as my wife causes me to fervently wish it were already so. It tempts me to act rather than speak." He watched her eyes for a sign of comprehension.

Elizabeth blushed.

He spoke quickly in a constrained manner. "You wish me to speak of duties. I *shall* speak. I hope you will not perceive any desires of mine as duties, Elizabeth. Unless you have strong objections, I mean for us to occupy the same bed always. I have been too much alone. Once we are settled at

Pemberley, you may find me sometimes indiscreet in my displays of affection. I want you to always let me know your feelings, your... desires as you learn what gives you pleasure, and certainly you must speak instantly of anything that does not." He stopped as abruptly as he started, turned away from her and drew in a deep breath.

She stepped to him, placing a hand to his shoulder, wishing to allay the disquiet of which she knew she was the cause. He was, after all, a man in love with a maiden. "Please allow me to apologise, sir. It was not my intention to discompose you."

He replied without turning, "No, Elizabeth, there is no need. If you will allow me to speak as much as I can, when I can, this conversation, although disjointed, may yield the information you deserve. If you are brave enough to ask, I must be brave enough to answer as truthfully as words can express."

Her hand remained on his shoulder, and after a moment, Darcy reached to cover it with his. "You humble me, Elizabeth."

She stepped closer to him and embraced the arm at his side. Their hands entwined. He was vibrantly aware of her breasts through her thick winter spencer pressed to his arm. It was the same embrace she occasionally bestowed upon him as they walked in the countryside before her dream, before she became distant. *We shall conquer this. She has come back to me in spirit, and soon she will be mine in fact.*

"I shall keep this secret." She smiled playfully at him, shaking the arm she held. "No one need know you may be humbled. Is it not also a wifely duty to protect her husband's weaknesses from discovery?" she teased. "You have so many; I shall be rather constantly on guard for you."

Darcy looked into her eyes, his darkened with passion. "Loving you is my weakness, Elizabeth. It is also my greatest strength."

They smiled fondly until Darcy said, "Let us walk. Our destination is close, is it not?"

Elizabeth looked about as they continued forward. "Perhaps when we reach the viewpoint, I shall devise another question to disturb us."

In a few minutes, Elizabeth and Darcy stood upon the rise, and they were presented with the tranquil prospect of Hertfordshire countryside in tawny autumn colours. Darcy stood behind her and wrapped his arms around her waist. They remained thus, contented with silence until Darcy cleared his throat.

"Are you certain you will not be sorry to leave this prospect, Elizabeth?"

"Indeed, I shall not. I have been on this spot perhaps fifty times in my one and twenty years. I shall not miss it but neither shall I forget it." Darcy was pleased and kissed the top of her head. "Besides, will we not visit the Bingleys occasionally?"

"Of course we shall, but I do not know how long they will last."

Elizabeth stiffened. Darcy felt her shock and recognised the implications of what he had said. *That was poorly worded, Darcy,* he cursed himself. He had no doubts about the longevity of Jane and Bingley's mutual affection. "Would *you* continue long at Netherfield with your mother not three miles away? That is my meaning. Even the placid nature of your sister seems to lose patience with your mother occasionally. Bingley is a difficult man to impose upon, but I believe your mother will apply herself."

Elizabeth visibly relaxed and even started to chuckle. "Ah, sir. I take your point. Do you think we could convince them to settle nearer to us?"

"I would wager by the end of the coming year, Bingley will approach me for my opinions of estates in Derbyshire."

"You think it will need so long as that? I shall take that bet, sir! A sixpence says that if they join us in midsummer, the topic will be broached sooner."

"It is indeed my intention to invite them to spend some weeks with us around the time of the 21st of July, so I agree to your wager. But only a sixpence?"

"I would not wish to bankrupt you, and I am certain I shall win. On the 21st of July? Fitzwilliam, what does that date signify?"

"It is *our* anniversary, the date upon which we met at Pemberley. You have had the effect of my becoming a highly sentimental man where I was never one before."

She turned in his arms and asked playfully, "Perhaps we should postpone our wedding until then?"

Darcy's cheeks warmed instantly. "No, indeed not. I have waited for you entirely long enough, *more* than long enough. It is sweet of you to offer, madam, but no, that will not be necessary."

Elizabeth stepped back as he sought to tighten his embrace. She was laughing. He lunged after her, realising she was teasing him yet again, and he smiled as he caught her. "Elizabeth! You must not test me on this point. You would deny a thirsty man water?"

They stood suspended in time; she was laughing into his eyes, and he was cherishing holding her. After a long moment, Elizabeth reached up to smooth the curls from his forehead, tucking them under his hat, and her fingers lingered on his cheek. Darcy was deeply moved when she continued to hold his gaze and whisper, "No, Fitzwilliam, I would not. If you believe it within my power to make you a felicitous marriage, I shall endeavour to repay your conviction." She paused as he drew her more securely into his arms. "Please tell me what I must do, other than marrying you on the date we have affixed *already*, to ensure your happiness."

Darcy threw off his hat. "For now, kiss me."

It may be assumed the practice of kissing now occupied much of the remainder of their time upon Oakham Mount, and when, at last, they mastered the delicate art of breathing whilst kissing, and how to respond when one's cheeks and ears were so anointed, Darcy complimented Elizabeth, saying she was in a fair way to becoming proficient. "Indeed, dearest Elizabeth," he breathed into her hair, "I believe you have it within you to become truly adept."

"Such praise!" She smiled in a way that reminded him of the disastrous —by his reckoning—Meryton assembly, when she danced with Bingley after he himself had so ridiculously insulted her. She had glanced his way as he watched her with his friend, as if to draw attention to her virtue as a partner, knowing the lively dance flattered her.

"I am not teasing you, Elizabeth. I am serious."

"Much too serious, Fitzwilliam. Now where is your hat? We should start our return."

He did not move or allow her to, saying only, "Oh, hang my hat . . ." He kissed her laughter away until he felt her responding. Her arms crept around his waist and back under his great coat.

All will be well, Darcy. She will let me teach her all I want her to know.

When he ended the kiss, she remained in his arms, her face upturned, eyes closed, and silent.

"Elizabeth?"

"Shh . . . I am savouring this," she whispered.

"What pleases you?"

"Being alone with you, being in your arms. The quiet when we do not need to speak." She laid her head on his chest.

Darcy took her hint, and held her for some minutes, leaning his cheek on her hair, until she sighed.

"We must go," they both said and laughed. Their walk back to Longbourn was brisk, contented, and mostly silent.

Chapter 9

His Daughter's Worth

"When you depart from me, sorrow abides
and happiness takes his leave."
William Shakespeare, *Much Ado about Nothing*

The Bennets and Gardiners were invited to Netherfield for another musical evening and supper. After his late morning walk with Elizabeth, Darcy sent a note to Mr. Bennet asking for Elizabeth and him to arrive earlier to finalise the marriage settlement and explain it to Elizabeth.

Mr. Bennet was surprised to receive the note. He was of the opinion that Darcy and he were agreed on all of its generous terms, and he assumed Darcy had already acquainted Elizabeth with the knowledge that she was about to become a woman of substance. There was nothing more than for the documents to be drawn and signed.

Once they were settled in Bingley's study, Mr. Bennet asked, "Has my Lizzy given you reason to over set the marriage settlement already, Mr. Darcy?" He smiled at his future son-in-law, but behind the smile was some concern.

"Indeed not, sir, but I believe you and I will benefit from informing her together." He looked at Elizabeth with a broad smile.

Mr. Bennet glanced at his daughter, interested in her reception of the particulars. She seemed curious and oddly, he thought, embarrassed.

"Eliz... Miss Elizabeth," Darcy corrected upon seeing Mr. Bennet's raised brow, "I have not yet made you aware of the terms of the settlement between myself and your parents. Has your father mentioned any part?"

"No, Mr. Darcy, and you may well imagine my curiosity. I assumed I would have a chance to read the document before being required to sign it." Her tone was slightly playful.

"I think you may gather after our conversation this morning, that I have decided to acquaint you with the particulars sooner rather than later. I hope you will find everything to your liking. I hope...I hope you will see reflected here the faith I have in you."

Mr. Bennet suppressed a chuckle. He knew very well what his daughter's reaction to Darcy's largesse was likely to be.

"I am honoured, Mr. Darcy. My father will be pleased at this further proof of your confidence in me."

Mr. Bennet watched the young people exchange a significant look of pride in each other. He leaned forward in his chair as Darcy explained the terms. This was likely to be a spectacle.

"Miss Elizabeth, the agreement states that I will settle twenty thousand pounds upon you at the time of our wedding"—Elizabeth gasped, and drew a hand to her bosom in surprise—"to which will be added five thousand pounds every year for the rest of your life. You see, I have a bit more than ten thousand a year."

Elizabeth's eyes were wide, and she gave her head a little shake of disbelief. Mr. Bennet chuckled, having already been apprised of how much over ten thousand a year Darcy was worth.

"It is your money; you should think of it as yours. It is separate from your personal allowance and the household funds." Darcy took a breath. "At the time of my death, as the agreement states, you will become the legal owner of Pemberley in trust until our oldest male child should come of age. If we have no male children, then the oldest female child inherits. Pemberley is not entailed away from the female line but each generation *has* managed to produce a boy."

She was aghast but managed to stammer, "I–I will do my best."

"Now she will tell you she does not deserve it." Mr. Bennet could no longer restrain his amusement at the turn of Elizabeth's countenance. He took his daughter's hand. "But you and I know better." He nodded at Darcy.

"Indeed, sir. Your daughter has consented to become my partner in managing the estate. She has agreed to let me teach her. I am delighted she is willing to assume a role that is similar to my mother's place with my father.

"And once I am gone, Eliz...Miss Elizabeth will direct the future of

Pemberley as she and I will have planned, assuming our heir is not old enough and has not completed his schooling."

Elizabeth leapt to her feet and began pacing behind her father. "First, sir, we *must* cease speaking of your being dead. We simply must." She looked beseechingly at Darcy. "And secondly, I did not apprehend so much as this." She continued to pace.

Mr. Bennet chuckled at the forlorn look on Darcy's face as he watched Elizabeth pace the room.

"Mr. Darcy..." Elizabeth seemed to cast about for the proper expression of her astonishment and alarm. "Is there any circumstance that would allow me to ask, without appearing avaricious, just how much beyond ten thousand a year you are worth?"

"You have every right to know. I am...*we* will be, worth a little over twenty thousand a year." Darcy's voice had quieted. "There are investments, other smaller holdings...you will know all of it as soon as may be, after the wedding and our honeymoon. Unless you wish me to enumerate now..."

Her pacing grew more pronounced, and Mr. Bennet was glad of the thick carpet that deadened a sound with which he was quite familiar: the stomping of his daughter's feet when she was most agitated.

"Surely, Lizzy, you understand the even greater honour Mr. Darcy is prepared to bestow upon you. It is not like you to shrink before a challenge."

Darcy caught Mr. Bennet's eye with a brief nod, and the men watched Elizabeth carefully.

"Papa...Mr. Darcy... What will people say when they learn of this arrangement? Of what mercenary motives will I be accused? What will people assume I have done to *earn* this? Fitzwilliam..." At her father's censorious look, she amended, "...Mr. Darcy." Elizabeth took a deep breath, enquiring into his eyes. "You know what your aunt has said of me already. Oh..." Her pacing was rapid but her gaze remained fixed upon Darcy.

Mr. Bennet turned in his seat to follow her, and with the increased velocity of her steps, he realised he and Darcy might appear to a disinterested observer as if they were watching lawn tennis. Elizabeth and her betrothed remained with fixed gazes upon each other, Darcy's head moving rhythmically from side to side.

"Elizabeth, you know I abhor disguise of any sort. I know you love me, and I know you love Pemberley. Let my aunt say what she will. Let her invite such folly upon herself. My cousin Richard and my sister agree with my wishes. They are all the family I need consult. They approve of everything about you."

"But my mother, Fitzwilliam... what of her? She will trumpet this all over Hertfordshire. Every shopkeeper, blacksmith and labourer will know your worth. Every stranger she meets will be told. She will announce it to our servants when she visits. I have no doubt of her insufferable, interminable bragging."

Darcy stepped around Bingley's desk and interrupted her pacing by taking her hand. "Elizabeth, stop yourself. Breathe."

Mr. Bennet decided that the darkened colour of his daughter's complexion approximated that of a beetroot. This opinion he kept to himself.

Darcy shook the hand he was holding, trying to move her to meet his gaze. "Is this the woman I have heard described as having a conceited independence?"

Mr. Bennet was pleased that Darcy would try to tease her out of her high dudgeon.

"Who has said this of me?"

Mr. Bennet believed he was about to learn to what heights of indignation Elizabeth could be provoked.

"A woman you will soon be calling sister, I am afraid. Do not worry. I defended you, even though, in this instance, the lady was not wide of the mark. But what she calls 'conceited independence,' I would call a refreshing lack of conformity."

Elizabeth raised an eyebrow. "Oh, would you! Faint praise indeed, Fitzwilliam. And yet you will marry me?"

Darcy laughed. "And never want for another."

Elizabeth fought a smile but ultimately lost the battle.

Mr. Bennet hoped he would remember to praise Darcy when they were next alone for how well he was already able to manage Elizabeth. This man would do very well for her.

With his bride-to-be once again cheerful, Darcy continued, "My aunt and your mother will be equally foolish, each in her own way. What does it matter to you and me? We shall know we have done the right thing by each other. The people we love most already understand us." He clasped both of her hands to his chest.

"Ahem." Mr. Bennet stood. He took one of his daughter's hands from Darcy and turned her to face him, drawing Elizabeth back from nearly entering Darcy's embrace. "Mr. Darcy—which is how you should address him in my presence until you are married—is perfectly right, Lizzy. Let them—whoever *they* are—say what they may. Let your mother and his aunt have their sport. You know the truth of your regard for each other. Let that be an end to it."

Elizabeth turned to face Darcy. Their eyes shared an embrace. "*You* will not mind?"

"No, dearest Elizabeth. I shall not mind. I consider myself a very lucky man. Bingley may smile, but I laugh."

She sighed deeply, still watching Darcy's loving brown eyes. "Did I not tell you, Father, he is the best man I have ever known?"

"Yes, Lizzy, I believe you mentioned it."

Darcy's blush was immediate and profound.

Mr. Bennet took Elizabeth into the Netherfield library while Darcy remained in the study to add a few notes to a letter he had already drafted to his solicitors. Mr. Bennet suspected correctly that a decanter of brandy could be found there and poured a portion for himself and a splash for Elizabeth. They each took a sip.

"Would you care to explain your comment about Lady Catherine de Bourgh, my love?"

Elizabeth nodded. "Do you remember, Papa, when you received that inane letter from Mr. Collins with his inference from his in-laws' gossip that Mr. Darcy would propose? You asked if Lady Catherine had come to deny her consent."

"Ah...I was not wrong? As I recall, you did not directly respond to that particular query. Had Mr. Darcy proposed already, and was awaiting an answer?"

"No, not exactly. Lady Catherine had indeed heard speculation. She was 'most seriously displeased.' She importuned me to promise I would never accept a proposal from Mr. Darcy, and I said I would make no promise of the kind."

"Of all the bloody—"

"—cheek," said Darcy, entering the room and finishing Mr. Bennet's oath. He had heard enough of their conversation from the open doorway to know its content. "Mr. Bennet, I caught your response to Miss Elizabeth's reference to my aunt. Lady Catherine was quite a matchmaker, though contrariwise to her own wishes. She would be equally 'seriously displeased' to know she has created quite the most amusing chapter of our courtship."

Elizabeth continued the tale. "After leaving me, she descended upon her poor nephew, announcing that since I would not promise *not* to accept Mr. Darcy, he must promise *never* to propose to me."

Mr. Bennet laughed. "It is a wonder so many negatives could end in such a positive way."

"It makes proposing much easier, I find, if one's aunt has revealed that one will be accepted in advance of taking the risk. She tipped Miss Elizabeth's hand, I fear. I tend to be a conservative gambler, and I much prefer a sure thing. My aunt's retelling of her dressing down by your daughter proved highly motivating. I hastened back to Hertfordshire the next day."

"And you got onto your hind legs with her, did you Lizzy? Of what did she accuse you?"

Both Elizabeth and Darcy responded by imitating the lady, "Arts and allurements..."

"Ah!" nodded Mr. Bennet. He was highly diverted. "Did they work?"

Darcy laughed, "Slowly, but yes. Evidently when a woman is artful enough to thoroughly and sincerely detest me, I find it alluring..."

Elizabeth was chuckling, but she also blushed. She had never told her father of Darcy's first proposal in Kent, and she felt Darcy was dancing dangerously close to revealing it.

Mr. Bennet thought the way Darcy spoke the word "alluring" too intimate. Fortunately for Elizabeth, he felt keenly that he had seen enough into their privacy and need delve no further. "Well, well, Mr. Darcy. You see us restoring ourselves. Will you take a small brandy to sustain you until our evening revels begin?"

"Aha! So *this* is where all of the interesting people are!" Bingley entered the room. "And they are pouring out drinks!" This last was addressed to Colonel Fitzwilliam, who was behind him. "I find, Colonel, one can generally locate lost Bennets or Darcys in a library."

Colonel Fitzwilliam added to Bingley's exuberance, "I shall remember it, sir, should I ever find one missing."

Now that the marriage settlement had been explained to Elizabeth, Darcy grudgingly decided he would go to London to prod the drafting in person. Once the news of his leaving was announced, he found himself quickly burdened with errands for others, and although he had planned to ride to London on horseback, he speculated it might take more than one carriage for his return, a second being needed to bear all the gifts for Elizabeth and Jane ordered by their relations and his.

Elizabeth was not pleased to be without him for a se'nnight, leaving only five days until the wedding after his return. Their leave-taking made her eyes sting, but she wanted him to believe that, while she would miss him dearly, she was not silly. There had been a dinner at Longbourn the night before Darcy's early morning departure, and although they had said their farewells publicly and properly in the drawing room, Darcy contrived a long wait for his carriage. Elizabeth likewise made an excuse to leave the room, and joined him in the torchlight on the Longbourn porch in the cold night air.

"Is it too late for me to leave with you?" She snuck up to him and embraced his arm. "It would take very little encouragement to convince me to elope."

Darcy chuckled. "Will the next week be such an ordeal? You *will* stay away from your Aunt Phillips, will you not?"

"Everyone seems decided that Jane and I shall not fall victim to her salacious prattling, but there is all of the rest of it; the minutia cannot be borne without our morning walks. Your company has me quite spoilt. It is no longer enjoyable to walk alone." She hugged his arm ardently before continuing. "And my mother..." Elizabeth emitted a resentful sigh. "Thank you for waiting to announce the terms of the settlement until your return. She seems to like Miss Elizabeth Bennet less and less, but she likes Mrs. Elizabeth Darcy more and more!"

Darcy took off his hat and bent to kiss her forehead. "It is only a week. Please write, or send an express if it all becomes too much."

"Oh, I am quite sure you will want as many details as propriety allows about the night Jane and I are to stay at Netherfield with Caroline, Louisa, and your sister. Indeed, I would not go were Georgiana not to be there. She has your wicked sense of humour; she has let me discover it."

"Ah, I am reminded to tell you. My sister is too clever, at least too clever for *my* own good. Two nights ago we sat talking—about you, as it happens —and she inferred, correctly, from an unguarded remark I made, that I have proposed to you twice."

Elizabeth looked a little alarmed. "Oh, dear...did you quote me? Tell me you did not."

"To relate the tale honestly, it is sadly necessary to quote us both." Darcy embraced her. "That event did neither of us credit."

"She adores you. Now she will like me less." Elizabeth looked down, studying the buttons on Darcy's greatcoat, suddenly trying not to cry. Although the proposal in Kent was now, in private circumstances, a matter of amusement between them, Elizabeth was not willing to have her faulty first impressions and the influence of a certain other man so widely known.

"I think you will be surprised, for I believe you will find her more impressed with you than ever, and a little less so with me. She kept saying, 'You said *what?*'"

Elizabeth wanted to read his eyes. His voice had a note of teasing. She learned nothing, for he closed his eyes and kissed her. She responded in kind, warmed by his embrace.

"*That* is the part of our walks *I* shall miss." Darcy lowered his head to whisper in her ear then drew her earlobe between his teeth. His breath on her neck made her shiver, and she noticed he did not ask whether she was cold. He knew better. He kissed her jaw, her blushing cheek, and finally her mouth again before asking, "You will not forget I love you, will you?"

"No, sir, I promise I shall not. But this may give Jane and Charles another chance to progress beyond us in their...courting." She kissed Darcy in return, her hands travelling up his well-clothed chest to the top of his cravat. Elizabeth longed to feel his skin and tousle his hair. Touching him was the one yearning she allowed herself. "Why is your cravat always so tight?" she muttered, exasperated.

"To torment us both, I fear. One might just as easily ask why your evening gowns are so devilishly low." His hand was on her shoulder, and he allowed one finger to drift slowly down her skin next to the lace at the edge of her neckline until he could feel the swell of flesh at the top of her corseted bosom. He had never before attempted such a liberty.

Elizabeth shivered again and felt somehow both alert and dizzy at once.

The couple pulled away from each other, shocked—Darcy by his near loss of self-control, and Elizabeth by the fierce desire he ignited. "I am sorry!" he blurted. "Now I must leave with you thinking me a terrible scoundrel."

She looked down, smiling. "No, sir, I would not have you think so." She paused before admitting, "I am rather wondering why you did not try something of the kind before. I see where your eyes wander, Fitzwilliam; I am not blind." She did not mention she would have allowed more; *at least a little more*, she admitted to herself.

Darcy's eyes narrowed, and he smiled only enough to deepen his dimples. "In a fortnight, Miss Bennet, you may regret teasing me in this manner."

"*I* am accused of teasing *you*? Oh no, Fitzwilliam, this will not do. My hand on your collar is not at all the same as your hand upon my"—she hesitated, but a better word would not arise—"collar." She could no longer meet his gaze. "I scare myself," she whispered somewhat ruefully, more to herself than him.

Darcy mistakenly inferred she was alluding to her dream. "I would like to imagine your dreaming of our wedding night again while I am gone if it no longer alarms you."

"It was not our wedding night, I think, in the dream." Elizabeth had not revealed to Darcy that she was experiencing many more dreams of their intimacy since the first, which affected her in so profound a manner. The recent dreams felt more romantic and less like reality, leaving her wishing for more sensation, such as she was experiencing at present. The touch of his finger near her bosom had produced such stirrings as she had never felt before, *except* perhaps in sleep.

The Darcy carriage came around the end of Longbourn from the stables. *Damn it!* "Dearest Elizabeth, if I am able to come back even an hour sooner than planned, rest assured I shall." Now there were footmen opening doors for him and waiting. He took Elizabeth's hands, kissing them reverently.

"I shall write to you," she smiled bravely, raising her chin. "I love..." Her chin quivered, and she could not finish. She took a deep breath, pulled the lapels of his greatcoat to lower his ear to her mouth and whispered, "How *dare* you begin to touch me in that way and just... leave?" She turned on her heel and returned to the house without looking back.

Darcy stared at the firmly closed door. *What did she say? She was not teasing; she was serious.* That much he knew. By the time the carriage reached Netherfield, he deduced he had been scolded for not seeking further liberties. "Ha!" he exclaimed as he exited the carriage. *She is a wonder...*

ELIZABETH FLEW UP THE STAIRS of Longbourn and went directly into her room. Although provoked to slam the door, she did not, for she did not wish anyone to know she was disquieted, with the exception of the man riding away in his coach. She had no doubt that, had she wished, she could have slammed the door full loud enough for him to hear it over the clopping of the horses' hooves. Without hesitation, she sat at her escritoire and pulled out a sheet of parchment.

14 November 1812
My dearest Fitzwilliam,

Elizabeth looked at her handwriting, and realised she was about to compose her first letter to Darcy, and a love letter, at that. She felt inclinations of desire adrift within her and decided, although it was against all notions of propriety to express such sentiments, she would not refrain.

You have just driven away, and I must let you know that your merest touch has awakened in me such feelings—I am shocked to admit it but shall not keep it from you. Until tonight, my waking thoughts of your expressions of affection have limited themselves to your warm kiss and the secret thrill when you breathe upon my neck. I have dwelt upon these things when alone ever since you first kissed me weeks ago, and these actions affirm my knowledge of your regard in a way much different from your words of love or any talk of excessively generous marriage settlements.

Tonight you went further. Your touch filled me with the strangest need for you, which I cannot explain away. To have it happen now, when you are to be gone from my side for a full week, is a torture most cruel.

These are feelings a maiden ought not express to her betrothed, yet there they are, and you have often said you wish to be told my sentiments and preferences, no matter the kind. My preference, my dearest, is for you to touch me as you did tonight, but not when you must leave me within minutes. Surely, such sensations deserve to be lingered over.

Often I find myself worrying what you would think of me if you knew my dreams. They are just dreams and do no harm, but I do dream of us. There have been other dreams since the first, though none so disturbing or improper. But your touch tonight was an all-too-brief waking version of similar liberties I have already allowed you whilst I sleep. Perhaps when you come back to me, I shall relive those recent milder dreams while awake? You are the experienced one, and I trust you will know best which expressions of love should be allowed between us, and which must wait.

When you return, there will indeed be a great deal less time to wait, and I feel I shall still have many lessons to learn about being a loving wife.

Your adoring pupil,
E.B.

Elizabeth sat, breathing quickly. Her desire was there on the pages for him to read. She felt the sentiments swirling within her would subside upon being put to paper, but they did not. Before she could think twice, she folded and sealed the letter, addressed it, and quietly descended the stairs to place it on the salver in the foyer for the morning's post.

She slept, when at last sleep did come, with her hand over the path of his finger.

Chapter 10
An Eventful Week…part one

"To be a well-favoured man is a gift of fortune;
but to write and read comes by nature."
William Shakespeare, *Much Ado about Nothing*

Fitzwilliam Darcy's mind was still enflamed by Elizabeth's parting words as he drove his horse towards London the next morning. His heedless touch of her neckline had opened a door of intimacy between them, and he wholly understood and shared her annoyance at the arrival of the carriage outside Longbourn. But if he had not tried her forbearance, he would not have learnt her desires. How delightful to know she would allow something more. He was well exercised and light of heart by the time he reached the cobbled streets outside town. Darcy went directly to his solicitors, Steveton & Sons, still grimy from the road but unconcerned. He had sent an express two days previously, alerting them as to what was required and stating when he expected to arrive in their offices.

After setting the solicitors to their task, he stopped to refresh himself at Darcy House and spent a pleasant hour in conference with the housekeeper, Mrs. Chawton, on making changes to his new bedroom. Darcy planned to move, at last, into the master's suite. Somehow, at Pemberley, it had felt right to change to the corresponding rooms immediately following his father's death, but in London, where he came and went in a random manner and lived a bachelor's life, the change had not seemed necessary. Now it was time for fresh draperies, better bathtubs, and new mattresses for both bedchambers. His first night in those rooms would be Elizabeth's as well. He smiled at the thought of selecting in which room to sleep—*mistress or master, or both?*

He entered the library, hoping to find any book on marital relations secreted there. Mrs. Chawton looked in to ask if he would remain at home for dinner, making him jump even though the book he was consulting at the moment was a recently arrived volume on the birds and flowers of Derbyshire. He thought he might send it to Elizabeth as a gift.

"I'm sorry to have alarmed you, Mr. Darcy. I ought to have knocked."

"Nonsense, the door was open. I was merely lost in my thoughts. Once I have written a note to Miss Elizabeth, I would like this book wrapped and sent to her. I shall ring when the note is ready. And yes, I shall dine in this evening."

Mrs. Chawton smiled. "Very good, sir. And may I say, sir, how delighted we are by the news of your wedding. If I may beg your pardon, we have just had word from Mrs. Reynolds at Pemberley, and she sends her unqualified approval of your choice of wife. Not that the approval of servants matters, sir, but we do want you to know we are pleased."

Darcy started to laugh. "You mean relieved, do you not?" Darcy had no illusions about how both Caroline Bingley and his cousin Anne de Bourgh —and her mother—plagued his servants when they were entertained at either of his residences.

It was not an easy thing to make Mrs. Chawton blush should one wish to do so, but she did. "Yes, sir. I shall not say more." She smiled and left him to his writing.

15 November 1812
Darcy House, London

For my dearest Elizabeth,

It is my fond wish for this volume to answer those questions about the natural surroundings of your future home that are beyond my knowledge. I can claim to know the best place to watch the Black Kites soar over the Peaks, which I know you will enjoy. I look forward to seeing Pemberley anew through your beautiful eyes.

With deepest love,
F. Darcy

Darcy folded the note and slipped it inside the front cover, then went to find Mrs. Chawton. He returned to the library until dinner was served, having been unsuccessful in his search for secret information in hidden books.

After dinner, in a moment of sudden inspiration, Darcy betook himself to the master bedroom's bookcases, where his careful father would have been more likely to have a cache of books he would not have wanted his son to find. On a bottom shelf, after moving the bed to reach it, he found a stack of books on their sides. He suspected the first one he opened might be identical to the volume of naughty French cartoons that Elizabeth had found in her father's desk. As he turned the pages, the pictures became exceptionally detailed and amusing, but not exactly informative.

Darcy picked up the second book, containing hand-tinted drawings of naked women of many body styles—flat chested, plump, buxom but long-legged, long-limbed but too skinny, perfect derrieres, and some less than perfect—some scantily draped with fabric, and although beautifully rendered, the images were not instructional. He wondered which image he would find his Elizabeth to most resemble. *I shall know soon enough.*

In the very back of the book was a surprising page tipped into the binding from some other source and on different paper, containing a pen and ink drawing of the surface structures between a woman's legs, quite medical in its thoroughness. He had not realised the maidenhead was so close to the threshold. This book he set aside for further review. The tinted pictures were lovely and he was inclined to learn the Latin names of Elizabeth's parts, but how such knowledge would help him comfort her on their wedding night, he knew not.

The last book was indeed a marriage manual, verbose on the topics of abetting conception and managing intimate congress with a woman already with child. In Darcy's opinion, it was far-fetched in how to stimulate an elderly husband, and gave no suggestions for the wedding night. The book seemed to take into account a lady's emotions and sensations not at all. It was published in 1782, the year his parents married. *This cannot have been much help even then,* he decided.

With a disappointed sigh, Darcy returned to his old bedroom with the picture book of female nudes. After pouring himself a half tumbler of brandy, he was ready for bed. It had been a long day; he had tossed and turned the night before, with Elizabeth's parting words echoing in his ears. No, she did not think him a rake for touching her intimately, but rather she was annoyed with him for not trying further, and for attempting anything at all just before departing. What a miraculous and confounding thing was the female mind, or at least Elizabeth Bennet's.

It was with these weighty but gratifying issues that he occupied his mind before falling to sleep.

MISS ELIZABETH BENNET STEPPED INTO the billiard room at Netherfield Park. Darcy straightened from aligning a shot, and bowed slightly. He had taken off his frock coat, and he was in his waistcoat with his shirt sleeves rolled up almost to his elbows. She appeared confused about what room she was in and met Darcy's gaze with a slight tilt of her head. She was wearing the elegant gown from the Netherfield ball, half of her creamy bosom exposed above pale yellow polished muslin. In the autumnal afternoon light, she looked ethereal, a shaft of sunshine in a dark masculine room.

"Miss Bennet!"

She started to back out of the room, stopped when he said her name, and bobbed a brief curtsy. "Mr. Darcy."

"Do you play?"

She eyed him warily. "If I say yes, I am too modern in my habits and not feminine, and if I say no, then I am a country miss with no experience of the world. Surely, sir, you know there is no billiard room at Longbourn, nor is it considered a woman's game."

"It seems I have earned your distrust. But be assured, I agree few women take the opportunity of playing. It is a relaxing pastime and, like archery, improves hand-to-eye coordination. Would you care to try?"

His tone seemed to challenge her and she took a step or two into the room, chewing the corner of her lower lip in the most beguiling manner.

"Perhaps if you cared to demonstrate, Mr. Darcy," she finally suggested, "I could answer you properly."

"I shall most happily oblige." He met her gaze with a slight smile that deepened his dimples. She coloured slightly, and he wondered why. He stood at the centre of the table end nearest him, and surveyed the balls on the felt surface. "The object is to use the cue stick to hit the plain ball, the cue ball, into the coloured and striped balls, knocking them into the pockets. After each successful shot, one reassesses the remaining combinations on the table, and selects the next shot

based on how easily one thinks another ball can be hit into another pocket." He pointed to the red ball.

"I have been amusing myself hitting in the solid colour balls first. The red ball is close to the pocket, and I should be able to tap it in with just a touch of the cue ball. However, one does need to think ahead to where the cue ball will roll after the shot, and perhaps if I hit the ball harder, the cue ball will come to rest in a way that will produce another easy shot."

"Like chess, then," she responded, "one thinks a few moves ahead?"

He was bent over the table, aiming, but looked up, reappraising her. "You play chess, Miss Bennet?"

"Oh, yes, I play with my father." She smiled a little.

"Somehow I find I am not surprised. Let me continue: in billiards, one always assumes one will make the next shot, and one's opponent will not." He leaned in, and with precise efficiency, pulled the cue stick back and took his shot with the desired result.

She was standing at the corner of the table where the red ball dropped smartly into the pocket. She widened her eyes. "Oh!"

He had been aiming at her.

The cue ball rolled to the centre of the table, and presented a fairly simple angled shot to put a purple ball into a side pocket. "Come, Miss Bennet, grab a stick."

She went to the rack of cue sticks affixed to the wall between two windows. As she stood, the afternoon sun revealed the outline of her legs under her gown, and Darcy quietly held his breath at the sight. He shook his head to clear his mind.

She selected a cue stick and turned. "What next?"

"Come stand by me." She did so. "Watch my stance, and mimic my grip on the stick. You are right-handed?"

She nodded.

"Good. Let your left hand guide the cue stick. Your right hand provides the power of the stroke. I have leaned over to sight the angle. When I see where I want to hit the cue ball, I pull back a few inches, and hit with as much force as I think is needed."

"What about the next shot?" she asked, leaning slightly over him, as if to see what he was seeing. The movement caused her breasts to swell towards the neckline of her gown. She stood again without seeming aware of her effect on him. How he longed to cup those breasts in his hands.

He exhaled deeply. "Let us walk before we run, Miss Elizabeth."

"I do have the unfortunate tendency to get ahead of myself." She smiled.

Darcy backed up. "Now you."

She leaned over, left hand resting in front of her on the green felt, right hand behind. She twisted her shoulders away from him, and it was then he realised that her hair was styled as it had been for the Netherfield ball—swept up and intricately woven with satin roses and ribbon—but three tempting ringlets hung down the back of her neck, dark... shiny... soft. She closed one eye to sight, and shot with rather too much force. The purple ball dropped percussively into the pocket, but the cue ball careened around the table so she and Darcy straightened quickly to avoid it.

"You do not know your own strength," he said, barely above a murmur.

But she appeared delighted to have made her first attempt count. She watched the cue ball roll to a stop. No further shots were obvious. She turned to him, questioning with her eyes.

"You have the additional options of bouncing the cue ball off of the bank, as the edges of the table are called, or you may ricochet the cue ball into another solid colour ball to make a second one drop."

"Ah," she mused. "That does not sound easy."

Darcy breathed in her scent of lavender, which was starting to fill the air. She moved down the table from him and leaned far over, looking for a new opportunity. As she did so, one foot came off the ground, the other leg bending at the knee to balance as she leaned on the table. She wore handsome little slippers with a slight heel, and pale pink stockings. Her ankles were slender and well turned.

This is why men do not play with women—they are too distracting! Do I watch her lovely ankles, or walk around the table to leer at her bosom? I wish I could be in two places at once!

"If we were competing," Darcy explained, "and playing the simplest version of billiards, I would be pocketing the solid balls, and you would be hitting the striped ones. The player finishing first wins. As long as one keeps hitting the pockets, one keeps trying. Once one fails to hit the pocket, the turn proceeds to the opponent. Did I mention one must declare one's intentions before each shot? In your turn, you would have said, 'purple ball in the side pocket.'"

"Declaring one's intentions? Fancy that: a game wherein gentlemen must constantly declare their intentions. Come then, Mr. Darcy, help me decide on my next move since I am helping you rather than competing."

He moved to her side. "Singular for us, is it not?"

She looked over her shoulder at him, her eyes merry. "So it is!"

She stitched her lower lip with her upper teeth.

"It looks to me, pray correct me if I misread what I am seeing, but the only shot is awkwardly situated. Is it allowed to partly sit on the table? I fear I must stretch over it."

Darcy inhaled forcibly. He cleared his throat. "It is allowed. You may even lean on your elbow to steady yourself. Indeed, I do not see any other possibility. Short of climbing upon the table on all fours, one may do whatever one thinks necessary to reach the shot and sight it. The only thing not allowed is to move the balls that are at rest."

He had moved behind her again. Infernal curls! She hitched a hip onto the table, stretching to keep the toes of her other foot solidly on the ground, her gown sliding up her lower leg. Her torso, leaning low over the flat surface, twisted to reveal a trim waist. The gown pulled tight, and he could detect no evidence of a corset.

Instinctively, and completely without heed, Darcy leaned over, put his hand on her waist, and crushed the three impertinent curls against the nape of her neck with his lips.

"Mr. Darcy!" She froze.

"Hang it, Elizabeth, you know your curls were meant to torture me!" He murmured with a caressing breath, not stopping his actions. "Did you not want every man in the room to be tempted when you were here for the ball?"

"No, sir, I had no such idea! Did I tempt even you?" She spoke in such low tones he was not sure he heard her correctly. She did not turn or move, but her breath quickened.

"By the end of our dance, I was angry with you, angry with Bingley, and angriest with myself. I wanted you then, and I want you now. I still love you." He moved his hand around her waist and pulled her to him. She did not resist. He was kissing her neck, then her shoulder. He opened his eyes and looked down the front of her gown. Her breasts were just shy of exposing their nipples at the neckline. He moaned, and realised she had also.

One hand supported his weight on the table while the other slid over the swell of her hip. Her derriere was round and firm. Her thigh felt warm through the gown. He bunched her skirt in his fingers, raising it until the hem was in his hand. "Do you love me even a little, Elizabeth? Did my letter at Hunsford, or our meeting at Pemberley, change anything?"

Her naked derrière was before him, and he rubbed his growing erection against her, undone by desire. His forehead leaned against her shoulder, waiting to hear her answer or a shriek of disapproval.

He instead heard the thud of the heavy end of the cue stick dropping onto the felt. Her hand sought his, and held it. "Indeed, Mr. Darcy, everything has changed."

"Elizabeth…" He said it like a prayer. "Please say you will be my wife."

"Indeed I must, sir. We must sanctify that which I hope and believe is about to take place."

He chuckled, almost giddy, into her hair but stopped as her hand stroked his where it rested on her bare hip. To his utter astonishment, she gently raised his hand to her lips then placed it on her breast. She sighed with a shudder.

"Fitzwilliam, I fear I am more bold than a maiden should be."

"I can find no fault with you." He was enraptured by her use of his given name. He kissed her shoulder and followed each kiss of her tender skin with another until he reached the nape of her neck behind her ear. She was moaning softly.

She rolled her hips slightly, repeatedly touching his covered manhood with her bare skin.

"Oh, yes! Fitzwilliam!" she murmured.

DARCY AWOKE ON HIS SIDE, panting and slightly sweating. His did not wish to assuage himself. It took several minutes and more deep breathing to lessen the intensity of his tumescence. This was by far his most realistic dream of her; yet, when he could regulate himself, he chortled. *Imagine proposing to Elizabeth while grappling on a billiard table!* He wondered at the juxtaposition of details, and her wearing her ball gown. He knew a long ago, fleeting encounter at Netherfield summoned the dream. *But her hair? The ball gown?*

Darcy considered. He had only danced with Elizabeth one time, and by the end of the half-hour set, they were barely able to remain civil. Yet she was a brilliant dancer and so refined. Darcy arose from his bed and went to the small desk in the room. He made two notes on a sheet of paper: "Ball gown—Jane?" followed by "Jewellers." He walked to the hallway door where his night robe hung from a hook. His eyes easily led him through the dark to his study where he lit a candle, then went to his larger desk and, from a deep bottom drawer, drew out a wooden casket. He opened it with a key hidden in another drawer.

Much of his mother's jewellery went to Georgiana, but there were a few pieces he imagined giving his future wife. He took the inner box covered in oxblood velvet and opened it. The first pouch contained a single strand of medium-sized, pale rose pearls. He smiled and set them aside, thinking *wedding night*. The next, smaller pouch contained a solitary emerald set in a gold band of figured leaves. He stared at it in wonder. *It could have been made for her. I wish I had remembered this weeks ago. When I return, I shall give it to her immediately.* He set it aside and opened another pouch, full of loose pearls. This he put into the pocket of the robe, *just the thing...* Another pouch held a much grander ring—a large diamond surrounded by smaller ones—his mother's betrothal ring. This he returned to the box with a note, *change small diamonds for emeralds, give at Pemberley, July 21.* The day he and Elizabeth stumbled upon each other as if by magic loomed large in his memory, and would always mean more to him than even his wedding day. The last pouch contained a pair of gold hair combs, each with a row of bright emeralds along the spine. There were earrings to match. *This first Christmas.*

How did I know when I was six and twenty, when Georgiana and I sorted these, that all of them would be perfect for my Elizabeth?

THE NEXT MORNING, DARCY DESCENDED to the small dining parlour with a jaunty gait. His frock coat appeared lumpy, its pockets filled with small pouches.

After breakfast, his first of many calls would be to the jeweller, where older items could be inspected for soundness and others enhanced. In the night, a scheme had come to Darcy for an entertainment at Darcy house while they were in London on their honeymoon. It would require some complicated planning—a conspiracy, in truth—but the project would give him a focus for his thoughts while waiting for the marriage settlement to be finalised.

As Darcy served himself a cup of coffee, a footman entered with a salver of the morning's post. He knew this would be the earliest possible arrival time for a letter from Hertfordshire, and was delighted to find one from Elizabeth on top of a blessedly small stack of business correspondence. He realised she must have written it shortly after his departure. He opened the letter, and upon reading the first sentence, sat down. By the end of the first paragraph, he was on his feet and aimed for his study, away from prying eyes.

Devouring the letter from beginning to end, his eyes then sought the more tender passages again and again: "...your merest touch has awakened in me such ardour—I am shocked to admit it..." "...The secret thrill I feel when you breathe on my neck." "My preference, my dearest, is for you to touch me again as you did tonight..."

Darcy became light-headed and breathless, running his fingers over her signature, "Your adoring pupil..." *What are you willing to be taught, delightful pupil?* He was not surprised to find himself aroused, and growing more so. He considered opening his trouser fall and relieving himself of his current tension but feared soiling her letter, which he was not willing to set aside. Darcy drew in several deep breaths and tried to consider all she said in a reasonable way, but his own desire trumped any attempt at logic. He could only savour her revealing candour and dear innocence. Elizabeth was willing to write—and articulately, too—words she was unwilling to speak. He studied her handwriting. It was clear and full of charming curves. *Just like the lady who produced it.*

Suddenly he was possessed by concern. *I must respond immediately! How she must feel, what anxiety, knowing she has written such a letter. She worries too much what I might think... I must let her know I cherish this evidence of her love and desire. The book!* Darcy leapt to his feet and ran calling for Mrs. Chawton, his hand still clutching Elizabeth's letter.

His housekeeper came bustling from her workroom inside the passage to the kitchen stairs. "What is it, Mr. Darcy?" She was alive to the slightly frantic edge in his voice.

"Has the book been sent to Miss Bennet?"

"No, sir. I have just finished wrapping it and was about to send for a footman."

"Thank goodness. Bring it to me first, please. Then we will send it express."

Mrs. Chawton retrieved the book and gave it to Darcy. "I shall be back directly," he said as he disappeared into his study.

17 November 1812
Darcy House, London

My dearest Elizabeth,
The first letter you have ever written me is in my hands. I have not set it down since opening it, as it is now my dearest possession. Your words have

given me such happiness that I must respond immediately. I would not have you in any suspense over their delightful effect upon me.

Indeed, my only sorrow in receiving your letter is that I must write my response and cannot take you in my arms to comfort any misapprehension you may feel for having written it. I cannot breathe upon your neck as I so wish to do, knowing now it pleases you. I dare not continue in this vein, or this letter will never be finished, and would certainly make you blush, though you must know I find you quite fetching when you do. But I know this of you —you do not like to be always blushing.

The solicitors are hard at work preparing the "excessively generous marriage settlement." How I smiled when I read this, my love—I could hear you say the words as plainly as if you were in the room. The solicitors are hopeful they can return me to you a day or even two earlier than we have been led to expect. Whilst they toil, I am consumed with the errands of others and also with preparing this house for our week here, blessedly alone together. How I shall adore having you all to myself. The only thing better will be our fortnight at Pemberley before holiday guests arrive.

Holding your letter in my hand, full of such sentiments as truly gladden my heart, I am more ashamed than ever of the one letter I had previously written to you. I recall asking you to burn it, and I hope you have done so. Keep this one instead to remind you of how I long for you when we are parted for even a few days.

Please accept the book accompanying this letter with my deepest affection. It was newly arrived, and I thought it would please you as you prepare to live at Pemberley. There is a note with it written earlier, and I am grateful your letter arrived before the book was put in the post, as it may serve to distract certain parties from this longer letter, which is full of my love for you with every line I write.

We must avoid being parted in the future, once we are married. It certainly does me no good.

With deepest love,
F. Darcy

He read the letter through once, and after adding a brief post-script, was satisfied it said enough. He consulted his pocket watch, finding it well past time for the jewellers to open. He slid the letter into the book, and Mrs. Chawton wrapped it again promptly. Darcy chose to take it to the express office himself. He also had an express to send to Bingley, who could be counted upon to assist in setting certain plans in motion.

Chapter 11
An Eventful Week...part two

"Done to death by a slanderous tongue."
William Shakespeare, *Much Ado about Nothing*

Jane and Elizabeth were in Longbourn's front hall while the family footman loaded their small valises into the carriage for their overnight stay at Netherfield when an express rider arrived with a package for Elizabeth. Mrs. Bennet swooped down from the stairs when she heard the commotion.

"A wedding gift from Mr. Darcy, no doubt! The first of many jewels to come, I am sure, Lizzy." She hovered as her second eldest daughter opened the package. "Oh fiddlesticks...only a book?" Mrs. Bennet turned away. "I do not see the romance of *that*. Only Mr. Darcy would think a book a fitting wedding gift."

"Yes, Mama," replied Elizabeth, "and only *I* would appreciate his thoughtfulness. It is a guide to the birds and flowers of Derbyshire." Lizzy pulled the single sheet from inside the front cover, feeling a thicker letter tucked further back in the pages. She read the simple loving words, which her mother snatched from her hand and read aloud.

"Pretty enough sentiments. Well, if you are pleased, my dear, I am, too. Bingley sent Jane a lovely bracelet last week, gold it was, but if you are happy with a book, far be it from *me* to complain." She handed the note back to Elizabeth and left the hall, calling behind her, "Have fun with Bingley's sisters, girls! Do not overdo and make yourselves ill..."

Elizabeth and Jane exchanged a look and climbed into the waiting coach, Elizabeth still clutching her gift.

"There is a longer letter here, too, Jane! I did not tell you. but I have written Fitzwilliam a letter—such a letter. When he left, I had myself in a state. All my thoughts spilled onto the pages, and I do not know whether he will approve or censure. I doubt he would have received it before this book was sent."

"Read the letter if you like, Lizzy; I will not mind, nor shall I snatch it from your hands to read for myself." Both sisters laughed.

"Thank you, but no, I can wait until I have a few minutes alone at Netherfield."

After the servants took their outerwear, Caroline Bingley and the Hursts ushered them into the drawing room. Caroline noticed the small thick volume Elizabeth was holding to her bosom.

"You are such a great reader, Miss Eliza. Pray, what is that book?"

Elizabeth looked at the book in her hand and was surprised to be still carrying it. "Mr. Darcy sent me a treatise on the flowers and birds of Derbyshire. It arrived just as we were departing Longbourn." With great reluctance, Elizabeth sat it on a side table as Hurst passed thimble-sized glasses of wine to the ladies before filling a goblet for himself.

"What a singular sort of gift," smiled Louisa Hurst. "So like Darcy. He knows your love of nature already." Elizabeth thought she detected a note of honest sincerity in Louisa's tone. Perhaps Louisa recognised her husband would never be so observant of her interests. Could it be that she was secretly pleased for Darcy in his choice of wife?

"Are there game birds listed?" Hurst asked, pursuing his current line of interest. The weather had turned warmer but stayed rainy, and he feared the fine shooting at Netherfield was over for the season.

"Indeed, Mr. Hurst, I do not know. I have yet to peruse it," Elizabeth responded.

At that moment, Georgiana Darcy entered the room. "You have come!" she cried, taking the liberty of giving Elizabeth a quick impulsive hug, met by Elizabeth's relieved and crushing embrace. "And Jane," Georgiana said, once Elizabeth had released her and she could again draw breath. "How lovely to spend time with you."

Caroline eyed Georgiana's reception of the Bennet sisters with deepening envy. No Darcy had ever welcomed her and Louisa so warmly.

Georgiana remained standing when the others settled again. "Elizabeth, since we have a few moments before dinner, would you join me in the music room?" When Elizabeth approached her, Georgiana whispered, "I have a duet I would like to try. It would please my brother to hear me play while you sing. We shall surprise him."

"Nothing would make me happier," Elizabeth whispered in response. Georgiana smiled. Elizabeth scooped up her book as they left the room but neglected to notice Darcy's letter slipping to the floor. Only Caroline detected the loss.

"Dear Jane." Caroline stood and casually sidled to the place where Elizabeth had been sitting. "Charles and Colonel Fitzwilliam are visiting with Sir William this afternoon. They should be here well before dinner. Would you care to rest until then?"

Why does she want to get rid of me? Jane wondered. Knowing Caroline had schemed to separate her from Bingley brought wariness to Jane's normally unsuspecting nature. "I am perfectly well, Caroline, but unlike my sister, I have neglected to bring a book. I will step into the library for a moment, if I may."

"Of course," Caroline replied coolly. "We are less than a fortnight from its contents being yours. Pray join us when you have made your selection."

Jane felt like a duck oiled for roasting, but she was not such a silly goose as Caroline surmised. Bingley had acquainted her with the entrances and exits of all the rooms during her previous tour of the house. She knew there was a connecting door to the library from the sitting room, and observed it was ajar. Jane left the drawing room by the hall door and entered the library by the next door down. She then hustled to the drawing room connecting door to listen. *What has become of my manners?* she thought, but her intuition begged she be on guard.

As soon as the hall door closed after Jane, Caroline bent to pick up the letter on the floor. *My Dearest Elizabeth* was written on the outside in Darcy's precise and even hand. Caroline pondered the several ways she might cause Eliza Bennet some trouble: she could unseal the letter, remove the salutatory page, and try to pass it off as a love letter from Darcy to herself; or the letter might contain revelations of improper behaviour with which to sully Eliza's virtue; or a page of it might be used to imply Eliza received a letter from some other source—Wickham perhaps?—but no, Darcy's penmanship was too distinctive.

Louisa noticed her sister had grown quiet. "What have you there, Caroline? What letter is that?"

Behind the library door, Jane's heart jumped into her throat. *She has Lizzy's letter from Mr. Darcy!*

"We might have some sport with this Louisa, if you are willing to assist me in making up a plot. It is a letter from Darcy to his 'Dearest Elizabeth'. It slipped out of her bird book." Caroline's voice dripped venom. Her ill humour overtook her wits as she tore the letter open. She did not see Hurst rise from his chair and stare at her in disbelief.

Louisa was shocked. She was not the quick and clever woman her sister was, but she saw instantly and with horror the ramifications of Caroline's angry actions. Caroline's nerves had become brittle to the breaking point as plans for the double wedding progressed—the wedding breakfast was to be held at Netherfield—and Louisa feared just such a situation as this might arise. In one motion, Caroline risked alienating their brother, his betrothed, and their brother's best friend, thus losing the condescension of Darcy in extending his considerable hospitality and connections to her and her husband.

"Shall I read it out?" Caroline did not wait for an answer. Her voice was loud and crackling. "'My dearest Elizabeth' . . . is it not too sweet? 'The first letter you have ever written me is in my hands. I have not set it down since opening it, as it is now my dearest possession.'" Caroline abruptly stopped. Her hands were shaking with jealousy edging close to lunacy.

"Caroline!" Louisa stepped forward and snatched the letter from her sister, unfortunately leaving the outer envelope page in Caroline's hands.

Caroline could see the hasty post-script Darcy had included. *Loveliest Elizabeth, while I am in London, please do not forget I love you. F. D.* Caroline burst into wailing tears. "How I hate her!" she shrieked.

Jane burst into the room just as Hurst reached his sister-in-law and shook her by the shoulders. "Stop this at once, you silly cow! Do you want to ruin us?"

Jane took the crumpled envelope from Caroline's hands and turned to stare sternly at Louisa, who meekly handed the pages of the letter to Jane.

Mr. Hurst released Caroline as she sank, still crying, to the floor. Hurst, Louisa, and Jane watched with disdain, alarm, and sorrow, respectively. Jane looked questioningly to Louisa, wondering why she would not help Caroline through this crisis. She knelt next to her, taking her shuddering shoulders into her arms, and looked up at Louisa. "Will you not help me console her?"

"I would sooner see her rot," Hurst fumed, holding Louisa's wrist.

Louisa looked up at her husband with tears just starting to spill. "Marcus, please, she is my sister. I know she has committed an unpardonable sin, but I fear for her senses. Please let me help Jane get her to her room and sedated."

Hurst released his wife's arm, and Louisa crouched next to Jane. Together they raised the whimpering Caroline to her feet. When the three women turned to the drawing room door, they were met with the shocked faces of Elizabeth and Georgiana, who had heard Caroline's anguished scream and proceeded from the music room with all possible haste.

"Oh, Lizzy, please help us." It never occurred to Jane that her sister, the obvious recipient of Caroline's unhinged wrath, would withhold compassion. "Find the housekeeper and brew the calming tea you make that so comforts Mama."

Elizabeth felt as if her own wits were wanting. She stared at Jane a moment until the words finally penetrated her comprehension. "Yes, of course." Elizabeth turned from the room in search of the Netherfield housekeeper.

"Lizzy, wait," Jane called. When Jane, Louisa, and the nodding, weeping Caroline reached the hall, Jane held the disassembled parts of Darcy's letter to her sister. "It fell out of your book. Caroline picked it up."

Elizabeth's eyes grew wide as she took the pages, but she merely nodded and continued on her way to make tea. She knew Jane would explain further once Caroline was safely settled. Georgiana followed Elizabeth.

When the tea was taken to Caroline's room, Elizabeth stopped outside the door and whispered to Georgiana. "Please take this in. I cannot. I know my presence will disturb her."

Georgiana held no fondness for Caroline Bingley. During her time at Netherfield, Georgiana was shocked by Caroline's continued pursuit of her brother despite his betrothal and the constant talk of his affection for Elizabeth. The depth of Darcy's adoration had become a continuing joke between him and Bingley, with much teasing and innuendo that both men thought the ladies of the household would not comprehend, but of course they did. Georgiana was astonished at her brother's forbearance in the face of Caroline's constant insults aimed at Elizabeth and her equally constant references to the Bennet family's want of connections.

Georgiana looked at Elizabeth, who wore an expression both compassionate and sad. Elizabeth was near tears, but Georgiana could not yet find it in herself to pity Caroline. If she thought Caroline truly broken-hearted, she might have summoned empathy, but Georgiana believed Caroline was merely thwarted in her social scheming, thus angered to the point of rage. She simply nodded at Elizabeth, took the tea tray and entered the room.

Caroline cried and tossed upon her bed. Jane stood aside, quickly discerning that she brought Caroline no consolation. Louisa sat on the bed, whispering in a soothing manner, and managed to get Caroline to take most of a cup of tea since it had been provided by Georgiana.

Caroline eventually grew still and sleepy. She glanced at Jane. "I am sorry, dear, sweet Jane," she said in a sluggish voice. "I have underestimated you. Please understand, it was never my intent to make you an adversary."

Jane nodded. "You brother loves you, Caroline, but you have tried him to his limits, and he will not be pleased to learn of this. I shall try to intercede for you, but you may need to leave for a time. Prepare yourself."

"Thank you, Jane." Caroline turned to Georgiana. "You cannot imagine my shame, Miss Darcy, that you have witnessed my undoing. What you and your brother will think, I know not."

Georgiana could find no forgiveness, but she thought of her brother and what he would want her to do. Loving Elizabeth had made him kinder. "Miss Bingley, you need to rest, and you do not need to worry about anyone's thoughts. But please, settle your own; my brother will forgive you, as will Elizabeth." She did not mention herself; she did not wish to lie. "But you must control your feelings and forgive yourself. We, all of us, court shame and are challenged at some time."

Caroline started to cry silently. Louisa cooed to her but looked at Jane and Georgiana, and they understood it was time for Bingley's sisters to be alone.

Elizabeth waited in the hall and stopped pacing when her dearest and her newest sisters emerged from the bedroom, affected by the churning chaos of Caroline's emotions. Elizabeth was alarmed that she had forgotten Darcy's letter, now shoved in her pocket. She was afflicted by an odd sense that she had somehow betrayed him with carelessness for allowing his words to fall into Caroline's malevolent hands. Such were her thoughts as the three women embraced each other, and Elizabeth finally broke down. She tried mightily to suppress sobs. Jane and Georgiana were quick to guide her to the room she would occupy that night.

"Oh, Jane, Georgiana. How will he forgive me?"

"Lizzy!" Jane sat on the bed next to Elizabeth and rubbed her sister's hands vigorously. "What is there to forgive? You were not careless. We must admit the entire fault lies with Caroline. That much is clear. She had every opportunity to return the letter to you or to me. Instead she got me out of the room as quickly as she could, and sought to form a conspiracy with Louisa. Fortunately, Louisa is good at heart—truly she is, Lizzy—and she retrieved the letter before Caroline could read much of it aloud. Have you read it?"

Elizabeth shook her head.

"Do so now, Lizzy. I heard her read the first sentences and it is such a beautiful expression of his devotion that even Caroline could not continue reading. In the face of such love, she had to admit her failure, which unleashed her rage."

With trembling hands, Elizabeth drew the letter from her pocket. It was not in her nature to be secretive with Jane. Georgiana sat to her right and Elizabeth supposed the younger woman already knew many of her secrets. "Do you mind if I read it aloud? I am sure he is not improper... 'The first letter you have ever written to me is in my hands. I have not set it down since opening it, as it is now my dearest possession. Your words have given me such happiness, I must respond immediately; I would not have you in any suspense over their delightful effect on me.'"

Elizabeth could read no more and held the letter to her chest. Finally, she whispered, "Is he not the best of men?"

Jane nodded to Georgiana and said to Elizabeth, "We shall let you finish this in private. We shall be in the drawing room awaiting Charles and the colonel. I would not have Charles hear of this event from Mr. Hurst. Please join us when you have finished."

Elizabeth smiled wanly at Jane and Georgiana. "Thank you. I shall not be but a few minutes." She returned to Darcy's words. The letter was everything she hoped it would be. He did not think the worst of her for having written in so forthright a manner—in fact, quite the opposite. She dried her tears, and knew Darcy would see this trying afternoon for what it was—the final act of Caroline's farcical one-sided courtship.

IN LONDON, DARCY'S BUSINESS WITH the jewellers went well. The emerald ring would be perfect as Elizabeth's betrothal ring. The jewellers ensured the setting was secure, cleaned and polished the stone, and returned the ring to Darcy in a brown velvet box.

He planned to give it to her as soon as they were together again, and he thought perhaps he might even preface the gift with a third proposal. His second proposal, Darcy still found wanting, though it certainly had the desired effect. He had merely stated that feelings he had at the time of the first proposal had not changed, which was hardly true as his devotion to her had become much deeper, joined as it was with gratitude. He had been warmed, and much relieved, by her uncharacteristically inarticulate but nevertheless positive reply. He now wished he had thought to bring this ring with him.

The diamond ring would be reset with emeralds encircling it, and he would give it to her at Pemberley in the summer. He had an idea about enhancing his mother's pink pearls and those would be ready for the wedding night. Darcy had taken a bag of loose pearls, and wished for them to be drilled and put onto golden hairpins for Elizabeth to wear for the wedding. Much to Darcy's surprise, the jeweller had slightly larger pearls already made up in such a fashion. He purchased a set to be sent to her directly by the jeweller's special courier with a note from Darcy. They even had a small room with just a chair and table where gentlemen such as he might compose a gift card in private, on the jeweller's stationary.

17 November 1812
Grandison & Co. Jewellers, Ltd.
Kensington, London

Dearest Elizabeth,

Several times I have told you how beautiful I thought you on the night of the Netherfield Ball. If you have not yet made other arrangements, I put this quite forward suggestion to you—knowing you may think it improper but also knowing you will try to humour your adoring bridegroom—that your hair be styled as it was the night of the ball and adorned with these pearls.

I know the custom is for brides to wear bonnets or veils or—horror of horrors—a conglomeration of both. Please give my suggestion your fondest consideration, but if you cannot find it in your dear heart to fly in the face of convention, please accept them anyway, knowing in our future life together,

*you will have many occasions when they may be of use. In any case, you will
be my beautiful bride.*

With deepest love,
F. Darcy

THE EVENING AT NETHERFIELD PASSED more calmly than the first hour
but was not without its trials. Bingley was mortified when he learned of
Caroline's actions. Elizabeth was amazed he could be so disturbed—not
supposing the always-ebullient Bingley had a breaking point—but was not
aware of all the slights and insults Caroline had been spitting at her with
unveiled contempt, and even at Darcy for appearing so besotted. Netherfield
seemed to bring out the worst in Caroline Bingley.

Colonel Fitzwilliam watched the family drama develop with no little
concern and now realised that Jane Bennet was bringing more civil relations
to her marriage than was Charles Bingley. He intended to write Darcy and
say as much. The colonel was most impressed with Jane and was sorry he
had not accompanied Darcy to Netherfield a year ago. As the story went,
Bingley fell in love with Jane at first sight, and the colonel could well believe
it. There was something remarkable about the two eldest Bennet sisters, and
he was sorry not to have been the first in line in either case.

Louisa stayed with her sister most of the evening, and Jane acted as
hostess, giving a good account of herself in the role. Hurst was as talkative
as anyone had ever heard him, absurdly currying Bingley's and Elizabeth's
favours with apologies for Caroline long after the subject had been worn thin.

Elizabeth longed to sit up late into the night with Jane, dissecting the
afternoon's events and deciding how to tell Darcy, but Bingley seemed
reluctant to relinquish Jane's attention or Georgiana's company. The party
grew quiet, and Elizabeth was left with the impression that everyone in the
drawing room wished to speak without her presence. She sighed and decided.
"I must wish you all a good evening, and I shall see you in the morning. I
shall draft a letter to Mr. Darcy. Jane, if you might tap at my door when
you come up? I may not have the tone of the letter just right and would
seek your good opinion."

"Of course, Lizzy. I shall join you presently."

As the door of the drawing room closed behind her, Elizabeth would have sworn she heard several sighs of relief. *Are they all so afraid of my response to Caroline that they will not discuss the matter in front of me? Am I thought such a harridan?*

The next morning, Elizabeth's letter was included in an express with correspondence from Bingley to Darcy, which Elizabeth assumed covered the matter of Caroline's behaviour and Bingley's explanation and apology. Elizabeth also noticed a letter to Darcy from Georgiana in the packet, and even one from Jane. Perhaps they all decided the best policy was to offer several accounts, letting Darcy seek the truth from many sources.

Chapter 12
An Eventful Week…part 3

"Tax not so bad a voice to slander music any more than once."
William Shakespeare, *Much Ado about Nothing*

Although Fitzwilliam Darcy fully understood his own definition of innocence regarding his beloved's knowledge of the sensual realm and marital relations, he would have been surprised to know that she defined *him* as an innocent in the art of the giving of gifts and in the understanding of their effect upon those who were not the actual recipient. He had no way of knowing the effect his presents had on anyone but Elizabeth, but had he sought that lady's advice, she might have warned him that her mother would respond in a way wholly unreasonable but not unpredictable.

It would not have occurred to Darcy that Mrs. Bennet would have an opinion on the subject of how his bride would style her hair on her wedding day, or that anyone, Mrs. Bennet included, would seek to be obeyed if their desires ran contrary to the wishes of a bride. And so it was, for the second time, that Elizabeth received a gift from Darcy that drew the disapprobation of his future mother-in-law. For Mrs. Bennet, the first gift to her daughter was not fine enough, and the second far too grand.

The courier from Grandison's arrived at Longbourn two days after Elizabeth and Jane returned from Netherfield. This auspicious person presented himself two hours after a box from a prominent London milliner had arrived, addressed to Miss Jane Bennet, containing two wedding bonnets, from which Jane was to choose one and return the rejected specimen.

Elizabeth, Mrs. Gardiner, Mrs. Bennet, and Jane were in Jane and

Elizabeth's bedroom, studying the two hats and watching Jane try on one, then the other, interminably. Three of the ladies found the simpler embroidered white veil over a low frame to be the most becoming to the lady and her wedding gown—of which she was not yet in possession, it being given its final hemming in Meryton—but Mrs. Bennet preferred the bonnet with a more pronounced brim that Elizabeth, under her breath, likened to the prow of a ship. It trailed an elbow length veil with rather more beading than suited the absent gown.

When Mrs. Bennet left to confer briefly about the evening's dinner, Elizabeth suggested to Jane that they and their sisters each wear a specimen of the more ornate bonnet and advertise themselves as "an Armada of Bennets." Jane was convulsed with laughter, and Mrs. Gardiner was chuckling as Elizabeth paraded around the room in the offending chapeau when Mrs. Bennet re-entered the room. She was instantly livid.

"Lizzy! You will ruin that lovely bonnet, and Jane will have no proper veil for her wedding. And we shall have to pay for it. I am sure, as Mrs. Darcy you will order whatever you want and abuse your clothes howsoever you please, but you are not married yet, *Miss Lizzy*..."

"Mama," Jane looked at her mother with heart melting sincerity, "you know Lizzy is right. The lower bonnet and longer veil will suit me much better. The larger white bonnet is, I am sorry to say, also uncomfortable." Jane took the hat from her sister's head, examining how it was fashioned inside. Whoever had sewn it had done so very ill.

Mrs. Bennet breathed a loud sigh and gazed with favour on her most beautiful daughter. "If it is uncomfortable, dear Jane, then I would not have you wear it. All of your tears that day should be tears of joy."

Jane stood wearing the veil she liked best, and embraced her mother. "Thank you, Mama."

As both hats were being packed into their boxes, a smart rapping was heard on the front door. Hill answered as the four ladies stepped onto the upstairs landing to watch. They could not hear what was said, but Hill turned and called up the stairs, "Miss Elizabeth, this courier has a gift for you from Grandison's Jewellers, *in London*."

Elizabeth blushed and started down the stairs, only to be edged aside by her mother. "Grandison's! I shall take the package, young man!" Mrs. Bennet rushed to the courier.

"Please, I do beg your pardon, ma'am, but are you Miss Elizabeth Bennet?" The courier tried to sound as civil and friendly as possible.

"Do not be ridiculous. I am her mother." Mrs. Bennet reached for the beautifully wrapped package.

The courier took a step back. "I am indeed very sorry, ma'am, but it is Grandison's policy to deliver our items into the hands of their intended recipients. I do apologise."

Elizabeth stepped forward. "I am Elizabeth Bennet, sir." She gave him a rueful smile.

"For you, ma'am, from Mr. Fitzwilliam Darcy." The courier executed a handsome and well-practiced bow. "You will find a card from the gentleman inside the package."

Elizabeth looked to Hill, not knowing whether a gratuity should be offered. "Ah, ma'am," said the courier, recognising the look. "I cannot accept a gratuity from you; it has been paid by the sender."

"Thank you," murmured Elizabeth. She was still blushing. The courier left, riding in a small, unmarked carriage with a driver and secretly well-armed footman.

"Open it, girl!" Mrs. Bennet was beside herself.

Elizabeth tore the wrapping, revealing a handsome wooden box with a hinged lid. Darcy's card was inside but Elizabeth tucked it into her pocket before her mother could abscond with it. Inside the box was a velvet pouch. Elizabeth could feel loose items in it and opened the drawstrings to withdraw a golden hairpin topped with a pearl the size of a silver tuppence.

"Oh, Lizzy! How lovely! How many are there?" Jane was at her elbow.

Jane took the pouch and poured it into her sister's cupped hands. There were fifteen perfectly matched pearl hairpins. Tears stung Elizabeth's eyes. "Jane, oh Jane." She looked at her sister with a smile starting to crumple around its edges. "He has said he loves my dark hair," she whispered. Her throat tightened.

The pouch was laid on the table and the hairpins arrayed upon the velvet. "We shall give you a moment to read your card, Lizzy," said Mrs. Gardiner. She pointedly placed her arm around Mrs. Bennet's shoulders and turned her away saying, "We shall be in the drawing room."

"What can Mr. Darcy have to say that needs such privacy?" groused Mrs. Bennet as Jane joined her mother and aunt.

Elizabeth read the card and did cry but smiled through the tears. She knew her mother would never allow the pearls to be worn for the wedding. After replacing them in their pouch and the pouch into its box, Elizabeth took a deep breath, preparing nevertheless to make Darcy's case.

AN HOUR LATER, ELIZABETH AND Jane were both in tears—Elizabeth from vexed frustration and Jane in sympathy. Mrs. Bennet was shrill and shouting. Mrs. Gardiner was quietly infuriated. It was she who finally said, "We do not need to settle this now. When the bridal gowns are delivered tomorrow and the girls try them on, we can be assured the selection for Jane is the best one. When you see Lizzy's gown, Fanny, you can judge what might suit her most. There is still fabric enough and time enough to follow our first plan to make her a proper veil to match her gown. Perhaps the pearls might be incorporated into it?"

"Mr. Darcy may spend whatever he chooses, but we must show him the Bennets are not so profligate. Lizzy may wear the bonnet Jane is not wearing. It will be less expense than making Lizzy a new hat."

Elizabeth began to protest but a hand on her arm stilled her as her aunt pursued their point. "Fanny, dear Sister. At your request, Lizzy is wearing a colour called candlelight. The bonnet is white. She cannot possibly wear it. If you would spurn Mr. Darcy's request, we must at least have Lizzy in a veil or bonnet matching her gown."

"Nonsense. No one will notice. Lizzy must wear the second bonnet."

Elizabeth eyed her mother warily and stood. "Madam," she addressed her mother formally, "had not Mr. Darcy given me these pearls and suggested I wear them for my wedding, would you so much as suggest I wear a white bonnet with a candlelight gown?"

Mrs. Bennet dithered before responding. "Your Mr. Darcy may be a man of fashion, Lizzy, but we are not without our own resources of taste."

"In what county is it the height of fashion for a bride to appear mismatched?" Mrs. Gardiner asked, incredulous.

"Oh bother!" Mrs. Bennet stood, trying to face down Elizabeth, who was two inches taller than her mother. "I won't have it, Lizzy. I shall not have you upstage Jane. You are always trying to put yourself ahead of her, and your father pushes you to it every minute. I suppose you will run to him now, *Miss Lizzy*, for his protection, but I shall not have it. *I shall not have it!*" She flounced from the room, and her heavy tread was heard ascending the stairs to her sitting room.

Jane and Elizabeth stared after her, their tears abated by stunned silence.

"Close your mouths, dears, you look like startled fish," their aunt murmured. "It is time to let the dust settle. Nothing shall be deemed decided until the gowns arrive. Do not fret, either of you."

The sisters nodded, and Elizabeth left the room to write the necessary thank-you note to Darcy. She settled herself in the small sitting room after drinking a glass of water to restore her equanimity. *Two lovely gifts and each creating havoc in their different ways. I pray he will send no more, poor dear man. How amazed he will be when he learns of it all. But what am I to say to him?* She sighed, trying to clear her head.

Elizabeth breathed deeply to calm herself, and closed her eyes. A vision appeared in her mind of sitting at a looking glass preparing for a ball, putting the pearl pins into her hair, and over her shoulder, Fitzwilliam Darcy's handsome face, with dimples pronounced in approval, watching her in the glass. She opened her eyes, the vision dissolved, and she laughed.

18 November 1812
Longbourn

My Dear Fitzwilliam,

Do not think for a moment, dear sir, that I do not see what you are about. Your generous and beautiful gift of pearl hairpins is clearly meant to help you improve your memory of past events. I know you do not yet follow my philosophy of remembering the past only as it gives us pleasure, and you seek to improve the future in order to banish the past. It remains to be seen whose way of thinking is best, but I am thankful for your gift and even more thankful that we have our entire future together to determine which of us has the better approach.

Matters at Netherfield seemed calmer when we departed, and Miss Bingley passed a quiet night. Do not disturb yourself overmuch regarding the events there. You and I must step out of the way and allow the Bingley family to heal itself with my dear Jane's gentle assistance. She has been very wise throughout these events, which is all one would expect of her, and yet I love my sister more as each day marches us closer to the altar. That day, I shall happily transfer myself into your tender care and wisdom.

I miss you dreadfully, my love, more than I dare say here. I pray your next letter will tell me that you will re-join us much sooner than expected.

With all grateful affection,
Your E. B.

Elizabeth decided she was not up to addressing his suggestion of wearing the hairpins for the wedding. She was hopeful that, with Jane and their aunt's help, they would prevail in furthering Darcy's proposition. She was quite sure it had never occurred to him that his desire for her to wear the hairpins would not find universal welcome.

ON THE MORNING OF NOVEMBER 18, Darcy received a note from the solicitors with news that the marriage settlement was already drafted, and he was welcome to review it at any time before the final copies were prepared. This visit was executed before eleven o'clock. Darcy was assured by the youngest Steveton that he could be on his way back to Hertfordshire on Monday.

"Monday! I would ask that clerks be paid extra to prepare the documents sooner."

"Very good, Mr. Darcy. We shall send the copies to you by special courier as soon as they are ready."

"Thank you, Steveton. I would be delighted to return to Miss Bennet on Saturday. I promised I would."

Mercifully, the remainder of the week passed without further incident and at Longbourn without the arrival of more gifts from Darcy. Letters continued to pass from Darcy throughout Meryton, and the Royal Post noted a boost in Hertfordshire to London revenues throughout the remainder of November.

DUE TO THE INCIDENT AT Netherfield, Colonel Fitzwilliam privately suggested to Elizabeth that Georgiana would enjoy a change of scene and asked whether it would be an imposition to have her stay at Longbourn for a night or two. The attitude of Caroline Bingley had become what could only be called servile towards Darcy's sister, and Georgiana longed for escape. Elizabeth remembered the spare bed in Kitty's room, as well as Georgiana's avowed desire for a sister. Given the current atmosphere at Longbourn, Elizabeth judged that, if the application to Mrs. Bennet came from Jane rather than herself, the scheme could be accomplished.

And so it was that Georgiana spent three nights at Longbourn. Mrs. Bennet extended every hospitality to the girl, thinking meanly that she scored some vague social victory over Bingley's sisters with Miss Darcy's visit. Georgiana's beautiful performances on the pianoforte filled the house, and by the end of the stay, she was calling Catherine "Kitty," and Kitty was calling her "Georgie." The roommates sat upon their small beds until late into the night. They spoke quite candidly of George Wickham, and Kitty was astonished to learn that the proper Georgiana Darcy had nearly eloped with him. Georgiana revealed, on pain of Kitty's secrecy, what she knew of her brother's involvement in Lydia's marriage arrangements. The report made Kitty reflective—quite a new sensation for her—and she came to realise that her favourite sister had behaved dangerously and married badly.

During the day, when she was not practicing at the Bennet instrument with Mary, Georgiana joined Elizabeth for turns in the garden if the weather was fair. It was calming to Elizabeth to have a Darcy with whom to pass the time, and Georgiana was happy to speak of her brother to his betrothed. Thus did Elizabeth learn many of his preferences—for food and drink, colours he preferred in his dress, books he enjoyed enough to return to, and his love of riding and swordplay for exercise—without having to ask the man himself. With Georgiana in the house, Elizabeth's longing for Darcy was not quite so keen, for she could speak of him openly and often.

Chapter 13
The Final Days

"There's little of the melancholy element in her, my lord:
she is never sad but when she sleeps and not ever sad then,
for I have heard my daughter say, she hath often dreamt
of unhappiness and waked herself with laughter."
William Shakespeare, *Much Ado about Nothing*

The marriage contract arrived at Darcy House late on Saturday afternoon. Murray and the household servants spared no effort to prepare for Darcy's speedy departure by carriage. However, the arrival of the documents coincided with the first winter storm of the season, and flurries of snow persuaded Darcy to spend another night in London. Beside himself to be thwarted by the weather, he was reminded of words he overheard from Bingley to Elizabeth describing what a fearsome object he was when finding himself with nothing to do, and he owned the truth of it through the long evening.

He sat in his bedroom with Elizabeth's letters, drinking brandy and jumping up frequently to curse the snowfall. By midnight it had ceased. *I could have gone easily. Damn!* He consulted Murray one last time, vowing, no matter the morning's weather, he would ride to Longbourn at sun-up. The carriage could follow. With any luck, he would arrive before matins.

By morning, the snow was melted, but the horse he selected was not the swiftest choice for dirty weather, and when he reached the wayside where a fresh horse from Netherfield awaited him, Darcy realised with annoyance he would be later than he wished. He had written an express to Elizabeth and Mr. Bennet the previous day saying they should expect him to call at Longbourn in the afternoon. Although he would have no time to tidy himself, he determined to slip into the back of the Longbourn chapel even though services were started. He had to see her—his Elizabeth—even if it was only to stare at her back whilst she was at prayer.

Indeed, by the time Darcy entered the little church, the final hymn was just beginning. He stepped inside and scanned the Bennet family pew. Mr. Bennet stood at the aisle, Elizabeth—in a pale green woollen gown and spencer that seemed somewhat familiar—was next to her father and, oddly, Georgiana. He heard the lovely voices of Georgiana and Elizabeth lifted in song above the congregation. The vicar, who would perform the double ceremony in less than a week, met Darcy's eye and nodded as he sang. When the service ended, the vicar shook Darcy's hand as he passed to exit the church.

The Bennets turned to leave, and Darcy was clearly visible, watching them. Elizabeth's heart fluttered, and her inclinations reminded her of the worst excesses of Lydia and Kitty as they squealed and chased officers; it was all she could do to refrain from gleefully giggling and leaping into his arms. She limited herself to a wide smile as Darcy met her gaze with an intense half smile, expressive of emotions one does not usually associate with churches.

Mr. Bennet looked from his daughter to Darcy and was entertained by insinuating himself in front of Elizabeth's precipitous approach to her betrothed, thus slowing her and reaching Darcy first with an extended hand.

"Aha! You have returned to us, Mr. Darcy. You have had ample time to escape the snares of the Bennet family, so I take it by your appearance that you really do love my girl." Mr. Bennet turned to see Elizabeth's reaction. She rolled her eyes and blushed; her father was delighted.

Darcy watched Elizabeth but answered her father. "Mr. Bennet, I have no intention of escaping your daughter. As I am thoroughly and happily ensnared, I believe the opposite might be closer to the truth. You have no idea the effort I have expended to convince her I am worthy. *She* may wish to escape *me*." Darcy paused from smiling at Elizabeth and looked to Mr. Bennet. "Sir, since the weather has improved, may I have your permission to escort Miss Elizabeth to Longbourn?"

"Certainly, sir! Nothing of an improper nature can possibly transpire in the three minutes it takes for the arduous journey from this church to

Longbourn house. I shall send our groom back for your horse." He leaned to Darcy and whispered, "Have Lizzy show you the long way around. It takes five minutes."

Elizabeth stepped aside as Georgiana approached and gave Darcy a brief embrace. "I have had a lovely visit at Longbourn, Brother. Kitty will join me at Netherfield now you are returned. I have learned something of what it is to behave like a sister with sisters! See? I have given Lizzy...Elizabeth a gown she admired!"

Darcy happily nodded at Elizabeth over his sister's head. *Ah, this explains why the gown is familiar. Georgiana bought it for herself last Christmas. How well the colour suits Elizabeth.*

He extended an arm to his bride-to-be, and they exited. After taking leave of the vicar, Elizabeth turned their steps away from the path taken by the rest of her family. The couple circled the perimeter of the village until they reached the path approaching Longbourn from its western fields.

When they passed behind a hedge, Darcy turned to Elizabeth, and she was on her toes kissing him before he could draw her into an embrace. He gave himself entirely to the feeling of her body pressing against his and was surprised when she struggled away.

"Oh, Mr. Darcy! Fitzwilliam...I should not run at you. What a week it has been. You must never leave again without taking me with you."

She was so seriously scolding him that he had to laugh. "The next time I leave Hertfordshire, you will be my wife—you may depend upon it—but if you need to kiss me to reassure yourself of this truth, then please do."

They continued walking and were soon at the south side of Longbourn in the boundary lane behind a hedgerow where they had often met.

Only one room of the house could spy them from this angle, and behind the curtains of his bedroom, Mr. Bennet watched. He was dumbfounded to see Darcy formally draw himself up before Elizabeth and open a small box.

"Dearest Elizabeth, I know you will think it an unnecessary foolishness," Darcy said earnestly. "But I should have done this weeks ago. This ring should have come to you when I last proposed. I am embarrassed it has taken me three attempts to get a proposal properly stated, but I hope your answer will be the same as for the second attempt. I love you so very dearly, and I am quite certain you are the *only* woman in the world I could *ever* be prevailed on to marry." He smiled plaintively at her.

At first, Elizabeth was shocked at Darcy's posture and expression, but as he spoke, tears gathered at the corners of her eyes, and a crooked smile formed on her face. He opened the box, revealing the simple emerald ring. She experienced a momentary fear that the box would contain an ostentatious jewel she would be hard put to live up to, but when she saw the modest, brilliantly green stone, her hands went to it immediately.

"Fitzwilliam! My only complaint of your second proposal is for myself, as I did not respond in anything like an articulate or eloquent manner." Recognising his playful reference to her refusal at Hunsford, she added, "Let me make myself abundantly clear, sir: I love you, and I am honoured to become your wife. My father has always said I must only marry a man I could love and respect, and I *never* disobey my father."

Darcy laughed at her. He would not have called Elizabeth an altogether-obedient daughter. He pulled the ring from its box for Elizabeth to see the exquisite workmanship of the band of gold wrought leaves.

"Oh, Fitzwilliam. Was this your mother's betrothal ring? It is so beautiful, so delicate. It is so—"

"So like you."

"It is so *perfect*, is what I was going to say."

"It was a ring of my mother's but not her betrothal ring. I selected this from her jewellery years ago when Georgiana and I sorted the pieces I might keep for a future wife. I did not know I would be adorning a wood nymph that I captured in the fields of Hertfordshire, but I thought it the prettiest piece in my mother's entire collection."

Elizabeth held out her right hand, but the ring was slightly too big for her ring finger, and she hastily moved it to her middle finger, which was an exact fit. "Does it matter to you that I shall wear it on a wrong finger? I love it."

"You may wear it on whatever finger you like, just so you wear it!"

Their eyes met, Elizabeth lifted her face, closed her eyes and parted her lips. Darcy's hands encircled her waist and he kissed her tenderly. Her arms came to rest upon his shoulders.

Mr. Bennet was still watching. He did not know what he would do if the contact of the lovers became more improper. He feared, given their separation and the looks on their faces in the church, that it would.

When the kiss ended, Elizabeth opened her eyes and held Darcy's gaze as she took his hands from her waist and placed them at her bosom, stacking them over her heart and holding them there, against her left breast.

"You make my heart race, Fitzwilliam Darcy," she whispered. Her eyes burned into his. *If he asks to meet me privately, I shall say yes. He must know I would say yes.*

Darcy's first thought was of how full and warm the flesh was over her heart, thumping like thunder under his hand. He allowed himself one brief moment of sensation before he carefully, and determinedly, pulled his hands from under hers, but continued holding one as he stepped a pace away.

Mr. Bennet breathed a sigh of relief after his initial shocked distress that it was his Lizzy who had instigated such an intimate moment. He found himself wishing more than ever that he had sired boys.

"Elizabeth..." Darcy continued to meet her gaze. "We must not tempt ourselves. I am well aware of the feelings I stirred before I left, and I should not have been so reckless. In our future life, we must have nothing with which to reproach ourselves."

Elizabeth's words stumbled upon each other. "But you must know... I... there is already such feeling... and you have waited so long." Her eyes were earnest, and Darcy felt himself falling into their darkness and sinking forever. "Fitzwilliam, I will deny you nothing," she murmured.

Darcy leaned his forehead to hers, mainly to prevent his own swooning. "Darling Elizabeth. Dearest." After inhaling a deep breath, he tucked her bejewelled hand into the crook of his elbow and they proceeded into the open garden, walking slowly to the house.

This was all to Mr. Bennet's great relief. He turned from his window.

Elizabeth looked down, trying to recover herself. *What have I done? Why did I not wait for him to try me? Have I always been so impulsive?* "I am sorry to have suggested any misbehaviour. It is from missing you. I have not been myself with you away."

Darcy stopped, but she would not look at him. "Elizabeth, I love you all the more for what you have said. But I know myself. Any liberty will lead to too much. I must be honest and not pretend otherwise. You are all that is generous and tempting, believe me. I desire... so much. But I shall not importune your innocence. My wish is that when we... eh... well, I shall just say it... when we consummate our marriage, we shall have all the time in the world. There will be no regrets."

She nodded. Her eyes fell upon her ring, and she marvelled at it until they reached the house. It made her feel safe—and made the coming wedding more immediate—to be wearing it. She paused when Darcy opened the glass door for her and handed her into the morning room. "Thank you for this, Fitzwilliam. It is beautiful, and I thank you for saving it for me. Me. Of all people."

They found their way to the drawing room with Darcy vowing silently that he would avoid being alone with her for any extended period before the wedding. He was too easily aroused, and Elizabeth was no longer inclined to stop him.

MRS. BENNET WAS THE FIRST to notice Elizabeth's ring when the family, including the Darcys and Mr. Bingley, sat down to Sunday dinner. Usually more impressed with size than quality, even she had to admit it was exquisite. "I believe it suits you quite well, Lizzy!" she exclaimed. "And no doubt there will be larger, later, when you are Mrs. Darcy."

Elizabeth looked at her plate in absolute mortification and hid her hand in her lap.

Mrs. Bennet prattled on, "I daresay, after Lizzy has produced a boy or two, Mr. Darcy, she will barely be able to move for the jewels you will heap upon her. You ought not judge my girls on what I have done, Mr. Darcy, nor you, Mr. Bingley..."

Seeing that his wife was causing those at the table who were engaged to be married to burst into fierce blushing, Mr. Bennet cleared his throat rather loudly before warning, "Mrs. Bennet..."

Darcy was on Elizabeth's left and also looked down. He reached for her hand and gave it a quick squeeze. *To have been raised by such a mother—my poor dear girl—with never a compliment that does not veil a slight. Perhaps we should have eloped...*

Elizabeth pressed his hand in return and moved it to his thigh before he released his grasp.

During the fish course, Mr. Bennet leaned forward and asked Darcy in a low voice whether he and Elizabeth wanted to meet about the marriage settlement with Mrs. Bennet after the meal was completed. Darcy was about to reply in the affirmative when a glance at Elizabeth's countenance changed his mind.

"Perhaps we should leave the Sabbath unsullied by what is essentially a business matter? Shall I come tomorrow after breakfast instead?"

Mr. Bennet's eyes twinkled. "That will suit me just as well. As you say, let this last Sunday as a family proceed in relative peace and quiet." Elizabeth looked from her betrothed to her father and back with a silent expression of thanks.

"Mrs. Bennet, may I assume you will spend tomorrow shopping?" Mr. Bennet asked his wife.

As had become her wont, she stopped chattering as soon as her husband began to speak. "Oh, no, sir! I do believe, according to my lists, everything we need has been ordered. Jane and I are to visit Netherfield in the afternoon to discuss the breakfast one last time, and Lizzy, too, if she wishes, but otherwise, I shall be at home."

"Excellent! Will you be available to join me after breakfast when Mr. Darcy arrives with the marriage settlement?"

Mrs. Bennet fairly beamed. She knew it was the settlement that had taken Darcy to town. She foresaw great pleasure getting rid of her most difficult daughter to a most surprising bridegroom, and at a most handsome rate of return. "Indeed, sir, for such an occasion, I shall wait upon you as early as you wish!"

Mr. Bennet turned to Mr. Darcy with a droll murmur, "You sir, would do well to hope for such a compliant wife as I have."

As ELIZABETH SAID HER GOODNIGHT to Darcy, she asked whether he would join her for an early morning walk. The weather turned clear and cold, and to Elizabeth, the brisk morning air was like a tonic, strengthening her for the rest of the day.

Darcy declined. He could only imagine the rosy bloom of her cheeks and the rise and fall of her invigorated breathing. He was still warmed by the feeling of her breast and heartbeat under his hand that morning. "Prudence dictates I should give the settlement one last reading before presenting it. Perhaps if you join your mother and Jane at Netherfield, Bingley and I can hang about and make ourselves annoying, and insist we walk you back to Longbourn."

Elizabeth had to laugh at this plan but was disappointed they would not be truly alone again soon.

THE FOLLOWING MORNING, SHE WALKED before breakfast and was irked to see Darcy and Bingley riding through the newly shorn fields around Netherfield. *What is he about? Why the pretence of reviewing the settlement?* Her wonder turned to exasperation, and she ran from the boundary of Netherfield to the side door of Longbourn to regain her poise.

Darcy arrived as the Bennets stood from the breakfast table and seemed very much himself when he entered Mr. Bennet's library. The presentation and signing of the marriage settlement between Mr. Fitzwilliam Darcy and Mr. Thomas Bennet went forward as three of the four parties would have predicted, unfortunately.

Once the highly advantageous particulars were repeated to Mrs. Bennet enough times that she finally comprehended them, the elevation of her spirits was nothing short of piercing. She fanned herself vigorously and smiled upon Darcy with every affectionate phrase at her disposal. No one was more generous, liberal, bountiful, charitable, or kind. She patted Elizabeth and rained approval upon her, telling Darcy what he already knew: he was marrying the most beautiful and charming of the Bennet daughters, the cleverest and best educated.

"And her temper—so easy, Mr. Darcy! Nothing disturbs her, and she never raises her voice. She has never spent an angry day in her life!"

At these words, Darcy, Elizabeth, and Mr. Bennet began to call out that she had now overstepped herself entirely, and betwixt them laughed her into a brief silence. Finally, Mrs. Bennet joined their laughter. "Well, perhaps I did err a little there. Lizzy *can* bear a grudge, but it is nothing a walk in the fresh air does not cure."

"*That* description of my future wife, Mrs. Bennet, I shall allow as more accurate," Darcy said with a chuckle. He patted his soon-to-be mother-in-law on the shoulder as he rose to leave.

Mrs. Bennet was vastly pleased. She looked at the clock on the library mantle and wondered whether she had enough time to visit her sister with the settlement's particulars before the appointment at Netherfield.

AND SO THE FEW REMAINING days before the wedding passed with Elizabeth and Darcy much in each other's company but rarely alone together—and never for longer than a few moments to say hello or good-bye with a kiss or two as one or the other came and went from Longbourn or Netherfield.

Elizabeth continued her morning exercise on the lanes of Meryton's environs. Darcy did not join her. She did not like it, but she understood him. A charming note arrived two days before the wedding with a gift of sheet music in which Darcy explained that, although he had resisted her the morning he returned from London, he did not suppose himself strong enough to do so again. He confessed to sleeping poorly, as he was visited by dreams of being alone with her that seemed alarmingly real. He asked her to bring the sheet music to London, so she could play the selections for him privately. He did *not* write that, while awake, his sustaining occupation was devising ways of seducing her just before the wedding—he had no intention of doing so, but it did not make him want to any less—thus passing the time in anticipatory reverie until the event.

Occasionally he spied her running away from the cares of wedding details on the lanes, or she saw him galloping across the fields. They waved to one another, but Darcy rode with Bingley and Colonel Fitzwilliam, and even once with Georgiana. At his sister's behest, they approached Elizabeth for a pleasant conversation, but the two Darcys did not dismount.

As they rode away from Elizabeth, who had climbed and sat upon the top tier of a fence to converse, Georgiana leaned towards her brother and asked, "Does Elizabeth often run? Is it a habit with her? It is a most unusual thing for a woman to do. I am only a month from turning seventeen, and I cannot remember the last time I ran."

Darcy smiled. "She says it disperses her ill humours. Jane says the activity subdues Elizabeth's excessively high spirits. I have seen her vigorously walk herself out of a fit of temper and into good cheer on more than one occasion. I hope she will be so happy at Pemberley that she will not feel the need, that she will not be vexed or frustrated in any way."

"But wait... Fitzwilliam, am I mistaken? It is my understanding that she is marrying *you*, so certainly she will lose none of her motivation—unless she is marrying another, more amiable man who plans to settle at Pemberley?" Georgiana was learning from Elizabeth that she could—and should—tease her brother.

"Brat." Darcy glared.

Georgiana laughed and found herself hoping Elizabeth would not give up the practice of running and that she might partake with her new sister.

UNBEKNOWNST TO DARCY, THE DAYS for Elizabeth were punctuated by regular skirmishes with her mother. All her sisters and Mrs. Gardiner had taken her part; Mrs. Bennet was beset on all sides, making her more stubborn. Mr. Bennet, who in this case decided not to enter the fray, was nevertheless aware there was, indeed, a combat to be avoided.

The wedding gowns were modelled by the brides-to-be for their female relations. Elizabeth and Mrs. Gardiner were relieved when Mrs. Bennet admired, if in a comparatively mild way, the style and detail of Elizabeth's gown, and complimented her sister-in-law for bringing the sheer fabric over-layer of the gown's skirt, which suited Elizabeth and drew attention to her "sweet little" emerald betrothal ring. For Jane, Mrs. Bennet fussed constantly at errant threads, worried over the symmetry of the beading —"Is there a bead missing from your wrist, Jane? Oh no, it is just a trick of the light."—and would not let anyone with food or potentially soiled hands near it.

Chapter 14
Two Beloved Sisters, One Doting Father

> *"You are thought here to be the most*
> *senseless and fit man for the job."*
> William Shakespeare, *Much Ado about Nothing*

The morning of their wedding at last arrived, and with sleep coming in fits and starts for both sisters, Jane rose early with Elizabeth. They went to the two window seats in their shared bedroom, one on either side of their dressing table, and watched for signs of the approaching dawn, each lost in her own thoughts.

Jane sat with her arms wrapped around her legs, her chin on her knees. There were no words, in French or in English, to calm or distract her from the evening to come. The wedding would be wonderful, and in no way a trial, but by lingering outside the Netherfield billiard room, Jane had ascertained Bingley's experience with women was rather chaste, and she wished he were more educated. Jane could not bring herself to examine her reasons.

Elizabeth stood in her nightgown, languidly leaning against the side of the window with the curtains pulled back. She wondered whether Darcy would ride that morning and whether he would see her. Elizabeth was not superstitious and was quite consciously titillated by the notion of revealing herself to Darcy from the safety of her maidenly bedroom.

"Oh, Lizzy," Jane finally groaned. "The day has come." Sensing disquieted spirits, Elizabeth immediately went to her sister's side.

"Yes, Jane!" She embraced her from behind with one of the exuberant hugs for which she was legendary within their family circle. Since girlhood,

Elizabeth was known to nearly knock sisters, parents, favourite aunts, and dear friends off their pins. "Are you not relieved?"

Jane turned to her. "I shall be lovely, Charles will be handsome, you will be beautiful, Mr. Darcy will be regal, the food will be marvellous and the four of us will hardly touch it. Then you and Mr. Darcy will leave, and I shall not see you for months, well, a month anyway, and I must stay and see to the remaining guests, and when they all leave, it will be my wedding night and, oh dear, Lizzy..."

No one blushes like Jane. Elizabeth smiled to herself. "We must not dwell on our wedding nights, dear. We shall not get through the day if we do. We must be done with that. I need my wits about me for one more bout with Mama, at least, and I trust you, this one last morning, to take my part."

From the distance of fifty yards, a handsome horseman watched from his hidden spot as the only woman he had ever loved moved from her window. Darcy would not have imagined that Jane could fold herself to look so small, and he wished Bingley were with him to see her vulnerability. Then with the boisterous actions of a mother hen—he could imagine her chuckle—Elizabeth's arms swooped in to surround Jane and wrap her in a jubilant embrace. Darcy could see the sweep of his beloved's dark hair engulf her sister—*tonight, this very night, her hair will enrobe me.* The embrace held for a few moments; then both sisters laughed and moved away from the windows. The parted curtains closed, and he smiled. Although Elizabeth did not appear to have seen him, it did not matter; he had seen her. And not just a glimpse, but he had witnessed her doing something so endearingly and characteristically Elizabeth that he found he was as amply comforted as Jane appeared to be. He rode back to Netherfield to make an attempt at breakfast and to dress for his wedding.

THOMAS BENNET, AWAKENING TO THE role of father of the brides, and who rarely insisted on anything except not being disturbed in his library, had demanded the night before that all his daughters, his wife, and his in-laws, come down early to breakfast. All were seated when he entered the dining room, already wearing his wedding frock coat.

"Now hear me, all of you." He stood formally behind his chair at the head of the table. Rather than looking at him, all eyes turned to Elizabeth as if she could explain his behaviour. Elizabeth turned her eyes to him with raised brows and the others followed her gaze. "I demand efficiency this morning. I shall not have Bennet daughters arriving late for their wedding when leaving from *my* house. Mrs. Bennet, I demand the maids be left to Lizzy and Jane. The rest of you can help each other." His wife nodded, speechless, drawing in a breath for a coming salvo. "And as their father, my last request is that I be allowed a mere quarter hour each with Jane and Lizzy before we depart. Can this be managed, Mrs. Bennet? Mrs. Gardiner, you will help me?"

"Of course, Thomas," nodded his nearly laughing sister-in-law.

"Mr. Bennet, how can you imagine so much can be accomplished?" ranted Mrs. Bennet, letting loose at last.

"Fanny!" Mr. Bennet fixed her with a sharp eye that would have opened an oyster at twenty paces. The room hushed. "Jane, Lizzy, eat as quickly as you can and get about dressing. The Bennet carriage will leave with the three of us promptly at nine o'clock. As you see, I am ready. Lizzy, Jane, you will join me in the carriage at nine o'clock in whatever state of dress you find yourselves. If the rest of you miss the proceedings, that is your head and your ulcer. Until then, I shall be in my library."

Jane and Elizabeth jumped from the table, each grabbing an apple and some tea, and dashed upstairs. The family maids, Annie and Sarah, followed them in a matter of seconds. Fifteen minutes later, Elizabeth and Jane were joined in their room by Mrs. Gardiner, who was herself ready for the wedding, but for her bonnet and gloves.

"Lizzy, I shall help you since I am familiar with your gown, and Annie, you see to Jane," instructed Mrs. Gardiner. Elizabeth had already put on her short-stay corset with Sarah's help; it only cinched in her ribs, and it was topped with short tight rows of ruffles under her bosom to hold her breasts up and out in the popular fashion.

Elizabeth fastened a petticoat around her waist, pulled up new pale pink stockings, and tied her garters. The gown was slipped over her head and settled about her with a whisper. The skirt was suspended from the bodice and comprised of several layers of sheer fabric over one of heavy satin. The outermost sheer layer also constituted the inner bodice of the gown, and quite scandalously, the usually proper Mrs. Gardiner convinced Elizabeth not to cover her bosom by wearing a fancy camisole under it. The separate outermost portion of the gown consisted of a matching long-sleeved pelisse of heavy satin, secured by seven tiny mother-of-pearl buttons and cut away to form an outer skirt with a box pleat reaching below the knee at the back.

The entire ensemble was a perfect example of what an elegant bride would wear, and despite Mrs. Bennet's mean intentions, the candlelight colour enhanced Elizabeth's warm skin tones and rendered her even more radiant than had she also worn white. She and Jane had exchanged gifts of small pearl earrings, and her only other ornaments were the garnet cross her father had given her when she turned sixteen and the betrothal ring from Darcy.

Elizabeth was dressed in mere minutes, and with a little assistance from Annie, began dressing her hair in the style requested by Mr. Darcy. On the dressing table lay Darcy's gift of the golden hairpins topped with pearls. Sadly, Mrs. Bennet was unmoved.

"Oh, Mama," sighed Kitty dreamily from the doorway of her sisters' room, watching as Elizabeth's hair was dressed. "It is so *romantic* that Mr. Darcy wants to marry Lizzy with her hair full of pearls. How can you oppose it?"

All spare hands were attending the complex lacings and buttons of Jane's gown.

"Indeed, Mama," added Jane, speaking in jerky breaths as her mother and aunt tugged at her corset. "It would be...wrong of you...to insult Mr. Dar—oof!—Darcy."

"He insults you, Jane, by not providing for your hair and jewels," Mrs. Bennet huffed. "He means for Lizzy to outshine you, and you should have precedence. You are eldest and far more beautiful."

"But he is not marrying *me*," Jane gasped as her mother tied the laces.

"It is improper for Lizzy not to wear a bonnet or veil. Whoever heard of just wearing pearl hairpins, even if they are real? It is not seemly to dress my daughter like an actress. I wonder you would consider it, Lizzy. I do not understand you and Mr. Darcy at all."

"Mama," Elizabeth made one last attempt at flattery, "you have been generous to me in every respect. I am sure I do not deserve your forbearance in this, but Mr. Darcy would be so grateful for this gesture. He is sentimental, and longs to be reminded of the night he fell in love with me. Your condescension would be greatly appreciated."

"My mind is quite made up, Lizzy. The lace bonnet will be good enough for you." Mrs. Bennet and Mrs. Gardener slipped Jane's petticoat over her head, laced and buttoned it, and followed it with the white gown. Mrs. Bennet made a great show of fastening the one string of family pearls around Jane's neck.

Annie finished Elizabeth's hair, which was at least styled as Mr. Darcy requested even if the pearls were not used. Elizabeth stepped away from the dressing table trying not to cry. Jane met her sister's eyes and took her hand as she sat at Elizabeth's place at the mirror.

Tears sprang to Jane's eyes. "Mama, it pains me you would discomfort Lizzy and me on our wedding day." It was as close to a serious complaint as Jane was ever to make to their mother and silenced the room for a moment.

"See what you have done, Lizzy? You have made your sister cry. Now her eyes will be all red when she faces Mr. Bingley," Mrs. Bennet screeched, oblivious that the wedding was over an hour and a half away.

Elizabeth's mouth assumed a flat line of dissatisfaction, her face a blank mask of disapprobation. In her hand was the pouch of pearl hairpins. She placed it in the fussy lace reticule that matched the ugly bonnet she would grudgingly wear. She walked to the door of the room. "Then I am ready. I shall go to our father as he requested." Her feet, in their satin wedding slippers, were next heard stomping—as best they could wearing such light shoes—down the stairs.

"That girl and her big feet..." Mrs. Bennet muttered as she fussed with Jane's veiling.

Elizabeth entered her father's library, slammed the door and flung herself into a chair. "Your mother?" Mr. Bennet asked.

"Your *wife*," Lizzy responded accusingly. She hopped back up, ashamed of herself for acting like she was fifteen again.

"Sit down, my love."

Elizabeth was already pacing away her vexation.

"Or not. Suit yourself. Mr. Darcy knows he is getting a pacing wife, surely? I believe he is also given to forceful pacing when agitated. Indeed, I have seen him do it. You must take care you do not both start pacing in crossing directions unannounced. Lives could be lost!"

Elizabeth stopped and smiled. She turned and was welcomed into her father's arms. "Oh, Papa..."

"Lizzy, the giving of such small but sage words of advice is not why I asked to speak to you. I have an important story to tell, and every word of it is true. I should have told you years ago. Pray, sit."

At last she did; he took the chair next to her and held her hand. "When

Jane was born, we were not at all concerned she was not a son. She was a first child, and there was no worry. But when your mother carried you, she was convinced you were a boy. I think I may safely say, of all my daughters, *you* are the one she has never forgiven for your sex, because she was found to be so loudly and completely mistaken. You did not have a name for two or three days, because you were not Edward Thomas Bennet. Your layette was even embroidered with the initials E. B. At the time, I was reading a history of King Henry VIII, and thoughts of the birth of good Queen Bess, his own second daughter, were much in my mind. He hoped for a boy but thought his second daughter quite a beautiful child, as she favoured him. She grew to be famously precocious. He saw she was intelligent and worthy of his attention. Of course, we know she lived to far outshine her siblings and was England's greatest monarch.

"Thus I named you Elizabeth, and would brook no quarrel. And it has come to pass, Lizzy, that you are the only child who favours my side of the family, dark in your features and lively. You are the most intelligent, and today and hereafter, you will outshine all your sisters. When you stand up with Mr. Darcy, Jane will pale by comparison for everyone except Mr. Bingley, no matter how you wear your hair. Mr. Darcy will never notice your bonnet for the sparkle in your eyes and the wit in your smile.

"He loves you dearly, Lizzy, as he has never loved before, I would wager. I only ask that you be kind to him. Do not be impatient. He may be as clever as you, but perhaps not quite, so be brave and kind, and he will always remain devoted to you. But he is just a man, so do not expect too much."

Elizabeth's quiet tears spilled down her cheeks, and he gave her his handkerchief.

"You will always be my confident Lizzy, my fearless and inquisitive girl. Mr. Darcy loves you for the same reasons I do. There may have been some reluctance on my part when the two of you came to me, but over the course of your engagement, it must be admitted, Lizzy, I now think that, had I the choice from a menu of attributes from which to select and construct you a husband, I could not have created better."

Elizabeth sniffed into the handkerchief. "I am keeping this."

"Yes, I thought you might. Your Aunt Gardiner had it made for me. See? It is the colour of your dress—candlelight. I have learnt something of lace after nearly twenty-four years with your mother. My last demand as your father is that you not tell her."

There was a tap at the door and Jane spoke from without. "It is I."

Elizabeth rose to leave but stopped at the door. "Thank you, Father. How could two such men love me so?" She turned to him briefly for a kiss on her cheek and then she was gone.

Jane looked at her quizzically in the hall. "What an adorable person our father is," was all Elizabeth could say, and Jane slipped into the library. Elizabeth was alone in the hall with her mother, who observed as Elizabeth dabbed her eyes in front of the mirror.

With a sigh, Elizabeth picked up her gloves and the dreaded white lace bonnet from the entry table.

"Oh, Mr. Bennet," Mrs. Bennet muttered under her breath. "Making your daughters cry on their wedding day... Hill! I have left my gloves upstairs! Hill!"

Elizabeth stepped outside onto the front porch to await her father and sister, and donned her gloves. The late autumn sun brightened the frosty ground with a glaring brilliancy. She did not trust herself to be alone with her mother for even one more moment, and perhaps she would not need to be so again for a very long time. Jane and Elizabeth would ride with their father in the Bingley coach. The rest of the Bennets would ride in their own carriage with the Gardiners.

Mrs. Gardiner joined her. "Lizzy, let me help you with the bonnet." They eased it into place and Elizabeth felt it crushing the loose curls on the back of her head.

Something in the construction of the bonnet poked her in several places, and she tore it off again. "This is a veritable crown of thorns, Aunt!" Elizabeth looked inside to see several joints in the construction were not properly finished with padding. "No wonder Jane rejected it."

"Oh, Lizzy," consoled her aunt, putting an arm around her shoulder. "It is cold. You should put it on."

"I shall not wear it one moment before I must."

The Bingley carriage could be heard on the drive. Mr. Bennet and a laughing Jane joined Elizabeth and their aunt. Immediately pulling up behind it was the Gardiner carriage. Elizabeth looked at her aunt in surprise.

"Like you, Lizzy, I am sure I do not want to spend any more time with *her* than is absolutely necessary. This bonnet dispute has disturbed me, and Edward suggested we leave for London immediately after the wedding breakfast instead of staying another night." She squeezed Elizabeth's hand. "Just because she can wail louder than everyone else does not make her right."

Elizabeth smiled. Her father handed Jane and her into the carriage, and they set off for the church with the Gardiner coach just behind them. They were ahead of schedule.

Chapter 15
The Wedding Breakfast

"We will have rings and things and fine array."
William Shakespeare, The Taming of the Shrew

The newly married Fitzwilliam Darcy stood just outside the formal dining parlour at Netherfield Park, waiting for Elizabeth to emerge from a small sitting room set aside for the use of the brides. The guests would arrive shortly and enter the dining room by a door near the main hall after greeting their official hostesses, a surprisingly composed —one might almost say catatonic—Caroline Bingley and an ebullient Mrs. Louisa Hurst. The door of the sitting room opened and Jane emerged first.

"Mrs. Bingley!" Darcy bowed. "Your husband awaits you inside."

"Thank you, Brother." She smiled and curtsied. Darcy was the first to call her by her new name and she coloured prettily. "Mrs. Darcy will join you directly. She is adjusting her hair." In an unprecedented action, Jane winked at him, and entered the dining room through the door Darcy had opened for her.

Jane winking! I wonder what causes such a singular action. This has been a day of surprises already—brides arriving early, Elizabeth in tears as she came with her father to stand beside me, now Jane winking at me...

Mr. Bennet had taken Darcy aside in the church before the wedding. "There has been a set-to about Elizabeth's hair, and I am afraid her mother carried the day. Your bride means your gift no disrespect, but I cannot say the same for Mrs. Bennet." Darcy rolled his eyes but made no other response. He had been warned that every wedding produced a silly story or two, and he had, at that moment, much more important matters to consider than the folly of Mrs. Bennet. His adored Elizabeth was about to become his wife.

And yet, when the processional finally began, there stood his magnificent bride, his woman and chosen partner, elegant in her charming gown with his pearls in her hair. Mr. Bennet brought Elizabeth alone up the aisle and met no one's eye except that of his wife. His stern and steely gaze effectively silenced Mrs. Bennet from pitching a fit and falling in it. The proud father deposited his dearest daughter next to her betrothed before turning to nod at the organist. Mr. Bennet then strode briskly back up the aisle and, within a moment's time, conveyed his eldest daughter to Bingley. It was a conspiracy planned from the start by Mr. Bennet and the Longbourn church musicians, as he was determined each daughter should have her moment to shine.

Even immediately after the fact, Darcy's memory of his wedding was a hazy muddle. The magnitude of the event seemed to inhibit all real experience of it. The only detail remaining with him was the phrase "happiness in marriage requires diligent practice to become truly proficient," offered by the vicar during his homily. It was all Darcy could do to suppress his laughter, and he dared not look at Elizabeth. She told him during their brief carriage ride to Netherfield that she felt exactly the same, and was afraid the congregation could see her shoulders shaking with stifled hilarity. Elizabeth rather hoped they thought she was crying.

She also explained why, despite the brides arriving early, the wedding started a few minutes late. Once all the guests had been seated, Elizabeth stood before a mirror in the vestibule and donned the dreaded white-veiled bonnet. She turned to her father with her chin up for courage, but Mr. Bennet could see her expression was fragile.

"Great God, child!" Mr. Bennet was appalled at the hat on Elizabeth's head. "What a dreadful spectacle. It does not match your gown. Jane, come. Are Mr. Darcy's pearls here? We cannot have Lizzy enter the church resembling a frigate setting sail at Plymouth."

And so, as quickly as Mr. Bennet and Jane could manage it, the bonnet was superseded by pearls. Elizabeth's relief and joy brought forth her tears. Darcy had yet to decide whether he was vexed to have been kept in ignorance of the contest with her mother or he was truly better off having not known.

THE HALL DOOR OPENED AND Elizabeth stood in the doorway looking for him. She was just as lovely as at the church, wreathed in bridal radiance, her hair shining and dotted with pearls. They smiled as their eyes met, and she held out her hand as she approached him. He intended to kiss her rather more thoroughly than he had in the open barouche that carried them from the church to Netherfield, but Mrs. Bennet burst into the hall.

"Mr. Darcy! Oh, Lizzy! Your hair, child!" She drew breath to launch into a proper tirade. Mrs. Bennet was waving the unworn white bonnet through the air.

Darcy would not hear it. "Madam... Mrs. Bennet!" His strong deep voice stopped her mid-inhale. "Mrs. Darcy has dressed her hair exactly as Mr. Darcy wishes. We, none of us, shall hear any more from you on the subject." He held out his arm, Elizabeth laid her hand upon it, and they entered the dining room affecting a regal hauteur, trying not to laugh. They were by no means successful.

Mr. Bennet smiled from behind his thwarted wife. *At last, Lizzy has a champion better than I.*

An hour later, Darcy stood by the far window of the dining room. He had taken coffee and noticed Elizabeth still carried a cup of wine punch, but neither had done more than push their food around on their plates during the meal. He watched steadily as Elizabeth circled the room, stopping to visit with friends and neighbours, and graciously accepting the many compliments on how well she looked, what a handsome couple she and her husband made, and how lovely the flowers were that arrived from the glasshouses at Pemberley. *She is my enchanting bride.*

On a sideboard was a display of fruit, also from Pemberley. Elizabeth stopped to sneak a late season strawberry, and then another. She turned to see if he was watching—*Of course he is watching me; he sees every little thing I do!*—and sent him a guilty smile. He smiled enough to deepen his dimples and send her pulse racing.

Darcy's look turned to a smoulder, and across the room, a slightly tipsy Mrs. Phillips nudged the arm of a friend, remarking on his countenance and pitying Elizabeth the trials of the coming evening. She did not remark upon, or even appear to notice, the sly look Elizabeth returned to Darcy.

With the most anticipated event of the day still many hours hence, Elizabeth was able to summon ample confidence to flirt with her bridegroom from across the crowded room. Whether she could maintain such command over herself in six or eight hours was quite another proposition.

How easy she is in company. Everyone seems to love her. As I do. Well, perhaps not quite as I do... Darcy glanced over at Jane, who sat in state in an armchair with Bingley standing at her side. They looked golden together with their honey-coloured hair. Jane's serenity greeted everyone who approached with the same smile and blush, and one might surmise Jane could still not believe such happiness was to be hers. However, she seemed a little nervous, and Darcy could guess why. Bingley fussed over her, touching her shoulder to draw her attention to someone or something, refilling her cup, taking her hand and releasing it again. *Poor Charles... he thinks he is steadying her, but I fancy she would like nothing more than to step outside and take a deep breath.* Somehow, his Elizabeth met the gathering with assurance, and any nerves she might feel about him or the coming night were well hidden.

As he returned his gaze to his bride, he felt someone take his arm. It was Georgiana.

"You have captured the prettiest and most charming Bennet sister, Brother! Look how lovely her hair is. How I envy her confidence. She has such gracious manners." Georgiana smiled mischievously and leaned in to nudge her brother's guarded composure with her shoulder. "The pearls are from you?"

Darcy did not take his eyes from Elizabeth as he smiled and nodded. "She will do us proud, Georgie."

The two siblings stood in admiration of the new addition to their small family. "How interesting it is, Fitzwilliam, that the two eldest Bennets have chosen men with the same colouring as themselves, or did you two men concoct the scheme between you? Jane and Charles so fair, you and Elizabeth so dark; you could be bookends. What lovely nieces and nephews I shall have."

Darcy was surprised he had never made such an observation himself. With a self-satisfied half smile, he whispered to Georgiana, "Indeed you will."

"How shall we manage the giving of my gifts for Jane and Elizabeth?"

"There is a small sitting room down the hall from the rear door of the dining room. I shall bring the brides there in five minutes."

Georgiana had ordered special presents for Elizabeth and Jane, but she could not abide the idea of making a show of presenting them. Darcy caught Elizabeth's eyes and silently beckoned her towards her sister. They met near Jane and Bingley, and he murmured, "Georgiana has gifts for you and Jane.

If we can ease ourselves into the small parlour, she will meet us."

Elizabeth leaned to whisper in Jane's ear, and she immediately stood. Sensing a conspiracy, Mrs. Bennet approached. "Mr. Darcy? Lizzy? Are you leaving so soon?"

"Indeed no, Mama," responded Elizabeth. "Mr. Darcy's sister has gifts that she wishes us to open in the sitting room."

"What nonsense! Have her bring them here so everyone can see."

Mr. Darcy stepped forward and fixed his new mother-in-law with an unyielding gaze. "Indeed she will not. But you may join us, Mrs. Bennet."

"It is quite rude to leave one's guests so, Mr. Darcy."

"It is equally rude to make a shy guest more uncomfortable by making a spectacle of the simple giving of gifts," Darcy responded and caught Bingley's eye. Each man took his new wife's arm and exited the dining room, with a clucking Mrs. Bennet following. No one noticed Mr. Bennet steal away in the curricle waiting for him.

When the couples entered the sitting room, they found Mrs. Gardiner already at hand. Georgiana handed a large box to Elizabeth, and another to Jane. "Mrs. Gardiner—whom I may now call Aunt?" Georgiana asked and Mrs. Gardiner nodded. "Aunt Gardiner helped me select and order these. We used her modiste since that lady has made gowns for Elizabeth and Jane before."

Elizabeth opened her box and lifted from its depths the most luxurious pelisse she had ever seen. It was a heavy matte satin in deep royal blue, padded with several layers of wool for warmth, and lined in a lighter-weight white satin. However, the spectacular feature of the garment was the high collar and front placket trimmed in ermine, as were the cuffs of the long sleeves.

Elizabeth was on the point of saying it was too grand to accept when, taking it from her, Darcy whispered in her ear, "For *my* Queen Elizabeth."

She turned her head sharply and met his shining eyes as he eased the garment onto her shoulders. "My father has been telling tales again." She smiled up at him. "Which of her many admiring courtiers would you have been?"

"Courtier? Ha! No, madam, I would have been her consort had I lived in her time."

"So she would not have been a virgin queen?" Elizabeth whispered.

"I should say not. Decidedly not..." Darcy breathed into her ear. He longed to molest the three curls reposing where he had flipped them free of the pelisse's collar, but stopped himself. *My self-control is ebbing. We should make our escape as soon as may be.*

"Georgiana, thank you," Elizabeth said in a louder voice, blushing. "It is beautiful. You are too kind."

Elizabeth's newest sister came forward and took her hand earnestly. "Oh, Lizzy," she began, using the family epithet impulsively, "do you really like it? I could not imagine your riding to London in your wedding costume during such cold weather. And you can wear this to the opera during your honeymoon."

Darcy hid a smirk. He had no intention of stepping outside Darcy House for the next week, and perhaps not even straying more than three steps from their suite of rooms. He would proudly escort his new wife to the opera when *next* they went to London.

Jane's gasp turned everyone's attention to her and the lifting of her gift from its box. Jane preferred a cape to a pelisse for outerwear, and her gift was a pale, dove grey taffeta cloak with a pink watermark sheen, its hood lined with misty grey mink. It was clearly the equal of Lizzy's in price, and complimented Jane's complexion. "Oh, Georgiana! I have never beheld anything so fine! How can I thank you?"

With uncharacteristic silence, Mrs. Bennet turned and left the room. No one noticed. She did not know what annoyed her more, that all the people she wanted most to impress had not seen the unveiling of such magnificent gifts, or that it was all arranged without her knowledge. To her credit, she did appreciate that Georgiana had not presented Elizabeth with a gift grander than Jane's. Mrs. Bennet entered the dining room in high dudgeon nevertheless, and hissed her disapprobation in Mrs. Phillips's ear. By all of those present who were close enough to overhear, she was roundly, if silently, censured as crass and ungrateful to the last.

"ELIZABETH, PERHAPS WE SHOULD TAKE this opportunity to make our escape. We shall make a brief pause at Longbourn first, as your father has a parting gift for us. I promised we would stop."

Before he could be harnessed, Bingley stepped into the hall and announced Mr. and Mrs. Darcy were leaving, unleashing a tumult of scraping chairs and the calling for this or that person to look sharp or they would miss the departure.

Just as Elizabeth and Darcy reached their carriage, the shrill voice of Mrs. Bennet could be heard. "Lizzy! Your bonnet! Here! She must have her bonnet." Elizabeth's heart sank as the crowd parted to allow the advance of her mother, waving the bonnet over her head.

Darcy ripped it from her hand and tossed it without ceremony into the waiting barouche. Some of the guests who witnessed the exasperated roll of his eyes were laughing. He bowed curtly to his mother-in-law, and handed Elizabeth into the coach. Darcy accepted a hearty slap on the back from Bingley, and a kiss on the cheek from Jane. "See you at Christmas!" "Write often, Lizzy!" "Thank you for everything, Charles!" "Thank your sisters, Charles!"

Georgiana worked her way forward. "Good bye, Sister! Good bye, Brother!" Darcy hugged her quickly. "You will join us in three weeks? At Pemberley?" She nodded, smiling. "This Christmas will be the best ever, I just know it!"

Darcy entered the coach, and Mr. and Mrs. Darcy left Netherfield. The last they heard from the waving throng was Mrs. Bennet crying, "Mr. Bennet? Oh, where is Mr. Bennet?"

Elizabeth and Darcy laughed.

Although Elizabeth sat on the ladies' side and Darcy sat opposite, he leaned forward and reached for her hands. They rode knee-to-knee, hands joined, and chuckled over their observations of the various wedding guests. Elizabeth commented that she thought the Pemberley strawberries would make a fine jam. They were soon at Longbourn.

Mr. Bennet was on the porch to meet them. When they disembarked and joined him, he said, "Now I do feel quite spoilt to have the newlyweds all to myself. Lizzy, look at your glorious coat! Does not your wife look like royalty, Mr. Darcy?" He caught Darcy's eye merrily. "Lizzy did not leave this house with that!"

"No, indeed, Papa! It is a gift from Georgiana. Is it not splendid? I think it much too grand for me, but Mr. Darcy says not!"

"I am afraid my gift is not so grand. You see the footmen loading a hamper of food into the storage box of the carriage?"

They turned to watch. "You have not eaten, the pair of you, have you? You must, so there is a picnic for you to enjoy on the road. It may be the only time you feel like eating today. I know you would not willingly starve my daughter, Mr. Darcy, but she might accidentally starve herself. I fear her mind is occupied with other things, which might render her less than her usual eupeptic self." This was the only reference he had ever made in her hearing to the coming wedding night and her concerns. Indirect though the remark was, she still blushed.

"Come inside. Do you need to freshen yourself, Lizzy, before you depart?" Mr. Bennet waved his hand airily towards the downstairs washroom as if Elizabeth were a new guest.

"I do, Father, but I shall step upstairs."

Darcy and Mr. Bennet looked at each other for an explanation that neither could supply. They did not notice the white lace bonnet she held away from their eyes.

The men entered the library. "Darcy, I apologise for my wife's behaviour. She has never been as fond of Lizzy as a mother ought to be, but I cannot account for the misery she made today."

"Every wedding has its stories, so I am told. Do not worry yourself, sir."

"Your equanimity will stand you in good stead in this family."

"Did I hear a rumour, Mr. Bennet? Is Mrs. Wickham with child?"

"Yes, her mother has so informed me and begins to make plans to travel northward when the time comes."

"If you do not wish to join her, you, and Mary or Catherine, or all of you, will be most welcome at Pemberley, or in town, if we are there for some part of the season."

Mr. Bennet was delighted. "That is one invitation I *shall* accept. Thank you, Darcy, thank you! Write to me. I do not promise a prompt response, but I shall read what you write with great interest when it involves either my Lizzy or any new books arriving in the Pemberley library."

"Very good, sir! I shall."

They heard Elizabeth's light step descending the stairs.

"Have my two dearest men been entertaining each other?"

"I have just invited your father to join us, wherever we are, when your mother travels north for Lydia's confinement."

Elizabeth looked shocked, first at her father and then at her husband. "This is indeed news, though I cannot think why I am surprised."

Darcy sputtered, "I only learnt it through overhearing at the breakfast, Elizabeth. Clearly, you were not told?"

Elizabeth raised a sardonic eyebrow. "It is a wonder my mother did not further demean this day by announcing it and ordering us to drink to the happy news." All three sighed.

"Let us not think of that couple. It will be nothing to me, for I am invited to visit my favourite daughter for the duration of the madness. Well, well, Lizzy, I am sure you and Mr. Darcy are anxious to be off. And I? I must return to Netherfield to observe Jane's nerves and Mr. Bingley's aggravation of them."

Once outside, Elizabeth stood looking at the carriage with the Darcy crest on its doors. She turned to her father with unsettled emotions and hoped she would not cry. Her two previous carriage rides with Darcy had been of short duration, but now they would be alone for hours on end. *What will we say to each other for so long?*

Mr. Bennet could read her distress. "All will be well, Lizzy." He kissed her forehead as he had since she was a child, filling her with strength.

Darcy watched from the door of the carriage as she said her goodbyes. From a distance of twenty feet, he could sense her disquiet. Her father kissed her; she stood up straight and lifted her chin to face her husband and her new world. *It is not me she fears*, Darcy reminded himself, *it is the unknown.*

ELIZABETH WATCHED HER FATHER RECEDE until she could see him no more and stopped waving. She sat back on the ladies' side of the coach, gazing at Darcy. Would he change sides now? Would he come to her?

He was sitting where he could watch the view, and did not look at her. *Can I keep myself in check until we reach London? If I sit next to her, I shall kiss her, and if she responds, I shall not stop. She is my wife. At long last, Eliza-beth Bennet is my wife.*

"Fitzwilliam?" she said encouragingly. "Will you join me?"

He blinked at her, trying to scatter his lustful daydreams. "Elizabeth, are you cold? Here..." He pulled a wicker bin from under his seat from which he selected one of several folded lap robes.

Elizabeth took it with a confused expression. "I am not too cold. But I thought you might wish to be more...companionable."

Agitated, Darcy took off his hat and shrugged out of his great coat. "No, I thank you, but I am not cold."

Indeed, you are flushed, sir.

Elizabeth could not withhold the exasperation she feared was creeping unbidden into her voice. "Why do we speak of being cold, when neither of us is?"

He finally met her gaze. "If I sit next to you, we shall hold hands, I shall kiss your hands, I shall kiss you, and who knows where it will lead?"

Elizabeth started to laugh but saw a certain pleading look in his eyes. She said calmly, "Where is the lauded Darcy self-control? Is all or nothing our only choice?"

"Do you really wish to be deflowered in a carriage, Elizabeth, as no doubt your sister was?" Like Elizabeth, Darcy heard the edge of petulance in his voice.

"Mr. Darcy!" She could not believe what she was hearing. "How could...? Why would you say such a shameful thing? To me...now?" *Is he angering me on purpose? Is he unnerved, too?* She fiercely balled her hands into fists, her nails impressing her palms.

Darcy saw some violent urge flicker across her face. He instantly regretted his words but felt he would regret it more if her first experience of marital relations was a ravishment in their carriage. He had longed to finally be alone with her, to possess her, but now felt barely under restraint. *How have I let it come to this?*

He had no answer, sighed, and turned to look at the Hertfordshire countryside. He had blundered this, the very start of their married life. Elizabeth slid to the opposite corner of the coach. He ventured a sidelong glance, and saw disappointment writ plain in her rigid posture.

What should I do? Darcy gave the appearance of calm as he raced through memories and dreams of Elizabeth, hoping for a clue.

Chapter 16
Darcy's Dreams

"But masters, remember that I am an ass."
William Shakespeare, *Much Ado about Nothing*

hen did I first dream of her?

When Fitzwilliam Darcy first dreamt of Miss Elizabeth Bennet, it was a fleeting vision. It happened the night following Elizabeth and Jane's departure from Netherfield after Jane's illness. During the visit, Darcy and Elizabeth engaged in several debates touching on numerous issues. Each left Darcy more intrigued. As her visit came hard on the heels of the Meryton assembly where Elizabeth had heard her feminine attributes roundly disparaged by Darcy, she was disposed to take offense and find fault, both with the man and his every utterance. At the time, Darcy did not apprehend her response to him as annoyance.

Darcy was merely enticed when he came upon Elizabeth as she approached Netherfield on foot. She had walked three miles at a vigorous rate. Her hair was nearly falling to her shoulders, her cheeks glowed, and her eyes were flashing. That evening, after Jane was asleep, Elizabeth stumbled upon him in the billiard room, mistaking it for the drawing room. She wore a simple gown slightly lower at the neckline than usual, and he was beguiled. Once in the drawing room, she defended her disinclination to play cards with a quick wit, which easily parried the viperous Caroline Bingley's verbal assault. Adding to enticed and beguiled, he then became impressed.

The next evening, Caroline acted on the misguided notion that if she strolled about the drawing room with Elizabeth on her arm, Elizabeth's lack of fashion would show itself to Caroline's advantage. Unhappily for the tall, stick-figured Caroline, Elizabeth's posture was refined and her figure just the sort to attract Darcy's silent praise, as he was now given the occasion to observe it carefully. Elizabeth had a lovely bosom and was slender enough to rarely wear a full corset, giving her gait a natural grace. He suspected she might have fine legs, for what he could see of her ankles appeared trim and shapely. Elizabeth Bennet radiated health, and although Darcy was not conscious of it, this attribute attracted him as much as her laughing, intelligent eyes and pert opinions.

The same night, Elizabeth challenged Darcy to enumerate his faults. As he sat with a book and brandy upon retiring for the night, he confessed she had bested him. He was embarrassed to admit that, in answering her queries, he had responded with pride and vanity—the very faults he told her he tried to regulate. He could just possibly be smitten. The next day he tried to avoid her, though he spent a tense half an hour in her company in the Netherfield library, where he was thoroughly aroused by nothing other than her proximity.

When Jane and Elizabeth departed, Darcy was fit only for brisk physical activity, and he spent the rest of the day riding. Before retiring that night, he had stolen unseen into the room Jane and Elizabeth had shared. Although the Bingley housemaids had tidied it, there was a faint hint of lavender in the air, which he had noticed in the library on the previous day. *Oh Darcy, this will not do. She is not for you, so do not dwell upon the simple country charms of Elizabeth Bennet.*

That night, he dreamt of one of the courtesans he had hired in Vienna, a redhead. She had the complexion of ripe peaches and an ample bosom with rouged nipples, which was displayed spilling over a pale pink corset. In his dream, as he kissed the thighs and dimpled knees of the exquisite and expensive harlot, he glanced from time to time at her face. Sometimes it was the red-haired strumpet watching him with encouraging smiles, and sometimes it was the brunette Elizabeth with her brows lifted in surprise. In his dream, when the face was Elizabeth's with those beautiful dark eyes, his breath quickened. He blinked and the harlot returned. In the morning, he awoke unsettled by the awareness that Miss Elizabeth Bennet had invaded his dreams.

THE NEXT DREAM WAS THE night after the Netherfield ball, and Darcy's last night in Hertfordshire before returning to London to attempt to convince Bingley that Miss Jane Bennet was an unsuitable match.

Darcy stepped away from the dance floor after dancing with Elizabeth Bennet to find a glass of wine. Although she was easily the most handsome woman in the room and an accomplished dancer, his set with her had been disappointing. She was attempting to sketch his character, and he felt that any effort to correct her impressions would imply he cared with a deeper regard than he could admit to anyone, least of all himself. He wandered back to the edge of the dance floor to find Elizabeth dancing with George Wickham.

At each turn by his partner, Wickham passed too close, as if hoping to brush her bosom or derriere. Bastard! Darcy stepped onto the dance floor, standing between Wickham and Elizabeth, interrupting their progress down the line of the dance. Elizabeth was making a turn in place and did not see Darcy until she came to rest. She slowly smiled at him. "Is this what it takes to draw your attention, Mr. Darcy? Must I dance with a blackguard?"

"Surely, Miss Elizabeth, you mean that he is the blackguard," sneered Wickham, and he moved to take her hand to continue the dance.

Darcy took her other hand, and turned her sharply away from Wickham and into his arms. In front of all the assembled guests, he kissed her with a passion he had never before expressed in any way to any woman. The assembled guests gasped, but Darcy did not care, and neither, it seemed, did Elizabeth. Magically, her evening gloves were gone and her bare arms climbed his chest, her hands finding their way to his hair. She opened her mouth slightly, it was all the welcome he needed. His hands slid down her back and grabbed her firm derriere. She did not release his lips but moaned and pushed her body against his.

"Mr. Darcy, what are your intentions towards my daughter?" boomed Mr. Bennet, sounding altogether louder than seemed possible.

"She deserves far better than that rake," Darcy responded, not releasing Elizabeth from his embrace.

"You are not behaving far better," she teased. "In fact, I would say the two of you were cut from the same cloth."

She looked up at him, the corner of her lower lip caught by her upper teeth, as if trying not to laugh. "Then damn you," he growled, and kissed her again with renewed ferocity. His hands slid up her back, around her ribs, and to the sides of her breasts, which were heavy and heaving, much bigger than he previously noticed. He looked down and her breasts were now bare, nipples rouged.

"Your intention had better be marriage, sir," bellowed Mr. Bennet.

"Do you want me?" Darcy whispered hotly into Elizabeth's ear.

"Take me, Mr. Darcy. Take me tonight and always."

Darcy had awoken in a cold sweat, with an erection requiring immediate attention.

As Darcy now reflected on the dream, he realised that, at the time, it had been easy to pretend that the larger part of Elizabeth's allure had been due to his jealousy. Wickham had charmed her using no more effort than it might take to drink a glass of water. Darcy had not wished to charm, tempt or encourage her in any way, yet the knowledge that his enemy had done so had made the bile rise in his throat. He had tried to think less of her for being deceived by Wickham's appearance of goodness, but the material point remained: he had not been able to stop thinking of her at all.

WHEN DARCY WAS LATELY IN London and dreamt of Elizabeth in the Netherfield billiard room, upon awakening, he felt he was seeing her more clearly. She was a woman worthy of being pleased, and he had improved himself sufficiently that she had accepted him. She was everything lovely. Her attempts to rise to every challenge had encouraged him to tempt her further, and her response to his touch before leaving for London had thrilled him.

So why am I now afraid she will spurn me? The steady clopping of horse's hooves on frozen gravel provided no answer, other than to offer nagging evidence that precious time, which might have been spent laughing with her, was instead wasted on contemplating how to right an insult.

ON THE NIGHT OF DARCY'S return from London, just five days before the wedding, Elizabeth had offered herself to him. Was this not her admission that she was ready to be awakened? She had said more than once that it was her own inclinations she feared, not him. Somehow, in the days of his absence, she had overcome her trepidation.

The dream that followed was another confounding combination of the actual past, an improvement of it, and a strange sensation of prescience.

As he rode away from Bakewell, where his sister remained to follow later, his thoughts turned, as ever, to memories of Elizabeth Bennet. It was a hot summer day. Darcy slowed his approach to Pemberley, sticky and uncomfortable in his riding clothes. He swerved his horse to the spring-fed pond hidden from the house by a copse of willows.

There was really nothing to be done about her. Although Darcy planned to convince Bingley to return to Netherfield for one more season of shooting before giving up the lease, Darcy did not think he could bear to be so close to Elizabeth and not see her. He had taken her criticisms to heart—such a perceptive woman she was—but he had no hope she would offer any opportunity to display his improvements of civility. He had insulted her and her entire family, even those members he had not met. His sweeping statements of disgust mortified him now, but it was much too late. No, he could only hope to restore Bingley to Jane Bennet's attention, and then Darcy would leave Hertfordshire. He was even undecided about the wisdom of standing up with Bingley, should a wedding take place, as Jane would surely wish to be seconded by Elizabeth. Darcy could not imagine standing at an altar in the company of such a bridesmaid without importuning the minister to state the wedding vows twice.

After his swim, a groom who was exercising Georgiana's new horse happened by. Darcy sent his mount off with the lad and approached his home on foot. The water had done him good; he felt refreshed and oddly hopeful. Perhaps he should be of a more positive opinion regarding Bingley's return to Netherfield. Perhaps he should convince Georgiana to accompany him. She might forebear the company of Bingley's sisters a little longer if it meant an introduction to the mysterious Elizabeth Bennet. Darcy had overheard his sister querying Bingley on the subject, and he was of the firmest belief that Georgiana and Elizabeth would become fast friends if he could effect an introduction.

Musing on the possibility of establishing a correspondence between his elusive beloved and his sister, Darcy strode smartly around a hedge, but he was stopped by what had to be an illusion borne of his speculations. He blinked, wondering whether something in the pond water might produce visions.

However, the vision abruptly halted her rambling approach and stood staring at him. She was above Darcy on the sloping lawn and a step forward caused her to stumble towards him.

"Miss Bennet!" Darcy exclaimed as Elizabeth landed rather forcefully in his arms. He unconsciously chuckled with the abandon of a boy with a new puppy.

"Mr. Darcy!" Elizabeth squirmed as he held her.

Remembering himself, he set her gently on her feet. With genuine concern, he asked, "Are you well? You are not hurt?"

She looked down, clearly mortified. "No, sir, I thank you."

"I...you..." He tried valiantly to gather his thoughts, but he had just held the woman of his dreams in his arms, and the urge to savour the moment nearly overcame the necessity of making a properly hospitable remark. "Welcome to Pemberley, Miss Elizabeth. What a delightful surprise! What brings you here?"

Her confusion was explicit in the blush advancing on her cheeks and the hand trying absently to force a dislodged ringlet back under her bonnet. "Oh!" Her startled eyes met what he hoped was a friendly aspect. "Mr. Darcy, had we known we would be intruding, we would never have come. Please... I apologise."

"Nonsense. Parts of the estate are open for anyone to visit. And as a friend," he looked particularly into her fine dark eyes, "you are all the more welcome."

Elizabeth seemed overly heated, and touched her forehead. Her spencer and gloves were too heavy for so warm a day.

Without a thought, Darcy took her hand, leading her the way he had come. "Do you swim Miss Bennet?" Darcy smiled at her over his shoulder.

"I can tread water."

"That is a good start. Come with me." He started running, and she could do nothing but follow.

As they approached the little lake, Darcy slowed. "This is where I swim."

"I had no notion Derbyshire could be so warm."

"It is rather hotter than is typical. I cannot control the weather!"

"I am all amazement. You try to control everything else..."

"Such irreverent remarks will not go unpunished, Miss Bennet." He turned and looked at her with an ardent desire flickering to life. He pulled her close, removing and dropping her bonnet. He helped her unbutton and remove her spencer, turned her to unlace her gown, and pulled it off her shoulders so it slipped to the ground.

"Mr. Darcy..." She started to move away but appeared faint.

"This heat will make you swoon. You must be cooled." He tried to sound kind yet authoritative.

He unbound her next layer, a petticoat. She wore no corset, and she was left in a plain thin chemise. "That should do. Come and sit on this rock. Take off your stockings and walking boots, and I shall escort you into the water."

"Wading will suffice, Mr. Darcy, if you will leave me to it."

"The bottom is slick, and I would not have you drown. Now that you are here, I do not mean to lose you so quickly."

"I am not afraid of the water, sir."

"Please, I shall lead you."

His eyes were voracious as he took in her figure revealed in the startling daylight. His intensity burned as he whispered, "Are you truly so luscious? This will not do. My intent was to behave in a gentlemanlike manner, but you thwart me at every encounter, loveliest Elizabeth."

She half smiled but said nothing.

He slowly led her into the water. It was not unpleasantly cool, and the sensation of muddy pond bottom between her toes made her giggle.

"Please, sir, not too deep?" Elizabeth requested when he led her in up to her waist.

Darcy took her in his arms, the water wicking up their clothes. "I plan to take you as deeply as possible." His eyebrow rose, but he soon realised she would not understand his double entendre.

"Silly man." She looked up at him. "I do not understand you. But I comprehend from your letter that I have never understood you. Even now, you should loathe me for my unkindness and prejudice."

"No, Elizabeth, that is not the way of it. I love you all the more for your honesty. Let me prove my love to you."

It felt heavenly to be with her in the water on such a hot day. He started squatting down, lowering them both until Elizabeth's bosom was wet. Then he slowly stood again until she was returned to waist depth. He kissed her with tender passion, and she responded, slipping her tongue timidly into his mouth. Darcy pulled his hands from her waist to her breasts, enthralled with their roundness under the wet fabric. She sighed. He moved to shallower water and lifted her onto the grassy edge of the pond. He stepped back to gaze in approval.

He untied the drawstring at the neck of her chemise, peeling it to her waist. Even in the sunshine of a hot day, his actions made her nipples pucker. "May I, Miss Bennet?" he whispered. His mouth was less than inches from her breast.

Elizabeth breathed, "You must, please. I feel I might die if you do not."

"I shall only proceed if you promise we shall wed."

Her smile was radiant. "Perhaps it was not a mistake to visit Pemberley after all."

"I do not wish to act upon a possibly mistaken assumption again. I must have you speak plainly." He took one breast gently in his hand, and with careful slowness, gathered it so the nipple was placed in the circle of his thumb and forefinger as his palm lifted the weight of it closer to his mouth. "I am waiting..."

"I am yours, sir. We are already wed. Although I cannot say I predicted such teasing, being your wife holds delights of which I was kept entirely unaware. Happy anniversary, Fitzwilliam. Happy 21st of July."

Darcy drew her peak into his mouth as she murmured his name.

Darcy had awoken writhing, with the corner of a down pillow well into his mouth and soggy. He spit it out and laughed at himself.

AS HE REVISITED THE ELIZABETH of his dreams, and the progression of their mutual regard, Darcy began to understand just how deeply he had insulted the real woman sitting with him in the Darcy family coach. *Of all the stupid things to do... mentioning Wickham at a moment such as this.*

This woman was not the wanton, almost slatternly, siren of his dreams. She was his unique and sometimes inscrutable Elizabeth. She was his lively, clever, beautiful wife, at long last, exactly the woman who could share his future with the necessary spirit of humour and affection in an enlightened, loving partnership. But in fearing the actions that could either make her his devoted lover or scar their intimacy forever, Darcy had reduced her to this, something much less than her dear confidant self. *Surely, a man can maintain control by simply not unbuttoning his trousers.*

He was ashamed. *To think, I have been so worried about frightening her that I have abandoned her! But how do I guide her from innocence to awareness? She expects me to know.*

Wake up, Darcy. She is your wife. Let her be your partner in this, too.

Chapter 17
Ice and Fire

> *"Why, what's the matter,*
> *That you have such a February face,*
> *So full of frost, of storm and cloudiness?"*
> William Shakespeare, *Much Ado about Nothing*

The day remained bright and clear. Every vista of the passing landscape was crystalline with persistent frost. Darcy glanced at his bride. Sitting by herself in one corner of the coach, staring beyond the far horizon, Elizabeth appeared smaller than usual and quite alone.

After briefly rubbing his mouth with the back of his hand, as he habitually did when he was searching for the perfect words to correct an awkward situation, he ventured, "The whole countryside is cold and glaring, is it not?"

"Indeed, sir, by your definition, the outside landscape greatly resembles the inside of this carriage."

His eyes snapped to her face. Elizabeth levelled her shot right at him, but just as their eyes met, hers darted away and looked out the window. Her mouth was a thin line, her profile otherwise impassive, and her eyes were blinking. She was fighting tears, and he had never seen her so angry. No, he *had* seen her that angry—at the Hunsford parsonage last April. *Darcy, you are an imbecile.*

With a quick agile motion, he slid from his seat and turned to sit on her side of the carriage, pulling her gently closer. She was rigid, but did not resist. With a sweep of his hands, he spread the ignored lap robe over their legs and tucked it under his thigh and hers, without, he hoped, appearing to take liberties. She was passive. He took her gloved hand in his, and laid them on his leg under the blanket.

Without a word, Elizabeth shook her hand free and held the coverlet to her neck with both hands. She *was* cold but could not discern whether the shivers she was trying so valiantly to hide were some symptom of temper or reflected true physical discomfort.

Given their amiable conversation from the church to Netherfield, and then later to Longbourn, Elizabeth never would have expected this. He had kissed her as they rode in the open, but once enclosed in the Darcy barouche, he became missish. That Darcy would choose to insult her deeply was unfathomable. Now he was next to her, perhaps wishing to make amends, but she could not conscience it. This was the start of their married life, and it was no better than their first meeting at the Meryton assembly.

"Elizabeth, you have taken a chill." He reached an arm around her shoulders.

She pursed her lips a moment before responding. She looked away from him to the carriage window, but spoke loudly enough to be heard. "It is my distinct impression that a cold wife is what is required. I would not wish to try your goodness, Mr. Darcy. We must not disrupt the careful regulation of your manners now that you are alone with your bride."

He inhaled as if to speak, and Elizabeth awaited his rejoinder with exaggerated interest. She sat with hands primly folded in her lap, with a countenance indicating he might be about to utter the most fascinating words she had ever heard. It was easier to be passionately angry with this man; any other passion was too unsettling...too mysterious. She rather hoped he would make some further blunder. Her father's words, *"Be kind,"* echoed in her ears, but she did not know whether it was in her to be charitable. When Darcy proposed, he had said she was too generous to trifle with him. *Who is trifling with whom? Is he so afraid of losing control? Surely, he would stop if I asked it of him.*

When Darcy did not speak, Elizabeth could not forbear filling the silence. "In case I have mistakenly given you reason to think otherwise, *sir*, it is not my intent to be taken in a carriage, as you so indelicately put it. I had hoped to avoid being *taken* at all. I thought when we arrived in London I would be asked to give myself...that you might do things that would coax me to give myself. You must see my predicament."

"Elizabeth..." Darcy whispered and tried to pull her closer.

She squirmed away. "Now I find I am not inclined either to give or be taken." No longer able to suppress the curiosity at what his looks might reveal of his thoughts, she turned. She wanted to appear haughty, but she had never practised that posture. She was therefore aggrieved when, instead of meeting Darcy's dark, distant, and disapproving gaze with a coolness to match his, she saw he was distressed. She burst into angry tears, and he folded his arms around her.

He rocked her with the rhythm of the carriage until she was no longer sobbing. "I am sorry to be so inept, Elizabeth. You see, I have never been married before. Do not think for a moment that I do not long for you."

She snorted softly, dismissive of his words. "And wounding me, reminding me of my darkest days, is how you choose to express this longing? I do not believe you." She struggled in his arms, but this time he held firm.

"It appears I should try arts and allurements other than those I have employed thus far."

For the past six weeks, any reference to Lady Catherine de Bourgh always made her smile when nothing else would. While still vexed, Elizabeth felt the contours of her face soften, but she did not allow herself anything further. *I will not smile at him.*

The blanket had slipped, and Darcy took her hand, kissing the back of her glove. She raised an eyebrow. "I gave you no leave to kiss me."

"I am attempting to earn a smile."

"Silly man. I smile rather constantly, or I did until entering this carriage."

"*Silly man?* I wonder no one warned you, Mrs. Darcy, that you have married a complete fool." He squeezed her hand. "Whatever do you see in him?"

She looked down, and a smile just started to lift the corner of her mouth. Without meeting his earnest gaze, she replied conversationally, "He has quite an astonishing smile, if you must know. It renders his entire countenance irresistibly handsome. When he smiles, I can deny him nothing, but fortunately for me, he is not aware of this great advantage. I have known him a little upwards of fourteen months, and have seen him smile six times, mainly while at Pemberley—*never* in Hertfordshire—though several more came earlier today, and one or two were even directed at me. I firmly believe that, should he and I take particular care of our health and live to be married fifty years, I may reasonably expect to see perhaps twenty more such smiles, principally when I present him with children, or so I imagine."

She succeeded in making him smile and felt an attendant sense of victory. How was it that he so constantly provoked her competitive nature? Why was the destruction of his apparently hard-won sangfroid so devoutly to be wished? She glanced around the interior of the carriage, marvelling at his largeness within it. That he was a tall, well-made man had never intimidated her, but he seemed suddenly a giant confined in an insufficient cage. *I ought to be grateful he is not a different sort of man.* Her considerations made her sober. *Yet, he concedes some power to me that I do not recognise. He protects me from something I would rather embrace than fear.* With quiet conviction, she determined to succeed in making him do something more than hold her hand.

"I *am* sorry, Elizabeth." Darcy lifted their hands from under the robe, removed his gloves, and then, more slowly, her left glove. He leaned over her bare hand, meeting her eyes from under his brows, silently requesting permission. She nodded and he kissed the back of her hand reverentially. With fingers entwined, he placed their hands back upon his leg and covered them.

Rather than disturb the warm intimacy of their joined hands, Elizabeth drew off her right glove with her teeth and tossed it aside while Darcy watched intently. She had often caught him looking at her mouth and knew her actions drew his concentration. She pulled the shared coverlet to her shoulders and, having turned slightly towards him, let her hand remain atop his frock coat. *And waistcoat, and fine linen shirt, and I know not how many more layers. Perhaps he wears more layers than I do. Why do I not know this? Why did I not ask Aunt Gardiner what men wear?* But she was happy with their present level of familiarity, happier still to be warmed by him and no longer competing for who could tolerate more cold; shivers were, she now knew, exceedingly hard to suppress. She leaned her head against his shoulder. "Do I endanger your equanimity if we ride thus?" The innocence in her voice was feigned.

Darcy covered the beguiling hand on his chest with his and sighed contentedly by way of answer. *I might have denied myself this?* He kissed the top of her head, once again appreciating the pearl-headed hairpins he had known would look becoming in her dark hair. His eyes travelled around the carriage absently until he noticed that a garment he expected to see was missing. "What has happened to your wedding bonnet?"

"When I went upstairs at Longbourn, I placed it on my mother's bed, upon her pillow."

"Elizabeth!" He was surprised and delighted. "Well done!" *And about damn time!*

"Hateful thing... I have never worn a more uncomfortable or ill-suited object in the whole of my life. I hope you know I never wanted it. My bonnet was to be made from the remaining fabric from my gown. Two white bonnets were sent for Jane to choose between. They arrived the same day as your hairpins."

"*Your* hairpins, Elizabeth," he corrected her.

"Mama was jealous of *our* lovely hairpins on Jane's behalf. Jane was not jealous; she does not know what it is to be jealous. But Mama was worried I would outshine Jane if I dressed my hair as you wanted. Me, outshine Jane?"

Of course, you would. You always will, and this morning you did. During their engagement, he learned he could not convince her of her superior beauty, at least not yet. His kissed her hair again. "And it was Jane's cast-off, too? That tops it all. I do wish I had known."

Elizabeth had been wonderful. "Today you were far lovelier than your sister. Jane always looks the same—an ornament from the Parthenon—no matter the occasion." He looked down at her with amusement and found her eyes were merry, yet she did not smile. "I have been told by men who know such things that no wedding ever runs smoothly. This will be the story we tell our granddaughters, Elizabeth. Why did you not tell me my gift had launched a battle of wills?"

"You think ill enough of Mama already. Up until the last possible moment, I thought surely she would relent. How could she risk demeaning a gift from her loftiest son-in-law? But her purpose was to ensure that I knew, to the end, that I am her least favourite daughter and must never think anything special of myself simply because I accidentally married well. Dear Papa saved me."

"A tempest in a teapot."

"A hurricane in a hatbox!" Elizabeth laughed.

"Ah! At last, you are smiling. Everything you said of my smile could as easily be applied to yours, dearest, loveliest Elizabeth. I live for your smiles."

She parted her lips, turned up her face, and closed her eyes. He leaned in to kiss her. As she wriggled more upright to deepen the kiss, he pulled back, ending it. Elizabeth sat motionless, ready for him to continue. *Let him see me after we kiss.*

"Elizabeth..." he whispered with a note of warning.

She could feel the hiss of her name near her lips, and parted them further, just managing a slight pouting noise. His mouth was on hers instantly. She made a low moan of approbation and traced his lips with the tip of her tongue. When he made a choked sound in his throat, she pulled away, opened her eyes, and beamed at him.

He narrowed his eyes as if aware of her scheming, and deepened his dimples. "Oh, is that the way of it?" He chuckled.

Satisfied with herself, she nestled against him again.

They had reached a state of cosy and amiable good cheer.

After a few more miles, Darcy needed to stretch his arms, and just as he stirred, so did Elizabeth.

"Now I fear I am too warm," she said.

She unhooked the blue pelisse given her by Georgiana. As she leaned forward to shrug out of its sleeves, the back of her head revealed, exactly as he requested, those three loose ringlets that captivated him at the Netherfield ball almost exactly a year before and again at their wedding breakfast —a little mussed to be sure, but bobbing against her smooth nape all the same. *There are my tormentors.* He grinned to himself.

Without allowing any reconsideration, Darcy murmured, "Do not move." He quickly drew down the shades on the coach windows, plunging them into near darkness. He bent to kiss the saucy curls into submission against her skin. He inhaled the warm scent of lavender and slowly nuzzled his face against her hair, at last indulging in the impulse that had haunted him for much of their acquaintance.

Elizabeth closed her eyes as she felt his breath on her neck. His nearness produced a warm tremble down her spine. *A frisson?* she wondered. "You know, Fitzwilliam, I suspected this of you when I first read your note that accompanied the hairpins."

"How is it that she knows me so well, and I know her so little?" Darcy was surprised to hear his voice murmuring his private thoughts into her ringlets.

She smiled but withheld speaking her own musings. *Yes, this is how I thought happiness would feel.*

He closed his eyes and slowly kissed the curls again, then sat upright against the back of the seat. "Dearest Elizabeth, I thank you. Perhaps our granddaughters do not to need to know about your impertinent curls and how they have tortured me."

Shaking her head with a laugh, Elizabeth settled back with Darcy's arm about her shoulders. "Did you not see them as part of my arsenal of 'arts and allurements,' Fitzwilliam?" *Who could resist such a sentimental man?*

He grinned and nodded against her head, then looked down and took an intimate notice of her wedding ensemble. Little shafts of light crept into the carriage from the edges of the shades. *If I unbutton those seven buttons on her bodice, what shall I find?* He did not resist looking at the top of her bosom, still inhaling her scent. It appeared as if the sun did occasionally reach her upper chest as the skin there was rosy and a little tanned. At the neckline of her gown, however, the skin was creamy, and the full curves hinted at further ampleness upheld by... *Hmm, short stays?* he wondered. He could see no evidence of a divorce keeping her breasts apart. *Arts and allurements she says...*

While he and Bingley tried not to lower their jovial debate of the relative merits of the two eldest Bennet sisters to an intimate level, Darcy did believe that his Elizabeth had the more generous bosom. Some men at his club held that, as regards a woman's endowments, anything more than a handful was a waste, and even though Darcy's experience was from long ago, he tended to agree. Of course, it was easy to concur when he knew himself to have larger than average hands, the palms of which were now vaguely itching with the stifled impulse to cup her breast.

Darcy had managed to kiss her ringlets and brush his lips over the back of her neck without unduly arousing himself—those actions were an expression of veneration—but now the view of her rising and falling chest in the flickering sunlight was arresting all thought. Elizabeth appeared to be sleepy. Her steady breathing held him spellbound. And so they rode, with Darcy's universe of awareness reduced to his virgin bride's bosom.

She was lulled to drowsiness from the swaying of the carriage and the contentment of their easiness together. She knew where his eyes were roving. The path on her chest, where Darcy's fingers had lingered briefly a fortnight ago, seemed to animate under his scrutiny. The nearness of his hand currently warming her shoulder heightened her memory of that first stroke. Since then, it took very little for Elizabeth to become distracted by acute remembrance. The thought of that touch, at once teasing and sincere, now created the necessity for more. There was an ague inside her ribs at the notion of further attention being paid to that portion of her person. If he could be lured to finish what was begun that night, if he would caress her bosom, she felt certain her desire would be alleviated. Why he would resist her in this, she could not imagine.

After a time, she felt her courage rise and shifted her position, turning slightly to face the windows. Her back was now against his chest, and she lowered and shrugged her shoulder, which caused the coverlet to slip, and his hand to drop from her shoulder onto her breast. She tried not to alter her breathing.

Darcy's, however, stopped—*can she read my mind?*

Elizabeth feared she had over-stepped what might be expected or allowed of a new wife. He was obviously attempting by every means at his disposal to ignore the temptation she presented without giving further offense. Perhaps if she could somehow convince him that her movements were guided by sleep, he would not say anything or attempt to remove his hand. Almost instantly, his warmth was pleasantly transmitted through the satin. *He does not know how little separates him from my skin. Oh, what have I done? Reckless girl! He will be nettled again.*

The joined sensations of pleasure and alarm coursed through Darcy with a speed that made his head swim. *Is she asleep? Should I remove my hand? This is astonishing. If I do remove my hand, will she awaken and know where it has been? I do not want to move my hand. She is my wife; we are alone in a carriage, why should I remove my hand? She certainly implied she would have allowed this before, had I but tried.* Darcy was desperate not to startle and reveal his surprise.

Although Elizabeth could manage her breathing, she could not control the blush that ignited in her cheeks and became a spreading heat flowing, as lava must, down her neck and across her chest, betraying her. When Darcy gasped, she knew the feigned innocence of her ploy was revealed for what it was: she desired this expression of his affection. *This is not how a bride behaves. What will he think of me?*

Fixed motionless in what seemed an endless moment, Darcy's eyes stared at his hand as if it were not his own. *My hand is on Elizabeth Bennet's breast!* As he blinked at the wonder of it, he watched the skin curving under the narrow lace edge at her neckline as it flushed to florid pink. He studied her chest as the jostled light altered with the pitch and roll of the carriage.

Darcy could hardly breathe, and felt his colour rising. He dared not move his hand, or even a finger. *She is awake! She must be awake. Or do women blush in their sleep?* He whispered, "Lizzy?" His mouth was at her ear. *Do I want to awaken her, if she is truly napping in my arms?*

Her heart skipped, and all things considered, she was certain he felt it, too. *He called me Lizzy!* She was nearly rendered insensible by the endearment. *Dearest Fitzwilliam, what should I say to you?* Her logic—such as it was—dictated that all she could do was continue the charade of sleepiness. "Mmm?" She turned her head towards his mouth and kept her eyes closed. She could feel each shallow breath he took. His hand grew hot, as did her breast beneath it, yet she felt if he moved his hand away, she would be inconsolable.

The turn of her head brought her temple to his lips. Elizabeth's drowsy response convinced him to move his hand. Certainly, as a husband he had the right to touch her, but not accidentally, not this first time, and certainly not without an explicit invitation. *May it please God, don't let her notice.*

Elizabeth felt his intention at its origin in his shoulder behind her neck. As his muscles tightened, she knew she must somehow confess that she had, with full awareness, initiated this moment of sublime but unsettling contact. Just as he started to lift his hand and inhale to speak an apology, she covered it with hers and held it in place, murmuring, "Please, Fitzwilliam, do not remove your hand. It comforts me." *Is comfort the word I want?*

Darcy smiled into her hair. *Ah... is comfort the word she wants?* "My dear wife, I am here for nothing if not to provide comfort where I know it is welcomed. It is a husband's duty."

Elizabeth grinned with relief—*he is not offended*—and her smaller hand pressed his larger one, encouraging him to truly grasp her. "Then see you do it, sir, but pray, try not to be too smug." She felt as much as heard him chuckle. But now that his hand had taken possession of one breast, the other rapidly developed an unanswered ache. This she had not expected. The word hung in front of her eyes and filled the air again: desire. *Where will this lead? The yearning does not stop. Dare I ask?*

Before she could form a coherent question, Darcy moved his hand. With his palm, he skimmed the satin at its fullest point, and quickly felt her nipple firm and pucker. He was led to suspect there was little or nothing between the fabric under his hand and her flesh underneath it. Her hand had fallen away from his; it was now fisted and strangling a gather of blanket in her lap.

Does she want this as much as I have assumed? Emboldened, Darcy slid his hand under the gown's satin layer. There was only a thin lining of lace or mesh, and he met no impediments to cupping her pliant breast and teasing the hardened nipple with his fingers. Elizabeth gasped, and he spoke low into her ear. "If you will trust me, Lizzy, we shall learn the things that bring you joy, and I shall repeat them for the rest of your life."

Aunt Gardiner said to trust him, and he has now asked to be trusted, so I shall. She cuddled her head against him, and found her wits enough to explain softly, "Fitzwilliam, I thought...if I could tempt you to touch me, the needful...relentless wanting you to would go away."

"It does not?" he murmured. He slowly blinked his eyes to ensure he was not dreaming. He was amused that she should be so much like him—if given more, she wanted more. Being a visual man, the sight of his hand disappearing inside her wedding gown caused a heightened tension in his trousers that he sought to ignore.

She paused, unsure of what words to use, or how much to reveal. "I ache. The..." *Take another breath for courage.* "My other...the breast you are not touching aches."

In an artful manner, Elizabeth had initiated their present situation, and Darcy sensed his gentle ministrations might be leading to an unfolding. She was revealing the tempestuous nature that drew him in even though she was, until now, largely unaware of its existence.

Darcy thought he might swoon at her candour and kissed her temple. All of the blood formerly reaching his head now settled in his crotch. He slipped his hand to her other breast and felt it tightening as he circled and brushed the peak with his thumb. "Better?"

Elizabeth felt she might catch fire. Her face hid in his shoulder. The blush had not subsided. "Yes...and no..." She quit her torturing of the blanket and turned, twisting and rising to face him. She again clasped one hand over his in her bodice, and with the other turned his jaw. Their eyes met. He had never looked at her in such a way before. *If this is truly love, what lesser expressions were all of those others?*

They kissed as he continued to entice her with both tender and robust applications of his fingers and palm. The heat of her soft skin, the weight of her breast in his hand, the pounding of her heart, and the taut buds between his fingertips were combining to crumble his reserve. He was intoxicated when she admitted longing for his touch. It was one thing to read it in a letter, but quite another, finer thing to hear it in her low, breathy voice. Her innocence was endearing, even as her body disclosed her secrets. When they paused for breath, he murmured, "Lizzy," just to watch her eyes widen before half closing as if drugged. He smiled at her, which elicited an expression he had not seen before. She looked full of wonder, and his chest swelled with a sense of accomplishment. If he did not know better, he would have called her besotted.

Darcy kissed her again, but removed his hand from inside her gown and held her waist.

"Oh…" she murmured, disappointed. There was a veritable fire in her belly, a deeper need. She watched his mouth as she murmured, "I do not understand myself. My aunt said this would all be very pleasant."

"You did not find it pleasant?" Darcy nearly smirked.

"I was… I am…overwhelmed." *Breath in, breath out, do not tell him you are most anxious to repeat it; he will think Elizabeth Bennet ruined and wanton.* "I had not expected this. You control yourself; I thought surely I could." She looked completely undone. "But I cannot."

His bright eyes nodded into hers. "Although not being a woman myself, Lizzy, I can only tell you so much."

"But you have been with women. You said—"

"Those were purchased women. I was young. There was no love. Those events were for my education as to the"—*How do I say this?*—"mechanics of…things, and to learn what constitutes my own pleasure. And it was long ago, years and years."

She considered again. "It would be of some consolation to me, sir, to know when—or if—you and I have done something, or may in future do something, you did not do before. I…" Elizabeth looked beseechingly into his eyes. "I would like to be special."

Darcy felt a tightening in his chest. For a moment he was speechless and found himself nodding at her. Her vulnerability revealed his. He leaned her body against his and pulled the lap robe over her shoulders. "Yes, Lizzy, I shall do that for you. I promise I shall tell you. You may be quite surprised at how often we are pioneers together." They were silent for some moments. "Warm enough?"

She nodded.

"With purchased women, it is difficult to know what they may be expressing just to earn their fees. My understanding is that they do not allow themselves the most profound feelings." He fell quiet. *But you will, dearest Lizzy. I know you will.*

Elizabeth waited, absorbing what he said with some gladness. She longed to be unique. She did not realise that he had thought her so ever since she laughed at him after his insult the night of their first meeting.

Women did not laugh at Fitzwilliam Darcy. It alerted him to the presence of a lady unlike any he would ever meet. He could not like being mocked, but he must own that he had not behaved well and had opened himself to derision.

Finally, he started again, "I have never felt such love for anyone in my life as I now feel for you. You are beyond special. You have made me feel like a king, Lizzy, a king. That I shall love you even more after what we share tonight seems impossible, but I know it to be true."

The thought of the evening to come caused her to blush furiously. Darcy noticed immediately, and hugged her tighter. "Please do not be fearful. I have never lain with a virgin. Like you, I have attempted research—in books—and it has mainly come to nothing. There is no man or woman in my life I would dare to trust or regard enough to ask. Not my cousin, and certainly not Bingley, who is less experienced than I. I might have asked Mr. Gardiner, but he is *your* uncle! It would not do!"

Elizabeth smiled. "The books in my father's desk disappeared after I told you of their existence." She paused, and briefly moved to fix him with a knowing eye before continuing, "They were not helpful, as it happens."

They both laughed.

She assumed a saucy manner. "And I am relieved no end to learn you have not been careering around the countryside ruining maidens in the interest of gaining practice, just to make the wedding night easier for me."

"Elizabeth!" he cried in mock horror. They laughed again. He continued calmly, "It did occur to me, you know, that I only have to 'ruin,' as *you* so indelicately put it, one virgin in my life. It is not worth becoming a proficient at something that will only be done once." His eyes burned into hers, humour fleeing before his consuming passion. "I promise to take great care and offer every comfort. *After* I have made you truly mine, then you will see the work of a true proficient."

Darcy took a deep breath. The carriage was slowing, but he had to ask,

"You will give yourself to me, Elizabeth?" He smiled nervously. He was relieved when her besotted expression returned.

"Yes, Fitzwilliam. I shall." She had never felt more in love.

The carriage rolled to a stop to rest the horses.

Chapter 18
A Picnic on the Road

"For I am he born to tame you, Kate, and bring you from a wild Kate to a Kate conformable as other household Kates."
William Shakespeare, *The Taming of the Shrew*

Darcy alit from the carriage and stretched then turned to look back inside as Elizabeth nudged her wedding slippers out of the lap robe and tucked her feet into them. He had not noticed her wriggle out of her shoes during their journey, but the glimpse of her pink-stockinged feet arrested him. *What adorable little feet...* Some protective instinct brought him back to the door of the carriage. It would not do for the groomsmen and driver to see the mistress of Pemberley's unshod toes. Darcy wanted the spectacle all for himself.

He watched as Elizabeth straightened her back, placed an open hand firmly at her bosom, and shifted her shoulders. He sucked his lips over his teeth to suppress a chuckle, but felt his brows climb his forehead. He had never seen such a thing before. *What I have done requires some adjustment to correct?* He did not hide his amusement quickly enough. Elizabeth pouted at him. He leaned into the carriage and spoke in a low voice.

"Do not trouble yourself, Mrs. Darcy. I plan to disarrange you again as soon as the next opportunity presents itself."

She blushed, shaking her head. "What a smug, disagreeable sort of man I have married. I cannot say I was not warned, but I defended you, sir." She thrust the ermine-edged pelisse at him. "Hold this and hand me down, please, Mr. Darcy."

Once she was standing on the gravel, and still blocking the view of her with his body, Darcy helped her into her coat. It was wrinkled, and Elizabeth fussed at smoothing it over her figure.

Darcy leaned to her ear. "I would dearly love to assist you, but to do so would cause a sensation with the locals."

"Silly man," she murmured in return. "You are too complacent by half."

The look in her eyes bespoke an affection her words could not belie. Darcy smiled before whispering, "If you hope to check my vanity, Elizabeth, you will need to cease looking at my mouth as if you wish me to kiss you." He breathed the words with some warmth of feeling.

"Oh!"

Now thoroughly delighted with having discomfited her completely, Darcy took her hand and said, "Your father mentioned there was something for our drivers in the picnic hamper. Let us see."

Together they stepped to the rear of the coach where a storage compartment revealed the wicker picnic hamper. Darcy unfastened the leather straps, and on top of the foodstuffs and serving ware was an envelope addressed in Mr. Bennet's hand, "To Mr. and Mrs. Fitzwilliam Darcy."

Darcy opened the missive and read aloud, "My dear Mr. and Mrs. Darcy." (Elizabeth chuckled. *How he must have loved writing that.*) "Within you will find, in addition to comestibles that I hope will be most pleasing and welcome to you, hand pasties filled with a savoury concoction known to warm the hands and spirits. These are enough for your driver, footman, and the four outriders with you, and are packed in the centre of this hamper in the hope they may retain some heat from the Longbourn oven. Pray distribute them straightaway when you reach the inn where you plan to break your journey."

Elizabeth began unpacking the hamper, and came to a package wrapped in parchment that was, indeed, still a little warm. "How like my dear father." She smiled as she opened the wrapping.

Darcy took the package, and called the men together, "Hodges! Sam! Here, these are for you with compliments from my bride's father. Sam, there is one for each of the riders." The outriders heard the call, and came back to take their share. All six men turned and tipped their hats to the new Mrs. Darcy.

Elizabeth repacked the hamper. Darcy lifted it out of the storage chest, and placed it inside the carriage. "Do you mind, Mrs. Darcy, if we eat once we are started again? I had not planned to stop for longer than to rest and water the horses, although now..." His eyes finished the message as his words trailed away.

Recognising his meaning, Elizabeth took a nervous breath. "I shall just freshen myself in the wash room, and perhaps have a drink of something cool."

Darcy left her briefly at the door of the inn, returning to the driver. He placed his hand on the man's shoulder, turning him away from Elizabeth. The driver nodded at whatever was said, and Darcy re-joined Elizabeth with a smile on his face.

"What are you about?" she whispered. "You look like the cat who stole the cream."

Darcy feigned alarm. "It is not my intention to steal anything. Well, perhaps a few kisses and another foray into your bodice." His voice was quietly insinuating.

Once inside the inn, Darcy and Elizabeth were led to a private sitting room with a blazing fireplace and a washroom door to one side. Elizabeth entered it directly.

There was a mirror over the basin of fresh water, and Elizabeth looked at herself carefully. *I do not look any different, but I do feel different*, she thought, squinting at herself in the poorly silvered glass. There were several reasonably clean-looking hand cloths hanging from the front of the washstand, and Elizabeth dabbed one in the water and unhooked the high-necked pelisse to cool her throat before opening the garment to its hem. She took a lavender sachet from her pocket and inhaled the soothing scent.

Darcy was near the sitting room door when she emerged and looked at him in query. His dark eyes smouldered into hers as he pulled the bolt on the door, locking it. He saw her cheeks grow rosy. *It is so delightfully easy to make her blush.*

"Is married life all you had hoped it might be so far?" he asked, taking her hand with merriment in his eyes and leading her to the settee in front of the fire. "If not, I can have the carriage take you back to your father. It is not, in truth, too late."

"Oh, I fear it is far too late for me, Mr. Darcy," she laughed in return. "I do not understand what magic is in your touch, but I intend to discover the source." She sat, and she was surprised when Darcy knelt on the floor before her.

"Surely, you must know it for love, Elizabeth." He pulled the blue pelisse from her shoulders, causing her breathing to deepen. "You might find the room too warm with that heavy coat." The garment was drawn down her shoulders and arms. He watched her bosom and detected hard points form under the satin.

Elizabeth licked her lips as she fixed her eyes upon his. She tucked up a corner of her lower lip absently, and pulled her arms free.

"Now..." Darcy's hands moved to the seven tiny buttons of her gown. "I sincerely hope your trousseau does not include too many of these cruel little buttons." He broke their gaze to attend to his work.

"But the carriage... They may call for us at any moment."

Darcy looked sly, but kept to his task. "It is *our* carriage, Elizabeth. It will not leave without us. We will continue our journey whenever we choose." *But there is one journey I wish to continue here.*

Under his hands, he felt the sharp rise and fall of her chest. Once the buttons were conquered but before drawing the garment open, he again looked into her eyes. For a brief moment, he feared she would stop him. Her mouth opened, but she did not speak. Her eyes flitted from his gaze to his lips. *Elizabeth speechless... how novel.*

He leaned to kiss her, pulling the halves of her gown's outer layer apart, and cradled her breasts as their lips met. He was glad his mouth dampened the sound from her throat, a mix of surprise and welcome that he found utterly disarming.

Elizabeth met his kiss with equal passion, and seemed to delight in teasing his mouth with her tongue. One hand toyed with his ear while the other caressed his cheek. She pulled away only long enough to whisper, "May I touch your hair, Fitzwilliam?"

"Of course. Whatever you wish. Anything."

Her hands grasped his curls, and she stroked his head in a way that made him wonder whether this was a desire of long standing.

He deepened their kiss.

With each movement of their mouths, Elizabeth emitted breathless sounds that further enflamed Darcy until his breathing was no steadier than hers. He leaned his forehead against hers. "My aunt was correct. With practice you have become a true proficient."

"I do not think we could ever hope to find an instance where she would be less pleased to be found useful." Her voice was husky in a way Darcy had not heard before. It pleased him.

At last the longing to see her became too great and he sat back upon his haunches. Her breasts were held in netting embroidered with leaves, the same as the over skirt of her gown. Her gathered peaks were rosy brown, and the remembrance of rouged nipples in a gentlemen's club in Brussels fled before the present natural reality.

The colour of her cheeks spread to her chest. "This is... I am so... Your staring is most ungentlemanly."

He pulled her forward with one arm, while massaging a breast with his other hand. "Surely you do not mean it, Lizzy. Perhaps what you truly intend to say is that you grant me permission to kiss you here." He was rolling a nipple between his fingers, and it tightened to a point.

She gasped as his hands embraced her back. She cried out rather loudly at the connection of his mouth to her breast. He planted several kisses around one peak, each time touching the tip of his tongue to her skin.

When she wriggled as if to escape, he looked up. "It is too much," she whispered.

"Is it unpleasant?"

She paused, as if considering. "Not exactly..."

"Let me continue whilst you deliberate. Take your time. If my attention does not comfort you, I will never do it again."

"Well... er..." she was sputtering until he lapped at a nipple briefly before it was pulled into his mouth. She moaned.

Darcy mindlessly moved from one breast to the other, and Elizabeth wrapped her hands around his head. Her fingers were embedded in his hair, and she held his head against her with such fierce determination that he could only move from side to side. As he suckled, he made low guttural noises of which he was not aware, but Elizabeth responded with coos and murmurs of encouragement.

Without conscious direction, one of Darcy's hands left her back and reached for her ankle. Upon realising what he had done, he began a wary ascent. As he cuddled and tasted her bosom, she had begun to writhe subtly, inching forward on the cushioned seat. The thought of lowering the fall of his trousers and sliding her onto his ready member was momentary, quickly banished to the future, when they had been united many times and she would expect it.

When the pressure of his touch reached her garter, Elizabeth hissed, "Fitzwilliam! Where is your hand?"

Diverted, he looked up from her body into her alarmed eyes. His dimples deepened as he suppressed a grin. "Both of my hands are at the ends of my wrists, my love, precisely where I left them. Of which do you inquire? This one?" He made a circle with his thumb over one nipple. "Or this one?" He moved his hand to the bare skin above her stocking.

Her lips parted, and she momentarily was caught unaware before saying, "Surely this cannot be proper."

"We are married. We are in a private room. We are quiet, for the most part. What is improper?"

"Your touch. Your mouth. You are trying to seduce me. I have married a rake."

"Nonsense. You have married a man anxious to please you. Or have you decided something is uncomfortable? What would you have me cease doing, exactly?"

"Oh..." She frowned a little. "I cannot think clearly."

"It appears that your thoughts are making you unsettled. I suggest you cease all thinking at once, unless you care to ponder where my hands are and what they are doing. I love you. Dwell on that if it is more acceptable, but I own I would prefer you concentrate on your present feelings."

When she only sighed, his lips again lowered to her breast. He continued to suckle as his hand reached the joining of her silky thighs. Her heat led him onward, and he tenderly moved a thumb and finger into the coarse damp curls between her legs.

Her hand at the back of his neck struggled under his collar, and he felt the prickles of her nails in his skin. Her breast was pushed more deeply into his mouth. "Yes, oh, yes," Elizabeth murmured.

Darcy moved his finger to her threshold. He inserted it to the first joint, and was pleased to hear Elizabeth's responding "Oh!" of surprise, then "Ooooh..." of pleasure. He eased the finger further as his thumb found the firm hot rise of sensate flesh where he might bring her some relief. *If she will allow herself... If she will allow me.*

A choked sob erupted from her throat. He felt a frisson shake her. Her thighs clamped together, pinning his hand in place. He opened his eyes to see the skin of her chest blotching with red, and the portion of her breast in his mouth seemed to expand. A deeper tremble began where his thumb pressed her, though she seemed to fight it.

Suddenly she was entirely aquiver and sobbing his name, or what sounded like his name, at his ear. With surprising strength, she lifted his face to her mouth and covered his eyes with feverish kisses. After several moments, when his thumb ceased its taunting, she stilled. He smoothed her skirt and embraced her.

Elizabeth pulled her head back and looked into his face. He was smiling as he watched the focus of those expressive eyes return to him from wherever it was she seemed to have gone. "So you have taken me after all?" she whispered.

His smile broadened. "No, dearest Lizzy, not really, not yet..."

She started to argue, but he wrapped her in a more crushing hug before sneaking a glance at his hand, assuring himself there was no blood on his fingers. He was relieved. Perhaps what would happen in the evening would not hurt her so much as he feared.

"But I felt... Oh my word..." She could not articulate what she felt. "What have you done to me? What manner of man have I married?"

Darcy grew serious. He pulled away, realising that, during their frenzy, the drawstring of the mesh bodice had come untied, and her breasts were bare. He was not aware of when or how it happened. He pulled the ribbons together, attempting to put her costume to rights as he spoke. "You have married a man who puts your happiness above all things. Upon reflection, I hope you will find what has just happened pleasurable, and you will grant me your favours as often as may be."

"I granted *you* favours? But I am not taken?"

"The instrument for that purpose remained in my trousers. It was my finger."

"I thought... I was led to expect discomfort, pain even." She relieved him of the burden of buttoning her bodice as they spoke.

"You will find a considerable difference in size..."

"Is there?"

She sounded incredulous, but Darcy looked suspiciously into her eyes and saw them sparkle with mischief.

Elizabeth looked rather arch. "If you do say it yourself."

Darcy blushed. They both laughed.

He stood and raised Elizabeth to her feet. "I think it is time to return to our carriage, Mrs. Darcy."

"They must be wondering what takes us so long."

Darcy smirked. "I do not think they wonder at all. Everyone knows it is our wedding day."

Elizabeth became distressed. "I told you this was improper! Do they think we...?"

Darcy chuckled indulgently. "Your hair is perfect, there is no bed in the room, and there is no other evidence. A keen observer may detect a glimmer of new wisdom in your eyes, but I do not intend to let anyone near you. Whatever is suspected, nothing can be proved. Let us ignore any speculations."

"Is this the fastidious, grim-visaged, sanctimonious Mr. Darcy?"

"No. This is the jubilant, impulsive, newly married Mr. Darcy." He bowed over her hand, turning it to kiss her palm. "It is a pleasure to make your acquaintance, Mrs. Darcy. I look forward to knowing you better."

DARCY HANDED ELIZABETH INTO THE carriage. They positioned the hamper of food between their feet. Elizabeth wrapped the lap robe around her legs and removed her shoes. She picked up her father's letter. "We have not read all of it."

"Elizabeth, are you not hungry?" Darcy asked. "You ate little earlier."

"I am famished, sir! Are you not?" She held the letter with one hand and rummaged through the offerings with another. "Father writes, 'I expect neither of you ate sufficiently, if at all, at your breakfast. Enclosed I believe you will find some of your favourite foods, and I hope they will sustain you through your journey, as once you reach London, you may again find yourselves too agitated to eat properly. Nothing worthwhile is ever accomplished on an empty stomach.'" Darcy and Elizabeth looked at each other like naughty children and laughed. "'There is a cold roast pheasant, which I know both of you prefer to chicken, and there is a cask of fresh cider for Lizzy. This reminds me to let you know, Mr. Darcy, that Lizzy has been known to partake of turned cider, an event that provided no little amusement when she was twelve years of age and about which I shall tell you at some later time.' Oh! I must read ahead with some censorship, or you will know all the family secrets!" She laughed again as Darcy snatched the letter from her hand.

He continued reading, after swallowing a bite of pheasant and crusty bread. "This becomes more interesting! 'There is cheddar for Lizzy, and our cook makes a fine loaf of bread with wheat from our fields. You will find late apples from the Lucases' trees, which I hope have not gone mealy, but if they have, Lizzy will enjoy feeding them to the horses when next you stop. You cannot use it now, but there is a canister of tea, the kind Lizzy prefers, provided to the family by the Gardiners. You might be warned, Mr. Darcy: Lizzy likes her tea the way most of us like our coffee—black and thick as tar with nothing added. Please warn your kitchen staff thereof. Lastly, Mr. Darcy, do not read this next to Lizzy'—Well I cannot stop now; you will hear it, Elizabeth—'you will find a half dozen jars of Lizzy's favourite strawberry jam. Hide it if you can and dole it out to her only when she has been very well behaved or has been exceedingly clever in company.'"

Elizabeth was laughing too enthusiastically to eat.

Darcy continued, "'Our cook will not reveal the recipe of this jam, but it does have a magical effect upon our Lizzy and makes her sweet, tractable, and eager to please if given in small amounts. Perhaps one of your cooks at Pemberley can assay the contents and reproduce it for you, but in the meantime, do not leave her alone with it or she will dose herself insensible.'"

They were laughing loudly enough to cause the driver and footman to look at each other with raised brows. "Never heard the master laugh like *that* a'fore," Hodges muttered to Sam, shaking his head at the wonder of the sound.

"'If your Pemberley staff do unlock the secret, instruct them never to make as much of it as Lizzy will order, as you do not want her tending to fat. I assure you, this jam is her one weakness...'" Darcy regarded his new wife with a raised eyebrow and gazed fondly at her bosom. "Oh, I think I may have discovered another."

"How sad to learn the two most beloved men in my life are conspiring against me." Elizabeth caught the corner of her lower lip to suppress a smile.

"Let me see... oh yes, '...this jam is her one weakness, but remember, sir, with great knowledge comes great responsibility. With love and prayers for a safe journey, T. Bennet.' This is unprecedented, Elizabeth; I do not know a father who loves a daughter more." He leaned across the food spread on the seat between them and kissed her. "Perhaps you will give me a few daughters?"

"To obtain that jam, sir, I shall give you as many sons or daughters as you wish."

"There is a postscript to me. Are you willing to hear it?"

"Surely even a coach as large as this is too small for you to keep it from me until London," she threatened with a chuckle.

"I expected as much. The postscript reads, 'Mr. Darcy, when you call Lizzy by her full Christian name, it is said with such regard and respect that I forget of whom you are speaking. We shall know you are truly part of the family when you start calling her "Lizzy." —TB.'"

Their eyes met, and Elizabeth, flushed and smiling, looked down. "Oh, my... Poor Papa. Fitzwilliam, I hope he never hears you call me 'Lizzy' the way you do. It would be mortifying to have my own father know what we are doing."

Darcy felt no response was necessary but to lift her chin and kiss her. "Lizzy," was all he said when his tongue had tasted her lips.

After finishing their repast and stowing the remains in the hamper, they pushed it aside and wrapped themselves in the lap robe again. It was so cold that, even in the sun, the frost seemed to persist, but they were warm against the icy landscapes, and soon were sleepy. Fed and at last easy with each other, they napped fitfully until the wheels of the carriage, gaining the cobbles of outer London, woke them with their changing rhythm.

Darcy awoke with his lips on Elizabeth's head and began kissing her hair until she smiled. "Although the beginning might be said to have been wanting, altogether I think our first journey as married people has been much more successful than not," she said as if she had been giving the matter no little consideration.

He kissed her mouth slowly. When the kiss ended, he glanced outside. "We are perhaps half an hour from Darcy House, Mrs. Darcy. The two front riders will have left us by now to alert Mrs. Chawton."

Elizabeth took a deep breath, feeling a little nervous.

Darcy noticed her discomfort. "We shall have a few lovely, lazy days here, Elizabeth. We shall make no visits and accept no callers, and we shall do nothing we do not both agree to do. When we are ready to travel to Pemberley, we shall go." He looked into her eyes. "My dearest Elizabeth."

They sat more upright, and Darcy could sense a heightened level of tension in his bride. "We shall meet the staff, and Mrs. Chawton will join us to see the master suite. I have chosen a maid for you from amongst the existing staff, but if she does not suit you, we can easily make a change. She is bright enough, and has been part of the London staff for four years. I have ordered a simple meal, and perhaps you might play and sing for me, or we might tour the house..."

Elizabeth thought what Darcy avoided saying. *And at some point we will retire to the same bed.* They travelled in silence.

Darcy looked out the window. "Only a few streets away."

Elizabeth shook the lap robe, producing only one shoe. "Oh heavens, where is the other slipper? Did we pack it with the food?" She made an uncharacteristically nervous giggle.

Darcy began searching with her, folding the lap robe. "You were wearing it when we left the inn?"

She laughed. "I would have noticed had I not!"

Darcy laughed, too. "Ladies lose gloves, Elizabeth, not shoes..."

She picked up his hat on the gentleman's bench. "Hmm, no..."

"My new bride will not exit this coach half barefoot. I shall carry you with my hat on your foot if I have to." He chuckled.

"Check your pockets," she suggested, relieved he thought their present plight amusing.

The coach slowed as it approached Darcy House. The staff waited outside at the entry under the portico, and a footman stepped forward to open the carriage door. Inside was muffled laughter. Finally, Darcy moved the hamper to discover Elizabeth's second wedding slipper pinned against the far wall away from the door.

"Oh, thank God!" Darcy exited the coach, laughing.

"Merciful heavens, how silly! What will they think?" Elizabeth emerged, chuckling, to the amazement of the awaiting servants.

"Everyone, inside! It is far too cold for such ceremony." Darcy beamed at them all, and motioning his arms as if to both herd and embrace them, moved the staff of Darcy House into the front hall.

Elizabeth bumped her bosom against his arm as she clasped his hand, caressing him for moral support.

He turned to her with a wide smile. "Mrs. Darcy?" He waved the way with his free arm, and in they went. He could not recall ever being happier.

Chapter 19
Welcome to Darcy House, Mrs. Darcy

"Time goes on crutches till love have all his rites."
William Shakespeare, *Much Ado about Nothing*

Mr. and Mrs. Darcy stopped before a half circle of servants in the elegant front hall of Darcy house. There was a glass skylight, and the house faced due west, so the last rays of the winter sun lit the assemblage, adding to the glow of wall sconces lit when the approach of the carriage was announced. For Darcy, it was as if his bride brought the light and cheer with her as she entered the house for the first time.

Servants stepped forward to spirit away their outer clothing, and Darcy began introducing Elizabeth to the staff. To spare her any feeling of intimidation, he requested only the household maids and footmen be present. The gardeners, stable hands, cooks, and scullery maids could wait for another day. The last four servants were the most important: Mrs. Chawton, the housekeeper; Mr. Lefroy, the butler; Darcy's valet, Murray; and Sarah, who had been selected as Elizabeth's maid for the week.

"Elizabeth, Mrs. Chawton and Sarah will join us as we tour our new rooms. Then there will be a few minutes for you to revive yourself before we have a light dinner. This is correct, Mrs. Chawton?"

"Yes, sir, Mr. Darcy," Mrs. Chawton agreed as they started up the stairs. "The cook has prepared a menu that can be kept waiting if Mrs. Darcy would like to rest, have a bath, or change clothes. We are here for your comfort, Mrs. Darcy."

Mrs. Chawton did not understand why the new Mrs. Darcy flushed pink

183

at the suggestion of comfort. She put it down to bridal nerves.

ON THE SECOND FLOOR, THEY turned to the left. "This entire wing is ours, Elizabeth," Darcy began, leading the way. "These were my parents' rooms. I have not moved into them until now, so they are almost as new to me as they will be to you, although I was certainly in and out of them enough as a child.

"We have fresh mattresses, new bathtubs, and some of the furniture has been rearranged to suit me in the master's bedroom, but you must tell Sarah about any modifications you desire quickly made to your rooms and Mrs. Chawton about any permanent changes. Please do not hesitate."

He opened the first door, which was his dressing room. It was Sarah's turn to blush as this was a room she had never entered. "From my dressing room to yours, at the end of this floor, we can walk from room to room through adjoining doors without going into the hall," Darcy informed his bride.

Elizabeth's head was a little addled. *Bathtubs... mattresses... adjoining rooms. This will be like living with Jane... only not at all.* She looked around the small masculine room with coat brushes laid on a side table, a full-length mirror, a rack holding a frock coat about to be brushed, and wardrobes and chests of drawers. Elizabeth noted the large, copper, claw-foot tub sitting in a tiled corner of the room. *My goodness, two could fit in there... oh...* She said nothing.

Darcy opened the door to his bedroom. It was a large chamber with a fire already blazing in the hearth. It was sparsely furnished with a large bed hung with curtains tied back at the posts. On both sides of the bed were simple tables, each with a single candlestick, and next to the tables were metal washstands, each with a basin of fresh water and towelling hanging from a metal ring.

Elizabeth studied the washstands. *Surely, these have been brought in, but why are they here?* She glanced at Darcy, who met her eyes expectantly as if he thought she might be forming a question. During the weighty pause, as Elizabeth noticed his always-immaculate appearance, she realised why the washstands were placed so near the bed. She closed her eyes, and drew in and emitted a deep sigh, aware all the while that her colour was again rising.

In front of the fire was a settee with a larger table to one side topped by a vase of roses. The scent was calming, and she was in need of it. Elizabeth touched them. "From Pemberley?" she asked.

"No, madam," replied Mrs. Chawton. "Unless something particular is wanted from the Pemberley glasshouses, we buy flowers locally. All the flowers available from Pemberley were sent to your wedding."

"They are beautiful." Elizabeth turned to the heavy, tawny-brown velvet curtains and parted them to reveal glass doors opening onto a balcony.

Darcy opened the next door. "That balcony connects to doors in this room. We can go from bedroom to bedroom from outside, or inside, or from the hall." He was watching her carefully, trying to measure her state of unease. *Is this overwhelming her? Is she going to blush forever?*

Elizabeth stepped into the mistress's room. Although it had a cheerful fire in a slightly smaller fireplace, the cream walls painted with murals of flowers were faded, and not to her taste even had they been fresh. *Too vivid, not soothing.* The wainscoting was lighter wood, and Elizabeth found she preferred the more masculine darker room. She felt there was too much furniture, and looked around appraisingly. "Is there a dressing table in the next room?"

Mrs. Chawton stepped back and nodded to Sarah to answer the question. "Yes, Mrs. Darcy," she said in a low insecure voice. "And the one next door has a larger mirror."

Elizabeth walked back into the master's room and noted there was a bookcase. She came back to the mistress's room. *No bookcase, and why all the side chairs?* She counted six. "Did Mr. Darcy's mother use this as a sitting room?"

Mrs. Chawton shook her head to indicate a negative response was in order, prompting Sarah to reply, "No, ma'am."

"What do you think, Mrs. Darcy?" Darcy thought this room confining, and he could see she put her finger exactly on the problem. He was pleased.

"Perhaps there is no need for a dressing table in this room if there is a better one just a few steps away? And I see no need for so many side chairs when there is a settee facing the fire and a bench at the end of the bed. Mrs. Chawton, I do think I would like a bookcase in here later." Elizabeth looked at Darcy. "Would it be too much to ask that the chairs and dressing table be removed whilst we eat? It feels crowded." There was another vase of roses on the table by the settee. Elizabeth walked to them and inhaled.

Mrs. Chawton smiled. "Easily, Mrs. Darcy."

The party moved into the mistress's dressing room, painted a peculiar shade of coral, now faded. Elizabeth wished it were a soothing pale green or blue. In one corner, as in Mr. Darcy's dressing room, there was new tile with a rather large tin bathtub, the equal of its copper twin in the other dressing room. Elizabeth peeked behind a screen to see a tufted stool, a clothes rack, a commode, and a metal washstand with a side shelf holding neatly folded towelling.

Elizabeth walked back into her bedroom and noted tables on either side of the bed, and matching washstands. There were also chamber pots just visible on either side of the bed. *I must stop blushing. It is only to be expected. Fitzwilliam and I . . . Mr. Darcy and I . . . oh, my husband and I, shall get used to each other's . . . functions.* She felt a shudder of nerves. The confidence gained by Darcy's reassuring caresses in the carriage was fast waning.

Darcy followed Elizabeth into the mistress's bedroom but stayed standing behind her and could not tell where her eyes wandered. When she turned around, he was there. "Are you unsettled?" he whispered.

She looked at him with a rueful half-smile. "Oh, I fully expect to be a good deal more unsettled than I am now, and rather shortly, too."

He smiled into her eyes. "I love you, Elizabeth." He took her hand and led her to the waiting servants.

"Sarah, would you wait in the hall for just one moment? I would speak to my wife, and then we shall call you to assist her." Sarah stepped through the hall door.

"Mrs. Chawton, you will see to the furniture removal? We shall be down to the small dining parlour, in what, Mrs. Darcy, half an hour?" Elizabeth nodded, and Mrs. Chawton walked back into the mistress's bedroom.

As soon as they were alone, Darcy swept Elizabeth into a passionate embrace, holding her around the waist and kissing her hair. He took several deep breaths of her scent, then pulled back and looked at her expectant, upturned face. Her eyes were closed and her tempting lips were half parted. *If you begin kissing her now, there will be no retreat, and no dinner.* "Lizzy."

Her eyes opened at his breathy utterance of a name he clearly intended to employ only during moments of utmost intimacy. She met his gaze.

"Lizzy, do not bathe now. And after dinner, do not undress. And most important of all, do *not* change your hair."

"Fitzwilliam, *you* will undress me?" She asked. *It is as my aunt said —"let him!"*

186

"Yes, I shall."

She blinked before raising her chin bravely. "Shall I undress *you?*" she asked. *Do I dare?*

"Not tonight, I think it might be the death of me after so much restraint already." He chuckled.

Elizabeth thought of Jane's elaborate ensemble with its complex undergarments. "Poor Mr. Bingley..." she murmured with a smile.

"Bingley?"

"Oh, Fitzwilliam"—Elizabeth laughed—"if he chooses to undress Jane, he will not finish until tomorrow at noon. She is wearing a prodigious and complex array of garments."

Darcy joined her laughter. "At another time I would like to hear the story of how you came to be dressed in such a wonderfully *available* manner." His hands roamed up her sides to her corset. "Short stays only?" She nodded. "I think I can manage that."

He smiled in what she thought a rather lascivious manner. Her eyebrows rose. "You are being smug again, sir."

"If you are planning to be more unsettled, rest assured I plan to become a great deal more smug." He let his hands slip down to her hips before reluctantly parting. "I shall be back at this door in half an hour to fetch you for dinner. Wait for me to come to you. I would hate to lose my wife as she searched for the small dining parlour."

He went into the hall. "She is all yours, Sarah, until I return." He walked away and descended the stairs.

"It seems you will have little to do this evening, Sarah." Elizabeth drew in a deep breath. "Evidently my new husband wishes to undress me and take down my hair, and he bids me not to bathe. Whatever shall we do with ourselves until dinner?"

Sarah, who was big and plain, stepped to the closest wardrobe and nodded vaguely to the door of the bedroom. "Should you need them, ma'am, your nightgowns and dressing gowns are here."

"Perhaps I shall need at least a dressing gown... later. Let us select something and place it... next door." Elizabeth could not quite force herself to say the word bedchamber.

"Which bedchamber, ma'am?" asked the more practical Sarah.

"Oh!" Elizabeth stopped to consider. It appeared the two rooms were equally ready for occupation. "Perhaps we need two dressing gowns, one for each?"

They looked into the wardrobe. There seemed an unnecessarily large number of night shifts and dressing gowns.

"I do not remember ordering so many, Sarah! Where did they all come from, do you know?"

"There's some as are gifts. We have put little papers on them so's you'll know. There's two negligee sets from Mrs. Gardiner and one from Mrs. Bingley—hers is the green velvet with white nightgown."

"Dearest Jane..."

Elizabeth selected Jane's gift for the master's bedroom—*I shall blend right in and maybe he will lose me in there*—and a dressing gown in a lighter gauzy fabric she recalled selecting herself for the closer room. Then Elizabeth stepped behind the screen to use the commode and basin to cleanse her nether parts thoroughly since bathing was prohibited for the time being. She noticed a bottle of lavender water and opened it, dabbing it on her neck to soothe herself. She looked from behind the screen to where Sarah stood, awaiting instruction.

"Is there more lavender water, Sarah?"

"Oh, yes, ma'am. We have put all that was sent from your home into the cupboard with your nightclothes. I thought you would prefer it behind the screen. Shall I put a bottle on the dressing table? I did notice you have no other perfumes."

"Yes, on the dressing table also, please. I take great enjoyment from making my own scents. Do you know whether there is a stillroom at Pemberley?"

"No, ma'am, I do not know. I have never been. I am part of the London staff. There's very few as travel back and forth."

A tap came at the door. Sarah opened it at Elizabeth's nod, and Darcy stepped just inside. "They are ready for us." He took her hand and turned to Sarah. "I do not believe Mrs. Darcy will need you again tonight." All three of them coloured to varying degrees—even Darcy, despite his best intentions.

Elizabeth looked at Sarah with mock surprise. "See? I told you!"

Sarah lowered her face so her master would not see her blush further, but nevertheless, she was pleased. She *did* like Mrs. Darcy; she had worried that she would not.

"In the morning, Sarah, Mrs. Chawton will give you your orders," Darcy said. "Do not attend us until she gives you leave to do so." Sarah bobbed a curtsy and stepped back into the dressing room. She would be gone when they returned.

As ELIZABETH AND DARCY WALKED hand-in-hand to the small dining room, she noticed footmen poised to swarm the mistress's bedroom to remove the unwanted furniture.

Darcy cast Elizabeth a sidelong glance. She was clearly growing more nervous but sought to distract herself by surveying the various details of the hall.

"Perhaps, sir, after we dine, you might give me a tour of the house?"

Darcy stopped and turned her towards him, whispering intensely, "Or perhaps not." He noticed her scent was stronger, and moved his hands to her sides, near her breasts. "I am able to resist kissing you, Mrs. Darcy, but I cannot keep my hands away. The sooner we are closeted together, the easier it will be for the servants." His dimples were pronounced, and his eyes were dancing. He ran his thumbs over her bosom. "It is best that I practice with these buttons behind closed doors. I feel proficiency is within my grasp if I apply myself."

Elizabeth looked up at him, breathless. She opened her mouth to respond but could find no words.

He stood drinking in the singular moment of having a speechless Elizabeth before him.

Finally, she managed, "It is my sincere hope, perhaps sometime in the next five years, that I shall stop blushing about every little thing."

Darcy chuckled as he embraced her, whispering in her ear, "Now where is the sport in that for me? It would be a bleak future for this marriage, indeed, if I thought you would become immune to my one seemingly innate proficiency, which is to cause your blushes. I shall know you no longer find me desirable when I can no longer raise your colour."

"As long as you seek to 'comfort' me, Mr. Darcy, as I have learned is another proficiency of yours, you will have no cause for concern on my account. You already seem to be expert."

Darcy sighed. "Mrs. Darcy, you cannot imagine how delighted I am to hear you find me so." He leaned behind her and kissed the curls at the nape of her neck, then stepped forward. "Dinner, Mrs. Darcy."

Glowing and again holding hands, they descended the stairs.

The first course was a light chicken and lemon cream soup, and both finished it, but as more food arrived, they became less inclined to eat. Elizabeth sat to Darcy's left and could see the clock on the mantelpiece over his shoulder. It was not yet seven o'clock.

Darcy pushed his plate of roast duck and potatoes away, having only done any damage to the braised carrots. "Oh thank goodness," Elizabeth said, doing the same. "If you are going to stop the pretence of appetite, I may as well."

Darcy leaned forward and whispered, "Make no mistake, dearest wife, I most certainly do have an appetite... It happens not to include food at present."

Elizabeth blushed and blinked at him. Darcy pushed his chair away from the table and gave her a look she had seen before. After a moment, her memory of him watching her walk with Caroline Bingley at Netherfield came to mind. The idea made her insides jump and dance. *Did he dare to think of this night, even then?*

A footman started to approach, and Darcy spoke to him. "We are finished here. Please tell Cook the duck was just the way I like it, but I find I am no longer hungry tonight." The footman nodded, bowed, and left the room with their plates.

A silence descended, which Darcy knew could be a dangerous thing. The carriage ride taught him that conversing with Elizabeth, especially if she had reason to be ill at ease, was far better than letting her mind wander. He looked over his shoulder at the clock. "Let me see... what was I doing at just after seven this morning? Oh yes, I was astride my horse and looking at a beautiful woman at her bedroom window. She was in her nightdress and I was scandalised." He said it in a way that indicated he was not in the least scandalised.

Elizabeth brightened. "Were you out there? I had hoped you would be. You will think you have married an unrepentant wanton when I tell you this, but I fancied it would bring a lovely symmetry to the day if the first time you saw me, I was in a nightdress, and then you would sleep tonight with your last vision being that of me in a nightdress."

"Lizzy... you are an astonishing creature." He reached for her hand and she put it on the table for his grasp. Her innocence touched him, and he was charmed that such a chaste allusion made her feel wanton. But he had seen true and unbridled passion several times in her eyes already and was certain she would not find the nakedness he desired too shocking. His eyes burned into hers. "That is indeed a lovely fantasy. But I am afraid I am more wanton than you. Once I have undressed you"—His voice was low and full of insinuation—"and we have been in bed, if you wanted to don a nightdress and then allow me to remove it, I would comply."

Elizabeth blushed and shook her head. "You are a silly man." As so often happened, her sudden ill-understood desires caused impulsive action, and she jumped up from her place at the table and began pacing. "Oh! *I* am the silly one."

"Have I unsettled you again?" Darcy grabbed her hand, catching her off-balance, and guided her as she stumbled onto his lap.

She unconsciously giggled, a sound she disliked but was powerless to si-lence. She studied him particularly and discovered she was enamoured of the lock of hair that dipped to his eyebrow. Her hands reached to his hair. She loved the feel of it running through her fingers. "I do admire your curls, sir."

"*Your* hair was quite ravishing this morning, Lizzy, as you stood at the window. I find speaking of it now reminds me of a request I want to make of you, as my wife."

She cocked her head, expectant yet instantly tense.

"As a very great favour to me, I ask you not to give in to the societal con-vention of married women wearing lace caps. It would be an unsupportable deprivation not to see your hair anytime I look at you."

Elizabeth relaxed a bit and laughed. "If I cannot wear nightgowns, and I cannot wear caps, well, you are starting to narrow my choices of clothing rather alarmingly, Mr. Darcy."

"Mrs. Darcy, I do not think my requests at all unreasonable." He fiddled with her hair, and within a moment, had made a pile of gold and pearl pins on the table.

"No, in truth, husband, you are not so very unreasonable, but you are in a fair way to having me wander the halls of Darcy House with my hair down. What will the servants think?"

"The footman who just left us should be the last servant we see tonight."

"Now *I* am scandalised." She was not, but coloured anyway, and felt several curls slide down her neck at the release of more pins.

Darcy leaned forward and kissed her, starting gently and gaining in urgency as more pins were added to the pile. He could feel her tresses falling. Finally, he stopped pulling at pins and locked his hands in her hair. "Would you like to know how *I* wanted this day to begin and end?" he asked, pulling away from her mouth just far enough to frame the question.

"Tell me," she whispered.

"I saw you hug Jane, and you enrobed her with your hair. It has been my wish since then that you would surround me with your hair tonight. Will you?"

Elizabeth kissed him with such ardour; they were both breathless. She looked him in the eye and whispered, "That does not seem unreasonable, either."

"Shake out your hair, Lizzy."

She did so, feeling a few of the plain hairpins used to style her hair at Longbourn were still there. She raised her hands to search for and remove them.

The action caused the front of her gown to bow out, and the opportunity to gaze at Elizabeth's bosom covered only by the inner lace bodice was not wasted on Darcy. At the top of her bosom lay the little garnet cross from her father. "Lizzy, there *is* one thing I should like you to remove from your person before I come to you tonight."

Elizabeth's eyes followed where he was looking. "You have been your father's Lizzy long enough. Now you will be mine." He leaned his head down, and moving the cross aside with a finger, he reverently kissed where it had been.

Elizabeth shivered, feeling his tongue slip through his lips to taste her. He looked up into her eyes, awaiting a response. "I shall, of course, Fitzwilliam, but am I never to wear it again?" The long-ago gift from her father had become a talisman for her.

"Oh, you may wear it whenever you please, only not in our bed."

His eyes were darker than ever. Elizabeth nodded as she looked away, her face heating yet again. Her hands returned to unpinning her hair. She shook her head again, and all of her hair fell around her shoulders and cascaded down her back, over Darcy's arm. Their eyes met as he brought his hands up to thoroughly ensnare them in her dark tresses. He kissed her neck, turning her head from side to side, distributing kisses around each ear.

Darcy's growing arousal had become obvious. In a low rough voice, he said, "Perhaps we should retire upstairs, Mrs. Darcy?"

She coloured further and nodded.

Upstairs, they passed the various bedroom doors until they came to Elizabeth's dressing room. Darcy opened the door but did not step inside. "I shall join you in a few minutes, Lizzy." He kissed her lightly, and she gave him a quizzical look. "I have something for you, and when I come back, I shall enter through your bedroom. Will you open that door now? The idea of you and me wandering in and out of each other's rooms pleases me, but do understand, my dearest, if I ever find your door closed, I shall always knock before entering, and I expect the same of you."

"Again, sir, a not unreasonable request." Elizabeth turned into the candlelit room, and saw the door to the bedroom was already open, but Darcy retreated to enter his dressing room from the hall.

Elizabeth decided it would not be a breach of his request not to undress if she took off her shoes. She opened another wardrobe, a match for the one containing her nightclothes, and saw two lower shelves where shoes, slippers and walking boots were lined together. She put her wedding slippers away.

She continued her idle peregrination of the room, and as she passed the dressing table, she caught the gleam of her father's cross about her neck, and sat to remove it. There was an empty glass dish on the table, and she carefully placed her only necklace there, along with her pearl earrings.

Looking critically in the mirror, Elizabeth decided she did not look *too* worried about what would occur in the next hour. She lifted her chin, and gave herself a little smile. *You trust him, and his intentions are all for the best. Indeed, they have always been so. He is a passionate man, but is it not endlessly diverting to be so desired? You have nothing to fear, Lizzy Bennet.* She picked up a hairbrush, and began, in a desultory way, to brush her hair.

How long she sat brushing she could not say, for she always found the action soothing, and she closed her eyes. "May I continue?" Darcy asked. "I would love to do something for you that seems to bring so much pleasure."

She opened her eyes, and could see in the mirror that he was leaning against the adjoining door frame. Their eyes met in the reflection. *He looks at me now as he looked at me in the sitting room at Hunsford, and in his aunt's drawing room at Rosings. Did he desire this intimacy even then? I was so innocent of everything that I mistook his ardour for censure.*

His face had been shaved. He was wearing a robe, and she could see his bare neck and upper chest. His curly hair appeared wet.

She twisted on the tufted bench to face him. "Oh, now, sir, I must protest. This does seem unfair. You have had a bath, and you are undressed."

Darcy smiled rakishly. "Men do not smell as pleasant as women after a day on the road. And you do not know how to undress a man..." He joined her on the bench, his back to the mirror, and turned to look her in the face. "Do you?"

"No, sir, and at this rate, I never shall!" She was smiling, and he was relieved when she did not retreat from him. He had given a great deal of consideration to what he should—or should not—wear.

"May I?" He held his hand for the brush, and she gave it to him, turning away. Darcy brushed timidly at first but soon was lifting tresses and brushing them vigorously. Laying the brush on the table, he parted Elizabeth's hair at the nape of her neck and kissed the exposed skin. He pushed the two halves of her long hair over her shoulders then reached around in front of her, unbuttoning the top covering of her wedding gown. He managed the seven little buttons with more dexterity than before. Proud of himself, he caught Elizabeth's eye in the mirror and tilted an eyebrow at her.

She shook her head slightly. "Smug. You are a smug and silly man. If I do not correct you now, then who ever will? You will become proud beyond all hope of amendment." She was smiling, her eyes sparkling only for him.

That is the look I saw from across the room at the Lucases' party, her fine eyes inspired to laughter. How I wished to secure their humour for myself, and here she is... Perhaps that is when I fell in love with her—at the very moment I spoke of her eyes to Caroline? Yes, I believe it is so.

Looking over his shoulder in the mirror, he watched her as he pulled the garment from her shoulders, and she lifted her arms free. He let it drop behind her, and returned to the vision in the mirror of his Lizzy, her bosom nearly bare, with her dark hair curling around her breasts.

"I knew you would be beautiful tonight, but this is beyond my dreams. If I could bear to share this vision with an artist, I would have you painted just as you look at this moment, but I doubt anyone, no matter his skill, could capture your eyes." He whispered in her ear, "Lizzy...my own loveliest Lizzy..."

Overwhelmed by his smouldering stare, she closed her eyes and leaned her head back against him, exposing her graceful neck and chest in the glass. Her bare neck, the first time he had ever seen it without the garnet cross, reminded him of the gift in his pocket, and he drew out the strand of pearls he had removed from his desk a fortnight ago. He had asked his jeweller to add a second, longer string of slightly larger, pale pink pearls to it.

"Do not move, dearest. Keep your eyes closed." He looped the pearls across her chest, and fastened the hook behind her neck, then rearranged her hair. He was happy to see the new, longer row grazed the top of her creamy bosom, and the pearls were perfectly matched to each other and the colour of her skin.

As the pearls touched her, Elizabeth's eyes flew open. "Oh! Mr. Darcy. These are too lovely..." Her hands reached to feel them.

"*Too* lovely? Too lovely for what? For you? Surely not, Elizabeth Darcy. But I should withhold them because you did not keep your eyes closed that I might tell you what these pearls mean to me."

Her eyes were fixed on his in the glass. "That requires closed eyes?"

"Your eyes distract me." Not breaking her gaze, he reached his hands around her and cupped her breasts, raising them slightly to lift the pearls. As he had hoped, her eyes widened and she shivered at his touch. Elizabeth lowered her hands from the pearls to press against his.

"Fitzwilliam...mmm." Her eyes closed again, and a frisson shook her.

With his hands uniquely placed to feel her pounding heart, he whispered, "The shorter strand was my mother's. I had set them aside for my unknown bride. The first night I was in London a fortnight ago, I had a particularly vivid dream of you...of us, and when I awoke, I remembered the pearls and fetched them. I decided my love for you was grander than a single strand, so I had a longer one added. The second strand is yours alone, my Lizzy."

As Darcy spoke, he rolled her nipples in his fingers, watching his actions and her blushing, breathy reaction in the looking glass. He felt his erection finding a way through the opening of his dressing gown, and hoped Elizabeth would not see.

She turned to face him, but rather than glancing down, she stared at the exposed skin of his throat. Just before her fingers touched him, she whispered, "May I?"

"I would be delighted, Lizzy."

She surrounded his neck, feeling the sinews and muscles. Her thumb slid over his Adam's apple. She moved her hands to his face, pulling it to hers and landing an ardent kiss on his mouth. Her tongue slipped between his lips and one hand slid down to the slight hairiness at the top of his chest. He was just able to discreetly pull his robe over his attentive member before returning her caresses.

Elizabeth finally pulled away. *Am I truly worthy of such love?* She looked at his eyes to find them closed, and realised he was concentrating on the sensations inspired by her hands on his skin. She pushed apart the lapels of his robe, exposing his bare chest. Expecting him to be as pale as she, it was intriguing to find him a little tanned.

"Somewhere, sir, at some time, you were not as formally dressed as I have always seen."

He assumed an air of mystery. "In the summer, next summer, you may catch me out. You know I swim. At Pemberley, I sometimes ride without a shirt, and I have even been known to join the men in the fields if there are no women present."

"I would *not* have other women see this." Elizabeth was startled to hear a note of possessiveness in her voice.

"As you wish, Mrs. Darcy." He was amused.

She began kissing her way nearly to his nipple, as if claiming him. "Does this feel for you as it does for me?"

Darcy whispered, "It fills me with a most exciting anticipation. My mind is racing ahead, thinking what you might do next. Or perhaps it is simply your candour and trust that thrill me."

She was embarrassed by her desires and wondered whether she would soon again experience the tipping-over feeling of her passion reaching its peak. Her tongue reached for his nipple while she found one of his hands and placed it on her breast. She suckled him as he caressed her.

Darcy opened his eyes, and was rewarded with the sight of her tender mouth on his chest. The sensation of his hand arousing her breast, combined with what he was seeing, was almost too much. *I have to slow this down.* He tried to regulate his breath and remembered the champagne in a cooling bucket that the servants had placed in the next room.

"Lizzy, we should get ourselves to a bedchamber," he growled, releasing her breast.

She was disappointed but stopped her actions and straightened. "Fitz-william, I am eager to comfort you the way you comfort me."

"Darling Lizzy..." His forehead rested on hers. "And I do desperately hope you shall, but we should be in a bed for that, at least the first time."

"Which?" She smiled at her own boldness. She stood and stepped towards the door. "The nearest?"

Darcy chuckled at her eagerness. There she stood before him, hair down, face flushed and smiling, bosom only thinly veiled. He looked down the length of her irreparably wrinkled wedding gown to her shoeless feet in their pink stockings. *Those little adorable feet...* She extended a hand to him. *Once again, she is leading me.*

Chapter 20
A Consummation Devoutly to Be Wished

"Lady, as you are mine, I am yours: I give away
myself for you and dote upon the exchange."
William Shakespeare, *Much Ado about Nothing*

"Have you ever tasted champagne, Elizabeth?" Darcy stood next to the round table in the mistress's bedchamber.

"No, sir, though I have heard it is the most festive beverage and difficult to obtain from France at present."

"My cousin . . . *our* cousin Richard returned with a case from his last campaign. Not everyone likes it, but I enjoy it, and I hope you will, too." Darcy turned his attention to unwrapping the cork and removing the muselet in such a way as to appreciate the deep pop of release without the cork becoming a projectile. He filled the tall, thin glasses and handed one to his wife. "The custom, madam, is to touch the glasses together so they ring." They delicately tapped their flutes, and he declared, "To Elizabeth and Fitzwilliam Darcy on the occasion of their wedding night!"

"To us!" She sipped her first taste of sparkling wine. The bubbles tickled her nose and tongue. Elizabeth found the sensation altogether to her liking, so much so that she laughed after swallowing. "Why, it is heavenly!" She took a larger swallow and involuntarily produced a burp. "Oh!"

Darcy immediately consumed half of his glass and belched deeply, then looked at her like an ill-bred, ten-year-old boy.

"Now we are both naughty children, and you think by your impressive display that you will absolve me of exhibiting crude manners?" She laughed.

"You are a silly man, Fitzwilliam Darcy. That you could encourage a sensible woman such as I to indulge in similarly silly behaviour is quite remarkable."

He was growing used to the label "silly man," and realised its utterance usually presaged the further granting of his Lizzy's considerable favours. He took the opportunity of kissing her rather abruptly before saying, "I am wondering, Mrs. Darcy, whether you would kindly sit as you finish your champagne. I wish to remove your stockings this instant."

As long as they were jesting, she felt at ease, but each additional level of undress reawakened worries she wished to deny. She smiled pertly, or so she hoped, and followed as he led her to the settee, where he knelt in front of her.

Darcy had carried the champagne bottle and refilled her half-empty glass. "This should do for now. I would not want to be accused of drugging my bride to gain her compliance."

She took another sip. "It would be a waste of medication, sir. I am a bit of a foregone conclusion, am I not?"

He chuckled. "Lizzy, my love, it is my profoundest wish that you are truly as sanguine about all of this as you appear to be."

Elizabeth leaned forward to kiss his cheek. "You promised to tell me whenever we are doing something you have never done before. In return I promise to tell you if I become too overwrought to continue." She sat back.

"Then I have been remiss. I must tell you, I have never completely undressed a woman before now."

"Truly?" She was surprised.

"Yes, truly. Harlots always keep some undergarments on; at least that was their mode of business eight years ago. Am I not a patient man?" He cast her a sidelong glance.

"Yes, sir. You have amply proven your patience. I do hope you find me worth the bother." She sipped her champagne and demurely looked away.

Darcy carefully, in as unhurried a manner as he could accomplish, lifted her skirts by gliding the layers up her legs. When the skirts reached her garters, he stopped, not wishing to alarm her unduly. He untied ribbons on both legs and slid the stockings down and off, one side at a time. As her stockings were removed, he kept his hungry eyes on the skin revealed, but twice stole glances at her face. She appeared spellbound. *I have seen such a look on rabbits before being struck by cobras. Please allow her to be as brave as she thinks she is.*

Darcy looked at her small feet and held one in each hand. "You have charming feet. Have I told you?"

"No, sir, you have not. I am glad to hear it as my mother always told me they are excessively large and unfeminine." She was smiling again.

"It has never been clearer to me than at this moment that your mother and I have quite the opposite view of beauty." He leaned over and kissed the top of one foot and then the other, as if kissing her hands formally. He looked with a smile into her watchful eyes and was surprised to see hints of distress.

His face is between my feet; it could be up my legs next! Elizabeth's mind projected a brief vision of her disturbing dream onto Darcy's quizzical and concerned countenance.

Thinking the memory of her mother's derogatory comments produced her disquiet, he rose quickly and sat next to her. He held aloft a long, elegant, bare-to-the-lower-thigh male leg next to hers. "Hold up your foot, Lizzy!"

She was startled by the nearness of him and his now more obvious nakedness under his robe, but the unexpectedness of the fastidious Mr. Darcy exposing a leg to compare with hers was so comical that she complied with an anxious giggle that surprised her. Elizabeth prided herself on not being a giggling sort of person.

"I must say, sir, of all the apprehensions I had about this night, I certainly never imagined this—to be sitting next to you, both of us in various stages of undress, analysing our feet!"

Darcy tried to look serious. "Since we do find ourselves so, let us proceed. Yours are small and a pretty shade of pink, toes in a somewhat pointed array, nails of even colour and pale shine—yes, in every way delightful. Just what a lady's foot should be.

"Now look at mine... quite hideous by comparison. Knuckles rather knobby, hairy on the top. Apelike, I should say. They look positively misshapen and ill used. Mrs. Darcy, feel free to jump in at any time to contradict me. You may tell me my large manly feet fill you with unquenchable desire..."

Elizabeth's giggle became laughter. "They are interesting objects, to be sure, but I am sorry to inform you, in and of themselves, they do not quite inspire the feelings you hope for."

"Lizzy," his voice lowered, his eyes jesting, "You *do* know what is said about a man with large hands and large feet, do you not?"

A slight frown creased Elizabeth's brow, and she tugged at the corner of her lower lip with her upper teeth. *Now to what is he referring?*

Idiot, Darcy! Thoughtless! Why would a virgin find virtue in a well-hung man? Maybe she has not heard the old wives' tale... Darcy's mind raced to redirect the conversation but not quickly enough.

The words of her Aunt Phillips blared in her ears. *"Big hands, big feet, big cock!"* Elizabeth shook her head, blushed more vividly than ever, and turned away. "Oh, yes," she sighed, speaking with a quavering voice. "I do recall that." She cleared her throat.

"Oh, Lizzy, what beasts men are... I am profoundly sorry. You have no idea how sorry. To be vulgar, now of all times..." He drew her head against him, her burning cheek resting on his bare chest directly over his heart. His action raised the exposure of his leg to the upper thigh, but they were both disposed to ignore it until the present uncomfortable moment passed. Darcy was only relieved that, for the time being, his erection had partially subsided.

"No, I am not bothered..." Her cheek against his slightly hairy, warm skin, over his thumping heart, was soothing. "Evidently there is a wider scope for amusement in marital relations than I had imagined."

"Since we are on the topic, dearest and most forgiving Elizabeth, I shall simply say this: It is marginally acceptable for a woman to laugh *about* the male appendage in general terms, for it *is* an odd thing at times, but she must never laugh directly *at* it."

Elizabeth opened her eyes, and viewed the magnificent length of his bare leg. *Now this does incite desire.* She looked up at him and smiled. "Ah... thank you, sir. I do comprehend the distinction."

Elizabeth reached up to tousle his irresistible hair, although she yearned to touch his thigh instead. In the carriage, he indicated much would be allowed her, yet he had been reluctant to demonstrate or describe what might please him.

Her eyes closed, her lips parted, and Darcy understood her silent invitation. They kissed deeply before his fingers slid down her silky throat, over her pearls, and rested at the top of her lace bodice. While his tongue traced her lips, he found the thin ribbons holding it together and pulled.

Elizabeth sighed against his mouth as she felt her bosom exposed to his touch. She pulled away enough to murmur, "Fitzwilliam...mmm." She widened the opening of his robe and could not resist the urge to rub her breasts against him. He was warm, and his arms opened to her. She felt

201

moisture between her legs as a frisson of deep desire shuddered through her.

"Fitzwilliam?" She did not look up, watching instead the arresting sight of her bare breasts mingled with the sheen of the pearls moving on his skin.

Darcy was barely breathing. "What, Lizzy?"

"Can you explain...oh." She sighed. *Do not be squeamish.* "What is this wetness that arises when you touch me?"

Darcy felt the room execute half a turn. He did not blame the champagne, but rather the woman. *The things she says...she knows so little of her own body. Her candour is unbearably sweet.* He took several breaths before replying. "It signifies passion. It signifies readiness for..." *Dare I say it?* "...For me, for joining your body with mine."

"It is your leg, you know," she confessed with a whisper in his ear. Somehow, such remarks were easier to express quietly.

"My leg what, my love?"

"It is quite...it is beautiful, handsome, like a statue come to life. It has undone me..."

To Darcy's surprise, Elizabeth turned to straddle his bare thigh so the seat of her desire was in contact, moist and lush, with his skin. Their lips met in a frenzied kiss until Elizabeth's arousal grew so great that her head fell back and she moaned, "Oh, Fitzwilliam, oh please!"

He knew what she wanted, and he lowered his head and lifted her to gain access to a breast to tease, nosing the pearls out of his way. She pressed against his leg, crying his name, begging in murmurs and holding his head against her. When the shattering pinnacle arrived, Darcy knew it. He released his mouth from her, laughing for sheer joy at the bliss he could bring her. He was thoroughly captivated.

Slowly her movements ceased. Finally, she drew a breath to speak. "You may laugh at me, you may torment me, you may undress me, you may say or do anything, Fitzwilliam, anything, only please, *please*, let me feel that again." She was panting against him, and his erection was now lying against her bare thigh under her bunched skirts. She realised what it was, but turned her attention to his face.

Darcy had never seen such passion in any woman's face, and certainly not in Elizabeth's. That he had inspired such a look from those adored eyes exhilarated him, and his chest swelled to take in sufficient breath.

"Will it hurt you if I touch it?"

Darcy's inhaled breath was interrupted as he blinked at her. "What?" He could not believe his ears.

She did not wait for his reply. Her hand moved under her skirts to touch his engorged member. As soon as she felt its heat and size, she pulled her hand away in timid recoil. "Oh. Oh, my. Oh, dear..." Having rubbed herself giddy against his thigh, she instinctively felt the potential for pleasure in using this new instrument for the same purpose. But that it was meant to go *inside* her was unfathomable. Yet, she felt too full of desire to be afraid.

"Lizzy..."

"Yes?" Their eyes locked on each other.

"We must proceed to the bed. We must. I cannot wait."

With his hands on her hips, he pushed her up; her knees slid from the cushions and she stood, the crushed layers of her skirt falling about her legs. As he stood, the robe covered his erection, tenting the heavy damask. He took her hand and led her the few feet to the bed. Earlier, as he passed through the room, he had paused to turn down the counterpane and arrange the pillows.

They stopped at the edge of the bed. Darcy sat and positioned Elizabeth standing between his legs with her back to him. He untied the laces of her gown, and when he slid the shoulder straps of mesh and ribbon down her arms, the whole of it whispered to the floor. Next, he faced the laces of her short corset. These, too, proved easy. When it was sufficiently loosened, Elizabeth raised her arms, and he lifted it over her head to toss it away. That his enthusiasm to be rid of the garment caused it to land on the bed's canopy was not noticed.

She stood before him in nothing but a demi-petticoat tied at her waist. Even in the candlelight, he could see where the ribs of the corset had worn grooves into her skin even though a length of soft flannel had been sewn inside to protect her. He rubbed her back where the marks were. "Better?" he asked.

She nodded, her hair bobbing in agreement. "Thank you."

Darcy could feel the grosgrain ribbon wrapped around her waist and tied at the front to secure the petticoat. He reached around to undo the bow, and the last covering of her body joined her gown on the floor. He parted her hair at her neck, and unhooked the pearls. "Place them on the night stand, Lizzy." She leaned to her right to do so.

He sat back to view her gently curved derriere. "Is there any part of you, Mrs. Darcy, that is not perfect?" Breathing deeply, Darcy rested his forehead on her back and closed his eyes, steeling himself to do what needed to be done, what he longed to do. His arms stole around her waist, encircling her and steadying his nerves.

After a moment, he realised Elizabeth's breath was heaving—she was in the midst of a wave of sensation. He could hear her softly moaning.

With one bold hand, she guided his fingers between her legs. Being undressed by him had again provoked her passion. She no longer remembered anything her Aunt Gardiner had said. Her concern was not what Darcy might wish to do to her, but what *she* craved. Slowly she shook her head from side to side, swishing her hair over his face as his cheek pressed against her back.

"Please, Fitzwilliam...please." She paused.

His fingers slid between her thighs, and into her, guided by her hand on the back of his. "There is more... Please give me more." She tried to catch a breath at the edge of her moment of supreme bliss. "How can I bear this alone? Join me. Feel this with me." He held her upright as she reached her zenith of desire.

Afterward she calmed only slightly, and held his hand in place. "Fitzwilliam...never, never did I dream of such love. That I would feel it so and share it."

"Lizzy, dearest"—he smiled behind her—"you must release my hand."

My astonishing Lizzy. What a journey she has made today, and I still feel stupid, as if trapped in a dream.

She relinquished his hand and turned around as he stood. She undid the button of his robe, and embraced him.

He strained to savour all of her, naked against him.

Elizabeth could feel his erection pressing her hip. She longed to encourage him, not understanding that she was already behaving in exactly the manner in which he had devoutly hoped.

Now... I must take her now. He lifted her into his arms and turned to lay her on the bed. "I love you. I do love you, my Elizabeth Darcy." He looked at her complete nakedness while shrugging the robe from his shoulders; it joined her garments on the floor. She was lovely, with her hair spread upon the pillows.

Elizabeth's eyes met his seriously. Her legs slightly parted. "Husband...

Fitzwilliam..." There were tears at the corners of her eyes, yet she did not appear afraid. "Mr. Darcy... You have given me so much. I only have this to give you: I come into this marriage with my promise I have been chaste."

Darcy gazed into her eyes with astonishment. He had no doubt of her.

She reached an inviting hand to him, and he laid down facing her. She continued in a rough whisper, "It does not seem nearly enough, but you must accept it. I give myself. My love for you is all I have." She kept her luminous eyes on his, not daring to look down at his fully aroused member.

She is breaking my heart; she is so serious and must think these words necessary. Darcy breathed deeply. "It is all I need. Lizzy... remember I love you. As we do... this, please remember, I love you."

He leaned over her, fervently kissing a nipple until she moaned his name. Raising his head to kiss her eager lips, he slipped an arm under her shoulders, pulling her towards him, and covered her legs with one of his. He slipped his tongue into her mouth and out again repeatedly, as she responded by stroking his chest. He touched her breasts and flat belly. The power of speech left him as he lifted his hips to settle between her thighs.

Elizabeth wrapped her arms around him. *He is so warm... and he is not heavy at all.* She did not realise most of his weight was borne by the arm under her shoulders. With his other hand, he gently lifted her leg to embrace his waist. Feeling her heel on his tailbone, Elizabeth tucked her head under his chin, readying for the consummation. She was overwhelmed by his scent, her wits at a loss to define it.

Darcy closed his eyes and touched between her legs, finding the wet opening. With a deep breath, he took his erection in hand, addressing it to her rigid centre of pleasure. "Oh yes," she murmured. He guided it to her entrance.

Exhaling, he started forward, and immediately felt her maidenhead resisting. He pushed further and heard her gasp, her hot breath searing his chest.

Elizabeth's passion contorted into this new stinging sensation.

Darcy felt her sharply inhale but he could not withdraw. Elizabeth's fingernails scratched his back. He did not notice.

The smarting in her deepest parts could not be ignored, but she resisted crying out.

A small voice whispered within him. *Be careful, you brute!* But the warmth and wetness of her tight flesh was thrilling beyond anything he experienced eight years ago. *This is much more than I remember, this is my Lizzy, I am in her... she is mine. She will always be mine. Yet, it is I who am possessed...*

Darcy lost control. With several brisk thrusts, he was completely within her, rocking their bodies with his desire, and he was amazed to feel her other leg wrap over his lower back, her heels spurring his buttocks, opening herself further.

Her fingernails were gripping his back and she thought she might be drawing blood. She drew him as deeply into her as possible and the pain lessened.

When he at last became aware of it, Darcy mistook her clawing at him for passion. He slid his hand under her body to her derriere, pushing her towards him to intensify their connection. He surrendered completely, thrusting mindlessly, driven by her heels digging into his haunches until he found his voice, gasping, "Lizzy, my god! Lizzy!" Although he wanted the moment to stretch on forever, his release was sudden and thunderous. "Lizzy!"

She felt his spasms and was gratified she had incited his moment of ecstasy; gratified more that he cried for her with such vehemence, and most pleasantly surprised when his seed was soothing to her stinging flesh. But for all that, she was glad the event was completed. She suspected she was bleeding from his actions, but this did not alarm her—she would know what to expect the next night. *It is over... He has made me his wife. Soon it will not hurt. Perhaps when he repeats this tomorrow night, it will be more pleasant. Certainly, everything else has been... extraordinary.* As his last thrusts subsided, she whispered, "I love you," without understanding why she needed to say it.

Her voice brought Darcy back to alertness. "Oh, Lizzy. I am so..."

"Stop! Fitzwilliam, do *not* say it!" She was as strident as he had ever heard her. She put her fingers over his mouth and lowered her voice. "Please, do not. This had to be done. My darling, I know beyond any doubt that I am taken. I am yours. How foolish I must have seemed, before."

Darcy looked at her sheepishly. "Taken? Quite ruined, I am afraid. You were adorable in your innocence. Oh, Lizzy, if only I had maintained control, you might have enjoyed it as I did. The feel of you was far more intense than anything I have experienced. You are in every way exquisite. Your kindness has humbled me once again." He smoothed the moist hair from her face and searched her eyes. "Was it so very bad?"

She pulled her other hand from his back, and seeing blood on her fingernails, smiled bashfully.

Darcy saw it, too. "Did you do that to me?" he asked, chuckling.

"I am afraid your back was sacrificed to prevent my whimpering. I did not want to alarm you. We may both be sore in the morning. Given what you had to do, and the, um...uh...relative sizes, shall we say, of yourself and myself, discomfort was unavoidable. You must not trouble yourself, Fitzwilliam."

He meant to kiss her quickly but her hands held his hair, extending the kiss, her tongue teasing him. He was pleased to see her confidence had not abandoned her.

"But it did hurt you?" he asked when she released his lips.

"It is my endeavour to think only on what makes me happy. When you were most deeply, uh...joined to me?" The hue of her rosy skin deepened.

Darcy nodded that he understood her meaning.

"It hurt somewhat less, and I am sure you will be pleased to know that when you..." *How do I say this? I am naked underneath my naked husband, and he is within me still. I suppose I can say what I want in any way I please.*

"Yes, when I what?"

"When you called my name..."

"Did I?"

"I mean, when your seed, uh, came out, it was like a balm."

"So you are optimistic about doing this again?" He watched her eyes.

"When? Tomorrow night?"

"No, sooner."

"How soon?" She stifled an inclination to wince.

"In a few minutes, I expect. We are still joined, you know..."

"You mean again *tonight*?" She was incredulous. Aunt Gardiner had not mentioned the event might be more frequent than daily.

"Lizzy, I *promise* you will like it better the second time." Darcy felt himself deflating but did not wish to move. "Am I too heavy?"

"No! Pray, do not roll away. The feeling of you upon me is comforting."

"Do you mean truly comforting, the traditional meaning, or comforting as I comforted you earlier?"

Darcy was amazed to see her expression change to desire. "As I was tremendously comforted at the coaching inn, and on the settee, and then here by the bed..."

"Answer my question."

She chuckled, and Darcy enjoyed the motion of her body laughing under his, though it caused his member to slip out. The wonderful sparkle in her eyes caught the candle flames on the nightstands. He gave her a smile of joyful love.

"As I remarked in the carriage, if you smile at me like that, Fitzwilliam, I shall deny you nothing. I merely was not aware this might happen more than once a night."

"You have been comforted three times today, and if you are a docile and compliant wife, I may choose to comfort you yet again this evening and well into the night."

She pinched his bottom. *Oh the pride of the man!*

"Ouch! Well, Mrs. Darcy, that is one less comforting for you!"

Elizabeth laughed. "And is there a point to this fulsome reckoning of your prowess?"

"*You* started it, Lizzy, and most charmingly, too. But yes, the material point is that *you* may be comforted more times than once a day—many more—and so may I. It simply takes a little time for me to recover. Unlike yourself..."

"Oh, you are too proud by half, sir!" Elizabeth was inwardly astonished. Her marriage had just been consummated, yet they were naked and teasing each other. She had not reckoned with this—had not apprehended that conjugal relations might be entertaining, or that Fitzwilliam Darcy, in a moment such as this, would be playful.

"Why should I not be? I have taken my beautiful bride to bed, and although this act was not everything I had hoped for her, she has learned to be comforted, and is willing to continue granting me favours. You see before you all the makings of a happily married man."

He bent to kiss her laughing lips, and nibbled first one ear and then the other. He was pleased to make her giggle. Their mingled sweat pooled at the base of her throat and he licked at it, then rubbed it over her chest and continued licking to her breasts. She wriggled under him, moaning and sighing as the warm air chilled upon the moisture on her tingling skin. He felt his arousal renewing.

Elizabeth felt it against her thigh, and asked huskily, "*This* soon?"

"It has been eight years, you know. You should consider yourself a lucky woman, Elizabeth Darcy."

"Perhaps when I have had time to become a true proficient, I shall."

"Practice," he said solemnly, and returned his attention to her breasts.

After several moments, Darcy changed position and tucked his mouth next to her ear. "Lizzy...now I have had you, I cannot resist. We may never leave this bed." He applied his swelling erection to her point of pleasure. "Does this please you?"

Elizabeth nodded, sighing as a frisson passed through her.

"Then I shall not stop until you reach your ecstasy again. Lizzy... tell me when."

She did not need to tell him. One of her hands clasped his hair, her back arched.

Darcy entered her at precisely the right moment, slowly, feeling the stickiness of various fluids previously combined, but still revelling in the tight warmth admitting him. His hand slid to her derriere as her legs tightened their grip. "I am going to roll us onto our sides, so I can suckle while we are joined." His voice was low and insistent.

The very notion of it caused her to explode with the anticipation of pleasure. She grew tighter inside and her toes curled and flexed on his back. His intimate words, whispered in her ear, made her delirious. She was crying insensible words with syllables of his name, unheeding the loudness of her utterances. The prickly sensation was ignored, easily overwhelmed by the ample demonstration of his desire. That he could take such pleasure from her was its own gratification.

Pushing with one leg, he rolled her onto her side. He did not need to ask her to arch her back to reach her nearest breast, since she was quaking with waves of longing. He captured a nipple and she gasped at the tender connection. "Fitzwilliam...mmm."

Gently he began pulsing within her, carefully pushing as deeply as possible. Her response to the combined connection indicated how he could prolong her rapture. Her hands were everywhere, his hair, his arms, his chest, until one hand grasped his buttock, impelling him deeper.

"Fitzwilliam...the other..." she moaned, and he knew the tension was rising in the breast untasted. Sensing his own mounting urgency, he gave several buried thrusts before quickly latching his mouth to her other breast.

They sighed together, suddenly out of rhythm but uncaring, unseeing, only feeling and hearing each other. Again, his seed was spilled as he growled her name. This time, after his spasms subsided, he grew soft quickly and pulled away.

She was still writhing and, without opening her eyes, murmured, "Oh my." Elizabeth slid her leg from under him and pulled his head down to rest on her chest as her breathing calmed.

This is a miraculous thing. That the pain of the act could be overset by such stirring sensations is a wonder indeed. She leaned her cheek against the top of his head. "I was wrong in what I thought before. *This* is what happiness feels like."

Darcy smiled; she could feel the action curve his cheek against her. She said, "I love you," and he said, "I adore you," at the same moment.

Chapter 21
Wonderment

"I will live in thy heart, die in thy lap,
and be buried in thy eyes..."
William Shakespeare, *Much Ado about Nothing*

Fitzwilliam Darcy dozed, his awareness rising to occasional wakefulness, reassuring him that yes, his head was resting on the chest of his beloved Elizabeth, and they were in bed together as husband and wife. His arm and leg were her only coverings. Her hands fiddled with his hair, stroked his cheek, or lay companionably on the arm crossing her waist. Darcy was drowsy and sated, and feeling no end of relief that, despite his abominable loss of control, she remained generous and forgiving. Even now, when she might still be in pain, or at least uncomfortable, it was Elizabeth who offered the solace of a warm shoulder. He had never felt such peace.

Darcy floated into a dream. *He was with her in this room on the settee. She wore her wedding gown and gloves but then her clothing melted away. He was kneeling, looking up at her as she sat, her hair spilling around her breasts. She stroked his hair and looked at him with her laughing, loving smile. He bent his head, her bare legs parted, and he settled a kiss on her slightly pouting belly, just above her triangle of dark curly hair. "Silly man," she chuckled, "I am your wife, Fitzwilliam. You may do with me what you will."*

ELIZABETH DID NOT NAP, HER mind instead scampering amongst new experiences, examining the many sensations of the day, and adjusting to being naked with a *very* naked man. She was amazed at her previous naiveté,

211

appreciating all the more Darcy's patience. Had anyone told her a year ago she would find the deepest love—the desire she had spoken of only to Jane —with the proud and brooding, aloof and disdainful Fitzwilliam Darcy, she would have laughed them out of the county.

Darcy's face appeared before her. She remembered his wounded aspect as he handed her his letter in the grove at Rosings Park. *Had I only known my folly then... How near a thing that this day might never have dawned.*

She shook her head to scatter the vision. All she could do was wonder at the several small miracles that kept him first in her thoughts and, finally, in her heart. In her effort to remember the past only as it gave her pleasure, she would forget his thoughtless dismissal at the Meryton assembly, his blistering retorts as she spurned him at Hunsford, and his initial coldness in the carriage earlier.

Now she comprehended him much better. He only appeared unkind or forbidding when he was expending every effort to maintain self-control. Now that this final barrier to absolute intimacy had been forever breached, he need never appear that way to her again. That in their present circumstances he would prove to be gentle, teasing, and irresistibly playful was wholly unexpected.

Elizabeth knew Darcy had fallen asleep, but the room was growing cold. *I should stoke the fire, and I am sticky between my legs.* She kissed his forehead but he did not stir. She slowly tried to ease herself from under him, but when she lifted his arm from her waist, he opened his eyes.

His vision dissolved from the dream and focused on the breast in his line of sight. "Elizabeth?" he murmured, resetting the arm she was trying to move to cup her breast in his warm hand. He felt her cool, pliant skin and lifted his head to look at her face. "Are you cold?"

"I cannot reach the bedclothes, and it was my thought to stir the fire and stoke it."

"Mmm," he lowered his head to its former place, petting her breast. "You may stir my fire and I shall stir yours, *again.*"

She smiled. "I do feel a need to clean myself, excessively prideful husband, even though we may likely make more untidiness later."

Elizabeth was surprised when Darcy startled and sat up. "Of course! I have been negligent. Let me tend you." He swung his legs over the side of the bed, moved to the closest washstand, and dabbed a piece of towelling in the basin.

"No! Oh no, Fitzwilliam, I should wash myself…" She drew upright onto her knees. *We are intimate now but this is too much…* The length of his broad back, narrowing to a muscular waist, and the seamless transition from flat lower back to firm vulnerable buttocks stopped her mid-sentence. He was as perfectly chiselled as any statue in her father's art books. There were trails of scratches on his back, some dark from bleeding. "And I should wash *your* back. Do you scar easily?"

Darcy laughed as he squeezed excess water from the cloth. "Scars I shall wear with pride. If you think you have seen me self-satisfied, wait until my fencing master notices. I must practice a knowing smirk to meet any comments."

Elizabeth shook her head and sat back on her haunches. "I should have guessed as much. You will not need much practice."

Darcy turned to her, still laughing. His eyes fell to the carnage on the bedclothes, and he stood stock-still, stunned.

"My god, Lizzy! Have your courses come, too?" It was the only explanation he could contrive for such a scene. He looked at her aghast. *What is keeping her from fainting from loss of blood? She appears so rosy and alive!*

She looked down at the sheeting, then back to him, and started to laugh. "Did someone steal in here and slaughter a piglet while we were distracted?"

Darcy's stare deepened to shock. "Elizabeth, how can you jest? Are you not in great pain? Did I do this to you?"

"Fitzwilliam, calm yourself. Who else did it? Silly man. Did you not know I might bleed?"

He sputtered, "Yes, I knew you might, a little, but I thought a rivulet, not the Thames!"

"I suspect I bled both times. It is nothing. We shall clean it up and clean ourselves, and that will be that. Now hand me the towel."

"No, you come here."

They met each other's narrowed eyes for a long moment.

Darcy went to the bed. "Lizzy, please. I do insist. Then, if my back is as bad as you say, you may tend to me. We shall remove the sheets and Mrs. Chawton will burn them in the morning. We can take ourselves to the other bedroom for the rest of the night."

Neither moved until Darcy smiled.

Elizabeth heard her aunt's voice, *"Let him!"* and she could not resist his dimples. "I never should have revealed to you the power of your smile. Please take note, Mr. Darcy: I am becoming a compliant wife." She walked on her knees to the edge of the bed, skirting the evidence of a thoroughly consummated marriage. She returned to mirth from annoyance.

"About damn time…" he muttered, his dimples deepening in a vain attempt to stop smiling.

Elizabeth chuckled.

Darcy knelt before her and wiped gently at the streaks of blood on her thighs. Then, to her utter mortification, he took up a candlestick and told her to sit at the edge of the bed and spread her legs. He intended to be meticulous.

"Oh, surely not," she said, her eyes pleading. "Please, sir, no. I can do it."

"I know you can do it; you have been cleaning yourself for years. Now you have me to attend to you." He looked up, waiting. Finally, he said, "Elizabeth, now it is you who are being silly. Sit."

She did so, grousing the entire time. "Please give me the towel. This is most improper. Mr. Darcy, you assume too much. I should clean myself. You had better not."

As she continued her litany of ineffectual protests, he gently spread her legs—she was strong, but he had more leverage—and lit her nether parts in the candlelight. He folded, wet, and refolded the towel several times to remove all traces of their humours.

She admitted only to herself that his tender attention was soothing.

"There…" He leaned back on his heels but did not move the candle. He gazed fixedly at her womanly parts. He was caught, quite immobilised, between his desire to kiss her on her sensitive places and tearing himself away.

Sensing his desire, Elizabeth whispered, "Do not, Fitzwilliam, please do not." *Oh no… I see it in his eyes. Someday he will ask me to make the dream I had come true… or he might not even ask!*

He looked at her as if he had forgotten that she was attached to the devastatingly desirable sight before him. He said nothing, but stood as she scooted back onto the bed. *You must walk before you run, Darcy. When she is ready, you will know.*

He heard her take a deep, relieved breath, saying in a rather more plucky voice, "Is there another clean towel there? It is your turn."

She approached the washstand as he sat on the bed. He knew her intent was to wash his back, but he had noticed streaks of her blood on his thighs, and decided not to turn around, at least not immediately. *How thorough will she be? This ought to be interesting.*

She turned, her eyes immediately falling to his lap—she could not help it, or avoid it. His thighs wanted a wash but there it was, fairly tumescent, his male part. "Ah..." She straightened as if to proceed in an officious manner. "There is the creature who hath wrought such havoc." She dabbed at him timidly, avoiding the culprit.

Darcy could not help smiling. *Yes, her courage always does rise in the face of intimidation.* Something of his was rising, too.

"Would you like my advice, Mrs. Darcy? Or better, my guidance?"

"Mr. Darcy, I would say yes, but must you leer at my hands? It smacks of ingratitude. It is in no way humble or becoming to you, and after all, I am the more injured party." Her eyes flickered to his face. *I have never seen him more handsome.*

"I do not mean to laugh at your discomfort, Lizzy, but you will need to get to know 'the creature' one way or another. It certainly wishes to know you."

She had to smile. "Oh, I would say it has explored its way around the territory with some thoroughness already." With a great breath, she laid the moist towel over it, and then clasped his covered member in her hand. The chill of the cloth caused a momentary reduction. "Fickle thing, is it not?" But as her hands gently rubbed around it, the towel warmed and growth began again. "Very fickle." Lizzy tended to her task seriously. After a few moments, she peeked at Darcy's face to see his countenance a map of surprise and desire.

This is a most promising start, he mused as he closed his eyes.

She raised a brow. "Stop looking like the cat that ate the sparrow. If we keep soiling ourselves then cleaning up after, we shall be locked into an unending cycle. At what point are we ever to dress and re-join the world?"

He lifted her hands and moved away the towel, letting it fall to the floor. "Never, Lizzy." He drew her between his legs. The height of the bed put her breasts near his face and he nuzzled her.

Elizabeth embedded her hands in his hair. *Is he to be at me again? Should I resist? How much* practice *do I need?* These were her last complete thoughts as his mouth found a nipple, suckling her as she moaned, "Oh, Fitzwilliam...mmm."

His hands caressed her derriere, pulling her closer still. As his hands embraced each half of it, with fingers near her cleft, she felt herself become eager. She could offer no resistance. She pushed his head more tightly to her chest. "Yes, Fitzwilliam, yes..." She hoped he understood she would welcome him again. His fingers wandered further into her, parting her, teasing her. She grimaced and Darcy saw it. He instantly removed his hand.

"Sir?" She heard her voice as if someone else were speaking.

Her hair partly covered her eyes, but there was enough candlelight to make out her countenance, and he saw worry there. "Lizzy? I need not be so selfish. I shall give you time."

"I would not like you to think I am refusing my husband."

"Your husband demands too much."

Elizabeth sighed. She was braver now and could see very well the stout evidence of his arousal. This strange part of him was another source of wonder—quite a curiosity—and it felt wrong to do anything but submit when he was visibly possessed by longing. It was not as if Darcy was unkind or heedless. "But you wish to."

"Lizzy, here. Now it is me with blood on my hand." Darcy showed her the evidence.

She looked away. "Women are accustomed to such things. I must bear it."

"No." Darcy stood. "Let us remove the sheeting and bundle the towelling. We shall sleep in the master's bed."

She turned to see his back. "Then please, Fitzwilliam, let me see to your scratches first."

Elizabeth stepped quickly around the end of the bed, prepared a towel, and returned to him. He sat and leaned his elbows upon his knees. She pulled his shoulder lower and washed the scratches. "This does not look so very bad," she said as she worked. "There is only one deep mark. Perhaps I have not maimed you irreparably."

"Oh." Darcy sounded distinctly disappointed.

Elizabeth felt the need for a visit to the commode. She chewed the corner of her lower lip, wondering how to mention it, choosing to be airy and vague. "I shall step next door for a moment, sir, and perhaps when I return, we can remove these bedclothes, as you suggested, and tend the fire in your bed chamber?"

"An excellent plan, Elizabeth." He was amused that she sounded suddenly formal.

Elizabeth noticed the robe Sarah had left out, and picked it up as she entered her dressing room. The candle on the dressing table had burned down, but she took it with her behind the screen. She refreshed herself with lavender water, holding the anointed towel between her legs for the span of two long breaths. She looked at it and saw a dark streak. Vexed with herself for still bleeding, she repeatedly applied fresh corners of the cloth until there was no mark.

Darcy could plainly hear what she was doing; aware, in spite of all that had passed between them in the past two hours, she was still modest about her body's functions and might not be ready to hear his. *And she calls me silly...*

Elizabeth donned the gauzy white dressing gown. It was of a Grecian style, with narrow gold cording tied below her bosom and at her waist. There was some fullness in the skirt but it was open from waist to floor.

Darcy saw flashes of bare leg as she walked into the bedroom. He drew in a breath. "Elizabeth, stop."

She did so, noting the use of her full name and that his look resembled the way he had stared at her as she played the piano at Rosings, a look she now understood was impassioned.

"You are a goddess. My raven-haired goddess..."

"Compliments such as these will go a long way to keeping your wife in good humour, Fitzwilliam. I recommend you continue. Today, I have been a bride, your queen, a wife, your Lizzy, and now your goddess. All new roles for me...so many in one day; I never imagined."

"Are you well? You are not in pain now?"

"No. I believe I am better."

Darcy nodded and put on his robe without fastening the front. In dance-like movements, they removed the soiled sheets from the bed, folding and refolding, stepping together and apart. They gathered all the soiled linen and made a tidy bundle to give Mrs. Chawton for disposal in the morning.

Darcy held the champagne bottle before the flickering firelight. It was only half empty. "Champagne does not keep; we do not want to waste it." He carried the ice pail. "Bring the glasses, would you, Lizzy?"

"I have them." She followed him into the master's bedroom.

Darcy stirred the fire. "There are more candles in the drawers of the night tables if these need replacing," he instructed. The candles on the nightstands were indeed starting to gutter, and Elizabeth lit new ones from the old, illuminating the bed.

As Darcy added logs to the fire, she wandered to the settee and sat down, pulling the fullness of the dressing gown over her legs more out of habit than a need to spare her modesty. *Am I already so changed?*

Once the fire was roaring, Darcy poured two glasses of champagne. "I have forgotten which was whose, Lizzy. Does it matter?"

"Silly man," she replied. "I should think not one jot by now."

"To us again. Husband and wife." He smiled, tinging his glass with hers. They drank and he sat next to her, pulling his robe closed only enough to cover his crotch. With one foot, he hooked a wooden stool and dragged it in front of them. He extended a long leg onto it, and Elizabeth impulsively stretched one bare leg and leaned it atop his.

The feel of his skin against hers was alluring, warm, and irresistible. "Mr. Darcy," she began flirtatiously.

"Mrs. Darcy?"

"You have not lately mentioned, given all we have done this evening—"

"So far…" he interrupted.

Elizabeth was chagrined to feel herself colouring. "Yes, *so far*, you have not lately said what it is we have done, if anything at all, that you have not done before."

Darcy finished his champagne and put his arm around her shoulders as he spoke. "I am afraid, dearest Elizabeth, I have stopped reckoning what is new. *Everything* is new. What I did or did not do eight years ago matters not to me now, nor should it matter to you. Do you not know—have I not told you—you are the love of my life? You bring joy to this house and to me, and your joy makes everything new. I do not wish to remember the tawdry brothels of Vienna." He kissed her temple, and continued speaking with his lips brushing her skin.

"I wish to remember this: the smell of your hair and its beauty as you shook it loose in the dining room, your eyes in the coaching inn when you first found passionate bliss, undressing you, hearing you burp and laugh from drinking champagne. I want to remember each time you laugh."

"I am all astonishment, Fitzwilliam Darcy. I have asked myself many times today how I have come to deserve such love. Except for a time when I was desperately afraid I would never find it, or thinking I had lost it without knowing it was within my grasp, I have done nothing to deserve it."

"Nonsense. Silly woman."

"I do hope I have sense enough to let you continue teaching me all those things you wish me to know. I shall no longer concern myself with your past or my lack of knowledge."

Elizabeth and Darcy sat in amiable silence before the fire. They shared the remains of the champagne in her glass, emptying the bottle. Each silently reviewed the day's varied events, developing questions for the other that would take some days to recall and have answered. But one question intrigued Darcy above all others.

"Lizzy," Darcy began, attempting a casual air, "there is something I must ask, something that has become a source of mystery to me."

"I cannot imagine what remains unknown to you, Fitzwilliam. It seems I have revealed everything, even things I did not comprehend about myself, and you have *certainly* sought to examine anything I did not think to share." She blushed in the firelight. "However, if you have discovered some further secret within me, I pray you: ask what you wish to know."

"I must confess, I was surprised you had not ever reached a level of hmm... let me rephrase. When I touched you... between your legs, your response led me to think you had never touched yourself there, to understand your own parts and their sensitivities?"

"No, never."

"Odd. Just a difference of the sexes, I expect. Men seem unable to resist their own parts. You are not aware that as a boy becomes a man, we may awaken ourselves after having reached a moment of discharge in a dream?"

She sat forward and stared at him. "I, uh, I know nothing of such things. I do... Oh, I *suppose* something similar *may* happen to young women. Speaking only of myself, for that is the only answer I can honestly provide, I can report that the one time I believe I felt anything like that was in the disturbing dream I had some weeks ago."

"You have told me little of that dream, Elizabeth. You know my arrogance, and will not be surprised when I tell you that I believe I might allay some of your disquiet if you choose to speak of it. But you must come to peace with it in your own time."

Elizabeth took a deep breath, pulled away, and watched his eyes. They were gentle with concern. *I shall tell him as best I can*, she decided. "I believe I have already explained that the dream involved you, and we, or you, were engaged in an activity upon my person that only shocked me when I awoke. In the dream, what you did led to something like the height of sensation I have experienced today, and it awoke me."

Darcy said nothing, waiting.

"What you were doing in the dream was something which, in the other room, I begged you not to do, and you did not." Elizabeth lowered her lashes.

"But Lizzy," his voice was hushed, "you have, with heart-rending generosity and courage, done everything I have asked and taken some initiatives that I would have guessed would take weeks for you to try. You would even allow me to risk hurting you recklessly until I came to my senses. I do not recall asking anything you declined."

She chewed her lower lip. "Perhaps you did not ask aloud, but I thought I saw an intention, and I responded to that."

Darcy tilted his head, looking at her and concentrating until he remembered. "Ah..." *I did long to kiss her there. Oh, how she must taste...* He was carried away in a reverie of longing, and whispered, amazed, "You dreamt of *that*? That I kissed you... *there*?"

She turned her head away. "The look on your face in the dream... At first, it was only the awareness, but then you leered at me. You were enjoying what you did with no regret. You seemed wicked, and you challenged me. When I saw your face, I had the coming apart feeling, but when I awoke, I was ashamed... to have dishonoured us both... or so I thought. Now I know not what to think."

Darcy embraced her. "Lizzy, when we are alone together as husband and wife, there is nothing to be ashamed of or to regret. I know I challenge you, but I hope, if there are things you truly find too alarming to contemplate, you will tell me. I would not force or coerce you. You have demonstrated such trust, my dearest Lizzy. How could I betray it?'

She hugged him tightly. "I do love you, Fitzwilliam."

They sat with arms around each other for several minutes. Finally, they leaned back in their former languor, legs entwined before the fire.

Elizabeth realised Darcy was nodding sleepily. "Shall we retire to the master's bed?"

He rubbed his eyes. "The champagne has made me drowsy. I could stay right here in your arms if you would rather."

Elizabeth sat up and turned to give him a light kiss, thinking *I shall get into bed first,* but as she leaned towards him much of a comely breast slipped from her low neckline.

Darcy was immediately alert, his eyes brightening. He cupped her breast as she met his lips. "May I comfort you on the new bed, Mrs. Darcy?" he asked when their kiss ended.

Elizabeth was thinking her dressing gown had outflanked her hope to merely go to sleep when she noticed a bump forming under his robe. She did not say yes but reached under his garment and began stroking his manhood. She was amused by his surprise. "Yes, but I must practice comforting you, too, Fitzwilliam, if I wish to become a true proficient." She would not disappoint Darcy again. She must learn to master the pain of joining with him, and if at all possible, hide it. Touching him so explicitly was not unpleasant, for she could see evidence of her handiwork enlivening his dark eyes.

He drew his robe open, watching her elegant and dexterous fingers, one wearing the betrothal ring, handling his erection. *My wife, my Lizzy . . . on our first night . . . Elizabeth Bennet is touching me.* His eyes half closed and he felt intoxicated. "You are well on your way to proficiency, Lizzy. I must get you to bed before I faint from pleasure."

They rose from the settee hand in hand. Darcy sat on the bed and pulled Elizabeth between his legs. He untied the gold silken cords of her dressing gown, releasing the smell of lavender water. "Have I told you I love how you smell? It is lavender?"

"Yes, it is." Elizabeth was occupied with his unruly hair and tender ears. Caressing his neck, she said, "And I love how *you* smell. Is it sandalwood?" She sniffed the collar of his robe, pushing it off his shoulders and down his arms.

"Um-hmm." He continued lines of small kisses over her chest, avoiding her puckered peaks, glancing up to her eyes, watching the heat build there. He pulled away to gaze at the length of her body from her knees to the top of her head. Darcy placed his hands on the gathered fabric on her shoulders and let the dressing gown fall.

Elizabeth tried not to blush, and her chin rose a little. She still needed to remind herself to be brave in the face of his need to look at her.

"Oh, how you tempt me, Lizzy." He pulled her hair forward, so the dark tresses curled over her creamy skin. He stroked her hair smooth over her breasts. "My goddess."

Elizabeth sighed. "Oh, I am quite mortal and far from perfection."

Darcy lifted her onto the bed. "Although we, neither of us, have easy characters, I find we are perfect for each other." He pushed her against the pillows, then stood and let his robe fall. He put a knee on the bed to join her, but she stopped him.

"Fitzwilliam, pause a moment. Indulge me."

Darcy stilled, a questioning look in his eyes. Elizabeth gazed at him, admiring the glow of the candlelight as it illuminated his chest hair, his long, well muscled arms, his thighs and erection. She said in a sultry voice, "I do not believe I have expressed to you sufficiently, dear husband, the admiration with which I regard your person. I understand you completely when you speak of being tempted. That explains what I am feeling."

She rose to her knees. "Stay just as you are," she instructed. "Do not move." Elizabeth ran her hands down his arms, then slid off the bed and moved behind him. She stroked his buttocks, murmuring, "I never imagined —how adorable..." She embraced him and brushed her breasts against his back. "No, I never knew a man could be beautiful."

Darcy reached for the bedpost to hold himself upright. He blushed at her attentions, but she could not see it.

She rubbed her cheek against his back, and then kissed where her cheek had been. Her hands felt the taut muscles of his chest, moved over his stomach, and finally stopped on either side of his hard manhood. *If he can touch me in my secret places with such ease, I must learn to touch him.* He was pleasingly hot to the touch, and she could feel him become even more rigid.

"I am pleasing you?" she asked, although she could easily anticipate his answer.

"Speechless..." was all Darcy could offer by way of reply. He was silenced by the sight of her hands. *It is Elizabeth, my Lizzy, bent upon pleasuring me.* He had not dared think such attention might become a reality on his wedding night. He would not have presumed to ask, at least not so soon. *Last night at this time, I was having brandy, hoping to sleep. Alone. Am I dreaming still?* She chuckled in what he thought a most delightful way.

She had removed his power of speech, and now he could not even breathe. Slowly, knowing she was enticing him. Elizabeth climbed onto the bed and straddled his knee that was still leaning on the bed.

Darcy was beside himself with exhilaration, and feared he might spend himself. With a dry desperation, he said, "Lizzy, I am sorry to end this, but

I must have you... I pray it will not be too discomforting."

They lay side-by-side on the bed and embraced. Her legs encircled his waist, hoping it would give him the deepest access and produce less pain. She was instead elated when his careful entrance produced little stinging. She laughed.

Darcy rose on one elbow to look at her. "Laughter? *Now?*"

Her face was suffused with joy. "It does not hurt! Nothing we are doing hurts!"

His response was a passionate kiss and slightly more demanding thrusts. He paused to ascertain she was still unharmed; she was chortling, her cheeks aflame. He laughed too and, wrapping his arms around her, rolled them so she was astride him. She sat up—"Oh!"—but he held her hips down and pushed deliberately into her, deeper than he had yet been.

Elizabeth looked down at his face. His eyes were closed, he was clearly enraptured, and she closed hers. His depth produced a more profound response. "Ooooh." A deep shudder announced her slide into oblivion, and as long as he moved in her, it did not end. She cried his name with each thrust.

When he pulled her down so their bellies touched, her back arched and he looked at her, realising she was far beyond delirium. Had she seen his gaze, she would have met a very smug countenance indeed.

"I love you," he whispered, knowing she might not hear or comprehend. "I love you, dearest, loveliest Elizabeth." He reached his climax with a final burst of force. A breast was near his mouth. He gave it a fierce tug.

"Yes, Fitzwilliam, yes, yes!" She collapsed, her long dark curls enrobing them both.

He smiled even as his body shook with its final spasm, thinking of Elizabeth only that morning, wrapping her sister in her hair. Here was the hoped for reality.

Elizabeth did not open her eyes or move. Even when his deflated manhood slipped out of her, she did not appear to notice. Darcy was afraid she would grow cold. He reached for the corner of the sheeting, wiping the excess liquid from his loins. He pulled the bedclothes he could reach to cover them. Elizabeth smiled, her cheek on his chest.

"Mr. Darcy, you must allow me to tell you how ardently I admire and love you."

His chuckle bounced her cheek. "If you had not refused me then, Lizzy," he said, recognising the words from his ill-timed and ill-judged proposal, "we might have started this most pleasing exercise in, what, perhaps June?"

"I do not believe we would have joined together in so profound a way as this. This is all as it was meant to be."

"I believe you are right."

Sometime in the night, Darcy awoke briefly. He did not know when they had rolled into a spooning position. One arm was behind Elizabeth's neck, warmed by her hair, and the other was wedged between her breasts, his fingers entwined with hers. *Even now that I have had her, I want her all the more... How splendid she is...*

Elizabeth Darcy awoke as a bright and cold winter's day was dawning. She was sensible to an ache between her legs, and realised it was not a lingering pain from her deflowering but something else, something more. *I want him. Is this proper? I want him to take me again—the way he did the last time with the stirring motion. What will he think? All I want is to feel him. What has he done to me?*

Darcy remained soundly asleep as she slipped out of bed. She dabbed water onto the towel at the washstand, soothing herself. The feeling of emptiness remained, and she was alarmed at the intensity of her desire. *I shall stir the fire and warm the room; perhaps that will distract me.* She found and donned the green velvet dressing gown—it would be warmer than the sleeveless gauzy robe on the floor.

After stoking the fire, she went to the windows and slipped the curtains apart. The pale winter light illuminated her as she studied the frost lying over the formal courtyard with its complicated knot of herbs. She folded her arms under her bosom, watching the sun peek over the back of the house. *He has done something to me... This is not at all what I was lead to expect. I am...yes...I am lustful. Can this be what he wants?*

Darcy's eyes flickered open, alarmed to find he was alone. He saw the roaring blaze. *Where is she? Did she let a servant in to tend the fire? I did not think I would awaken with empty arms this morning... Where is she?* As he started to move, Darcy became aware of the undeniable erection already much in evidence. *This reminds me of when I was seventeen. At least some part of me does not age!*

He raised himself on an elbow, his eyes drawn to the morning light cutting a sliver into the room, and saw Elizabeth profiled against the glass doors. He went to her.

She did not hear his approach until his arms encircled her from behind. "Good morning, Mrs. Darcy. I did not think I would awaken in a cold bed this morning. Are you not well?"

"Good morning, Fitzwilliam. I do not know whether I am well or not."

"Yes? Are you in pain?" His deep voice was full of concern.

"I do not know what you will think... I do not understand what you have done to me. I am not in pain, exactly, but I do ache. I want you. I have never felt such desperation. Something has changed in me. Since I have been awake this morning, all I can think of is how soon you may wish to..." Her voice dropped to a whisper. "Please comfort me."

Darcy strengthened their embrace, and pressed his tumescence against her derriere. He enjoyed the feeling of the velvet gown against his skin and over her soft bosom. He leaned to whisper in her ear. "You are wonderful... That is what I think of you. Should such a case arise again, please know you should wake me. Immediately. Most mornings you will find me instantly at your command, as I am now."

"Is it proper for a wife to make such demands? Is this what you want? You do not find my request unladylike? Too forward?" She pushed her derriere against him.

He felt her sigh of desire. "No, my dear Lizzy, to the contrary. In fact, I think you may justly accuse me of feeling a quite improper pride." He slid his body against hers, slowly.

"You, sir, are behaving in a most ungentlemanlike manner. I was not wrong after all. You know arts and allurements far beyond any meagre attractions I may claim, teasing man."

"Come back to our bed, Lizzy."

Her lips were dry. "I shall." She pulled him to the table where the ice bucket remained. "But first, I must have some water." She poured a little melted ice into a champagne flute.

When she had finished, Darcy downed the remaining gulp from her glass and led her to the fireplace. "Did you have a servant in?"

"Whatever for?"

225

"To tend the fire."

"You have married a country girl, Mr. Darcy. I know how to tend a fire." Smiling up at him, she took his hardness in her cool hands.

"Indeed, you certainly do. Your attractions are *not* meagre. And may I say, Mrs. Darcy, I find a certain smugness in *your* countenance that is irresistible. I would not dream of correcting your pride. It is well deserved."

Darcy unbuttoned her dressing gown and reached inside to grasp her waist. He gently pushed her down until they were both on their knees on the heavy plush rug before the hearth.

"Are we not going back to bed?" she asked, just loudly enough to be heard over the crackling fire.

"I pray you, indulge your husband's dreams."

She nodded, meeting his eyes, entranced. *One night... in just one night he has made of me something quite other than I was yesterday. It is a wondrous thing.* She was panting. "You were right, Fitzwilliam, that we should wait for this. It would not do for an unmarried maiden to feel as I do this morning. You may not be shocked at my feelings, but I am. I had no notion..." Her voice trailed off with a shake of her head.

Darcy slipped the robe from her shoulders and smoothed it with the velvet side upwards, then lay upon it. He returned her candid gaze. "I knew when I received your first letter. I was certain you would respond to me, that you would know this as an expression of love, not a demand of duty. Lizzy, join with me?"

She did so, gratefully.

Chapter 22
A Period of Adjustment

"For which of my bad parts didst thou first love me?"
William Shakespeare, *Much Ado about Nothing*

Nearly all Darcy's hopes had already been realised when he awoke mid-morning on the day after his wedding. Elizabeth's eagerness to please lent confirmation of her passionate nature. The taking of her maidenhead had given her pain—indeed, he had not expected such blood—but she was valiant. He was pleased she recovered quickly and continued to explore what fulfilled her desires. Even in this carnal realm, she was spirited and loving. That she awakened on their first morning together in a state of adamant arousal made him revere her all the more. *Darcy, you have no right to be so fortunate.* He was not ungrateful; indeed, he was erect again, but he was in greater need of food.

"Elizabeth?"

"Hmmm?"

"Are you awake?"

She was still cuddled next to him, both of them naked and warm under the bedclothes, where they had returned after their commingling in front of the fire at daybreak. He was alert, and she lethargic.

"I am starving, Elizabeth. Are you hungry?"

Elizabeth lifted her head, a considering sort of look on her sleepy face. "Since you suggest it, I am ravenous." She scrambled from the bed.

Darcy stood and picked up her velvet dressing gown, giving it a shake. Crushed creases marred it. "Is it ruined?" He handed it to Elizabeth.

"Nonsense. It can be steamed and will be as good as new," she said, though her look was dubious. She slid her arms into it with his gentlemanly assistance. He buttoned it under her bosom in a most attentive manner.

"My preference, Mrs. Darcy, would be to have breakfast here, and then perhaps we could bathe."

Elizabeth lifted her chin, which Darcy well recognised as the summoning of her courage. "Am I to assume you wish for us to bathe together in the same tub?"

He embraced her—she was so pleasing to hold in her velvet dressing gown—and murmured, "That is precisely correct. If I may say, Mrs. Darcy, in matters of conjugal intimacy, you are a delightfully quick study." Darcy nibbled her ear.

Elizabeth's cheeks coloured, and she chuckled, asking, "Are you going to eat *me* for breakfast?"

I would, if you would let me. Darcy envisioned the tempting sight of her womanly parts as he cleaned them by candlelight the previous night. "Lizzy, I am highly suggestible when we are alone together, and while *I* thought of Cook's special ham rolls, and trying some of your strawberry jam, I would be happy to consume you instead. Whatever you wish." He shrugged amiably.

She saw his rakish smile and shook her head in mock censure. "Perhaps you should ring for Mrs. Chawton, sir?"

"I fear I must, madam, for we need to fuel ourselves. What would you like for breakfast?" Darcy gave the bell pull a tug and then found his robe.

The housekeeper knocked discreetly on the door. Darcy opened it and spoke to her quietly. "Mrs. Chawton, we would like a tray of food. Some fresh fruit?" He looked to Elizabeth, and she nodded. "Bread and butter, some of Cook's ham rolls, what is left of the cheddar from Mr. Bennet's hamper, and some of Li... Mrs. Darcy's strawberry jam. I want coffee, of course. Mrs. Darcy? What will you drink?"

She hesitated before saying, "I shall also have coffee, Mrs. Chawton, with milk, please."

"Then in about an hour, if you would have Sarah prepare a bath."

"Sarah will remove the linens then, sir. Shall I ask Murray to prepare a bath for you, sir?"

Darcy looked down, his cheeks turning rather reddish. "No, Mrs. Chawton, just the one bath. I shall ring for Murray when I need him."

"I see." There was a moment of tension, most of it flowing between Darcy and Elizabeth. "Very good, Mr. Darcy." Mrs. Chawton turned to Elizabeth, "and ma'am. The food should be here in about half an hour but likely sooner. Much of it is ready."

As soon as she left, their eyes met, and they started laughing. "What will the servants think?" Elizabeth asked. At heart, she *was* a little shocked. Darcy seemed close to his valet and housekeeper, and she wondered what they would make of their master going far beyond the bounds of his usual unvarying and confined behaviour.

Darcy walked to the door of the mistress's bedroom and closed it. "Mrs. Chawton will have Sarah and an upstairs maid make up your bed and refresh the basins and linens in case we wander back in there." He sat next to her on the settee. "We might want a change of scene...eventually."

"Mr. Darcy, unless I very much mistake you, and I do not believe I do, I detect licentious intentions." She gave him a quick kiss. "You should be ashamed of yourself, but I know you are not. I know you that well, at least."

He held her in a longer, passionate kiss, then trailed kisses to her delicate ears. "Tell me, Lizzy, which bedroom do you prefer?"

"That I can easily answer. I have preferred this room since first I saw it. There is a warmth and simplicity that pleases me. I understand it is many years since the other room was occupied, but I find it fussy. A soothing atmosphere is my preference."

"Nothing needs to be decided now, but we could have it fitted over as a sitting room for the two of us. We could keep the settee, add a larger table and chairs with a sideboard for food, maybe a small pianoforte. We can remove the bed. Perhaps you would prefer plain painted walls to the murals?"

Elizabeth's brows rose. "A pianoforte?"

"Indulge me, Lizzy. Your singing pleases me. You perform with lovely *joie de vive*. And I must confess, it stirs my blood.

"I was thinking about it yesterday. When did I first start to love you? It is difficult to say, but I remember you playing at Lucas Lodge, and I told Caroline Bingley how I admired your eyes. The irony is not lost on me, I assure you, that she, of all people, was the first to learn of my admiration of you. But I have never since dreamt of any other lady's eyes."

Elizabeth looked at him in amazement. "You loved me as long ago as *that*? And when I played for your cousin at Rosings?"

"This is the beast you have married, Lizzy; you must know the truth. After that first song, I wanted nothing more than to kiss you violently. During the second, when I approached, I wanted to take you by the hand and drag you to my room to make you stop mocking me. Oh, Miss Bennet..." He leant his forehead to hers.

"Mr. Darcy! Most unseemly..." Elizabeth started to reach up to his curls, but she was interrupted by tapping at the door.

"Damn..." they both muttered, before looking at each other with renewed laughter.

Darcy rose and bid the servants enter, one with the coffee service, one with the tray of food. "Excellent, thank you!" Darcy ushered them out again with all possible speed and poured a cup of coffee for Elizabeth. "How much milk?"

"Let us say, I take a little coffee with my milk."

Darcy smiled, "Ah." He handed her the cup. "The opposite then, of how you take your tea."

My goodness! He forgets nothing. "Light caramel-coloured, sir. Perfect on the first try."

Darcy poured himself a cup and sat next to her. As they finished their coffee, they could hear servants moving in the next room. Elizabeth went to the closed door, and opened it enough to call in, "Good morning, Sarah."

Sarah straightened from making the bed and curtsied. "Good morning, Mrs. Darcy. Oh, ma'am?"

"Yes, Sarah?"

"Is there a box for the pearls?" Sarah held them out to Elizabeth.

"Mr. Darcy?" Elizabeth looked back into the master's bedroom. "Have we a receptacle for my pearls, or are we to keep them in the pocket of your robe?"

"Ah, yes!" Darcy jumped to his feet and disappeared into his dressing room, re-emerging in seconds with a brown velvet box. "Here." He stopped next to Elizabeth and gave it to her.

Elizabeth handed the box to Sarah, who blushed to see the master so informally attired.

"Excuse me, sir," Elizabeth said, looking over her shoulder at Darcy. She stepped into the bedroom and shut the door behind her. Leaning back against the closed door, she met Sarah's eyes and beamed. "It all went rather well!" she whispered happily. Taking Sarah's arm, she pulled her into the dressing room.

"He wants to bathe *with* me, Sarah!"

"So I have been told, ma'am."

Elizabeth blushed and shrugged off the velvet robe. "I think the creases can be steamed?"

"Easily, ma'am." Sarah noticed evidence that the dressing gown had been used more as a towel than a garment.

Elizabeth opened the wardrobe containing her nightclothes. She grabbed a nightgown of deep pink satin with long sleeves and a drawstring under her bosom. "Help me into this, though why I bother, I cannot say..."

"Elizabeth! I am waiting to eat!" It was Darcy, impatient on the other side of the bedroom door.

"Oh, for heaven's sake..." Elizabeth muttered. She hurried behind the screen, freshening herself with more lavender water. Sarah handed her the sheer dressing gown meant as the partner for the nightgown as Elizabeth dashed back to the closed bedroom door. "Sarah! Knock on this door when the bath is ready...then you may go." She stopped at the door, donned the dressing gown, and took a deep breath before opening it.

Darcy stood on the other side, a handful of late grapes from Pemberley's glasshouse in one hand, and a half-finished ham roll in the other. "You look beautiful," he said with his mouth full.

"You said you were *waiting* to eat." She swept past him, stealing his grapes.

He swallowed. "I did not say I was doing it well."

Elizabeth began to eat the fruit. Darcy met her at the settee and refilled her coffee. Elizabeth knelt upon the settee, leaning over its arm, selecting morsels from the tray. Finally, she slathered a thick slab of bread with strawberry jam, and sat back on her haunches to savour it.

Darcy poured his second cup of coffee, admiring his wife. "You are a vision. You have had a costume change to match what you are eating? I do call that the height of fashion..."

"If I were any less pleased with you—and being married, and my jam, and everything—I would scold you for teasing me. That the first nightgown I came to matches my jam is a happy accident, sir, nothing more."

"Would you scold me? I was complimenting you, you know." He wandered around her, drinking coffee and observing. "I have been thinking about what we should do today."

"And?" Elizabeth asked between mouthfuls.

"I would like to show you the house after we bathe, but that means getting dressed. Or do you think the servants would mind if we wandered about in our robes?"

"*I* would mind."

"Would you?" He set down his cup, took another ham roll, and turned to her with a smile. "I could ask that they scatter and stay below stairs until a given time—"

"Oh, no, sir! That would be even worse. I would indeed like to see the house, and I would like us both to be presentable. I shall ask Sarah to dress me after our bath, and I am sure your valet is wondering what has become of you."

"He knows full well that waiting for you to become my wife has long since exceeded the limits of my patience, and I very much wish to be making up for the lost time." He sat down next to her.

Elizabeth finished her bread and jam and settled beside him, disturbed to think what his most trusted servant might know. She noticed a drip of jam upon her bosom, and leaned towards the table to retrieve a cloth. "It seems I *do* need a bath!"

Darcy reached for her. "Let me do what I can." He was grinning as he licked the offending sweetness from her scented skin.

Her inclination was to respond that he could not possibly lick all of her clean but thought better of it. Given his present mood, with his passion rising again, he would try her if challenged. He had already disarranged her nightgown and was fondling her. She felt herself giving over to desire when there was a rap on the mistress's bedroom door.

"You are good, sir, to be so very solicitous, but our bath is ready, and you need not trouble yourself further."

"I intend to trouble myself a great deal further, Lizzy, unless you truly perceive it as disagreeable."

When they reached the bathtub in Elizabeth's dressing room, it was half-full of warm water, with two more copper ewers of hot water waiting nearby and one sitting on a metal rack in the small fireplace amidst the blazing logs.

Darcy threw off his robe and stood in the tub. "Come to me, Lizzy. Be my frolicsome naiad. Cavort with me."

Elizabeth looked at him, his face so boyish and expectant; she could not help but chuckle. Together they undressed her, the pink silk shimmering to her feet. She stepped into the tub with a hop, and he hugged her. She returned his embrace and looked into his eyes. "Your... um, creature is recommending itself to me. Is it always so demanding, or may I take this as a compliment?"

"My male part cannot believe my good fortune. To have so beautiful and comely a wife, so generous and willing a wife..." Darcy sighed. The feel of her body against his bare skin was intoxicating. He whispered hotly into her ear, "Oh, Lizzy. Elizabeth. What a fool I have been. A year ago, I told myself to get to London to escape you. Then, although I put my words to you poorly at Hunsford, I had come to think you were exactly the sort of woman who would suit me. And even though I did not know *much*, at least I saw by then that I had gotten it all wrong at Netherfield. Had we never met again after Hunsford, I never would have married. No woman could displace you.

"But now, you are here, allowing my dreams to come true." His fingers explored her while his lips stroked her shoulders, punctuating his speech. He knelt, lowering her with him. "May I comfort you again, dearest Lizzy?"

"Silly man, you may ravish me at your will," she murmured.

"It is not ravishment, Lizzy, if you do not resist."

"What *was* I thinking?"

"I *hope* you were thinking of me..." Her legs embraced his waist as she held onto his shoulders. He sat on his heels and bounced her on his thighs, holding her tight.

The warm water splashed onto her toes, and lapped at his thighs and her derriere. Alternating hands, Darcy scooped water onto her breasts and stroked them reverently.

Elizabeth moaned repeatedly, unaware she was calling him "Mr. Darcy" and impelling him more deeply inside her. Their mouths met in a slippery kiss, and Darcy spent himself as her tongue invaded his lips. Elizabeth reached more than one blissful peak.

They slid apart, laughing, into the water. Both ends of the tub were slanted, and after Darcy added more hot water, they lolled with legs entwined, looking fondly at one another through the steam.

"Lizzy..." Darcy drawled in a speculative manner.

"Yes, my husband?"

"It occurs to me that we have been united in three rooms of the house already, and we have not yet been here a full day."

Elizabeth rolled her eyes and turned her head to give him a flirtatious glance. "I reckon what you are about to propose will make a tour of Darcy House take much longer than one afternoon, sir."

"Although I admire your initiative, I was going to suggest, as we tour the house *fully clothed*, we might note the other rooms that we want to *explore* at night." Elizabeth had no doubt of her husband's intentions.

They separated to dress. Elizabeth was keen to take a turn in the courtyard, the day remaining crisp and clear. She chose her pale green gown of fine wool with a heavy petticoat beneath and a chemise, but no corset.

"We must have pity on my poor husband, Sarah." Elizabeth smiled dreamily.

IN ARCHAIC TIMES, THE BEDCLOTHES from the marriage bed of an elevated bridegroom such as Fitzwilliam Darcy would have been displayed, but he thought the custom disgusting. Nevertheless, in the privacy of her workroom, Mrs. Chawton examined the linens in front of Sarah that the women could act as witnesses and vouch for the consummation of the marriage should that need ever arise. Who would doubt such obvious lovers had completed their marriage, Mrs. Chawton could not imagine, but she felt it her duty to verify Mrs. Darcy had come to be mistress of the house with her virginity intact. She and Sarah were both significantly alarmed by the ample nature of the evidence.

"Poor Mrs. Darcy..." Mrs. Chawton tut-tutted.

"She seems in good spirits, ma'am, I must say," Sarah said with wonder. "She told me she thought all went well. I would have never guessed at *this*." She grimaced at the bedclothes.

"We are uncommonly lucky in Mr. Darcy's choice of wife. She makes the best of things, I think. It is in her nature to be pleased and easy with servants, and to make no upset. This morning she joined Mr. Darcy in his coffee, but I believe she would have preferred tea. Tomorrow, no matter what, I shall send both. There was special tea in the hamper her father sent. It must be a family blend."

Mrs. Chawton began bundling the linens to burn when a short-stay corset dropped to the floor. "How did this get here?" She looked surprised, and Sarah blushed. "Please explain, Sarah."

"When the chamber maid and me was tidying the bed, the thing dropped from the canopy. I snatched it up quick before she saw it, and tucked it in last night's bedclothes. Then Mrs. Darcy came in, and we had to store her pearls, and find her fresh nightclothes. I forgot it was there."

Both Sarah and Mrs. Chawton stared at the garment for a moment.

"What were they thinking to put it on the canopy?" Sarah asked.

Mrs. Chawton burst into laughter. "*They* were not thinking at all! I would assume this is the master's doing!"

"We must never tell Mrs. Darcy, ma'am. She would be embarrassed."

Mrs. Chawton pondered the statement before shaking her head. "I am not so sure, Sarah. It is just possible our new mistress would be entertained. I have overheard her tease Mr. Darcy. She may have provoked him!"

Sarah considered what she had heard between the master and mistress, and decided the housekeeper was, as ever, probably right.

"The mistress seems to want to confide in me, Mrs. Chawton." Sarah looked at her warily. "Should I discourage it? She is open in her ways, and it seems to comfort her to speak her worries."

"Mrs. Darcy comes from a large family of women and is, I think, accustomed to confiding much to her sisters. Do not discourage her, Sarah, but also do not take it too much to heart. You may only be serving her for this one week. She may impose upon you as ever she wishes, but *you* must not presume too much."

"Yes, ma'am." Sarah left to tend to the velvet robe.

Chapter 23
Exploring Darcy House

"For a man is a giddy thing, and this is my conclusion."
William Shakespeare, *Much Ado about Nothing*

Darcy was surprised to meet Elizabeth at the top of the stairs dressed for the outdoors. Murray quickly fetched a hat, gloves, and great-coat for his master.

"I should have surmised you would need a breath of fresh air, Mrs. Darcy." Darcy extended his arm, and they descended to the ground floor. He showed her the formal entrance and the courtyard, and Elizabeth thought it all delightful.

When the cold finally penetrated, they returned inside. Darcy was keen to acquaint her with the ballroom, which adjoined the formal dining room.

Elizabeth expressed an interest in seeing the kitchen, so they briefly visited below stairs and Elizabeth complimented the cook.

They wandered upstairs to the drawing rooms, one large and formal, another smaller and intimate. "For family," Darcy said.

They proceeded to the study. "Would you disapprove, Fitzwilliam, if we had a small desk brought in for my use?"

"No, certainly not, but would you not prefer a private study of your own? There is room for one, across the hall from the master's . . . *our* bedchamber."

"I would rather be with you. After the past day, I foresee very little about myself that will survive your scrutiny. That is, unless I would be a distraction to you. There is *that* to be hoped."

He returned her devilish smile. "If you wish to be in my company whilst writing your letters and arranging our social engagements in London, I suppose I can endure the risk. Please notice I have had a rather capacious settee moved in front of the fireplace, and a fur rug."

"My goodness!" Elizabeth could not resist teasing. "What a hopeful man you are! You have presumed a great deal."

"I am not sure I can allow your use of the word *presume*, Elizabeth. I made quite a study of you, you know. I presume little."

"Yes, sir. Your dedicated and constant observation of me in company was remarked upon no end in Meryton society. What were you hoping to gain by it?"

"Evidence of an affectionate nature, willingness to express affection. Perhaps that you might let slip the tendency to sensual appreciation in an unguarded moment."

"Mr. Darcy!" Her expression of shock was not entirely feigned for his benefit. "And I but a maiden! What conclusions did you reach?"

"Oh, I think you know. I need not say, unless you wish me to later when we are back in our bed. Then I might be most particular."

"But we may assume the conclusions impressed you? You do not regret proposing again?"

Darcy was charmed to see her evince a coquettish expression.

They had been wandering around the study separately, but Elizabeth perceived, as their talk of Darcy's observations proceeded, that he was following her, and she moved away, initiating a slow, unspoken chase.

"No, indeed, madam. Quite contrariwise. I was confident enough of you to rearrange the furniture in this house less than a fortnight ago. Let me recommend the jaguar-skin rug in front of the fireplace. It is from America, and quite thick and soft."

"Ah..." She scampered away from his reach, putting his desk between them. "Perhaps it was admirable foresight rather than presumption."

Elizabeth rushed for the study door, but he caught the ties of her dress as they fluttered behind. He pulled her to him as she giggled. He abruptly brought her backside into contact with his eager erection. "Caught you!" he chuckled with tense desire.

"Oh, yes, I am well and truly caught," she chortled.

"Shall I lock the door?"

"I would like to see where the library is, Fitzwilliam, and after my curiosity is satisfied, we can return to our rooms and satisfy you."

"You ask a great deal of me, Mrs. Darcy. You should know, there are a new chaise lounge and another fur rug in the library. There is also a fire laid; we have but to strike a match."

"I think the match has already been struck." She gave him a look meant to enflame.

Elizabeth reached for the door, but Darcy stilled her hand. "We can enter the library from this room." He led her to a side door.

Once inside the library, Elizabeth was anxious to explore for the sake of the books therein and no other reason. But Darcy would not be denied. She heard him shoot the bolt of the lock to the study door. A moment later, another lock clicked on the door to the hall. Elizabeth continued to drift amongst the bookshelves.

As she stood leafing through a book of essays on classical art, in which a rendering of a statue recalled the buttocks and legs of her husband, he again embraced her. This time she knew he would not be dissuaded. If she had hoped to win a respite of a few hours by an exploration of the house, she betrayed no disappointment. She was enthralled with the novelty of being the object of such intense passion, and felt she was in danger of becoming obsessed with the summits of sensation first awakened at the carriage inn between Longbourn and London. With her dress already untied, Darcy easily loosened the lacings, and slid it down her shoulders. "Are you in there somewhere?" he asked, feeling a petticoat barring easy access to her coveted bosom.

"There is no corset, Fitzwilliam, and you are clever enough to conquer what garments I wear. I daresay you will find a way to work around what you choose not to remove." Elizabeth leaned back against him as he cradled her breasts through the layers of fabric. He kissed her neck and shoulders and she sighed.

"I find I do not have the patience I had last night," he confessed. He breathed into her ear as he unbuttoned his trousers.

She knew his tolerance for her teasing had reached its limit. "You know full well how I may be persuaded," she said with a throaty chuckle.

Darcy rested his forehead between her shoulders. "I *am* a savage," he said with a ragged voice. "It seems I cannot get enough of this, of you..."

"I am your compliant and dutiful wife in all things, Mr. Darcy," she replied in a soft voice, facing him with a sly smile.

The fire was lit, and they lay on the fur rug. They did not leave the library for several active hours.

WHEN THEY DID FINALLY EXIT, Mr. and Mrs. Darcy returned to the master's bedroom and slept in each other's arms without further congress. It was shortly after nine o'clock in the evening when they awoke. Elizabeth arose, making vague excuses to escape to her dressing room. Darcy found it diverting given the many ways she had allowed him to enjoy her. She still shied from any nearness of his mouth to the territory between her legs, but given all she was willing to do for his pleasure, and how demanding she was in achieving her own, he had no complaints. In fact, when she was not watching him in an almost feral manner, he was lost in admiration of her and found himself grinning stupidly.

"I shall order some food. What will you have?"

"Happy thought. I shall eat whatever is presented to me."

Darcy rang the bell for Mrs. Chawton and put on a robe before hearing the knock on the door.

"I am afraid we have slept through the excellent dinner I had ordered, Mrs. Chawton. First, I pray you, send our apologies to Cook."

Mrs. Chawton shook her head. "Poor Cook, sir. She has had nothing but apologies since you arrived. And I suppose *now* you want something to eat?"

"Yes, we do. Please bring whatever can be managed on a tray, another bottle of champagne, and fresh drinking water. That should see us through the night."

"You are not, either of you, eating enough, sir," Mrs. Chawton said rather sternly.

Darcy smiled in agreement. "Then pile it on, Mrs. Chawton, and we shall do our best."

In her dressing room, Elizabeth found Sarah dozing on a stool by the fire. Elizabeth's arms were full of the clothes she had not put on again after waking. "Oh, dear, Sarah, you need not wait here for me. I can ring for you when I am ready."

Sarah took the clothes and Elizabeth slipped behind the screen. When she emerged, Sarah held the velvet dressing gown, steamed smooth after its trials. Elizabeth selected a sheer nightgown to wear under it, with an alluring low neckline. It made her breathless to think what Darcy might attempt when he saw her in it.

There was a tap at the open door from the mistress's bedroom, and Darcy stepped inside. Elizabeth was charmed that even with the door open, and wearing only a robe, he was gentleman enough to knock upon approaching where he had every right to enter.

"Mrs. Darcy, I was just coming to enquire whether you would like to bathe in my dressing room after we eat. I shall alert Murray if your answer is yes."

Elizabeth blushed. "My answer *is* yes." Taking a deep breath, she smiled sheepishly at Sarah. "That will be all, Sarah. Thank you for working your miracles with this dressing gown."

Darcy took Elizabeth's hand and gave her a half turn, reviewing the restored garment. "Yes, Sarah, thank you." Darcy smiled at his wife.

Sarah bobbed a curtsey. "Goodnight, ma'am, sir." Her eyes barely flickered to Darcy as she hurried from the room.

Darcy and Elizabeth heard the rapping of the servants with food at the master's door, and re-entered that bedchamber. After eating nearly everything brought to them, Darcy carried the champagne in its ice bucket into his dressing room. Once she was certain Murray had left the room, Elizabeth joined her husband with the flutes.

Standing several feet from the tub while Darcy kneeled in it, she slowly took off the velvet dressing gown, laid it over a chair, and turned to face him.

He drew in his breath. The sheer fabric did not adequately cover her bosom, and only where multiple layers folded over her body was any detail hidden.

Feeling her power over him, she stretched her arms up as if tired. She pretended to yawn, and shook herself. "Fitzwilliam," she said lazily, "perhaps I shall precede you to our bed." She shrugged a shoulder, dislodging a strap and completely revealing one breast. From beneath her brow she looked at him, and finally smiled.

"Elizabeth," he murmured. He stood, revealing his reaction to her little charade, which brightened her eyes. "You have had ample sleep, so do not trifle with me. Let me comfort you."

"Again? You are not bored with me?" She held his gaze, and slowly slid the gossamer gown down the length of her body.

"Lizzy... step into the tub. I shall show you how bored I am."

THE NEXT DAY AND THE day after, several more rooms were *explored*, including the study and the music room. The next attempt at an evening meal in the small dining parlour was interrupted by Darcy pulling his wife onto his lap, disordering her hair, and lifting her skirts. Elizabeth and Darcy were rarely out of each other's company, even for the writing of letters, and a second desk was indeed moved into his study.

Elizabeth could not convince Darcy to walk in Hyde Park—"I most fervently do not wish to see anyone to whom I am not married, Mrs. Darcy" —and when the weather turned foul, she stopped asking. She did not really mind. Elizabeth wondered how they would find a normal rhythm to life at Pemberley when such ample joys were so readily available and tempting.

On the fourth night in Darcy House, as they sat before the fire in the master's chamber, Elizabeth asked why Darcy had not shown her the rooms where he had resided prior to their wedding.

"I have a special curiosity about the room in which you slept as a bachelor. I want to see where you struggled against loving me and where you dreamt of me. May we go there?"

Darcy paused, his mouth half open in awe.

Elizabeth misunderstood his silence. "We need not of course, but I have imagined you there..."

"Miss Elizabeth! You continue to astonish me. That a maiden would imagine a bachelor's bedchamber never occurred to me. Let us make haste." He was well on his way to becoming fully aroused.

The halls were dark, and although they remained on the same floor, his previously occupied rooms were down a hall that turned twice into the opposite wing of the house. Elizabeth was not sure she could find her way back.

Once they entered his former bedroom, Darcy produced matches and they began lighting every candle they could find. Soon the room was brightened, and Elizabeth could take in some details. There was only one large chair in front of the fireplace, and all of the fabric in the room was dark green, wine-red, and rich brown. Over the mantle was a portrait of Pemberley, and next to the bed was a landscape Elizabeth recognised as the view from Pemberley to a lake, which Mrs. Reynolds insisted Elizabeth see when she toured the home with her aunt and uncle.

Bookcases flanked the fireplace, but as in the master's bedroom, furnishings were simple. Darcy turned down the counterpane and bedclothes as

Elizabeth inspected the room. There were double glass doors opening onto a small balcony overlooking the courtyard garden. She looked out at the winter night. Across the courtyard, she could see a set of windows from which the glow of candles emanated. Otherwise, the house was dark and quiet.

"Is that our room?" she asked.

Darcy joined her. "Yes. It is many years since I have stood in this window and seen it illuminated." He kissed the top of her head. "You, Miss Elizabeth Bennet, have illuminated everything."

She glowed with his praise. "Hmm! How sweet you are! What a lovely thing to say. Perhaps we should move you back into this room?"

"I have said nice things to you in other places, I hope."

"There was something boyish in your tone just now. Quite youthful." She led him to the bed and pushed him to sit before stepping away. "May I assume, sir, in some of your dreams we were lovers without benefit of marriage? Were your dreams so improper?"

"Miss Bennet! Can you read my mind?"

"You have married a woman with a passionate nature, Mr. Darcy. I might not have comprehended it fully at first, but you have encouraged me, and I understand myself better. How you saw so much in me, I hardly like to think."

He smiled and reached for her, but she maintained her distance.

"In your dreams, Mr. Darcy"—she said his name in a most enticing way —"did you undress Miss Elizabeth, or did she disrobe herself?" She began to unbutton the velvet dressing gown, which had become a great favourite.

He tried to clear his thoughts, but her tempting query brought more than one dream to mind. "I should blush to admit it to Miss Elizabeth, but Mrs. Darcy will be hard pressed to imagine anything we did not do, in various and numerous combinations."

She parted the velvet, and slowly drew the long sleeves down her arms. "Tell me a recent dream, then."

"We were alone in the billiard room at Netherfield."

She meant to be seductive, but the memory of stumbling into that room and finding Darcy apparently austere and disapproving was now extremely diverting. She laughed. "Tell me more!"

"I was teaching you billiards, and you were wearing the gown from the Netherfield ball." He had to be careful not to reveal too much. There was a surprise coming for Elizabeth later in the week that he did not wish to spoil.

"Were you?" She had removed the dressing gown, but turned partly away, and drew it in front of her, hiding what he most wanted to see. Her face was coy. "Was I an apt pupil?"

"It seemed so, as I recall, but the dream ended with us lying upon the table, and I was about to enjoy you from behind, as I did in the library on...whatever day that was. The second time in the library, I mean." It was Darcy's turn to blush.

"I understood your meaning perfectly well." She gave him a long fiery look before turning away, allowing the dressing gown to trail behind her as she neared the fireplace. There were enough candles in the room that he could see her derriere through the sheer fabric of her white nightgown. "Were we married?"

"No, but before importuning you, I did propose." Darcy's mouth was dry.

Elizabeth's dark hair hung down her back in wavy tresses. He was torn between the enjoyment of studying her as an *objet d'art* and wanting her to come to bed.

"I am relieved to know that you are not entirely lost to propriety in your dreams. And did I say yes?" She looked provocatively over her shoulder.

"Yes, bless you, you did." Darcy stood and removed his robe, revealing his potency.

Still Elizabeth did not approach. The candlelight outlined every detail of her profile. She noticed a little casket on the table next to the armchair. It was unlocked. She picked up a letter, recognising her own hand, posted during the week he had been in London.

"You have many endearing habits, Mr. Darcy. That you have kept my letters where you might easily revisit them deserves recompense, I think."

Darcy sat back onto the bed as she strolled slowly to him. He found his breath growing shallow.

"Was there a dream of me in this very bed?" She leaned against the bedpost.

"Dozens of them, but none as enticing as you actually being here." Darcy crawled along the bed towards her. He reared up onto his knees, and she did not resist when he pinned her body against the curtained post, entwining his hands in her tresses. He whispered in her ear, "I always dreamt of your hair."

He turned her head, lifting her hair from her neck. He tickled her shoulders with his lips and tongue then met her mouth in a long rapturous kiss. As their lips parted, he asked, "You are here?"

She looked at him fondly. "Yes, my love, I am here."

Darcy slid the nightgown from her shoulders, but its downward progress was hung up where she leaned against the bedpost. He delicately tucked the fabric below her breasts and gave each nipple a thorough kiss. He looked into her smouldering eyes. "You are truly here?"

"I am completely and utterly present, Fitzwilliam, I assure you. You have my fullest attention."

Darcy pulled her against him and the nightgown slithered to the floor. He lifted her in his arms and turned to plunk her on the bed. She laughed. He lay next to her, stroking and petting his favourite parts as she writhed in approval. As his hand slid along her thigh, her legs parted.

"I am not dreaming this? Elizabeth Bennet is here, allowing me every liberty?" Darcy repeated.

"If you comfort me, perhaps *then* you will believe I am not an apparition."

"I must be awake. In my dreams, the succubus never refers to what I do as comfort. Only Mrs. Elizabeth Darcy does so. My voluptuous wife."

Chapter 24
Mrs. Darcy Hires a Maid

"If she and I be pleased, what's that to you?"
William Shakespeare, *The Taming of the Shrew*

In their final three days in London, Darcy and Elizabeth succeeded in becoming less nocturnal and less random in their meals. They had upset the schedule of the servants long enough.

A wedding gift arrived, which afforded some entertainment by producing a pair of uncommonly ugly, porcelain Chinese dogs sent secretly by their cousin Anne de Bourgh.

Darcy quizzed his wife about when her last courses had been—while he was in London, most conveniently—and wondered about conception. Being a fastidious man, he wanted to know when the glad moment would occur, but Elizabeth held no womanly secrets on the subject. Thus, he was forced to accept what his own discreet enquiries confirmed—there was no way to know. He decided to continue as if each union could be the special moment. No matter how playful and teasing Elizabeth chose to be, Darcy was aware that, at every instance, they might be creating their first child. It pleased him to think of it, and increased his attentiveness to Elizabeth.

On their final night, Darcy stood from their early dinner and drew Elizabeth to her feet. "I hope you will not mind too much, Elizabeth. I have prepared a special event for tonight. You have been patient to tolerate no company except mine all week. Your attitude has been in every way compliant." He was full of mirth, and a chuckle crept into his voice. "Tonight will be a reward for surviving an entire week of marriage to me." He kissed her hand lovingly.

Elizabeth laughed. "What—are we to share an entire jar of strawberry jam? What will my father think if he hears of it? He will have harsh words for you, sir, if you spoil me so."

They walked hand in hand into the hallway. "No, Elizabeth, nothing so profligate. You have not behaved *that* well."

Elizabeth grumbled good-naturedly.

"Sometimes you have been quite...provoking," he whispered in her ear. "Which deserves a special reward."

She looked at him questioningly. "You may have me compliant, or you may have me provoking, Mr. Darcy, but I fear you will never have both at the same time as long as *I* am your wife."

"Lizzy..." His lips nibbled her earlobe. "When you provoke me, no matter how you do so, you are indulging my wishes and are, therefore, by definition, compliant." He marked a line of kisses from ear to mouth, enveloping her in a passionate embrace with one hand squeezing her derriere. *Stop, Darcy; go slowly, or you will never get through this night.* He released her. "But for tonight, I hope it will not bother you to have guests. This may come as a surprise, but I find myself wishing to dance with you, Mrs. Darcy!"

"Indeed! Are we to have a ball for two, Fitzwilliam?" She gazed at him with astonishment.

"We shall have a small orchestra, and I have invited Georgiana's dance master, who will teach us a scandalous new dance: the waltz. Have you heard of it?"

"Indeed, I have! It does not seem so very scandalous if I am to dance it with my husband."

"Would Miss Elizabeth Bennet have danced it with Mr. Darcy at Netherfield?" He took her hand as they began to ascend the stairs.

"I find it difficult to imagine Mr. Darcy asking Miss Elizabeth to waltz at that time, especially if, as you have said, he was trying to resist her."

"Had I known the steps, I might have. What a scandal it would have bred! You *were* bewitching—by far the most captivating woman in the room —and although I had allowed no self-revelation, I was already in love with you. I knew you did not return my feelings, and in my prideful ignorance, I thought it for the best—that it made resistance easier. I thought I would forget you. I have dreamt of that night countless times since."

"Do I assume correctly how you wish Sarah to style my hair?" she asked, her eyes sparkling.

"Sarah has been well instructed in every particular of your dress. I own I have made some decisions for you."

Elizabeth stopped. "You know I think we should only remember the past as it gives us pleasure. Perhaps both of us left our one dance in some ways dissatisfied. I believed at one time that you were angry at its end. If your scheme is to create a better memory, I am your willing partner in every respect." She bounced up on her toes to kiss his cheek. "Have I time for a bath?"

"Yes, if you bathe alone," he said, using the voice that made her breath quicken. His eyes expressed his desire eloquently. "If we bathe together, the dance master will find us unpardonably late. I shall knock on the hall door to your dressing room in one hour and a half. Our lesson starts at eight o'clock."

Darcy turned into his dressing room, leaving Elizabeth to walk down the hall alone. As she entered her sanctum, she was amazed to see the ball gown she had worn over a year ago—and not donned since—hanging from an open wardrobe door. "Where did that come from, Sarah? I thought it was sent to Pemberley."

"As I understand it, ma'am, Mr. Darcy arranged with Mrs. Bingley to have it sent. It arrived during the week before your wedding."

"Did it indeed?" Elizabeth began to sense a larger conspiracy. Jane had helped pack the trunks of possessions and clothes to be sent to Pemberley. Clearly one box had been addressed differently from the rest. *Jane! You sly thing!*

Sarah helped her mistress undress; the tub was partially filled, and more ewers stood nearby. The lady's maid had learned Mrs. Darcy preferred her baths deep and steaming, an indulgence she was never allowed as the second daughter at Longbourn.

"Aye, ma'am. I am to dress you to the master's exact orders, as you was that night, excepting you are to wear your pearls what he gave you on your wedding night."

Elizabeth nodded, as if knowing what Sarah was going to say before she said it. "Has he provided white ribbon roses for my hair?"

"No ma'am. He requested the pearl hairpins from your wedding day."

Elizabeth nodded again. "And did Mr. Darcy specify as to my undergarments?"

Sarah's cheeks coloured slightly. "No, ma'am, he did not. He asked me to ask you... um, he said I should request, was his words, that you wear the same as you wore at the ball a year ago."

"Did he, indeed?" Elizabeth raised her brow. "Well then, Sarah, if he chooses to attend to undressing me tonight, he will find the task a great deal more challenging than it was on our wedding night!" Elizabeth started laughing at Sarah's shocked face. "Do not worry, Sarah! You may chuckle, or giggle, or simply smile knowingly. It would seem Mr. Darcy and I have few secrets from you and Murray."

Sarah smiled. "You are newly married, ma'am, and you love each other. It makes for a happy situation for us below stairs. This is a joyful house."

As ELIZABETH WAS SEATED IN her bath and lathering her hands with a cake of soap, she found herself making a decision. "Sarah, I know this is hardly the time or place for such an interview, but would you draw up a stool and sit for a moment while I soak? I have something I would ask you."

"Yes, ma'am." In a moment Sarah was seated next to the tub.

Elizabeth chuckled. *It is only fitting I am naked for this... Sarah has seen me thus more often than she has seen me in clothes! What a thought!*

"Sarah, do you have much family in London?"

"Oh, no, ma'am. My family is from Kent. Two of us worked at The Bell in Bromley where Lady Catherine de Bourgh preferred to break her journey whenever she travelled to London. She gave my name to Mrs. Chawton when there was a situation here."

"Ah. And have you had any further contact with her ladyship?"

"No ma'am. We had a long interview before she gave my name here, is all."

Elizabeth smiled ruefully. "Yes, I would wager you did. Sarah, did you happen to overhear a conversation, probably rather one-sided, between Mr. Darcy and his aunt some two months ago?"

Sarah blushed deeply. "I must confess, Mrs. Darcy, it would have been impossible not to. We all heard, who had business above stairs that afternoon. It made me glad I warn't workin' in *her* house." Sarah's eyes widened, and she put her hand over her mouth.

Elizabeth was indulgent. "I can well imagine. And may I assume you know that I was the bone of contention on that occasion?" Sarah appeared not to take Elizabeth's meaning. "I was the lady who profoundly wounded

Lady Catherine's pride."

"Oh, yes, ma'am. They said your name. You was Miss Elizabeth Bennet before you was married."

"Yes, I was. Now you must answer me honestly, Sarah. Did anything Lady Catherine said cause you to wish not to attend me this week when Mr. Darcy asked that you should?"

"Oh, no, ma'am, not at all. After Lady Catherine left the house, Mr. Darcy seemed to change completely; happier than *I* had ever seen him, he was. It was like he was a different man entirely before he left London. Then Mrs. Chawton got word Mr. Darcy was to be married, and when we learnt you was the lady, all of the staff was relieved."

Elizabeth blushed. "I see. But none of you *knew* me, only *of* me."

Sarah rattled away. "Mrs. Chawton had a note from Mrs. Reynolds at Pemberley soon after, saying as she warn't surprised. She said she met you and thought the master in love with you last summer. She wrote she liked you; you seemed sensible and kind and not taking on airs because you knew the master. Oh... I should not have..."

"True enough, Sarah, but I appreciate hearing it." Elizabeth considered. "Sarah, I would be pleased to have you continue as my abigail after this week is ended. Would you consider a move to Pemberley? Would you miss your family too much?"

"Oh, Mrs. Darcy..." Sarah's eyes widened, but she was clearly pleased. "Oh yes... I mean no, I would not miss my family. I am grown now; I make my own way. I could see those I want to when you come up to London, when there is time." She jumped from her stool, curtsied as she beamed her delight, and sat down.

"Sarah, you already know how... impulsive my husband and I are. We are not always discreet in the ways we express our affection for each other. One could make the case that we are too self-indulgent. You have already had to overlook a great deal. I fear, once we are at Pemberley, this situation will not improve. Although it might not seem fair, we would expect you to be much more discreet than we shall be. We must be able to rely upon you as we rely on Murray."

"Oh, yes, ma'am. I understand. I *do* understand. I am honoured, ma'am." Sarah repeated her curtsey, and seated herself in agitation.

"And I may ask you to withhold information from my husband, Sarah. I say this because I wish you to understand that *I* shall be your employer, not Mr. Darcy. If I ask you to keep a secret from him and it angers or frustrates him, remember, it pleases me. He cannot dismiss you without my agreement."

"May I ask, ma'am, what sort of secrets?" Sarah's voice betrayed a slight suspicion.

Elizabeth tilted her head, pondering. "Woman things, Sarah, mostly. Or, gifts I have ordered for him, surprises I might plan. When I do suspect I am increasing, I may wish to keep the news just between you and me for a time. It is my belief that once I am known to be carrying the Pemberley heir, Mr. Darcy may become quite smothering in his attentions." Elizabeth produced a private smile and settled lower into the water. She looked forward to the many new opportunities she would have to exasperate her husband once she fell with child.

"Oh, of course, woman things. I understand, ma'am." Sarah stood again, curtsied again, and sat again.

Contented with her arrangements, Elizabeth splashed her toes in the bubbles at the end of her tub. "We shall consider it settled then, Sarah. I shall speak of this decision with Mrs. Chawton. Mr. Darcy will be informed that I am hiring you away from him."

WHEN ELIZABETH AROSE FROM HER bath, she instructed Sarah as to her undergarment requirements. "We shall have a chemise first, then a full corset and a petticoat, then the ball gown, stockings and garters. I do not know whether he noticed my shoes, but he seems to notice *everything*, so I shall select a pair most like the slippers I wore then."

"A full corset, ma'am? But you are slender enough."

"It is what a proper country maiden wears to dance." The corner of Elizabeth's mouth curved up. "It seems we are to be accurate in all things."

When the ball gown was slipped over Elizabeth's head and fastened at the back, she and Sarah looked at the refection in the full-length mirror. It was too big.

"My goodness, ma'am!"

"Oh, dear, Sarah!"

"Was you taken ill, between then and now, ma'am?" This was the only plausible explanation Sarah could conjure for the noticeable loss of weight.

"No, indeed." Elizabeth sighed. "As I left Pemberley last summer, my family received some harrowing news about one of my sisters. My alarm caused a lack of appetite for many weeks. When Mr. Darcy came back into the neighbourhood, my disquiet continued but for a far happier reason. What shall we do? I do not think loosening the corset will help enough."

"The only quick thing I know is to set the buttons over ma'am. There is a sewing box in one of the wardrobes. Let me fetch it."

They removed Elizabeth's gown, and Sarah set to work, seated on her stool. Elizabeth pulled the bench from the dressing table and began pulling up her white stockings, which also seemed to fit rather ill. She heard a floorboard creak, and looked into the mirror. There she saw the reflection of Darcy's face peering through the partially opened door to the mistress's bedroom, looking ever so much like a curious boy in evening dress. He was watching her hands smooth the stockings up her legs. Their eyes met in the refection, and Elizabeth suppressed a smile, shaking her head as if cross. Darcy started to blush from his immaculate cravat, the heat moving into his face.

"Silly man." Elizabeth carefully mouthed the words into the mirror, so Sarah would not be disturbed.

Darcy smiled, giving an unrepentant shrug, but backed away from the door.

In a few minutes, Sarah was ready for Elizabeth to try the gown again. The effect was somewhat improved. "Thank you for your clear head, Sarah. The dress did fit a little better before, but our only other alternative would be to sew me into it. We had better not." *No wonder Darcy was attracted that night,* she mused. *I must have been the very picture of a buxom country maiden. I had no idea I had lost so much weight.* She remembered all the mornings she had set out from Longbourn as the family awaited news of Lydia, and how her walks had invariably become sprints to expend the bottled frustrations and unease.

Sarah turned her attention to Elizabeth's hair and drew from a chest of drawers the box containing Elizabeth's pearls and hairpins.

They had just fastened the necklace, and Elizabeth pronounced her three saucy curls perfect, when a polite tap came at the hall door. Elizabeth stepped into the middle of the room, feeling her cheeks colouring as she nodded for Sarah to open the door.

Darcy stood bewitched as the opening door revealed his smiling Elizabeth. She waited a heartbeat before extending her gloved hand to him. "Mr. Darcy, I am ready."

Chapter 25
Mr. Darcy Learns to Waltz

> *"Friendship is constant in all other things*
> *Save in the office and affairs of love.*
> *Therefore all hearts in love use their own tongues."*
> William Shakespeare, *Much Ado about Nothing*

"Miss Bennet, I have never seen you looking so well." He folded Elizabeth's hand in his elbow and addressed the maid. "That will be all, Sarah."

Elizabeth turned to her and winked. It was anticipated that Sarah might be needed later, assuming Darcy would be confounded by the number and complexity of his wife's layers of clothing.

Of course, he can get between my legs easily enough. Elizabeth smirked. *Oh, how you have fallen, Lizzy!*

She joined in the game of being Miss Elizabeth Bennet with alacrity. "May I be so bold, Mr. Darcy, as to tell you that you are looking more than merely tolerable this evening? I believe you may be handsome enough to tempt me."

He gave her a look of mock surprise. "I suppose I should have expected a comment of that nature. Surely, Miss Bennet, you do not intend to fling a gentleman's ill-chosen words back in his face."

"You have never specifically apologised for it, you know." She smiled provocatively before looking down with a poor semblance of maidenly modesty. "I trust you will judge my nature forgiving, eventually..."

"Miss Bennet, you are everything that is generous."

"Thank you, sir. I do not wish to encourage your vanity, but in truth, you are more handsome than ever. I thought so particularly when you were spying on me just now." She still did not meet his gaze.

"Miss Bennet! Whatever do you mean? Of what are you accusing me?"

Elizabeth could only laugh. "Merely that you tend to a dangerous curiosity, sir!"

"Surely not more dangerous than yours, Miss Bennet."

FOOTMEN OPENED THE BALLROOM DOORS. The room was ablaze with light. The orchestra began playing the music that Elizabeth and Darcy had danced to at the Netherfield ball. An elegant gentleman in evening dress bowed. "My dear," began Darcy, acknowledging the man's bow, "allow me to introduce the dance master, Mr. Leigh. Mr. Leigh, Miss Elizabeth Bennet."

Elizabeth blushed that Darcy would continue the charade with a relative stranger, and Mr. Leigh seemed disconcerted.

"Excuse me," Darcy fumbled. "Mrs. Darcy, now. You will both pardon me if I confuse the past and the present. Indeed, it is my purpose to do so all evening."

Both Elizabeth and Mr. Leigh nodded their amused acceptance.

"If sir and madam would be so good as to demonstrate the dance you shared previously, I can assess your talents."

Darcy stepped in front of Elizabeth, and bowed politely. "May I have the honour, Miss Bennet?"

"It will be my pleasure, Mr. Darcy."

He led her to the middle of the room, and they pantomimed the complicated steps as if joined by a line of imaginary dancers. At one point, Elizabeth and Darcy joined hands and paced four steps forward towards the orchestra, then turned and walked four steps away. As their backs were turned to the musicians, Elizabeth heard the swish of skirts and dance pumps quickly approaching, and was elated to have her free hand taken by a beaming Charles Bingley. Elizabeth heard her sister Jane's melodic giggle as she took Darcy's hand. Elizabeth stopped, too delighted to continue, and prepared to embrace Jane in a fierce hug.

Darcy noticed Jane plant her feet to brace for the onslaught.

"Ahem! Mrs. Darcy! You do not attend to your dancing!" Mr. Leigh scolded, beating the rhythm with his cane.

Radiantly smiling at Darcy, tears of happiness in the corners of her eyes,

Elizabeth resumed her place. The Bingleys and Darcys continued the figure for several more measures before all were again pacing forward, away from the ballroom doors. Elizabeth heard more commotion, and when the two couples turned to execute the next figure, she saw—with uncontainable joy—that their set was joined by Georgiana dancing with Colonel Fitzwilliam, and Mr. and Mrs. Hurst. "Oh, Mr. Darcy, this is in every way wonderful. Thank you so!" She squeezed his arm when the dance presented the opportunity.

"Mrs. Darcy!" censured Mr. Leigh.

Elizabeth laughed, uncaring.

The next time the couples progressed away from the doors, it was all Elizabeth could do to not turn her head. She heard more footsteps approaching and, when allowed to, saw Mr. and Mrs. Gardiner had joined the dance with Charlotte and Mr. Collins lined up behind them.

"Now our little party is complete," Darcy informed her.

Elizabeth nodded towards Mr. Collins and murmured to Darcy, "This shows great forbearance, sir!"

"He has been thoroughly schooled by his wife, Georgiana, and your aunt, let me assure you. He will not fawn over me or cast improper glances at you. Whether he treads on his wife's feet is for Mr. Leigh to attend, not you and me!" Darcy smiled. "But I wanted all of the people you love most to be here, and I would not deny you your Charlotte. She was more instrumental than we know, I think, in bringing us together, Miss Bennet."

"Indeed, Mr. Darcy, I believe she knew your heart well before I did. She suspected you even at Lucas Lodge."

The couples executed all the figures of the dance several more times before the music ceremoniously ended.

"*Now*, Mr. Leigh, may I embrace my guests?" Elizabeth challenged the dance master.

"As you wish"—he bowed—"but quickly."

Elizabeth bestowed her enthusiastic embraces on everyone, even her cousin Mr. Collins.

"Ahem, ladies and gentlemen, if I may have your attention. First, Mr. Darcy has allowed me to employ an assistant for the evening. Let me present to you..."

Mr. Bennet swept into the room, executed a practiced twirl, and arrived next to Mr. Leigh, ending with a deeply exaggerated bow. Elizabeth squealed with delight and ran to embrace him, then returned to her husband, nearly knocking the wind out of him as she flung her arms around his chest in as crushing an embrace as a smallish woman could administer to a tall, well-built man who was not expecting it.

Darcy gasped, laughing. "So this is what it takes for me to receive a famous 'Lizzy Hug'?"

Elizabeth was crying and smiling. "Is there such a thing?" With her husband in her arms, she looked at her surrounding friends and family. They all nodded, even the Hursts.

Jane was crying because Elizabeth was crying. "Indeed, Lizzy, the enthusiasm of your embrace has been spoken of in Meryton for many years."

The appropriate gentlemen produced handkerchiefs for their tearful ladies as all gathered around Mr. Leigh. "Now, if Miss Darcy will step forward, she has already had a lesson, so she will demonstrate with me. Could we have just the melody line on the pianoforte please?"

The three-quarter rhythm was beat upon the floor with Mr. Leigh's cane by Mr. Bennet. Georgiana straightened her back, lowered her shoulders, and lifted her arms. At arm's length, Mr. Leigh assumed the same posture, taking her right hand in his left, and putting his right hand just above her waist, with her left hand resting gracefully upon his shoulder. "*One*, two-three, *one* two-three," he counted as he and Georgiana twirled.

Anticipating his direction, the married couples joined hands, waists were encircled, shoulders embraced. Mr. Leigh handed Georgiana to her cousin and bid the entire orchestra play. Mr. Leigh walked amongst the dancers, offering suggestions and encouragement, though often saying to Darcy, "Sir, you embrace your partner too tightly. The torsos should not touch. It interferes with your frame and mars the elegance of the dance."

After such advice was given several times, Darcy muttered, "Miss Elizabeth, cannot the man see I simply do not care?"

"Mr. Darcy," Elizabeth responded, her eyes twinkling, "what will people say?"

"That I adore you, Miss Elizabeth? That I am captivated? That I have been willingly ensnared? They say nothing I have not said myself, so let them say what they will."

At the end of the tune, Mr. Leigh gave each couple a critique then bid the orchestra play another one suited for the waltz. During this dance, Bingley said something that made Jane chuckle and blush, and Charlotte Collins did *not* have her feet trod upon by her husband, even once. At the end of the second waltz, Mr. Leigh pronounced the lesson an unqualified success for all concerned.

"Now there will be one more waltz, during which my esteemed assistant will pass amongst you, and he will judge your dancing to award a prize to the best couple."

There was some murmured grousing that he would undoubtedly choose Elizabeth, but as the dance progressed, Mr. Bennet appeared to be impartial.

Comfortable now with the posture and steps, Elizabeth and Darcy covertly eyed the other couples and exchanged whispered commentary. "What I should truly like to know is how Papa escaped Mama, how the Hursts escaped Caroline, and how Jane and Charles escaped Netherfield."

"All I can ascertain is that there was surprisingly little prevarication all around. Truths were stretched, but I believe there was no outright lying. Are you happy with our anniversary celebration, Mrs. Darcy?"

Elizabeth leaned towards him and whispered, "I am happy with *you*, Mr. Darcy." Moistening her parted lips, she closed her eyes for a kiss.

Darcy complied. They managed to continue dancing, but when they passed Mr. Bennet still kissing, he was heard to say, "That, I am afraid, is a disqualification."

Elizabeth and Darcy smiled as their lips separated.

Soon after the kiss ended, so did the music. The couples assorted themselves in front of Mr. Bennet. He straightened his back and swelled his chest, making the most of the opportunity to hold forth. "Ladies and Gentlemen. If we could give a prize for the most passionate execution of the dance, I think there would be little disagreement as to who the winning couple should be." All eyes turned to Elizabeth and Darcy, who made a great show of curtsying and bowing, his arm still firmly around her waist.

"However, that is not my charge. If I were to give a prize to the couple who blushed simultaneously and giggled throughout, there can also be little doubt of the victors." Jane and Bingley obliged by turning several deeper shades of crimson.

"And if I could give a prize to the best lady, regardless of her partner, Miss Darcy would certainly be my choice, but sadly I am to give the prize to a couple, and Miss Darcy was saddled with a dancing bear." Georgiana blushed and Colonel Fitzwilliam laughed, enduring the criticism with amiable grace.

"And the single best gentleman would be Mr. Hurst, who dances elegantly yet with a most disinterested manner."

"Damned silly waste of an evening, as far as I am concerned," Hurst responded, his cheeks colouring slightly at the praise. Even Louisa laughed and nodded.

Mr. Bennet continued. "I know most of you have had little practice, but if I had been asked, and I was not, to give a prize to the most improved dancer, then surely my cousin, William Collins, would earn that honour." The plump vicar looked to his wife, and much to everyone's delight, Charlotte kissed his cheek. There was general applause.

"So, one and all, I am quite pleased to present the first annual Darcy dance prize, a magnum of champagne, to the graceful, and entirely unassuming, Madeleine and Edward Gardiner!"

There was applause, and all gathered around the Gardiners to congratulate them. "May we open the champagne?" Colonel Fitzwilliam asked Mr. Gardiner.

"Aye, sir, I think we must. Mrs. Gardiner and I could never hope to consume so much ourselves, especially since she is in an interesting condition."

Darcy and his cousin advanced to the ice bucket standing against the far wall of the room. Colonel Fitzwilliam lifted the bottle and unpeeled the muselet. A footman came forward with the colonel's sword. In what he assured his audience was the authentic French manner, Fitzwilliam made one sweeping motion with his blade, which grazed the cork and sent it shooting across the room. "Cousin Richard!" Elizabeth exclaimed. "I am quite impressed. However did you manage that?"

"Cousin Elizabeth, that performance represents countless hours of tireless practice!"

Darcy whispered in her ear, "I opened champagne on our wedding night whilst carrying a sword."

He brushed her derriere with what she judged as a modest blade, given that of which he was capable. Elizabeth's eyes widened, and her gloved hand flew to her mouth to prevent her own bawdy guffaw. "Mr. Darcy... how easily your jealousy is *aroused*," she hissed. She gathered her composure and stepped forward to direct the champagne's distribution.

All eyes turned to Darcy as he raised his glass. "It must be admitted that

Miss Elizabeth Bennet and I had a courtship fraught with misunderstandings and mistakes—indeed, I think most of the time we did not realise it *was* a courtship." He looked at Elizabeth and she nodded. *That is my wife, my laughing Elizabeth.* "But it can happily be said that she has endured her first week as my wife with unfailing generosity and grace. Please drink with me to Mrs. Elizabeth Darcy."

"Hear, hear!" chimed in Mr. Hurst, and all laughed and drank amidst the tinkling of one glass touching another.

After everyone had consumed as much champagne as they dared, Mr. Leigh cued the orchestra, and stood in front of the gathered couples. "We shall have a mixture of dances now, which I shall call, and at eleven o'clock, supper will be served." He bowed, and the couples sorted themselves. Mr. Bennet stood to one side watching, vastly entertained. Several couples changed partners: Jane danced with her uncle, and Bingley danced with Charlotte Collins. Mr. Collins danced with Mrs. Gardiner. The colonel asked to dance with Elizabeth, but Darcy would have none of it.

"It is *my* house and *my* ball and *my* new wife, and I do not mean to share."

Colonel Fitzwilliam shook his head knowingly. "Then I shall wait until the Season, when my parents give my new cousin a ball. There I shall dance with her when you cannot object."

Darcy nodded with feigned haughtiness. "And so you may, Cousin, unless it is a waltz, or the first dance or the supper set or the last dance."

Darcy had never enjoyed a better time dancing. Elizabeth was the accomplished partner he remembered, and he wondered where the Bennet girls had learned to dance. He glanced at Jane and Bingley from time to time, and he was again surprised that Bingley could look so buoyant and besotted while Jane merely looked serenely pleased with him and everyone. Darcy could not believe she was a passionate wife, but he expected there were many details he would never, and *should* never, know.

Elizabeth also observed the other dancers when her husband was not whispering seductively in her ear. She particularly noticed how carefully Colonel Fitzwilliam regarded Jane and Bingley. It was not the first time she had seen her new cousin gaze upon her sister with a look that could best be described as a leer. *That man needs to marry, and soon!*

Mr. Leigh called for a waltz just before supper. Darcy had returned their champagne glasses to the side table, and as he crossed the room to take

Elizabeth's hand, he and all the others were dumbfounded to see Mr. Bennet approach his favourite daughter and, bowing slightly, ask her to dance. Elizabeth glanced quickly at Darcy, who stopped abruptly. His dimples revealed he had no serious qualms. Elizabeth curtsied. "I would be honoured, Papa."

They formed the proper frame, the music started, and off they went, father and daughter, swirling around the room. The other couples watched for several bars before joining them. "It has been a long time since we danced together, Lizzy." Mr. Bennet smiled. "I think you were ten and stood on my feet."

"I do remember, Papa. We were in your library before there were so many bookcases. One could not dance there now. What was the music? I do not remember."

"I think Jane managed to play loudly enough that, for once, we heard her."

"Ah yes, that would have been before Mary took over the pianoforte and Jane gave it up. Papa, I really should scold you for the letter you included with the picnic. I never had any notion of you continuing your dominion as the family rascal into my marriage!"

"I knew you would take it in good part. I was highly entertained by the thank you note Darcy sent and surprised he would take the time away from you to write. The story of your lost shoe, and nearly appearing as the new mistress of Darcy House with a hat on your foot, was most diverting."

"He wrote to you about *that*? I wonder when he did it!" She sighed loudly in mock perplexity. "Are both the men in my life in need of scolding?"

"It was most generous of him to return the hamper loaded with his fine port. I am much in his debt...again!"

"Did he? He is a man too full of surprises by half!"

They laughed together until Mr. Bennet sensed the music was ending. He had one important question to ask while he could. "Lizzy, are you as happy as you assumed you would be? You look thin! Of course, perhaps you had grown thin before, but now I have not seen you for a se'nnight, and you seem worn. Tell me, is he still the best man you have ever known?"

She saw the loving concern in his eyes. "Oh, Papa, do not worry about me. I am eating." She sighed dreamily. *And getting a vast deal of exercise!* Her eyes found Darcy's as he watched her dancing, "Yes, he is still the best man I have ever known. As you said, he is most generous."

"Yes, I see the lovely pearls. They suit you."

"No, Papa, that is not my meaning. He loves me just as I am. He *wants* me to tease him. We challenge each other. He is careful to solicit my opinion, even when the topic in question does not concern me. He wishes only to please, Papa, and he does, without fail."

"Then I am likewise pleased."

The music ended, and the footmen opened the connecting doors to the grand dining room. Mr. Bennet took Elizabeth to Mr. Darcy, and together they escorted her to supper.

Elizabeth was too excited to partake of the meal, even though Darcy had a menu prepared that included many of her favourite dishes. Elizabeth caught Jane's eye, and the sisters rose to visit a saloon set aside for the ladies. Darcy and Bingley locked eyes.

"What can they have to discuss? They have only been apart a week." Bingley smiled tensely.

"Us," Darcy replied, and both men shrugged.

Darcy watched Elizabeth leaving the room. He noticed the odd styling of the back of her gown, and remembered Sarah had been working on it while he watched Elizabeth adjust her stockings. *Has she lost weight? Enough weight to alter a ball gown she has not worn for a year?*

THE SISTERS HUGGED AGAIN ONCE they were alone.

"Oh Lizzy! I can see you are very much in love. You did appear so before, of course, but as Mr. Darcy said, your courtship has been tumultuous."

"When I spoke to you of marrying only for the deepest love... remember? ...I had no idea what I meant though I am sure I thought I did. Fitzwilliam may seem difficult to others, but he suits me perfectly."

"Did you get through the first night well enough?" Jane blushed but did not shy from the topic.

"It was certainly a night of revelations, I must say!" Elizabeth shook her head in wonder, meeting her sister's eyes with mischievous glee. "But is it not gratifying to be the object of such desire?"

"Lizzy!" Jane's blush deepened and she lowered her voice. "Charles actually left me for his own bed after a while... after the first time, which did not please me. He thought he was supposed to. Half an hour later he returned, declaring sleeping apart was stupid. We awoke later and consummated our marriage again, which surprised me. But he has not left my bed since."

Elizabeth's competitive nature surfaced. "Between dinner and breakfast our first night, Fitzwilliam had me, well, we were at each other, really, four times." Jane looked sufficiently alarmed to suit Elizabeth immensely.

After Jane had a moment to absorb this information, she asked, "And how was the first time?"

"It was somewhat painful, but not unbearable at all, and Fitzwilliam was so...concerned. I felt such a need to console him! It was absurd, but he was so very dear, and I was sufficiently brave. And you, dear Jane? Did you master your nerves?"

"I *was* nervous, even though Mama lent me the use of Annie for the night. Charles wanted to undress me, but you know what my wedding costume entailed." The sisters laughed. "But he did the most remarkable thing. I should not speak of it, but it was so unexpected. I tried to discourage him... and I am sure this was quite improper, but it was so soothing when he, and I, were joined the first time, it hardly hurt at all, and I did not bleed but just a trace on my nightgown. Nothing Annie could not rinse away."

With a strange feeling of déjà vu, and the room slowly starting to spin, Elizabeth asked, "What did Mr. Bingley do, Jane?" She anticipated the answer, and she was not found wrong when Jane whispered her reply.

"Colonel Fitzwilliam told him what to do. He...Charles, kissed me, after a fashion, between my legs." Jane's cheeks had never burned hotter—she had consumed sufficient champagne to let down her armour of perpetual serenity. "He assured me it would ease everything, or so he was told. It was disconcerting, but only in the feelings it aroused in my heart, not in any painful way. And it seemed to make...what happened...much easier."

Steady, Lizzy, oh brace yourself. What am I hearing? It must be so if Jane is saying it. Elizabeth endeavoured with every fibre of her being to not appear dumbstruck.

"Are you surprised at me, Lizzy? Surely, with your adventurous nature, you have granted such favours to Mr. Darcy."

Elizabeth nodded, unseeing. *I? Adventurous?* Elizabeth felt faint, and took Jane's hand, saying only, "Thank you for your candour. My Fitzwilliam would not ask his cousin for advice. Jealousy, you see." She thought of how the colonel continued to look at Jane. *No wonder. He knows more than a man ought of another man's wife.* Elizabeth stood suddenly, energy and alarm joining to produce impulsive movement. "Surely, they will be waiting the remainder of the dancing for us."

As Elizabeth said the words, the saloon door opened and Georgiana ran a few steps into the room. "Ah! This is where my new sisters have got to!" She approached and took their hands. "I so look forward to all of us being together for Christmas at Pemberley. It is the family I have longed for." Georgiana's joy lightened Elizabeth's strained spirits, and with arms entwined, the three women returned to the ballroom.

WHEN ELIZABETH, GEORGIANA, AND JANE reappeared, Darcy and Bingley approached with mock reproofs. "We shall not let the two of you out alone together ever again!" Bingley chided them, betrayed by a laugh.

Darcy started to make a similar comment to Elizabeth but caught the strange cast of her eyes. She brushed past him and made for the champagne table where she poured herself a glass and drank it quickly, suppressing a burp behind her gloved hand. He took her hand and looked into her face with concern. "May I have the next, dearest Elizabeth?"

The light came back to her eyes. "Of course you may. I would like nothing better." The orchestra struck up a simple country reel, and the couples danced boisterously. There was a gathering around the champagne table when the dance stopped, and Mr. Leigh called another reel. Mr. and Mrs. Gardiner, used to keeping early hours with their children, sat out the dance and announced at its end that they would say their goodnights. Elizabeth and Darcy saw them to the entry hall and waited with them for their carriage.

"I would not presume to speak for my dear wife," Darcy said, "but I think in this instance she will agree. We are both keenly aware of our debt to you for understanding our feelings before we did ourselves." He kissed his new aunt's hand, and slapped Mr. Gardiner on his back.

"Aunt, Uncle, this has been a divine evening, more so because you could be here. That you would do this for me... other than saying thank you and agreeing with Fitzwilliam, I am at a loss as to how to repay your kindness." Elizabeth held her aunt's eyes for an extra moment. "It will be delightful to host you and the children for Christmas. Please come as early as may be."

There were tears of happiness in Mrs. Gardiner's eyes as she looked at Darcy and Elizabeth.

Elizabeth managed not to cry and laughed instead.

When the door closed behind the Gardiners, Darcy took Elizabeth's hand.

"Are you well, Elizabeth? I realised Sarah was altering your gown when I peeked in upon you earlier. You have lost weight? I had not noticed until tonight. And since returning to the dance, you have been quiet."

"I am well, Fitzwilliam. My appetite abandoned me entirely whilst we were waiting for news of Lydia. Her visit to Longbourn as a married woman disturbed me further. Then you came back to Meryton, and that was unsettling, too, in its way. I am quite sure once we are at Pemberley, I shall become the plump and buxom minx you fell in love with. You must not concern yourself."

Darcy gave her a searing look. He gently slid the tips of his fingers from her neck down her chest, over the pearls, and finally hooked his fingers inside the low neckline of her gown. "I would not call you less than buxom now, Lizzy. My imagination ran wild when we danced at Netherfield. How I longed to touch you like this. I shall remember it the rest of my life."

Elizabeth met his gaze. "*This* is a night I shall remember the rest of my life. Much about myself has been revealed to me. Who stays with us besides Jane and Charles?" She wanted to understand how much, or how little, privacy was to be theirs for the night. They began making their way back to the ballroom.

"I hope you will not object. Georgiana is to stay, as are the Collinses, until late tomorrow morning when they will return to Rosings. The Bingleys wish to remain for a day or two, that Jane may do some shopping without having to answer to...*anyone*. I have given them leave to stay as long as they wish, just so they join us, without fail, at Pemberley in a fortnight. I hope you will not regret delaying our departure another day. It is already a late night; we shall not want to begin a long journey tomorrow."

"You have made the arrangements admirably, Fitzwilliam. I am in every way pleased. Now I know, in addition to your many other talents, that you possess the ability to execute a delightful gathering, including all our dearest friends, and keep it an absolute secret. You are a marvel. Six months ago, I would not have believed it." She embraced his arm, her bosom clasped to him as if they were walking to Oakham Mount, their fingers entwined.

"Shall we waltz all night then, Mrs. Darcy?"

Elizabeth decided many things in an instant. "One way or another, yes we shall."

Darcy breathed in her scent. "My Lizzy..."

At last, the Darcys and the Bingleys were alone in the ballroom. Darcy asked Elizabeth whether he should order another bottle of champagne opened as they continued to waltz. "Not if more will make you sleepy, sir. We already know its effect on me is something opposite to the effect on you, but I feel certain I shall not need its enhancing properties tonight."

Darcy raised an eyebrow, intrigued. "Oh?"

Elizabeth replied with a curt nod, looking self-satisfied. Then she smiled at him.

Darcy embraced Elizabeth as if Jane and Charles were miles away. He kissed her deeply. She returned his passion unreservedly, moaning as one of his hands slid down her back, the other pressing the three ringlets hanging from her head into the soft nape of her neck.

When they parted breathlessly, Elizabeth whispered, "Fitzwilliam, it is nearly twelve hours since you have comforted me. We have not been apart that way for this long the entire week. I have an empty sensation that renders me distracted. I can think of nothing else."

"Lizzy..." Darcy's lips and throat were suddenly dry.

"Make my excuses. I must find Sarah. Come to me in half an hour?"

"But I would undress you."

"Indulge me, husband. I promise not to take my hair down, if that will console you. And I suppose I must confess another transgression. I have hired Sarah as my lady's maid, and she will travel with us to Pemberley. She is no longer employed by you and will be paid from my funds." She skipped from the room without a backward glance at the Bingleys or Darcy.

Oh, she is proud of herself. He laughed quietly.

Darcy turned to his guests, who were waltzing intimately, and moving rather suggestively. "We must allow the musicians to leave, Bingley."

"Let them leave, Darcy. We do not need them, do we, Jane?"

Jane's only response was a throaty giggle into the curve of her husband's neck, a sound that Darcy had not imagined her capable of producing. With a nod to the concertmaster, Darcy signalled the end of the evening and took out his pocket watch—two thirty in the morning. Elizabeth was correct. They had not shared their favours for over half a day.

He bounded up the grand staircase to his dressing room. Murray stirred from the straight chair by the fire and assisted Darcy in disrobing. They agreed a shave was needed.

Elizabeth had long since reached her room. Sarah began to unbutton the ball gown, standing behind her mistress as Elizabeth surveyed her selection of nightclothes. Elizabeth chose a white shift of the thinnest silk with a deep V neckline. Undergarments were removed with all possible speed, and Sarah laced up the back of the nightdress so the fabric hugged Elizabeth's bosom and trim torso.

"Shall I remove your pearls, Mrs. Darcy?"

Elizabeth sat at the dressing table. "Yes Sarah, but leave my hair, please."

Elizabeth removed her stockings. "I think that will be all, Sarah. Mr. Darcy and I shall join our guests for breakfast, so I shall need a morning dress...for once." Elizabeth caught her maid's eye in the glass. "Until morning, then, Sarah. Late morning..."

Sarah curtsied and left the room.

Elizabeth viewed herself in the full-length mirror. *You can do this, Lizzy. You can stop being a little fool. To imagine you thought yourself adventuresome.*

She took up a beautifully embroidered handkerchief. Sitting at the dressing table, she poured lavender water onto fine cloth. She heard the telltale floorboard creak; it was a sound that made her heart race. In the mirror she met her husband's ardent gaze. Darcy was wearing a robe, and she could see he had been shaved. *Blessings on Murray!* She smiled.

Darcy saw the barely perceptible shake of her head as their reflected eyes met. She mouthed the word, "stay." *She wants me to watch her. How delightful. That I shall remove a nightgown instead of a ball gown is of little matter. My beautiful wife...*

Elizabeth swivelled on the padded bench to face him, the moist hanky in her hand. Her eyes did not leave his face. She extended her legs, pulling her gown to the top of her thighs. Darcy's eyes flickered to the movement of the gown, inching up her elegant legs. He could not look away and believed she did not want him to.

Elizabeth began pressing the handkerchief against the creamy skin of her thighs. Darcy appeared spellbound. Elizabeth was pleased. Her eyes never left Darcy's face; his eyes never left the motion of her hand.

She is touching herself for the thrill of me watching. What has possessed her? It is as if she is preparing herself. Will she let me taste her? Is this her sign of permission?

She dropped the hanky. "Mr. Darcy..." His eyes returned to hers, two sets of brown eyes alight with passion. "Mr. Darcy, will you not come to me?"

Darcy began to breathe again, and in an instant, he was kneeling before her parted legs. "Miss Bennet! You are full of surprises!"

"Kiss me!"

He embraced her as she sat. Their kiss ended in his sucking her plump, bruised lower lip. His breath was ragged. One of her legs was around his waist, under his robe.

When he pulled back, she was half smiling. "My mouth was not where I meant you to kiss me. You misunderstand me, Mr. Darcy." She pushed his robe off his shoulders.

He picked up her hanky, inhaling. Her fingers tousled his curls, then slowly pushed his head down until he resisted. She opened her eyes. He was looking up at her, trying to comprehend her wishes.

"You will not?" she asked.

"You truly wish me to?"

"My only explanation"—she toyed with his ears—"is that I have been foolish. I have been senselessly missish. Make of it what you will. How was I to know there are so many ways to express love? Do you require a candle, sir?"

Darcy smiled and shook his head, saying nothing. *No madam; you will see for yourself that I know my way around quite well. At this, you will find me a true proficient.*

Elizabeth watched his actions as he kissed her belly, stopping just at the top of the triangle of dark hair where her legs joined.

"Are you certain?" Given how reluctant she had been, he could scarcely believe she was willingly allowing him this last intimacy.

Her breathing came in gasps. She trembled as her body released the liquid heat announcing her readiness. "I am. I am sure of you."

Darcy allowed himself a smile. He saw his lovely Elizabeth become his wanton Lizzy. He kissed her thighs, moaning at their softness.

Elizabeth's hands were still in his hair. "Fitzwilliam, why have I been so foolish?"

"This is yet another dream come to life, but yours this time. It scared you. I have no wish to do so."

"Please? I am not afraid of *you*."

Darcy lowered his head, placing his face at the heart of her desires. Using fingers and mouth, he applied himself where her sensations would be strongest. He kissed these other lips and folds reverently as his tongue entered her.

The result was a shattering explosion of bliss. When she could reason clearly, the dream was forgotten, and she wondered why she had denied herself such pleasure.

Darcy wiped his face on her breast. The fabric over it absorbed the moisture and adhered to her skin. The tossing of her head at the moment of deepest provocation had scattered her pearl hairpins to the dressing table and floor, and one was captured in the sweat on her chest. With his mouth, he plucked it from her and spat it on the floor, laughing.

"I love a very silly man," she murmured. "I cannot pretend otherwise."

Darcy fingered the edge of the nightgown. "How do we get you out of this?"

"It laces at the back."

"I do not have time for such finery," he growled, and with both hands at the deep neckline, he slowly ripped the fragile silk, exposing her breasts, capturing one of her tight points in his mouth.

"Poor nightgown," Elizabeth sighed. "I shall not bother again."

Darcy lifted his head, "No. Buy another. Buy a dozen just like this one —as a gift to me. I like it."

"Barbarian…" she scolded. "No wonder they do not let you into polite society." With a deft motion, Elizabeth wriggled completely off the bench, impaling herself upon his proud flesh with a throaty moan of completion.

Her precipitous action sat Darcy abruptly back onto his heels. "You, madam, are *not* polite society."

Elizabeth chuckled and bit his sweaty neck. She did not let go.

Darcy whispered, "I am going to attempt a rather delicate manoeuvre, Lizzy…hold on, while I try to stand and remain joined with you. I want to get to our bed."

"Mmm-hmm," was her eloquent reply.

Darcy lifted them carefully, steadying their rise with one hand braced on the padded bench. When he was standing, Elizabeth released his neck, admiring the love bruise she had raised. "It would appear sir, that we think each other quite delectable." She kissed the bruise then kissed his mouth as he began a slow progress through the mistress's bedchamber.

It was not his intention to stop there since they both preferred his room, but Darcy had not reckoned with the torn remains of her nightgown. It was bunched around her waist and draping hither and yon. He trod on it, changing their direction in a precipitous manner. Feeling a fall imminent, Darcy careened to the bed. They landed, unjoined, in a heap, laughing.

Darcy stood and pulled the nightgown down Elizabeth's legs while she mocked him. "It has had its revenge upon you, sir."

"Ha! Do I want a wife who sides with her clothing against her husband?" He tossed the garment back to her.

Elizabeth looked at him admiringly. He loomed over her: tall, lean-muscled, admirably well hung, and ready. Her voice dropped to a whisper. "Will it help my case if I tell you that I find your naked form beautiful, and the sight of you fills me with desire?" She rolled over and knelt on her haunches.

"You might have to remind me of it several times before I forgive you." He moved closer and her hands pressed his potency against her belly.

"How shall I know when you have forgiven me, and that I may stop saying it?"

"When I do this..." Darcy pushed Elizabeth back down on the bed, and carefully arranged her hair on the pillows and draped the nightgown as if posing her for a painting. He took an unused pillow and lifted her hips, sliding it into place. As she watched, he settled between her legs with renewed kisses between her thighs. Elizabeth groaned and parted her legs further. He nuzzled the source of her sensations.

Her hands sought his hair. "Fitzwilliam!"

He rose up and met her gaze with a look of such love and adoration that she gasped, nearly giddy.

"What do you think, Elizabeth? Should I continue?"

She returned his smile, sighing. "I pray you, sir, never stop. If I am dreaming, never let me wake."

Epilogue

1813

> *"Marry, peace it bodes, and love, and quiet life,*
> *and, to be short, what not that's sweet and happy."*
> William Shakespeare, *The Taming of the Shrew*

After spending their first winter together at Pemberley, Elizabeth and Darcy travelled to London in March and stayed six weeks. Darcy's uncle and aunt, the Earl and Countess of Matlock, held a ball in Elizabeth's honour, at which Elizabeth comported herself most impressively.

That is, until her admiring husband—driven to distraction by the tantalising neckline exposing much of her bosom, as was then the fashion, and by the continued irksome spectacle of his wife dancing with other men, including an all-but-drooling Colonel Fitzwilliam—convinced her to step into a sitting room in Matlock House away from the crowded ballroom, to speak urgently about a most pressing matter, which she, in turn, found to be a deeply penetrating topic. They were then discovered partly undressed and in a position vaguely reminiscent of one of the illustrations in her father's exotic "art" book.

They were found out, in fact, by Caroline Bingley, who made an assignation to be in that very room with the third son of a duke, whom she was hoping to ensnare into matrimony. Old habits do indeed die hard, and Caroline's reputation as a mercenary flirt was becoming legendary.

Elizabeth and Darcy emerged from the room a full ten minutes later, dishevelled, mirthful, sated, and unrepentant, each teasing the other for not locking the door. The responses of the guests were varied—most somewhat envious one way or another—but only Miss Bingley was truly scandalised, in her heart now relieved to not have married a man who would demand such performances from a wife. Indeed, she said so, and thus proved herself the butt of amusement for everyone else. Darcy insisted that all Elizabeth's remaining unspoken-for dances be his. If any man were to have so intimate a view of his wife's beautiful bosom, it would be him.

Given the timing of future events, Elizabeth believed they owed the conception of their first child to Caroline Bingley, the inviting fire in the Matlock House sitting room, and a revealing ball gown.

On July 21, 1813, Fitzwilliam Darcy awoke happily agitated. It was the first year anniversary of what he now termed "the Pemberley Miracle," the day he and Elizabeth had surprised each other—he by returning to Pemberley a day earlier than stated, and she by being there at all.

In the earliest months of their marriage, Elizabeth nearly always awoke before her husband and nearly always sought to be comforted by him—using her own definition of that charming word—as he roused. Now, Elizabeth consistently awoke later to find Darcy observing her, and if the bedclothes were disarranged, ogling her. So it was on this morning.

Darcy smiled gently upon his sleeping wife, lit by the morning sun streaming through the sheer summer curtains. It was proving to be an uncommonly hot summer for Derbyshire, and Darcy opened the glass doors onto their private terrace, surprised by how warm the air was already. *This makes it more likely that she will join me in the pond after we replicate meeting as we did last year.* He stepped back inside to await the opening of his wife's expressive eyes.

He was determined to be deliriously happy all day.

Elizabeth, lying on her side, opened her eyes and smiled. "You are a smug and silly man." She often remarked thusly to him upon waking. The role of a teasing wife was one she took very seriously.

Darcy had never lived with an expectant wife, and he was learning the signs, such as Elizabeth sleeping late. She quite inexplicably developed an aversion to her beloved strawberry jam, which the denizens of the Pemberley kitchens did manage to faithfully reproduce in the Longbourn manner. She suddenly preferred instead the tart bitter-orange marmalade made from citrus grown in the Pemberley orangery. Elizabeth's nausea had been mild.

She now entered that period of time when some expectant ladies feel quite fit and become exceptionally randy.

Darcy knelt at the edge of the bed and took her hands in his. "You see me more than a little silly just now. Happy Anniversary, Miss Elizabeth Bennet." He kissed her hands.

"Will you come back to bed, Fitzwilliam?" She lifted aside the bedclothes to reveal both her body with its fecund belly, and the tattered remains of yet another thin white silk nightgown. She pulled it to her, covering only the patch of dark hair between her legs, and gave Darcy a ripe look.

"Miss Bennet!" Darcy leaned away. "Have you no sense of occasion? Would you have behaved so a year ago?"

"You may assume you are affecting a shocked expression, sir, but in fact you look more than usually desirable." She held his gaze as she parted her legs. Her eyes grew more serious. "Let us join together, on today of all days."

"Miss Bennet! You are too wanton. Later. Later, I promise."

Her eyes narrowed. "Fitzwilliam, this is too silly, given the evidence before you, sir."

"Miss Bennet..." Darcy smiled, took a deep breath, and stepped further away.

"You have become a teasing sort of man, Fitzwilliam Darcy." She threw the nightgown at him with a laugh.

"I am keeping this one. 'The nightgown she lobbed at me on our first anniversary.' I have a little chest of such unusual treasures."

Elizabeth pulled a sheet over herself. *He must have plans for later that require we wait...dear man. I shall play along.* "May we at least take our breakfast together?"

"Certainly. I shall ring that we are ready, and I shall dress."

"You have plans?"

"Indeed I do. I mean to go riding, and at eleven o'clock, I shall make a cooling dive into the little spring-fed pond, and at half past eleven, if you would meet me on the west sloping lawn?"

"Am I to wear sprigged muslin and my brown spencer and bonnet?"

"How did you know?"

"You are not the only one with a sentimental attachment to the day."

Darcy beamed. "I *am* pleased. I was beginning to worry for your memory, Elizabeth."

She smiled fondly. "Dear man...you know those clothes will no longer serve me, at least until next summer unless you prove so potent that the remainder of my summers will see me in this same condition."

Darcy bent and nuzzled her temple. "Wear what you will, Lizzy, but meet me on time. We shall go for a swim."

When the breakfast tray arrived, there was a green velvet box at the centre, on its own little plate. Darcy peeked at Elizabeth through the crack of the door hinge between their bedchamber and the mistress's room, where they often ate when wanting to be truly left alone. He saw her pleased blush, and she picked up the box and looked around for him.

"Fitzwilliam? Darling?" she called lightly.

He stepped into the room, dressed for riding on a warm day. Elizabeth had put on the Grecian dressing gown. It was the coolest garment she owned. She felt the hot summer during her pregnancy was a punishment for some sin she had committed; she knew not which one.

"Miss Bennet?"

"Is this for me?"

"Yes, Miss Elizabeth, open it."

Inside the box was the diamond ring surrounded by emeralds that Darcy had altered to his specifications in London He intended for her to wear it on the hand opposite her emerald and leaf ring.

She looked into his eyes. "How lovely this will be with my betrothal ring. But it comes with no proposal?"

Darcy attempted exasperation. "How many times must I propose?"

"I have yet to decide, so you must keep at it."

Darcy leaned into her ear, his hands untying her dressing gown, and he pulled her against him with hands hot against her skin. "How is this proposal? Miss Bennet, I adore you passionately. I spend my days thinking of ways to touch you and taste you that will give you pleasure. I seek your happiness so that when I wish to join with you, you will always accept me. Tell me, Miss Bennet, are you willing to become my wife? I promise to maintain you in grand style." He kissed her neck.

"I am sorry to tell you, sir, I have taken a lover. He is tall with soft dark hair and devastating brown eyes, and *very* well hung." She chuckled and touched him where she could best emphasise her meaning.

"Nonsense. You have loved me since the moment you saw me."

Elizabeth laughed with delight. "Your arrogance is astonishing. You seek to lure me from him with this ring?"

"With the ring and whatever else may be needed." He paused, smiling sheepishly. "'Devastating brown eyes'? You think so?"

She huffed. "Vanity is *still* a sin, as I must so often remind you." She felt Darcy's erection through his breeches and started to unbutton them. "No," he panted. "We must wait, Lizzy." He stepped back.

"You have no one to blame but yourself that I have come to be such a demanding wife."

He nodded with a self-contented smile. "You have yet to become insufferable."

"Go ride your horse then, and stop pestering me." She shrugged vigorously, and her dressing gown fell to the floor.

Darcy slowly reached out to her with one hand. His fingers caressed her breast, and slid to her belly. He patted her there. "What a good wife I have," he dimpled.

He turned and exited the room like a man fleeing demons. He heard her laughter and her slipper hitting the door just as he closed it. Her aim was deadly, but fortunately, she threw only shoes or other items of clothing at him—nothing breakable—and only when he was teasing her.

Fitzwilliam and Elizabeth Darcy were happy.

A YEAR EARLIER, MRS. REYNOLDS, about some task at the time, had chanced to look out a window to see her master's unexpected approach. She watched as the young woman who had been touring the house wandered into view and saw the shocked posture of both as they greeted each other. When Mr. Darcy walked away from the guest, he grinned in such a way that she had never seen on his adult face. Mrs. Reynolds knew instantly he was in love with this self-possessed and unassuming young woman.

Mrs. Reynolds positioned herself in a chair near the same window, watching. What a difference a year made. Mr. Darcy, again wet to the skin in a linen shirt and riding britches, appeared from the shrubbery. Elizabeth, in a capacious new gown meant to see her through her confinement, approached, but lost her footing on the slopping lawn. Mrs. Reynolds stood, instantly fearful her mistress would fall while with child, but she underestimated Elizabeth's balance and agility. With a controlled fling of her arms, Elizabeth righted herself and remained on her feet, although moving forward at rather a higher velocity than she intended, sliding into Mr. Darcy's embrace. He seemed delighted. Mrs. Reynolds smiled and returned to her work.

THEIR FUTURES:

Jane Bingley bore to Charles Bingley eight children, all but the last, Elizabeth called "Betsey," were boys. Jane was six months gone with child when she and Bingley arrived at Pemberley on July 22, 1813. Within moments of their arrival, the Bingleys urged Darcy to assist in finding them an estate in Derbyshire. That night, Elizabeth found a sixpence on her dressing table as she prepared for bed. When the Bingleys were settled in an estate some fifteen miles from Pemberley, Darcy and Elizabeth confessed to each other a sadness to have never sampled the comfort of the bed in the room Darcy had inhabited when he stayed at Netherfield from late September through November of 1811, and again before their wedding a year later.

Mr. Thomas Bennet outlived his nervous, frivolous, and later, constantly hysterical, wife by more than ten years. Mr. William Collins did not live so long a life, obesity cutting short his expectancy of inheriting Longbourn. Charlotte bore him only one child. That son, Thomas Collins, was due to inherit Longbourn, and since none of the Bennet daughters were still at home when Mr. Collins and then Mrs. Bennet had died, it was Charlotte who nursed Mr. Thomas Bennet through his final month, aided by Thomas Collins's young wife—with Elizabeth and Jane arriving for the last week. But the elderly gentleman had enjoyed good health until his final weeks, and mental acuity to the last breath.

Mr. Thomas Collins had been urged from a young age to go into the clergy as had his father. He was a sensible young man, more like his mother in temper, but surprisingly better favoured than either of his parents—for which everyone excepting one elevated personage was exceedingly grateful —and the boy loathed Lady Catherine de Bourgh, striking up an aversion to her almost from infancy. He was heartily glad to leave Hunsford and reside, as the heir of Longbourn, with his mother after his education was complete. Thomas Collins fell violently in love with the young Betsey Bingley when she came to visit her grandfather. Betsey and Thomas were the parents of five sons, which was the source of great amusement to Betsey's mother and her Aunt Darcy; her doting grandfather lived to see the first two sons born:

twins. "Exclamation points!" cried the old man, when he was told the news.

Georgiana determined to act as her brother had done; she would only marry for love. Thus, she married much later in life, at age thirty-three, to a man eleven years her junior, one Benedict Gardiner. Yes, *those* Gardiners.

Elizabeth Darcy bore to Fitzwilliam Darcy seven children, a boy first —Charles Bennet Darcy. Mrs. Bennet attended none of the births, some other daughter always having a more prevailing need, though Mr. Bennet visited both Pemberley and Darcy House at will and often unexpectedly.

Darcy and Elizabeth agreed at the time of her second confinement that they would be ever vigilant of each other to avoid exhibiting favouritism amongst their children, but in truth, their eldest was slightly foremost in their hearts. They never did conceive a child on July 21, but not for lack of trying. A few years into their marriage, Elizabeth and Darcy forgot to celebrate their actual wedding anniversary, and July 21, 1812 became the de facto day from which they counted the beginning of their happiness together.

CPSIA information can be obtained at www.ICGtesting.com
Printed in the USA
BVOW05s1050061014

369643BV00005B/471/P